Past Lives, Present Tense

Contents

Soulmates   *Elizabeth Ann Scarborough*   1

A Rose with All Its Thorns
   Lillian Stewart Carl   37

Silver Lining   *Elizabeth Moon*   61

Shell Game   *Margaret Ball*   79

Renaissance Man   *Jerry Oltion*   99

Luck of the Draw   *Thomas W. Knowles*   125

Divine Guidance   *Sharan Newman*   153

Eye of the Day   *Janet Berliner*   169

Voyage of Discovery   *Nina Kiriki Hoffman*   189

Relics   *Kristine Kathryn Rusch*   209

Night Owl   *Carole Nelson Douglas*   233

Who Am a Passer By   *Gary A. Braunbeck*   255

Forever Free   *Rod Garcia y Robertson*   279

Stepping Up to the Plate
   Sandy Schofield   309

Sittin' on the Dock   *David Bischoff*   321

Contributors' Notes   337

Acknowledgments

"Soulmates" copyright © 1999 by Elizabeth Ann Scarborough.
"A Rose with All Its Thorns" copyright © 1999 by Lillian Stewart Carl.
"Silver Lining" copyright © 1999 by Elizabeth Moon.
"Shell Game" copyright © 1999 by Margaret Ball.
"Renaissance Man" copyright © 1999 by Jerry Oltion.
"Luck of the Draw" copyright © 1999 by Thomas W. Knowles.
"Divine Guidance" copyright © 1999 by Sharan Newman.
"Eye of the Day" copyright © 1999 by Janet Berliner.
"Voyage of Discovery" copyright © 1999 by Nina Kiriki Hoffman.
"Relics" copyright © 1999 by Kristine Kathryn Rusch.
"Night Owl" copyright © 1999 by Carole Nelson Douglas.
"Who Am a Passer By" copyright © 1999 by Gary A. Braunbeck.
"Forever Free" copyright © 1999 by Rod Garcia y Robertson.
"Stepping Up to the Plate" copyright © 1999 by Sandy Schofield.
"Sittin' on the Dock" copyright © 1999 by David Bischoff.

Soulmates

Elizabeth Ann Scarborough

Part One

Even before Tsering developed the procedure, his reflection no longer looked right. Chime really had been his other half, and when she died, leaving behind a pale and waxy shell that, unanimated, bore no resemblance to the woman he loved, his face in the mirror looked at least half as empty as hers had.

Still, he could not bear to let go of her shell. His family was long dead and he had no close friends to urge him to let the past go and allow her remains to be cremated. That was not in the old way of his people anyway. In the wintry times in Tibet, when the ground was far too hard to bury ordinary folk, bodies would be given to the wild animals. All life was one, a flowing stream of consciousness, if only a person had the discipline to swim that stream; and so giving the vessel of a departed spirit to other living creatures was a good act.

Perhaps, but Tsering could not part with her. So he did his own variation on another tradition, that in which the beloved rimpoches, the holy lamas, were mummified, and their remains would help guide the way to their next incarnation. The mummification techniques had been crude, but he had the means to have her body cryogenically entombed in the underground laboratory he had built for himself on the site of a former underground bunker the US government had built during the Second World War.

Then he calmly turned his back on her and returned to work. Unlike many Western scientists, however, he did not feel that science and faith were mutually exclusive. He had perfect faith that in the manner of the old high lamas, Chime would show him where next she should go and how to find her.

Her work sat as she left it when she became ill. Behind her tomb was the great image of the lotus, which, when lit, you could see was contained within the pupil of an eye, reflected in the pupil of another eye, to infinity.

Chime and he had met in premed classes at Columbia, but as he branched off into genetics research, she became intensely interested in opthamology and in repairing and rehabilitating diseased and damaged eyes and optic nerves. The minute ways image and light were transmitted to the brain fascinated her. Later, she delved into how that stimulation affected not only visual perception but other sorts of psychological perception as well.

Of the two of them, though his name was better known, she was the more brilliant. Even such deep and groundbreaking research as she worked on was not enough to entertain her active mind (now quiet?), and she had begun expressing the more spiritual side of her work in her art. The lotus was an older piece, but one it was easy to live with.

They had no children. Her eggs were stored, of course, along with his sperm. To make use of them would make him a single father. He had no experience, and no beautiful Chime to use her insight and strength to raise a child. Cloning was an option, even though it had been outlawed in the civilized world, at least for animal life, but he did not want a child replica of Chime. He wanted her. He wanted the Chime he had lost, mature of mind, heart, and spirit. In a way, she was still with him.

Chime always used to remind him when to eat and sleep and bathe, and it seemed to him, when he looked at her floating in her tomb, that when mealtimes came, her head was slightly inclined toward the stairs. When he had been working too long, the repose on her dead face reminded him to sleep. Sleeping, he dreamed of her.

He usually did not dream. He rarely remembered his dreams. Generally they were extremely abstract and convoluted, which was fine with him. He had always been surprised that Chime dreamed in color, with sound and, sometimes, she said, taste, touch, and smell. But increasingly, since her death, he had been having those sorts of dreams. Usually, they were like memories, but on this night, when she appeared, he knew somehow that this was no memory, but a ghost.

"You have to take better care of yourself," she said. "We have a lot to do." She was wearing something white. Her lab coat.

"I miss you so much," he said in the dream, and reached for her. "I don't want to wake up."

"If we're going to be together again, you have to wake up," she told him. "If you want to free me to be with you, you must look not only at your own work but at mine. Come, I have something to show you."

She actually took his hand this time. It was very cold. He still wore his clothes—he always slept in them these days and he stank, but he didn't care and it didn't seem to bother her. In this dream, she didn't smell very good either. She didn't stink so much of death as of the chemicals used to preserve her body. He followed her down the stairs, and he knew that his feet weren't touching steps, so he must be dreaming. She took him to her worktable. Her computer was on.

She didn't go to her computer, however, but picked up an oddly shaped piece of glass, faceted. "You see this?" she asked.

"Yes. It looks like those crystal sun-catchers you liked to hang in our windows." They shot rainbows throughout the room on sunny days. She loved the rainbows on rainy days, too. They sent her into blissful speculation about light refraction, which he often ended with lovemaking.

"That's where I got the idea. It's of a very special sort. You see here, the honeycomb effect? It's a prismatic in a way, but instead of sorting light into its colors, it separates other things into their essential components."

She handed him the glass, and he held it up, looking at her through it. But the ghost in the lab coat had vanished, and he found himself looking at his wife's corpse in the tank-tomb, through the glass. Her face was reflected in the facets, each facet the same face, another expression, each pore, each hair, containing many many faces. He realized the expressions weren't different, but as soon as he focused on each enough to see it, it had changed from the one he had focused on before. There were living Chimes in motion in each tiny segment, magnified for him to see.

"What is this?" he asked, and, sadly, did not expect an answer from the dead woman in the tank-tomb.

But there was a note written on the computer screen. "There is only one moon, but it reflects in many lakes." He remembered this saying from the teachings of the lamas and nuns who had taught Chime and him as children. It was the poetic explanation for the Tulku, the survival in a new living being of the soul of a deceased person. Commonly, the Tulku appeared in only one living person in each lifetime, but sometimes, it scattered and parts of it appeared in several people. He looked up, back through the prism, and the message was suddenly very clear to him.

Now he struggled to awaken as he had struggled to sleep before. When he did wake up, he was surprised to find that he was not in bed, but where he had been in the dream, standing beside her worktable. The computer was on, but there was no glass such as the one he had held in the dream. The image of such a glass, reflecting the same person millions of times over, was beneath the Tulku proverb. It did not take him long to discover what this represented, nor to coordinate it with a facet of his own work that had eluded him previously. But once he knew what it meant, he knew one other thing. This was nothing that could be done in a basement laboratory, no matter how well equipped. To make this manifest was something that would require money in far greater quantities than he possessed.

He used his computer to send a message, explaining what he needed to a former colleague who was now majority stockholder and CEO of a corporation with laboratories almost as multifaceted as the glass in his dream.

☐

They sat in darkness, having come in after the promotional video had begun, dominating one wall of the boardroom.

They were featured in the video, in life and in death, showing the inspiration and instigation of the blending. The film Wilhelm Wolfe had made was a re-creation of their first meeting when Tsering explained what he needed from the company, to the completion of the blending, when the material taken from a few of Chime's cells allowed her to join Tsering at long last.

The members of the audience were among the wealthiest people in the world, people who had gathered in person at the invitation of their friend and/or business associate, Wolfe. He had insisted that they must come personally and also insisted that they sign a complicated document forbidding them to disclose anything they heard in the room. In an atmosphere where industrial espionage was the rule rather than the exception, it was rather an empty gesture, but a dramatic one.

The drama was further enhanced when Wolfe began the film by saying, "The information contained here is so revolutionary, so challenges what we know of the corporeal and psychological aspects of life itself, that it should not leak to the public. If it does, there will no doubt be a cry from the segment of the population that closely resembles the peasants with torches in Frankenstein movies to ban its development and use. Its applications would be as bound up in government regulation as cloning, and its potential never fully realized. And yet, ladies and gentlemen, this discovery comes closer than any other to proving, for the first time, the existence of what the religious call a spirit and its survival after death."

The audience buzzed with varying degrees of disbelief.

But the film was persuasive in its scientific explanations of the process involved. The film explained what had been done under the company's auspices to develop the discovery and demonstrated why Wolfe's claim might be valid.

Afterward, the disbelief was replaced by a still rather skeptical wonder and in some voices, on some faces, the beginnings of a sort of hopefulness.

Wolfe thanked them for their attention, and said, "I'm sure that now you would all like to meet our expert—or experts, as he—they—prefer to be called. Ladies and gentlemen, may I introduce Dr. Chimera. Doctor?"

They rose and walked with Chime's grace to the podium. Reflected in the mirror that had formerly held the images from the video was a seemingly ageless and sexless Asian individual who only slightly resembled the scientist who often appeared in the film. This person, unlike the scientist in his initial interview with Wolfe, was no longer careworn and stooped from exhaustion and depression.

This person instead exuded the serenity that one always supposed a true Zen master would possess, smiled with a quality the audience members had never or only rarely seen before—a true and deep happiness so compelling that no one wanted to turn from it. To do so would be to miss learning how it might be attainable for themselves, or at least how it had come about. In this world, such happiness was the closest thing to magic any of those who could buy anything they desired had ever seen.

The audience, as jaded and skeptical a group as ever was asked to weigh the merits of thousands of programs begging for their money, applauded once more, for no reason except to welcome the charming person before them. Dressed in a plain black tunic and trousers, wearing instead of a tie a round pendant of faceted crystal, the person's twinkling, kind brown eyes tilted shyly from under square-cut black bangs in a stylish version of a bowl cut that gave this person the look of a tall Asian child—a child young enough to be androgynous in appearance. But the hollow cheeks beneath the jutting cheekbones lacked the roundness of youth and spoke more of many kinds of long hungers than of fashion.

"Greetings," Dr. Chimera said. The voice was somewhere between a tenor and a contralto, with both a light breathlessness and smoky undertones. "As you have seen in the video, the discovery that one's life memories, as well as the memories of the shape and health of one's ancestors, are encoded in our DNA happened early in this process. You have seen how that particular sequence was isolated, decoded, and rendered transmittable in our laboratories. There were aspects of the project, however, which could not be tested on animals or by computer, but had to be tried first on a human being. This is not legal, of course, and one cannot do it unless one has the power of the government, perhaps, with a captive prison population or armies to play with. But this process had great personal implications for us and so we decided that we would experiment first on ourselves—on myself. As you can see from the lack of bulky bandages, it did not turn me invisible, from my stature that I was not shrunk away to nothing, and from my smile, I hope, that I have not become a monster."

Chimera said all of this with great good humor that caused a ripple of laughter in the audience.

Dr. Wolfe had carefully choreographed this presentation. It was his idea to rename as Chimera the being that had been Tsering before he adapted Chime's research to allow him to take into himself that part of her DNA which retained who she was—her memories, inherited and acquired, both nurture and nature.

"Of our own transformation, Dr. Wolfe made more videos. Few births have been as well documented as our rebirth and reunion!"

Wolfe showed more film clips of the Tsering he had known, of Tsering and Chime's wedding, which he had attended. Of Tsering as he had been before the research and the transformation took place. Of the process itself all they saw was Tsering sitting in a chair while a machine that looked like a highly specialized version of the one an optometrist used to examine the eyes was fitted to his face. Immediately afterward, he fell asleep to awaken sometime later as the person presently addressing the audience.

"You see us now as we have become once rejoined, ladies and gentlemen," Chimera continued. "Whole at last—again, but in one body rather than two. No, we do not have conversations within ourselves any more than Tsering did before, or than Chime did—there are always those inner voices, in all of us, making choices, plans, and decisions. The difference we have as Chimera is that now the voices more often agree."

There was polite laughter around the room. "Now we will retire for a commercial break brought to you by Dr. Wolfe and his laboratories."

Half the room turned to watch Chimera stroll—practically float—out the door. The scientist exuded so much that each of them had longed for, worked for, that had eluded them throughout their lives. Two or three rose as if to follow, and question.

Wilhelm Wolfe cleared his throat. "I apologize for not having a longer question and answer period. But both Tsering and Chime, as I knew them before, were intensely private people. It is a mark of how critical this research is that they came to us to develop it and permitted all aspects, including the final joining, to be filmed and documented. I will avoid being overly technical in my explanation, though technical data will be available for any of you who choose to invest in this process for yourself. As you have seen, once the memory code has been rendered transmittable, the process is a simple matter of a painless retinal scan imprinting the new code through the optic nerve into the brain cells, much as *visual* experience is processed. The sleep period is required for the brain to integrate the new memories and process the material it has received. As this discovery has taught us, the brain is only the most immediate receptor and transmitter of the data and memory that an individual uses in making decisions, developing attitudes, and exhibiting what we call personality. All of that material, and this is the crux of the initial discovery, ladies and gentlemen, I repeat, *all* of that material, and the way it was processed by the brain, is also stored in each and every individual molecule of each and every cell in the body. Of course, with the death of the body, there is cell death, and the loss of much of the material. But some cells essentially remain intact long after death and it was these we used to find the memories of Dr. Chime.

"As you have seen in the film, after awakening from the sleep, Tsering immediately began exhibiting characteristics formerly identifiable as those of his late wife. The results of their integration you have already witnessed. The complete fulfillment of finding—or in this case recovering—that missing part of himself has caused Dr. Tsering to become Chimera, a result which, as you can see, has resulted in a joy seldom witnessed in this day and age, and also, I can tell you, in his intelligence being more than doubled, as well as his energy—and incidentally, his fortune. Since becoming Chimera, my friend has developed broader interests than the science that consumed both Tsering and Chime and has prospered because of it.

"But as amazing as Chimera is, he—they—are only one example, one experiment. What we need to do here today is to find an ethical way to recruit volunteers as well as to market our research without attracting undue attention from the media until we are ready to do so. You all know what happened with cloning and the universal banning of the cloning of human beings, depriving the world of any possible benefit from the process. We must be very careful that our investment in this project is not similarly disregarded by political peasants with torches before we have explored its full potential value to humankind."

"Fine, Wolfe. But what about the hazards? What if with someone else, the—er—union isn't as happy? After all, Drs. Tsering and Chime seemed to be pretty happy and knew each other pretty well before all this happened. Is the process reversible?" The speaker was Andrew McCallum, whose talent for helping money to breed money had made him, by the age of thirty, one of the wealthiest single individuals in the world. He had begun as a boy with an investment of a hundred-dollar inheritance from a grandmother and with care and an uncanny intuition that looked a lot like luck had nourished that meager amount into his current fortune. The only formal education he had was the beginning of a liberal arts degree and his CPA certification. Like many self-made men, he was a skeptic.

"We believe that it is, yes, for a brief period of say, three to six weeks after it takes place," Wolfe said carefully.

"On what do you base this belief?" McCallum asked, leaning forward slightly.

"There's already been a significant body of medical work to eradicate other sorts of memories and experiences, or at least prevent them from unduly affecting a personality. Great strides have been made in subduing naturally occurring multiple personalities as well these days. This, after all, is the introduction from the outside of a code not naturally occurring in the individual's own genes. It is entirely possible that in the case of Chimera, the results were made more dramatic by the close association of the two subjects, as you've suggested. We have also had some limited success with temporary restoration of normalcy in two cases of Alzheimer's and a head injury resulting in total memory loss of members of our staff. I say temporary because the disease and the injury continued to cause deterioration of the mechanisms that encode and retain these memories onto brain cells and ultimately the subject's own DNA—the material was introduced repeatedly and lost repeatedly. But should the body's mechanical functions be restored, we could also restore the memory at this point."

A murmur went through the crowd, many of whom were of an age to have parents succumbing to Alzheimer's.

"Perhaps our first investment should be in repairing the damaged mechanisms then, Dr. Wolfe," Miriam Markowski suggested. Both of her parents, from whom she had inherited the bulk of her personal fortune, including her interest in the corporation, were under care at the moment.

"We are pursuing that already, Ms. Markowski," he said. "But we can do much more than that. We could become our parents if we wished—"

She shuddered elaborately. "Who would wish that? I've lived all my life with a horror of becoming my mother!"

Light laughter again, and agreement.

"But there is no reason why we could not also become anyone else, as long as there is enough DNA surviving sufficiently intact to retain the code. We have already taken the liberty of examining specimens from several sources deceased for varying lengths of time and find that what we require remains for hundreds of years after death. By which I don't mean that one would actually become someone else, of course, simply that one would retain their memories and understand attitudes and characteristics from an insider's viewpoint."

"Like mind reading across the centuries?" Lady Margaret Dooley-Smythe asked. Lady Margaret was the financial *and* astrological adviser of the richest woman in the world, the present queen of England.

"Or past-life regression? As in the Bridey Murphy case?" Ms. Markowski asked.

"Bridey Murphy hoax!" scoffed Finn, a rock star with Ph.D.s in corporate law and electronics and who was *not* known to blow all of his money on drugs or trashing hotel rooms.

"Or is this more like channeling or—excuse me but one has to ask, Wilhelm, possession?" Lady Margaret asked.

"You are referring to psychological processes and possibly pathologies, Lady Margaret," Wolfe said. "Whereas the process we're discussing is totally biological—albeit biology that somewhat controls the psychology of human beings. There are always variables, of course. That's why we are trying to find more subjects—more people who feel that their lives could be more complete if joined with that of another, not in marriage, as Tsering and Chime were at first, but within the same body, enhancing abilities, expanding the scope of knowledge, talents, experience. For the sake of legalities, the donor subject must be deceased, of course, and, if a person existing in this lifetime, would need to be your own next of kin. Otherwise, the next of kin of the deceased donor might be expected to raise objections in the event that the 'joining' became public knowledge. But think of it, ladies and gentlemen. Other donors, not next of kin, could be anyone from as recently as thirty years ago to several hundred years ago. The only condition is that there are some viable cells remaining."

"Who'd you alloy with yourself, Wolfe?" McCallum

asked. "P. T. Barnum? Excuse me but I have a few other things to do."

Shortly afterward, during the film that showed busy men and women culling samples from clothing or other personal items in the basements of museums or ancestral homes, the room was empty.

Wolfe returned to his office, where Chimera sat sipping tea, reading some of the reports of cell-gathering expeditions McCallum's films would not allude to—grave-robbing expeditions, essentially. Bribes to groundskeepers and local politicians, significant donations to churches whose yards, walls, and floors contained suitably celebrated remains, and even larger donations to the charities, governments, or pockets of officials of third world countries had gleaned twenty-three specimens of verifiable authenticity.

Chimera smiled at Wolfe, who frowned in return. "We should like to go on some of these field expeditions ourself," Chimera said. "These people have had some wild adventures acquiring the donor cells. We're rather tired of being cooped up in laboratories all the time."

"Think you could use a breath of some fresh mausoleum air, eh?" Wolfe asked.

Chimera wrinkled his nose, one of the less masculine facial expressions Tsering had been sporting since the blending with Chime. "No, perhaps not. But some of the remains are buried in fairly exotic places, and we have been so involved with our work, ever since college, that we have not traveled much. It would be good to visit some of these museums and monuments, to learn a bit about the outer culture of humanity as well as the inner workings of its tiniest components. It occurs to us that seeing our fellow beings through a microscope is a bit like only seeing the world through a camera lens. Enlightening, perhaps, but limiting."

"Well, after that"—Wolfe jerked his head in the general direction of the boardroom—"you may have a lot of time on your hands, once the project folds. We may have the discovery of the millennium on our hands, but there's no viable market for it. Given security restrictions, we made the best presentation we could make and no one believed us."

"They believed us," Chimera said. "Some of them did, anyway. But surely you anticipated that they would be confused and even frightened by what they heard and saw?"

"No, not really. I suppose I could have had a psychologist present but that's all subjective anyway and, besides, *I* wasn't frightened or confused by it—I was tremendously excited. I expected the same reaction from other people of imagination and intelligence."

"Ah, good," Chimera said. "Then who of these donors do you think you will choose to join you?"

"Andrew McCallum suggested I'd already joined with P. T. Barnum," Wolfe said with a derisive snort.

"Barnum isn't on the list," Chimera said levelly and quite seriously, Wolfe saw.

"Just a moment—you aren't suggesting that I—?"

Chimera shrugged. "Not at all. *We* had a deep and urgent need for this process—so deep and urgent that we created it, something we were uniquely able to do. Others who have had the same need have not been so lucky. They have had to live on, perhaps go crazy, die maybe, from the loneliness."

"That's right," Wolfe said. "People lose husbands and wives all the time—other family members as well. It's part of life."

"And yet—we had each other before Chime's death, which was more, much more, than most people ever have. Did we feel the loss more deeply than they because we had once had the emptiness inside ourselves filled by each other? Or do others feel it as deeply and are never able to fill it?"

"I like it," Wolfe said, to cover his embarrassment at being talked to in this way by his old friend. Tsering had always been the listener in their college days. The most he had spoken to Wolfe in all the time the two had been acquainted had been when he came to ask him to help finance the research. The two had become closer in some ways since then—had spent more time together, certainly—but none of this psychological sort of thing. A chill went through Wolfe as he realized that Chime really *was* part of who Tsering was at every moment, in every thought, not just as part of their mutual science project. That reality had not occurred to him before. "Why didn't you bring this up to them?"

"Perhaps we would have if we had thought of it then. It was only now, speaking to you, friend, that it occurred to us."

"Well, bringing back any of my wives wouldn't help, even if any of them were dead," Wolfe said, laughing.

"That's true. You've not had happy marriages, have you?"

"No," Wolfe said flatly, and began shuffling papers on his desk.

"But marriage, romance, these are not the only relationships people would find what they lack, surely? More often, would it not be with a great teacher, someone you admire, probably even someone of the same sex who chose a different path than you?"

Wolfe looked up impatiently. His impatience did not seem to register with Chimera at all. Chimera was staring out the bank of windows behind Wolfe, over the tops of the other buildings to the sky beyond. "I really wish you had brought all this up to them instead of now. Maybe I should have given you more time to prepare but we need to start recouping some of our expenses soon."

Chimera looked back at him, the almond brown eyes both laughing and sad. "You will, Wilhelm," Chimera said with surprise, as though there had never been any doubt. "They will go home and think about what we told them and talk to the people in their lives and think of what it would be like if there were someone altogether different involved, who would change all of the things that make them unhappy—who would make them like us. And one or two at least will be courageous enough, unhappy enough, to return and want to know more. We will talk with them then, and they'll decide to do it. And if all goes as we have every reason to think it will, they will be happy and they will tell others . . ."

Wolfe thought that was an unusually naive view of humanity for such a brilliant person—people—as Chimera, but then, both scientists had isolated themselves with their work and each other for most of their adult lives. Didn't even watch much television or pay attention to the news, from what Wolfe gathered. And yet, they had found a peace and wholeness twice in their lives that totally eluded Wolfe. He had never considered his restless energy as anything but a positive driving force before, but looking at Chimera, who was anything but a failure by anyone's standards, he began to wonder.

"You're serious?" he asked. "You think I should think about going through the process? Finding—someone else?"

"Certainly not, if you don't feel the need of it," Chimera said. "It would be a mistake for someone who already has everything he needs." Chimera laid his—their—hand on Wolfe's arm, again in a very feminine gesture Wolfe would never have associated with the reserved Tsering. "It's only that, well, if you had been through what we've been through, you wouldn't need a sales pitch with those people, and you wouldn't need to think about the bottom line. You would be able to tell them what you received in your own words, from your own heart."

"Yes, but *you* didn't tell them that, not the way you're talking to me."

"Maybe that's because they were in a group. Maybe we should have done this one at a time. Anyway, we'll be seeing some of them again soon, and we can talk to them this way then. Excuse us now. We haven't had much to eat today. Would you care to join us?"

"No thanks," Wolfe said, and returned to his work, relieved that Chimera said nothing else about him personally undergoing the process. After all, who *would* he want to share his consciousness with? Not Barnum or his ex-wives, certainly, but who?

Part Two

Andrew McCallum, financial prodigy of untold wealth, would never have admitted it in any of his interviews with the *Wall Street Journal*, *Financial Times*, *People*, *Newsweek*, or *Hello*, not even to Barbara Walters, but he had never aspired to be a billionaire broker. It was rather like sports were for some people—he had a talent for money, and so he naturally fell into positions where he could use his talent, and so it went, him getting wealthier and wealthier. And the novel still wasn't past page two.

Despite the houses he had built for her in New York and San Francisco, the manor house he had remodeled for her in Edinburgh, the town houses in London and Paris, his mother was disappointed in him. She had been a folksinger in the sixties, and as soon as she finished exclaiming with motherly glee over his latest gift, she would say, "But Andy, you're only twenty, (twenty-five, thirty, thirty-five and now, thirty-six). You've made all this dosh. Why not settle down and do something really significant now?" Really significant to Mother meant creating, writing, playing a musical instrument, being an artist. Mere money, she explained, while it bought lovely things and gave her aging bones some comfort and provided plastic surgery to hide the fact that the bones were indeed aging, was superficial. It didn't last. When he was a child she had sung him songs she gleaned from the Minstrelsy of the Scottish Borders by Sir Walter Scott—well, or recordings made by other folksingers based on songs collected in the Minstrelsy and recollected, with tunes this time, by someone named Child. She had read him *Lay of the Last Minstrel* and *The Lady of the Lake* and sung the ballads of Thomas the Rhymer and Tam Lin. Endlessly, as he remembered. It had taken him tremendous effort to learn to speak as his classmates spoke rather than like a nineteenth-century-ballad Scotsman—as if fitting in hadn't been difficult enough with an IQ of 195!

Of course, he always intended to finish his novel. He had started several, but none of them had gone farther than a couple of pages. He knew if he could only find the time that he could do it. Maybe someday when he retired. But by then Mother would be gone, and it wasn't so much to please her as to *show* her he could do it if he wanted to that he wished to write a novel. The truth was, he hardly ever had time to *read* a novel, much less write one. Not since he had received a stack of steamy ancient Harold Robbins paperbacks in partial payment for a trade he'd made for some freebie computer games he'd received as partial payment on another trade for a used computer his uncle had given him to do homework on. By the time the Christmas present had come, he already had a state-of-the-art computer he'd received in trade for something else—he forgot what now—and it already had all the freebie games loaded. He'd read part of one of the paperbacks, was the point. He knew he could do that, too. If he could ever get off the phone, off the net, or out of meetings.

He had dinner with his mother the evening after he'd attended the "briefing" at Nucore. It was her birthday dinner. He'd known when he signed the security agreements at Nucore that he was going to regret it and he already did. It would have made a great story to entertain his mother with. She tuned him out when he tried to tell her about his deals, and right then she was going on and on about some poet or actor she had been having an affair with.

"I don't see what you get out of that, Mother," he said. She looked very nice—she was tall and thin and still wore her gray-streaked pale brown hair long, though for formal occasions, such as tonight, she looped it up. She was wearing a soft flowing dress she probably bought at a vintage clothing store. His mother was not extravagant when it came to clothing. She was a perfect size 9 and able to find lots of used dresses she liked, and she was very into recycling. He supposed that was creative, too.

"These men are exciting and dynamic, Andrew, and whether or not you think it has anything to do with the real world of materialistic commerce, I *need* that kind of creative energy in my life," his mother said so passionately that her voice rose, as it usually did in public places, embarrassing him, as it also usually did. Just as quickly she dropped her voice to its lower register—contralto, she called it—and took his hand in hers, which was long and elegant and cool as ever, though she'd had a Celtic knotwork ring tattooed on the top knuckle of her right middle finger. "I wish you could understand that, Andy. I wish you had a drop of—"

"Wouldn't you be happier, Mother, if it were *you* who were—creative?" he asked, feeling he was reaching an interesting solution. Whether or not Chimera's process really worked, his mother was suggestible enough (to everyone but him) to believe in just that sort of thing. He'd just have to make sure she didn't decide to be creative with someone like that Sylvia Plath she had thought was so wonderful, it seemed to McCallum, chiefly because the woman was so "tormented" she'd stuck her head in an oven.

His suggestion, subtle as he thought it was, did not meet with an even remotely favorable reaction. "What do you mean *if*?" she demanded. "I am a singer. Just because I'm retired doesn't mean I'm no longer creative. You keep me so busy decorating new houses that much of my creative energy flows into those, these days."

As did a great deal of Andrew's money, he thought. Not a great percentage, actually, but his mother was his only real extravagance. He didn't care much about status for himself, beyond being as comfortable as possible, and making his business negotiations convenient, and looking sufficiently prosperous to broker his deals. He was past the stage where he really needed to worry about appearances, however, as he had a reputation for being someone whose investment in a project practically guaranteed its success. Besides, most of his deals these days were brokered over the phone, fax, and computer.

Giving his mother the houses and the money to do with them as she liked was an investment in his own mental health, actually. While she was busy with the houses, she wasn't nagging him about his novels or to back some "creative" jerk or other she'd taken an interest in.

He didn't mind the expense really, though. She hadn't been a professional singer when he was a child because she was working as an aide in a nursing home to make a living for the two of them. She told him his father died in Vietnam, but she had been a peace activist, and he suspected that actually he was conceived in somebody's secondhand school bus and she didn't have a clue which flower child *was* his father. He had had a lot of "creative uncles" when he was a kid, but they seemed to have all died or disappeared in the intervening years. Good thing, too, or they'd be living off his mother. She found plenty of deadbeat dependents and causes as it was.

"I know, I know," he said soothingly. "But—well, wouldn't *you* maybe like to write a book yourself? You know, there'd be quite a market for it—"

"You mean just because I'm the mother of the great financial genius—puh-leeze," his mother said.

"Well, of course, I guess that's why you want me to write something. Because you can't," he said.

Her face grew very still, and he thought for a moment she was angry, and then the skin around her eyes suddenly was wet. "No, I'm afraid not."

"But what if you could?" he asked, a little desperate now, thinking he'd hurt her feelings instead of making her angry and would pay for it with a weeklong depression. It was her fifty-fifth birthday after all. He was supposed to be celebrating with her. He was trying to give her a gift.

She shook her head. "I guess I just have never had it in me. Any more than you have. I thought your father might have been a writer but then—well, we never knew, did we? And when I realized you were so bright, well, I just wanted the joy of it for you, sweetie. The sense of accomplishment— of leaving an artistic legacy like Sir Walter Scott or Kipling or even poor tragic Sylvia."

"Mom, what if you could have it in you? Would you?" She looked blank. How to continue without breaking the security agreement? Though of course it would have to be broken to some extent if he was to have his mother go through Chimera's process. "Say, for instance, you uh—went to one of your psychics?" Psychics were another big benefi- ciary of McCallum's generosity to his mother. To give her credit, she was not a fool, and she did not go to the worst of them. McCallum, after living his teen years with her and having her friends who claimed various degrees of "talent" come and go, realized that there were people who seemed genuinely to know things that they had no reasonable way of knowing. His mother only frequented, he supposed, the more respectable of them, the best astrologers and so forth. It wasn't like she had huge phone bills from psychic phone net- works.

She was looking defensive again. This was *not* how her birthday party was supposed to go. McCallum wondered how it was that a man like himself, who could convince people that he was going to take their money and make more for them with it, was having so much trouble communicating with a woman who adored him and whom he, for all of her flakiness, adored.

"No, I mean, went to one of the real ones and they did, say, a past-life regression on you and found that you had been, oh, Jane Austen in a former life. And that when you woke up you'd remember all about being Jane Austen and would be able to *write* like Jane Austen. But you would also still be yourself. I think."

His qualifier was drowned out by his mother's protests. "No one can do that. Not anyone legitimate. And it never turns out, when you're really regressed, that you're someone special. It's always like it was with the case of Bridey Murphy—you know, ordinary housewife turns out to have been ordinary Irish peasant girl."

He opened his mouth to tell her he thought he knew a way, but she stopped him by adding, "Besides, it's too late for Jane Austen or anyone. It would be very unfair to bring them into this life just to pass on again so soon. My best hope at this point is that someone in the future—someone pretty and brilliant and creative, I hope, won't be too disappointed if they're regressed and find that they were once—me."

"What do you mean too late? You're only fifty-five!" he said.

"It's what I've been trying to tell you, honey. Why I want so badly to see you truly on your way to being happy before I—well, what I mean to say is, I'm dying."

"*Mo*ther!" he said as if she had annoyed him. But she was nodding slowly. "Really? According to whom? Which doctors have you consulted?"

She told him, and they were the ones he would have recommended. They had no further recommendations for her except that she put her affairs in order. She had a rare form of cancer of the liver too far advanced and metastasized at this point even for a transplant. Ironically, her adherence to a healthy regimen had kept her looking and feeling good long past the time when the disease was treatable. "But it's all right, sweetie, really it is. I am very curious about the next life, and I'll certainly send you a message if I can at all and *not* through a medium because I know you wouldn't consult one. I have a few months yet though, and I just wanted to let you know—well, that it's the last chance you'd have to show me—that you can't put it off any longer—I know you say you don't have enough time, and now it's me, I don't have enough time. If you're going to realize your potential, baby, you'd better put the pedal to the metal because Mama's going to glory, and soon."

For someone as pale as Mother was, she sounded very much like Della Reese.

☐

Later that evening, McCallum called Wolfe, and said, "Look. This process of yours. Does it really work?" Wolfe started into the song and dance again, but McCallum asked for a simple yes or no and got a "Yes, as far as we know. You saw Chimera."

McCallum had. "I want to talk to both of you again. Where can we meet?"

Wolfe was still in his office, and Chimera was working late in the laboratory, so they agreed to meet at Nucore.

"I'll get right to the point," McCallum said when he had seen evidence enough to convince him, finally, that the process had worked at least in the case of Chime/Tsering/Chimera and had a good chance of producing a similar result again, varying, of course, according to the personalities involved. "I want to undergo the process, and I want to do it now. I have to make an 8 A.M. meeting and need to start a novel in the meantime. Who have you got on tap? Can you get me Sir Walter Scott, Rudyard Kipling, somebody like that? No Sylvia Plath or Hemingway though. I'm in no mood for another downer tonight."

"I'm very sorry, Mr. McCallum, but even P. T. Barnum wouldn't be able to promise such haste. Unless you're a very fast sleeper. Remember we did mention that there was approximately a thirty-six-hour deep sleep period following the process."

"Thirty-six hours is out of the question. I can postpone the meeting until tomorrow afternoon, but twelve hours is all I can spare. Can we get started right away?"

Wolfe flipped open a phone and spoke sharply into it.

"Ian? We have a team on standby in London, right? Get them up to Scotland pronto." He covered the speaker, and asked McCallum, "Scott? Scotland, right?" McCallum nodded, and Wolfe removed his hand from the speaker, and continued, "Sir Walter Scott. Keep the jet on tap at Edinburgh to bring the specimen straight to our strip. If you need to go to the Highlands or whatever to get it—"

"Borders," McCallum offered. He remembered that much from his mother's reading. "He lived in the Borders. Probably buried there, too."

"Thanks. The Borders, don't ask me borders of what. That's your department. Use the chopper from the Edinburgh airport. We need the specimen ten minutes ago."

"I suppose this is going to cost me extra?" McCallum asked.

"Nope, the cost of acquisition is included in what we quoted you. What can we offer you while you're waiting? Coffee? Tea? Haggis? A Scotch maybe, to get in the mood?"

"No, I'll just make a few calls myself and rearrange that meeting if you can loan me an adjacent office," he said. Several million dollars' worth of negotiations later, Wolfe knocked and poked his head in the door of the office McCallum was using. "The jet just landed. Come on down to the lab now, and Chimera will prepare you."

McCallum thought of retorting that he was always prepared—for anything, but in this case that wasn't actually true. There was nothing terribly daunting or *Star Trek*ish about the preparations, however. Chimera took him to a quiet, carpeted room, sat him down in what looked like a nicely upholstered dentist's chair with a contraption nearby similar to the one he had seen in the film. Chimera turned on the machines and waited.

"Don't we need more people in white coats running around, checking dials, like in the film?" McCallum asked.

Chimera looked over from making some small adjustment and smiled reassuringly, "That film was taken during the developmental phase of the project. It is all quite convenient for us to handle alone now, fortunately."

The door had been left open, and Wolfe arrived, carrying a small package, which he gave to Chimera, who removed something from it, inserted it in one of the machines, a moment later extracted something from the same machine, and placed that in the machine beside McCallum's chair.

"Now then, Mr. McCallum, I am going to tape your eyelids open. You may lose a lash or two, but otherwise this won't hurt a bit."

McCallum was glad he was not restrained in any other way as it was disorienting not to be able to blink. A helmet was fitted over his face, and moments later he heard a hum and saw a light, first a pinprick, then a brilliant blossom that rushed toward him, at last becoming a deep and consuming well that swallowed him whole.

☐

Chimera removed the helmet from McCallum's head and gently unstuck the tape from his eyelids. McCallum mumbled an automatic thanks, and allowed himself to be led to the sleep chamber. He was asleep even before he was fully prone and remained where he landed, without moving, except for the typewriter-carriage-like REM twitching of his eyelids. Despite the man's insistence that he could only sleep twelve hours, nobody set an alarm clock.

Wilhelm Wolfe debriefed his staff on the acquisition of the Scott material, then retired to the apartment he kept in the Nucore compound for occasions when he worked late and had early meetings and did not feel like driving the fifteen miles to his home on the city's outskirts. He did set an alarm clock for himself, but was awakened much earlier by a call from one of the other attendees at the meeting the day before, also requesting a private meeting with him and Chimera. They had a noon meeting with the queen's astrologer and came to an agreement, but this time were able to schedule the transfer for the following day, and fortunately the astrologer was authorized to select a donor whose material they had previously acquired. The recipient of the material would be neither the queen nor the astrologer, but a third party.

As the meeting was ending, Chimera's cell phone rang, and the scientist excused himself with a nod to Wolfe. McCallum had awakened.

By the time Wolfe arrived at the lab, McCallum was up and surveying his surroundings, not with his usual twitchy impatience but with an expression of both wonder and amusement. The man was barely five-nine, but seemed much taller somehow, despite the fact that his step was hesitant, as if he had hurt his leg, but then was even stronger and surer than ever.

"Gentlemen, this is amazing," McCallum said in a pleasanter tone than Wolfe had ever heard from him before. "What a pity that establishments such as this are commonplace these days. Really, you must bring a French fellow—oh, you'd know him, it seems—Jules Verne—to see all of this. He'd be fascinated."

Wolfe's personal assistant arrived to say that McCallum's personal assistant had sent a car for him to drive him back to his office in time for a meeting.

"Meeting?" McCallum said. "Oh, yes, of course. That meeting. But my appearance is hardly suitable for an important meeting."

"You may use my own flat to shower and shave if you wish, McCallum," Wolfe offered, more from curiosity than from courtesy, though he felt more inclined to be courteous to the new McCallum than to the previous version.

"That's decent of you, man," McCallum said, and Wolfe detected a trace of Scottish brogue. "Thank you."

McCallum/Scott seemed to have integrated with each other well enough that he had no problem with the modcons. Wolfe knew very little about the life of the early nineteenth-century Scottish author, except that he was prolific, had written a dense medieval novel that made great television but was a groaner as required reading for schoolchildren. But happily, as had been the case with Chimera, the blend seemed to produce an even more alert and intelligent individual than the original host had been. The new McCallum looked at the clothing he had slept in with distaste. He regarded with surprise and something akin to alarm his own reflection in the mirror while Wolfe offered him a change of underclothes from new ones still in the packages in his own chest of drawers. While McCallum was showering, Wolfe had his suit pressed by the service he retained for himself in the event that he slept over.

There was a brief exclamation of surprise from the bathroom when the water taps went on and another as the electric shaver started, but after that, nothing that suggested anything out of the ordinary except that McCallum sang in the shower—loudly—and in unabashed brogue this time—something that sounded like an old Scottish song with a true love and blood among its more prominent lyrics.

The man—or was it men?—at least donor and host were the same sex in this case, which made it easier than Chimera—emerged from the steamy bathroom wrapped in Wolfe's robe and beaming. "Did you hear that, man? I can sing! I suppose it's only natural what with—Mother—being such a fine singer. But while I was in Scotland, I collected songs but never could carry a tune, and from the time I was a schoolboy here, for some reason I don't seem to have tried. But it's most enjoyable and—well, yes, Mother *will* be pleased. In fact, I must—telephone her—at once and arrange another dinner, this time at my home, so that we can sing together properly."

Still wearing a large and sincere grin, McCallum impulsively grabbed Wolfe by the upper arms and gave him a friendly shake. "Oh, my dear Wolfe, this is *wonderful*. Thank you so much for bringing us together."

"My pleasure—and, of course, McCallum, it's not exactly free,"

"No, no, of course not. A moment then while I pull my trousers on and I'll find my purse and pay you—it seems I have ample funds."

When Wolfe's guest had finished dressing, however, he amended the statement with an expression that was almost pure McCallum. "That purse business was only a figure of speech, of course. Let me at a computer, and I'll transfer the funds right now."

Wolfe had expected an argument or at least an attempt to bargain and thought he saw it coming when McCallum turned back from the screen, and said, "You know, yesterday, when I made that jest—the crack, I mean—about you channeling P. T. Barnum?"

Wolfe nodded noncommittally.

"I—er—queered your pitch somewhat with that, didn't I? Everyone else left soon after—oh yes, I noticed. I have had a change of heart. This process does not seem particularly dangerous or harmful to me. Quite the contrary. I'm feeling very good, and being able and willing to sing, if nothing else, should accomplish much of my purpose in coming here. So perhaps you will not take it amiss if I ask if Nucore has room for an outside investor in this project? Judging from the preparations you made last night, your overhead seems to be quite high. And I have the feeling this has legs up to its armpits, uh—so to speak. I know you'll have to consult with the board on this but how about if I leave, say, forty mil in escrow for the project right now and when you have the word, we can have the lawyers draw up the papers?"

Wolfe, speechless, nodded as if he had expected such a proposal all along.

☐

McCallum couldn't remember when he had been in such a good mood. It was probably relief. The whole procedure hadn't amounted to all that much, really. A little tape, a little light show, a nice long nap after which he felt extremely refreshed and not a bit sleepy. The shower had felt better than he could ever remember, and he had also forgotten how fine his voice was. His singing voice was baritone, he found, well suited for the ballads he remembered. He thought Mother would be pleased. He was a tenor as a child.

As for the "new" personality, he wasn't really troubled by it. He did know an awful lot about historic Scotland, and found himself slipping into that kind of speech if he wasn't careful, but it was as if he'd been reading a lot of books on the subject, except that he saw everything at least as clearly as if he had watched it on television. Not that his own imagination had ever been lacking. Even Mother knew that. It took great imagination to see profit from a simple idea or the merging of two ideas.

On the way back to the office he obeyed a sudden urge and asked the Afghanistani driver if he recalled any of the songs he had learned as a child, and when the man obliged, asked him what the lyrics meant and then tried to sing along with him. He stumbled only a little over the lyrics. He was, he was surprised to learn, rather good at pronouncing foreign words. The teleconference was hooked up and ready to go when he arrived.

He turned to his assistant, "Well done, Miss Collins, well done indeed."

"Thanks, Mr. McCallum," she said, surprised.

"Why, all of this electronic equipment and so forth. It must have taken a team of engineers to set this up," he said, realizing he had always taken it for granted.

"No, sir. Just me, as usual."

"And do you have a degree in engineering, Miss Collins? I don't believe I noticed that in your personnel file."

"No, sir. Business, sir." She sounded puzzled, and Mr. McCallum realized he was laying it on a bit thick. "And—

er—you've always just called me by my first name before, sir, Collins. Why this 'Miss' all of a sudden?"

"Would you prefer—uh—'Ms.'? It only seems courteous when you refer to me as 'Mr.' You're an employee, but not a servant, after all."

"Uh—no—but it sounds a little old-fashioned is all. I mean, if you were going to call me 'Ms. Steinmetz' I guess that would be a mouthful, but just 'Collins' will be fine."

"That's your first name then?"

"No, actually, my mom named me Colleen but Collins sounds more—"

"Upmarket, eh? I believe I understand. Very well, Collins, since you prefer it. I think calling me 'Mr. McCallum' when it's just the two of us is possibly a bit dated as well. Could you manage 'Andrew' perhaps?"

"Uh—sure, Andrew. It's time to start now, sir."

He turned his attention to the screen. He was able to converse directly with LeClerc in Paris and Guitard in Montreal, much to their surprise. Collins Steinmetz slipped in unobtrusively and clicked off the on-screen interpreter. He was also gratified to see the shock in the face of Ariostos, the Greek shipping magnate, when he answered him in somewhat dated but nevertheless quite clear Grecian. Using the native languages of these business associates gave him a new insight into their communications, he found, and into the characters of the men with whom he was dealing. He didn't like the guys much. In fact, he didn't like this deal much, after all.

"Gentlemen, now that you've all met each other, why don't you talk among yourselves? I've some other pressing work to attend to, and a family emergency has come up. Ms. Steinmetz will be here to monitor the meeting and answer any questions if that's all right with her."

Collins nodded, expertly streaked honey blond curls bouncing.

McCallum returned to his own office and placed a call to his mother, who was out. He left a message that he wished to dine with her that evening at her own home in the city, if that was convenient for her. She had all the songbooks, the piano, and could still play guitar herself.

He found his fingers twitching in a strange way as he sat at his desk, and he pulled out a sheet of paper. "Must remember to pick up a journal someplace," he said to himself. He glanced at the computer screen. It would be faster, but less private. He wanted to keep the journal and see if he could tell any changes other than the singing, of course, from how he had been yesterday. He felt surely there were some, but he couldn't be sure unless he recorded them and then, maybe, cross-checked them with his mother. It was important to do this, along with many other things, while she was still here. After filling a page with handwriting that perhaps a graphologist could have identified with his own cubist scrawl but that was otherwise graceful and quite legible, he turned at last to the computer.

"Sir Reginald had gone to the Highlands in hopes . . ." he began, and then hit the backspace key. Too dated. Same story, same characters, but it needed to be more with it.

After several more tries, he began, "Shetland Islands, March 23, 2000. The oil rigs fell like giants slain by the fire of some invisible dragon as Bentley Harper, corporate attorney, watched. Sabotage? Or had he really seen the cylindrical objects in the sky, the slash of laser-bright lightning, just before the first rig exploded?"

He continued happily in that fashion, ignoring messages. By the time he had printed out the first chapter, he found that he was an hour late for the dinner at his mother's— three of the messages had been from her.

He had the vague feeling that he ought to be better dressed, with shoes that had proper buckles and perhaps a bit of lace at his throat. His business suit was really too drab.

"What am I thinking?" he asked out loud. "Oh boy, I guess that process or whatever is finally taking hold. Look, Sir Walter, we don't do things that way anymore. I dress *down* to see my mother. The truth is, she hates suits. She wants me in jeans or sweats so I can sit on the floor and watch her friends gaze into crystals."

He gave his reflection a quick look in the bathroom mirror and frowned. "Of course, one can't really blame her for disliking suits when they're so dull," he muttered—back to himself. "Perhaps it's time to start a trend . . . ?"

His mother was practically alone—just her current poet, who was also a musician and actor, so she didn't need several, he supposed, and a girl who looked about twelve years old.

His mother was dressed in something handwoven in Guatemala on top and jeans on the bottom. When she held her arms out to him he noticed how thin they were and could have kicked himself for not noticing before. "Sweetie, this is Lawrence Lassiter, *the*? I'm sure you'll have seen him on television either in *Real Police Car Chases*, his successful series, or on all the greatest talk shows. And Lawrence, love, this is my son, the capitalist." Indicating the twelve-year-old with a graceful flip of her hand, she added. "This is Lawrence's daughter, Chanel."

"I pronounce it Channel," the girl said, pumping his hand with one daubed with ink. A pad and a Bic pen whose clear cylinder had turned dark with spilled ink lay beside her seat on the floor. *Another* poet? "My friends call me TV."

"What were you working on?" he asked. Like he cared. In fact, he was amazed that he had bothered.

"Lecture notes," she said.

"Chanel is an associate professor of English literature at the U, sweetie," Mother said.

Not twelve years old after all then? While he was digesting this, his mother said, "*Honey*, I thought the idea of you coming to dinner tonight was so we could spend time together. What's with the sheaf of paper you're clutching? *Don't* tell me, please, you just have to make five or six short calls and then you'll be right with me?" The words were the same nagging ones he'd learned to tune out, but now he looked—

really looked—into her face and saw the sadness and resignation there.

He grinned and handed her the papers he actually hadn't been aware he was clutching until she mentioned it. "It's the first chapter of my novel."

There was a small groan from Chanel, who suddenly became very busy with her notes.

"And—uh—no, I didn't bring work," he said, while his mother was staring uncomprehendingly at the papers and trying to bring her lower jaw up from chest level. With some effort, he turned to Lawrence, who was tall—no doubt worked out from the look of him—had chiseled features, and except for the long white hair tied back in a ponytail could have passed for thirty. "You're a musician, Mother said. What instrument?"

Lawrence shrugged. "Guitar, piano, a little fiddle."

"Would you feel too much like it was a busman's holiday if we had a little singaround after dinner? I thought Mom might want to sing some of the old ballads with me like she did when I was a kid. I'm getting kind of interested in them again."

"Surely there's not a new market coming open for them now, is there, Andy?" his mother asked. "And you haven't called me Mom since you were eleven. Honey, have you started therapy?"

"No, no," he said. "Well, not exactly. But after our conversation last night, I realized that life is short, and my focus has become kind of narrow. I decided to—er—broaden my horizons. And once that decision was—implemented, I guess you could say—the novel just started coming. Hope you like it."

"When did you find the time?" she asked, scanning the page.

"Oh, you know, I let Collins take the meeting. I sometimes do that when I'm developing a new enterprise."

"Oh, but, honey, you're always telling me that writing is

for people who don't need to pay attention to their own business to survive. I mean, I'm delighted but . . ."

He gave his mother a peck on the cheek and put his arm around her, then pointed to page one. "Thrillers make money, and this is going to be one of those. See, the lead character is a lawyer and it's in the wilds of Northern Scotland so there's lots of room for chases and that sort of thing, and on oil rigs, so it starts off with a nice explosion. Besides, I hardly need to worry about where my next meal is coming from and I've been told I need to learn to delegate authority. *And* if I can't interest a publisher, I'll buy one and market this appropriately myself. It's a win-win situation."

"Not exactly," Chanel said. He looked down at her where she was still seated on the floor and realized, perhaps, that probably his mother had invited her along as a prospective date for him, and he had been ignoring her. She looked slightly pissed about something, anyway. "Publishing must not be an area you've dealt with much, McCallum. It's not very stable now. And even very *good* writers who've dedicated their lives to it and yes—have had trouble surviving because of that dedication—have suffered from the ups and downs of that business. Sir Walter Scott, for instance, spent his last few years writing himself out of debt because he lost all of his money when the publisher he invested in went broke."

"He—did?" Andrew felt as if someone had slammed into him with a truck. There was a lot more happening to him than just being able to start the novel to please his mother and getting a singing voice. He was going to have to look at this very carefully. He felt physically ill remembering how long and hard he had talked to set up the meeting he had blown off earlier in the day. His hands shook and his mouth went dry and his knees felt so weak he found himself dropping onto the floor beside Chanel. His mother, oblivious, sank gracefully into the cradle of one of her retro beanbag chairs, her nose in his prose.

"What—uh—what else do you know about Scott? Did he do anything else stupid? Was he an alkie?"

Chanel looked offended. "Absolutely not. He drank, of course, but very moderately for his day. He was a very generous man and a bit extravagant, but he simply had a failed investment. It could happen to anyone."

Andrew, who had never had an investment fail in his life, licked his lips with a tongue that felt like sandpaper. "You sound like you know a lot about him."

"I did my doctoral thesis on the traumas of his early life and how they related to his poetry," she said stiffly, as if she had been accused of a crime.

"That's very interesting. Because I am in need of a consultant who is an expert on the man."

"Really?" That seemed to please her. "Is he going to be the author the movies go nuts about next? Like the resurgence of interest in the Brontës?"

"Something like that, but not quite so related to trend. Have you—have you considered doing consulting work?"

"I'm afraid my class schedule hardly leaves me time—"

"It would be pretty much full-time, actually."

"I can hardly give up my career," she began. Andrew was thinking that he had just met her, did not know anything of her personality, character, bad habits, and should have her thoroughly investigated before he made a commitment.

But though he didn't know her, he had a terrible feeling she knew him better than he knew himself right then, and he needed to know what she knew. Furthermore, he needed her with him to tell him when he was acting more like Scott than himself. "I think I'm about to make you an offer you can't refuse," he said. And added, because it seemed the right thing to do, "That is, if you'd be so kind as to indulge me."

A Rose with All Its Thorns

Lillian Stewart Carl

Suffused with the arctic gleam of self-possession, Virginia clasped her hands in her lap and asked, "You're sure you have the correct DNA?"

Wilhelm Wolfe wasn't quite smiling back at her. His face was twisted into that expression of ghastly affability men use when confronting a competent woman. Theseus had probably looked like that at the point of the Amazon queen Hippolyta's spear, Virginia told herself. A shame she hadn't gone on and run him through, but that was Greek tragedy for you.

What had brought Virginia to Wolfe's office was a Tudor tragedy. Whose participants would certainly have recognized the classical names, even as they made the deplorable mistake of ascribing contemporary motives to historical figures.

"Quite sure," Wolfe replied. "We compared the DNA sample we retrieved from the excavations at the chapel of St. Peter ad Vincula in the Tower of London with a sample of the DNA from Thomas Boleyn's tomb at Hever church. The DNA sequence is Anne's, no doubt about it."

"Then I'm ready for the procedure." Virginia started to stand up.

Wolfe raised a cautious hand. "Ah, just one moment, Miss Follansbee."

"Dr." Virginia rolled her eyes. Of course Wolfe wouldn't acknowledge someone so much younger than he was, and a woman to boot, as his equal.

"Dr.," returned Wolfe, clearing his throat. "I really must ask just why you want the DNA of Anne Boleyn, hardly the happiest person in history."

"That's just the point, Dr. Wolfe." Virginia sat back down and leaned forward, her pale blue eyes emitting the frostiest of glares. She'd learned how to use such glares the last few years. Only the strongest survived the jungles of academe. "It's history, isn't it? Anne Boleyn was a prototypical victim of sexual harassment. Used, abused, and ultimately executed on trumped-up charges by a megalomaniacal Henry VIII because she bore him a daughter, not the son he wanted."

"I always thought it was ironic that the daughter he rejected turned out to be Elizabeth I."

"More than ironic. More, even, than poetic justice. Divine retribution. Henry changed the history of Europe to serve his own ego, claiming he was acting according to the will of God. Typical, for a man to think his own desires are God's."

Wolfe's expression stretched. He almost seemed to be holding back a laugh. Odd, how people's physiological reactions to stress often resulted in laughter.

"But then," Virginia went on, "it was an age when women were forced to act on men's orders, not on their own desires. Anne's crime was in challenging Henry's image of himself. No wonder he explained away his infatuation by blaming her, saying she'd bewitched him. Now, of course, we realize women are a colonized race. It's time for herstory to be told accurately. It's time for a victim like Anne to have a second chance at living her own life on her own terms, not on a man's."

"You've made a study of her life, haven't you?"

"Sixteenth-century sexual politics was the subject of my

Ph.D. dissertation. I now have a publisher waiting for me to finish an expanded version concentrating on the martyrdom of Anne Boleyn. How better to research a subject than to see her life through her own eyes?"

"And," Wolfe went on, "I believe you're being considered for a tenured professorship in Women's Studies at Northeastern Liberal Arts University? A truly seminal work would send you to the head of the list, wouldn't it?"

Virginia raised her chin, visualizing it as the bow of a battleship. " 'A seminal work.' Why not 'an ovular work'? You see what I'm up against, Dr. Wolfe. Even the English language is sexist. If I'm named to the professorship, I'll be in a position to serve womankind."

"Yes, yes, of course." Wolfe grinned, then hastily sobered.

He'd done a background check on her, hadn't he? Well, what could you expect? He had to make sure he got his money. And the money was there, no problem. Virginia's hands knotted together so fiercely her knuckles cracked.

She could still see her father sitting smugly behind his huge desk, its mahogany top a trackless waste of old-growth forest brought down to feed his ego. How excruciatingly embarrassing it was to be the recipient of a trust fund fattened by his investments: pharmaceuticals such as Viagra and Propecia. Anheuser Busch. General Motors. And (Virginia cringed) the Dallas Cowboys football team.

When she'd come into the money two years ago, at age twenty-three, she'd realized it was her moral duty to cleanse and redeem it.

Anne Boleyn. The feminist martyr. "I'm ready," Virginia said again, and this time did stand up.

The door opened, Dr. Chimera glided into the room. He—she—it was even more objectionable in person than in photos. That sublime smile was just what you'd expect from a man who'd swallowed his wife's independent existence as heedlessly as a gourmand swallowing an oyster.

Chimera waved one graceful hand toward the door. "This way, please, Miss Follansbee."

"Dr.," Virginia said. Evoking the ghosts of her foremothers Emmeline Pankhurst and Susan B. Anthony, she walked toward her destiny.

□

It wasn't that she was dreaming. It wasn't that she was having nightmares. The images, the sensations, came so thick and fast Virginia felt the familiar narrative thread of Anne's life and untimely death tangling and knotting in her hands.

She smelled open sewers and pomanders and her own mother's perfume. She tasted M&Ms and fresh apples. She heard voices, hoarse male voices shouting and children laughing, crowds jeering and dry professorial tones fading into fall afternoons.

She remembered birthday parties and the Field of the Cloth of Gold. Spotlights, open fires, candles. Fever and chills. Insects biting. The pain of childbirth. Sweat-soaked sex . . .

Those last two weren't hers. Neither of them, not hers. Virginia realized she was hyperventilating, whimpering in her sleep. She bore down, gritting her teeth against any show of weakness, even to herself.

She was running through the hedge maze at Hampton Court, her embroidered velvet dress twisting around her ankles, her athletic shoes thudding on the ground. A tourist guide spoke arch Oxbridge through a loudspeaker. Horses whinnied and weapons clashed in the tiltyard behind the wall. She turned this way and that and every way led to a dead end, but still the footsteps came on behind her. Until she reached the center and stopped, threw back her head, and laughed in a fierce joy and a fiercer madness.

A spring morning, sunlight gilding the ancient walls of the Tower, her heart hammering—at last at last—in resignation and relief mingled. The faces, eager faces, grim faces, were turned toward her. All the faces she'd wooed and won and lost again were here at the end.

The blindfold closed her eyes, erasing the walls and the watching faces. She heard a step behind her. A blow slammed her forward into nothingness. Her consciousness spattered into stars, drifted, fell, and coalesced again.

When, where, how? Memories of Virginia's own life cascaded through her mind. Again she heard Wolfe's condescending voice. And something deep in her mind sighed in comprehension.

She opened her eyes and stared at the ceiling. It was an ordinary plaster ceiling, with a couple of nails working their way loose and a cobweb trembling in one corner. Tentatively, like probing a sore tooth, she poked through her own head. The other awareness was there, a resonance below her own thoughts.

She hadn't expected it to be like this. It wasn't like reading a reference book, or watching a movie, or interacting with a Web site. She felt.

She'd been sick the first time she crossed the Channel. It'd hurt falling off her bicycle and splitting open her knee. Warm mulled wine reminded her of Dr Pepper. Henry's large but delicate hands played with her body . . . Yeah, she remembered Matt's clumsy efforts, too, and what a waste of time and energy that had been.

Laughter bubbled through her mind, laughter with a tart edge. Something warm and bittersweet curled through her body, making her stretch like a cat. She rolled over on her side, nestled her cheek into the pillow, and went back to sleep.

☐

Virginia stared at her own face in the bathroom mirror. And it was her face, pale and pinched, capped with short brown hair looking like the nest of some particularly inept bird.

Anne had been olive-skinned, with lustrous black eyes. Her dark hair had hung luxuriantly to her waist.

Virginia tugged at her own short strands in something between frustration and puzzlement. But short hair was easy to take care of. Why bother with rollers and perms? Why bother with cosmetics, for that matter, just to live up to the artificial body image men demanded for their own selfish pleasure?

She turned away from the mirror, intending to take her usual brisk shower, and found herself contemplating the felicities of indoor plumbing. She turned the taps on and off and flushed the toilet, almost giggling at the rush of water. At last she climbed into the shower, adjusted the spigot to different strengths, tried various temperatures, and settled on a slow pulse of hot water. She'd never noticed just what exquisite sensations hot water made as it flowed down her body. She lingered until she was wet and sleek as a seal.

When she dressed in her practical and professional clothing her fingertips itched. Silk and velvet, she thought. Bright colors and the shine of jewels.

Anne had been brainwashed by the standards of beauty of her time. Men dressed their women in fine clothes and jewels to show their power. The woman was as much a possession as the clothes and jewels. Virginia threw on her clothes with less attention than she'd throw groceries into a sack and left the laboratory.

Chimera was hovering. "How do you feel, Dr. Follansbee?"

"Great. Would you call me a taxi, please?"

"You're going back to the States today?"

"No. The annual conference of Tudor historians is here in the U.K. this year. A preliminary seminar at Hever Castle, appropriately enough, starts this afternoon. I have to . . ." She almost said, "impress several people." "I have to present a paper, part of my upcoming book."

"Of course." Smiling inscrutably (if you could still use "inscrutable" about an Asian person), Chimera passed her on to a flunkey.

Virginia shouldn't have answered "great." Her hip joints seemed to be attached differently, so that her usual no-nonsense unisex stride had become shorter and slower. Some aftereffect of the procedure, she told herself. No need for Wolfe or Chimera or their technicians to fuss over her any longer. She swung her legs gracefully into the taxi, smoothed her skirt, and told the driver, "Victoria Station."

Several minutes later she spotted the mock-Byzantine towers of Harrods and heard her voice saying, "Wait! Stop here!"

□

Virginia arrived at Hever Castle breathless, dazed, and mortally embarrassed. She'd never missed an appointment in her life, let alone shown up three hours late for a conference. She only hoped she could get checked in before anyone saw her.

Before anyone saw her festooned with green-and-gold Harrods' bags. Wearing lipstick, blush, and eyeliner. Her hair colored a golden blond and swept back with gel. She could hear the jeers of the male academics—"intellectual lightweight" and "frivolous" would be the least of them.

She'd expected she'd feel a bit schizophrenic her first few hours with Anne's personality. But during her shopping spree she'd felt like she was possessed by a demon child on Christmas morning—Oh, how pretty, feel, smell . . . Okay, she thought. The poor woman was relishing her second chance. Her freedom. Once she realized what important issues were at stake she'd settle down.

Virginia paid the taxi driver, gathered up her suitcase and her shopping bags, and started toward the castle gates. Tourists wandered past her, stopping to take photos of the medieval church and its lych-gate, which in the late-afternoon sunshine looked like a British Tourist Authority travel poster for Merrie Olde England.

Had Wolfe's men bribed the vicar for access to Thomas Boleyn's grave inside, Virginia wondered?

Or had they indulged in a bit of grave robbing? Not that Thomas Boleyn deserved to rest in peace, the way he'd thrown his daughter to the wolves of ambition.

How it must've hurt to see her fall faster than she'd risen, than they'd all risen, a shooting star flaming and then burning out. Thomas lost everything, not least Anne herself, and his only son, her brother, done to death at her side. No wonder both Anne's parents were dead themselves within two years, and Hever itself in Henry's vindictive hands . . .

Thomas Boleyn brought it on himself, thought Virginia, with his pride and ambition.

My pride and my ambition gone to ashes, whispered that resonance in her mind.

Virginia tried to drown it out, shouting silently, money is power! Power is masculinity! For Thomas Boleyn, for Richard Follansbee, for Wilhelm Wolfe.

For William Waldorf Astor, who'd bought decrepit Hever Castle at the turn of the last century and restored it. With unheard-of sensitivity for a man he hadn't slapped a crenelated Victorian monstrosity onto the ancient structure to house his guests but had built a mock Tudor village next to it.

Which, Virginia thought as she stopped dead at the top of the walk, actually worked. The different roof angles, the variety of chimneys, the muted colors blended in with rather than overwhelming the moated stone square of the castle itself . . . She went giddy. "Déjà vu" was as inadequate a description of the sensation as "a couple of snowflakes" described an avalanche.

She'd been here before. It'd been different: a real, smoky, offal-filled village in front of the castle, not behind. Trees and fields instead of the formal Italian garden. A muddy stock pond instead of a lake.

It'd been the same: the ivy-hung buttresses. Ducks pleating

the still waters of the moat. The soft green hills rolling away north, toward London.

She'd been a child catechized in the Catholic faith and the Boleyn name. (Boleyn, her father decreed, much more elegant than Bullen.) She'd been a girl returned from France, exiled from the court in London, bored to tears with country life. She'd been a young woman, watching as her sister Mary grew great with the king's child, until the king himself turned to her, and her parents urged her into his arms.

Your wife I cannot be, both in respect of my own unworthiness and also because you have a queen already. Your mistress I will not be.

But those brave words had been no more than the frightened squeak of a small animal caught in the talons of a predator. A sexual predator. Anne was doomed from the start. What Henry wanted Henry got—God himself wanted Henry to have his desires—and what was a woman's purpose but to provide first amusement and then sons?

A brilliant gamble, my nerve set against his. Or so it would have seemed, had I won.

Virginia shook herself, wishing that Wolfe or Chimera had warned her about these awkward side effects. Wondering if anyone had ever sued them for misrepresentation she walked purposefully past the shops and restaurant to the Tudor Village Conference Center.

☐

"Yo, Virginia! Looking good!"

She glanced over her shoulder. It was that twit Edmund Gooch from California Humanities, homing in on her like a moth to a flame. Funny, she could've sworn he didn't know what her name was.

Oh. She'd tried to wash off the makeup, but succeeded only in giving herself the dewy fresh cheeks and wide eyes of a Hollywood ingenue. And she hadn't made her escape from the bedroom without substituting teal silk for her white cotton blouse and draping her shoulders with a long scarf in a multicolored impressionist print.

Feeling some gaseous emotion between irritation and contempt, her mind shaped the retort, "It hardly matters what I look like." What came out of her mouth was, "Why thank you, Edmund!"

His face twitched like a basset hound on the scent. "On your way to the banquet?"

"Where else?"

"Good." Gooch opened the hallway door and ushered her across the lamplit courtyard. "Chilly out here with the sun going down. Would you like my jacket?"

She snorted derision. All this pseudo-chivalry crap was designed to keep women at a disadvantage by making them appear weak. She managed to get to the next door ahead of Gooch and opened it herself.

They were inside the castle. It was a much restored interior, but the intricately carved beams and tapestries were of the period—firelight and cooking meat and a bit of embroidery in her hands . . . She stumbled and Gooch caught her arm. "Mmmm. Nice perfume."

She'd tried to wash that off, too. Just as well she could still smell it—it helped cover up the memory of unwashed bodies.

Several of their professional colleagues were gathered in the entrance hall, serving themselves from an array of bottles. Among them was Elise Rossiter from Midwestern Tech, her cosmetic mask even thicker than usual and her leopard-print dress even tighter. Overwrought, Virginia thought, oversexed, and (unfortunately) over here. Disgusting, the way she draped herself over the male scholars and breathed suggestive alcohol fumes into their faces, as though they'd ever respect a word she wrote after that.

Much more important to her purpose, though, was Arnold Pickering from Northeastern, Dean of History, head of the professor of Women's Studies search committee. He looked like a self-satisfied walrus surrounded by younger members of the historian herd.

"Virginia!" he declaimed. Voices fell silent. Heads turned. "I'm looking forward to your paper tomorrow evening. New insights into the life of Anne Boleyn? That should be interesting—she's a much-plowed field, I'm afraid." He guffawed, looking around to make sure everyone else did too.

Virginia opened her mouth to say, "Yeah, it suits the male ego to think of her as a vixen rather than as a victim." But her lips said mildly, "Good to see you again, Arnold. Elise. I'm going to have a look around since I missed the tour this afternoon." And her body swiveled and carried her away.

Behind her Pickering stage-whispered, "Whoa—did somebody spike her granola with estrogen?"

Virginia plunged through a sitting room and up a stone spiral staircase. At the top she stopped to catch her breath. Don't do that! she ordered the echo in her mind, but even as she formulated the thought another rose in its place: *It is honey that draws the flies, not vinegar.*

Men. Flies. Yeah.

She was standing in a little panelled room with a half-domed ceiling, filled with the rosy gold liquid light of the setting sun. Portraits lined the walls. A glass case held the prayer book Anne had carried with her to the block.

Here she'd slept and dreamed, read and wept. Here was her prison until she recanted her love for Henry Percy—her king had other plans for her, and forbade the match. Here she'd seen her life lying before her. A dead end. A trap.

One portrait was that of Henry himself. Virginia was all too familiar with its reproductions—the old goat in his bestriding-the-world pose, his codpiece like a battering ram.

I never wanted to love him. But he walked the Earth like a god, a sun in splendor, and I was only a woman shadowed by his glory.

He was dynamic, conceded Virginia. Dazzlingly intelligent. His moods were quicksilver and his ego granite. In masquerades he played Theseus, Alexander, Hercules.

He fell from the firmament like Lucifer himself, angel becoming devil, until both he and I no longer loved and so was my eclipse accomplished.

Virginia felt not the painted eyes but the living ones of the autocrat (absolute power corrupts absolutely) as they watched her, narrow and calculating. Tension swelled inside her head as her belly swelled beneath her gown. She wanted to shout, to throw something, anything to relieve the anxiety.

Something had to give, she thought. And what gave were the pregnancies, three of them after the first, all males.

I miscarried of my savior, sighed the resonance in her mind.

Anne had laughed hysterically when she'd at last been arrested and sent to the Tower. When for the first time in years she'd known her future as a certainty, not as a gamble.

Shuddering, Virginia turned around and faced the portrait on the opposite wall. A woman, redheaded like her father, intelligent, cunning, a queen. The name swept through her on a gust of passion:

Elizabeth!

"Whoa," Virginia said beneath her breath, and staggered out of the tiny room into the sitting room next door—twentieth-century couches, a medieval tapestry—and through another door into a hallway lined with the sort of historical artifacts a few minutes ago she'd have genuflected in front of.

Now she wanted to get away. But the house was arranged around a courtyard and she kept walking in—well, not in circles, in squares. More than once she tripped over sneaky little steps. Massive bedsteads leaped out of musty shadows. Display cases gleamed spectrally. In the distance she could hear the voices of the others—of the court—but she couldn't find them. It was like her dream, Anne's dream, of the hedge maze. Except nothing was following her. She was alone and lost.

In the long gallery mannequins loomed through the shadows, in their Tudor robes reenacting episodes of Anne's life. Thomas Boleyn—it was her own father's face Virginia saw, furrowed with worry over his investments. Henry and all of his six wives. Francis Weston and Henry Norris and George, her brother George, three of the five men accused of adultery with Anne and therefore treason against Henry. A man— especially a king—who sleeps around is a stud. A woman who sleeps around is a whore.

How clever to accuse George as well. Even if Anne had argued that her marriage with Henry wasn't legal (Henry's first wife Catherine unreasonably refusing him a divorce), and therefore no adultery took place, incest was enough to condemn her.

A mere waxwork figure would but melt and flow away in the heat of our passion.

"What?" Virginia said aloud.

It was Mark Smeaton, mind you, with his musician's fingertips—although Norris was quite adept—how strange, to hold the slender young bodies and taste the freshness of their kisses after Henry's stale, bloated embraces.

Well yes, Virginia rationalized, in the sixteenth century bawdy byplay was accepted, and women gave as good as they got. Verbally. And yet—she frowned, chasing an elusive memory—everybody knew the charges against Anne had been trumped up merely to get rid of her. *Why dare anything, if not to dare all?*

Virginia remembered what Anne had dared. She blushed red-hot. "Shit!" There was a stairway in the corner. She blundered toward it—at least the charges about George were false, thank God for that.

When we were children I put a dead fish down his back.

At this point she wouldn't have minded breaking her neck on the dark, narrow spiral staircase, but no, she shot safely out onto the main floor of the house and stood grasping the newel post as inchoate thoughts of refunds flooded her mind.

This wasn't what she'd bought and paid for. She'd spent good money to have her prejudices confirmed, damn it!

Her body trembled with a disconcerting sexual hum, probably as much the heat of her preconceptions crashing and burning as the memory of lovemaking past. Norris, Smeaton, Brereton—surely they'd realized they courted death by accepting Anne's invitation?

If Henry had power over her, then she had power over him. And when that was gone, still she had power over other men. The gamble made the encounters all the more passionate, moments of pleasure stolen before the game itself came to an end.

Here came Pickering down the corridor, Rossiter simpering on his arm, Gooch and the others dancing attendance. "Virginia!" Pickering bellowed. "Time to eat!"

She let herself be swept into the dining room and seated at the low end of the table (below the salt) while Pickering wallowed in prestige at the top.

Sitting down with her colleagues had always before meant picking a fight or two—sparking discussions, she corrected—but tonight amiable phrases rolled off her own tongue. Amazing. Gooch's work on the Pilgrimage of Grace was a lot less pedantic than she'd assumed.

Servers began carrying in the "Henry VIII" feast that was part of the conference package. When one young woman bulging out of her "saucy wench" outfit whisked away a metal dish cover Virginia thought, what a shame she hadn't had the chance to replace the rib roast with one of the mannequin heads from the gallery. The look on Pickering's face would've been worth a little vandalism. And suddenly she was laughing, happy in the moment as though she'd never before been happy.

A relaxed Anne Boleyn. Practically a contradiction in terms. But not as big a contradiction as a relaxed Virginia Follansbee.

Usually she didn't bother to eat. Enjoying food was self-indulgence. Now she stared as the elaborate dishes were arranged down the table. When had she last eaten? A mouthful of dry bread that morning in the Tower?

The meat was succulent, dripping juices down her chin. The potatoes were crackling crisp outside and mealy within. The spiced wine (all the spices of Arabia, present-day oil prices notwithstanding) warmed her stomach—which was quite warm enough already, thank you—and vaporized in her head, so that steam filled the inside of her skull. She swayed to the period music coming from the minstrel's gallery, and her toe tapped beneath the table.

Ah voilà, quel beau homme! Even Virginia with her tenuous grasp of French caught the meaning, accompanied as it was with the unmistakable damp flare in her gut. She looked up.

Was he gorgeous or what? Young, slender, with a tidy beard and an earring, dressed not in the wretched-excess ruff and pantaloons of the Elizabethan gallant but in a jerkin and breeches. His hands caressed the lute he held, and his lustrous dark eyes were looking directly at her.

Licking the grease from her fingers, she smiled back. And from the corner of her eye intercepted a look of pure hatred from Rossiter. What?

Oh. The woman was clawing at Pickering's arm, trying to get his attention, but the walrus, too, was watching Virginia. She was the only young woman in the room. She was wearing flattering colors. She'd had her hair done in a modest but chic do.

Poor Elise. The woman was using every weapon she had—every weapon she thought she needed—and found them coming up short. While for once Virginia wasn't even fighting. It wasn't fair, was it?

Anne had watched and listened and waited, on tiptoe, holding her breath, gauging each word and each action until at last she no longer cared what people thought. For a time she savaged her enemies with impunity, pushing Henry further and further—would he go so far as to execute his first wife for her?—enjoying that power all the more for knowing it could be snatched away at any moment. *I miscarried of my savior. So did I challenge fate, and lose.*

The young musician set aside his lute and began to sing. It was "Greensleeves," of course, which according to legend Henry wrote for Anne although there was not one jot of historiography to support that contention. His eyes were focussed on Virginia, and his vibrant voice made her shoulder blades tingle . . .

What the hell? Some vestige of her former self protested, but the woman she was now mouthed the words with him: ". . . delighting in your company . . ."

He segued into "The Death of Queen Jane." Henry had announced his betrothal to Jane while Anne's body was still bleeding. Jane had given him the son he craved and then obligingly died before he had a chance to get tired of her. But then, she was a historical lacuna, with no discernible personality—the perfect woman, Virginia supposed.

Pickering gestured abruptly at the serving wench—so it wasn't time for the after-dinner drinks, he wanted his now. And suddenly Virginia saw truculent Henry, frightened witless. Frightened? Yes. That someday he would lose the respect of his court and his people. That someday he would make a mistake. He was a king. He wasn't allowed to make mistakes. When he did, he had no choice but to make other people pay for them.

"A rosebud in June," sang the young man, conjuring up images of couples rolling moistly (in more ways than one) across an English greensward.

Dinner was over. They were going back into the other room. Somewhere between buzzed and blitzed, Virginia followed. Usually at this point in a conference she'd slink off to her room to nurse her grievances. Tonight, wonder of wonders, she had no grievances. The world was a bright and pleasant place. She wondered why she'd never noticed that before.

In the doorway stood the singer/musician, offering her a silver salver piled with candy. "Would you care for a Godiva chocolate truffle?"

"What's your name?" she asked, her hand hovering between the plate and the half-open placket of his shirt. He exuded a spicy aroma, like the wine.

"Owen Harper."

"Do you do this for a living?"

"Not a bit of it. I'm a graduate student in Elizabethan politics at Cambridge. This is what I do for the ready." His dark eyes met hers and sparkled. "Have a sweet, lass."

Not "madam" but "lass." A few days ago she'd have been insulted. Now she took a morsel of candy, lifted it to her lips, and bit.

Her mouth filled with sweet dark warm chocolate (like Owen's eyes, and Anne's). Her throat opened. Her stomach softened. Savoring every molecule, she at last ran her tongue between her lips and smiled up at his enthralled face. "I didn't think I liked chocolate," she murmured confidingly. "I guess I never had any good chocolate before."

He grinned. "We aim to please."

She took another piece and nibbled at it while she watched his lithe body move across the room.

He's no competitor, is he? And if my purse outweighs his, then my advantage cancels out that of his sex.

Time, Virginia thought, had already cancelled out a lot of the advantage of his sex. With wide smile and glittering eye, she schmoozed her way through the group, making as many wordplays as serious comments on historical minutiae, asking Rossiter's advice on her upcoming paper, complimenting Pickering's tie (printed with the posturing macho figures of the Bayeux Tapestry) and then reminding him gently that she was ripe for a full professorship.

When she got back to her room it was late, and she was much too tired to get out the neat stack of pages that was her paper, let alone analyze just what had happened to the cool and orderly habits of her mind. She was losing her head, it seemed . . .

Her laughter was every bit as hysterical as Anne's. And yet hers signaled not a prison door closing but one opening.

☐

In the June sunlight the gardens of Hever Castle made a sight calculated to gladden the heart and sharpen the pen of any romantic poet. Virginia was no romantic poet. If she had been—or if she'd paid her good money for, say, John Keats—she'd be dashing off a ditty about storm clouds and lightning.

Muttering to herself, she plumped down on a bench and examined her options.

She'd made a real exhibition of herself last night. Compromised her principles. She'd blame drunkenness except she knew damn well she hadn't had that much to drink. She'd blame Anne, except she'd asked for Anne.

How facile to claim principle when vanity is truly at stake.

Vanity?

Is not clutching one's preconception to one's heart a form of vanity? Could not compromise be itself a higher form of principle?

Well, yeah. Was it really conceding her feminist credentials to have listened to everyone else's point of view at the banquet—even Arnold Pickering and his stupid sexist jokes. If he didn't realize the only reason everyone laughed at his jokes was because of his position, he was a fool. If he did realize it, then he was pathetic.

Is it better to be a woman, trapped by the limits of power, or a man, goaded into madness by its demands?

Even if that question had had an answer, Virginia's answer wouldn't have been the same as Anne's.

But Virginia couldn't blame Anne for being a product of her times. She shouldn't feel guilty for being a product of her own. If she worked it right, she could have her principles and eat them, too.

Across the way, in the garden gate, a young couple were arguing with each other. She gestured abruptly. He gestured broadly. Virginia wondered what the issue was.

Yesterday she'd have said the issue was that half the couple was male. Today she wasn't so sure. Today the issue for her was what to do about her paper.

She'd managed to drop enough hints last night that to-night she'd probably have everyone hanging on her every word instead of greeting her with garlic and crucifixes. She needed to take advantage of that interest, and she had the queasy feeling that going with the original fire-and-brimstone polemic wasn't going to do it. Would it be cowardice to tone down the rhetoric?

Not when the rhetoric was in defense of a position she now knew to be untenable, that Anne had been an innocent victim, acted upon but never acting.

I confessed my sins before God, should I be loath to confess them before man? And woman as well? An instructive tale, I should think.

Yeah right. Virginia was going to stand up before the group, and say, "Fellow scholars, let me introduce Anne Boleyn, erstwhile queen of England."

No. That was one secret she intended to keep. But every historian knew the whys and wherefores of "allegedly" and "it might be" and "it is thought that." Historical truth was slippery at best, and even now Virginia (Anne in tow) was operating within a cultural context. Why not turn today's postmodernist cultural context to her advantage, and empha-size Anne's ambiguities rather than her victimhood?

The woman in the gate shoved at the man's chest and stalked off around the corner. Crushed, he sagged against the brickwork.

"She kicked him in the nuts, right enough," said a mellow voice in Virginia's ear.

She looked up. Owen was standing over her, offering her a red rose. Torn from a nearby bush, she figured, but what the heck. She took it. "Thanks. Just tell me one thing. Why do men so often use that particular physical context in their metaphors?"

"If you had nuts, that wouldn't need asking. Do you mind?" Without waiting for her reply, he sat down beside her.

She couldn't help but appreciate how his snug jeans set off the objects under consideration . . .

Again she blushed, redder than the rose. Damn it, she'd never gone around blushing before.

Not enough blood, I warrant.

Owen was looking down at his thumb. A drop of blood looked like a tiny ruby on its tip. Shrugging, he thrust the thumb in his mouth and glanced over at her, a gesture that was anything but childish.

"Catherine Howard, Henry's fifth wife," she told him, "was billed as 'the rose without a thorn.' "

"Until she pricked him. Poor old beggar, convincing himself he'd finally found a sweet young thing who loved him for his own gross self and then he learns she's having it off with the young stallions amongst the courtiers."

Henry's illusions were as great as his temper, and in as great a need of cosseting.

Virginia shook her head. She should've come back with some retort about Catherine merely expressing her sexuality and yet . . . In another minute she'd be feeling sympathy for Henry. Talk about ideological whiplash.

She gazed at Owen, her interest level fast approaching lustful. Last night his beard and earring had been nice period touches. Today, with the boots, the jeans, and the leather jacket, they looked stylishly contemporary. Smart. But then, that word applied to mental faculties, too.

He inspected his thumb, found it acceptable, reached over and took her hand. His musician's fingers traced subtle little patterns across the palm. His dark eyes gleamed. "I see by the conference schedule you're giving a paper tonight. What's your subject, then?"

"My subject," she said, "is Anne Boleyn. Who was neither saint nor sinner but, like most of us, a mixture of both."

□

Spending the afternoon tearing the guts out of her paper and rewriting it had been well worth the effort, even if the keyboard of Virginia's laptop had been hot to the touch by the time she was done.

Now every face in the room was turned up to her, faces she needed to woo and to win. And, what was surprising, faces she now knew how to woo and to win. Including Owen Harper's. He'd slipped into the back of the room right after she'd started her presentation. Already in his period costume for the evening's festivities, he looked like an amiable ghost, smiling encouragement. Except the ghost was in her own mind, offering her own encouragement.

Virginia was closing in on the home stretch. "And so the people in the streets, especially the women, hurled abuse at Anne as she passed. And no wonder. If the king could put aside his first wife for failing to bear a son, what about the shopkeepers and the blacksmiths? Yes, the wife had a long list of obligations to her husband, but the husband had obligations to his wife as well."

The door opened. Goneril Pickering walked in and sat down beside her husband. She'd probably missed last night's banquet because she was singing Brunhilde somewhere. Arnold deflated. His eyes darted right and left.

"In her days at the French court Anne heard of and met many powerful women—Louise of Savoy and Margaret of Austria, to name only two. But no woman was strong in her own right. She had to ally herself with a man to be powerful. Going to court, attracting the eye of a powerful man, was the only career open to a woman. For once a woman was powerful, then she would—probably—be safe."

Elise Rossiter nodded. Today she was dressed in black, trying to appear more slender, maybe, but actually looking like a crow. Virginia resolved to give her one of the silk scarves Anne had chosen at Harrods.

"Anne saw her own sister Mary used and discarded by the king. She didn't want to follow that path.

"But Henry's game was the only one in town. Once Anne realized she was trapped, her maidenhood forfeit, perhaps she resolved to bargain it away for as high a price as possible. If she'd borne a son, she'd have been set for life. But she didn't. When did the tantrums she used to manipulate Henry become genuine outbursts of fear and frustration?"

Edmund Gooch was hanging on every word. At least Virginia hoped he was hanging on her words, and not on the light coating of makeup and heather-colored tweed jacket.

"But if Anne was frightened and frustrated, how much more was Henry? He'd mortgaged not only his soul but that of England for a son, and failed. That magnificent codpiece, and yet he had no legitimate son when his glorious ancestors had so many sons they battled each other for the throne. Fear makes people self-centered and cruel. Like Henry. Like Anne."

Virginia remembered Thomas Boleyn, jostling for power and position and dying a broken man. She remembered Richard Follansbee, dying of a perforated ulcer after years of jockeying for position and power. She remembered Henry Tudor. He'd been trapped, too, between the codpiece and the crown, two symbols of power, and the fates (women, in Greek mythology) who seemed determined to take it away from him.

"Catherine of Aragon held out for respect and dignity and died a lingering death of a broken heart. Did Anne perhaps, engineer herself a quicker death by throwing herself into the embraces of Henry's courtiers? Was she making one last cut of the cards to get herself a strong son? Was it simply one last spasm of a rebellious nature she'd never been able to express? Or was it one last desperate grab for the pleasure her sensual nature demanded, but her culture denied her? At her trial, her aggressiveness was used as a sign of her wickedness."

Arnold hadn't blinked for the last three paragraphs. Goneril inspected her fingernails. In the back of the room Owen's eyes flared.

"Norris, Brereton, Smeaton, Weston. They had their choices. And they chose to be as dazzled by Anne, by her vitality with its acid edge, as she'd been dazzled by Henry. As we choose today to be dazzled by her. Thank you."

Virginia had expected a polite smattering of applause, but the clapping was actually enthusiastic.

Propelled by Goneril, Arnold Pickering scuttled toward her. "Virginia, my dear, we must have a very serious talk. Are you coming to the reception?"

"Of course. Wouldn't miss it."

Glancing over his shoulder—Goneril was smiling, every tooth gleaming—he went on, "I don't know what's gotten into you, Virginia, but I'd just about written off any possibility of your coming to us at Northeastern. I mean, we have several of those man-hating bra burners already."

"Pesky bunch, aren't they?" she returned. "Give me just a minute, would you please?"

Pickering turned, was pinioned by his wife, and carried away.

Virginia started stacking her pages. Yeah, money was power. Daddy's money was power, which had backfired for Anne but worked beautifully for Virginia. And where to go from here? Women's shelters, prenatal programs, scholarships. Odd, how she had so little interest in womaning the barricades anymore. She was now much more interested in tearing them down.

Everyone had left the room except Owen. He sketched an elegant bow. "*Brava!* Well done!"

"Needs some more work, but thank you." Also odd, how she'd thought she didn't like men.

Maybe she'd just never met a man before.

There are always men. It is the woman who throws the dice.

Virginia smiled. "I need to get over to the reception—drinks, snacks, acclamation, job offers. When do you get off work?"

"Elevenish. There's some lovely champagne in the storeroom. If I pinched a bottle, do you think you'd still have space for it?"

Ah sirrah, what quantity of my space do you intend to fill . . . "Can you get some of those chocolate truffles, too?" asked Virginia, a little louder than was necessary.

Owen took her hand and raised it to his lips. His warm breath tickled her knuckles. "Whatever my lady wishes. Anon."

She wishes to explore her own ambiguities, Virginia said silently to his retreating back. And the resonance in her mind murmured, *O brave new world, that has such joys in it.*

Reminding herself to send Wilhelm Wolfe a thank you note and a box of chocolates—and a dozen roses, thorns and all, for Chimera—Virginia walked on toward her destiny.

Silver Lining

Elizabeth Moon

Clyde Jenkins peered through the steel mesh of his mask at his opponent, and tried to guess which thrust the old geezer would throw next. Sweat trickled down Clyde's neck, and tickled his ribs; the expensive velvet doublet he wore—scarlet with black fur edging—was soaking under his black leather jerkin. His left arm ached from the unaccustomed weight of his new buckler.

His opponent, a paunchy older man in yellow-and-green leathers, should have been dead by now. Clyde had seen him strolling around between matches, his graying hair blowing past his bald patch, beer in one hand and barbecue sandwich in the other, accompanied by a gaggle of laughing girls. His age, the way he ate and drank and—whatever those girls implied—the old coot couldn't possibly have the stamina to keep fighting. But he wasn't dead yet. The best attacks Clyde knew kept landing on the man's battered green buckler.

Clyde took a breath and rushed forward, only to feel his sword thwack into the buckler again. Something nudged his belly, and he realized that somehow the old man had rolled a thrust underneath, where he couldn't see it.

It was only a brush; Clyde didn't call it. Even a real sword, he was sure, would have done no harm with such a light touch. Instead, he lunged again, this time using his height and reach to whip an overhead toward his opponent's helm. But the green buckler flashed up, deflecting his blade, and at that moment a blow he could not ignore took Clyde's breath away. Voices nearby cheered.

"DAMN!" Clyde threw his blade on the ground and yanked off his helmet. "Dammit! It's not fair!"

"It was a fair shot," the safety marshal said.

His opponent had pushed his mask up, revealing all too clearly his amusement at Clyde's reaction. "Good match," he said, holding out his hand.

"It's never a good match when I lose!" Clyde said, grabbing up his blade. He stormed off, but not fast enough.

"Then, sirrah, you must have many bad matches." He didn't know which of the group around the older man said it, but he wanted to cram his weapon right down the scum's throat till the hilt broke his teeth.

☐

Halfway through his second beer, Clyde was still fuming. It wasn't fair. He was tall, strong, handsome, athletic—the perfect figure of a fencer. He had taken fencing as an elective in college, and as usual with any new enthusiasm, had gone out and spent top dollar for the best equipment, the best clothing, and then the best private instructor he could find.

Dressed in formal whites, with a curl of black hair over his forehead, he had impressed his then-current girlfriend Sheila, and Sheila's roommates Celeste and Gail; there had been many a private joke about swords and scabbards before they discovered that he was sleeping with all of them and turned on him in a storm of female hormones.

And then he had come in only fourth in the regionals, and the coach refused to have him on the team any longer, just because he'd said what he thought about the puny little Jap who beat him out of third place, and the rotten, politically correct judges who thought they had to kowtow to public opinion.

So he had broken a (cheap) practice foil over his knee and walked out, and ignored sports entirely for the remainder of college. He'd emerged with a very useful Business Administration degree and—four years later, when his grandfather died—a fortune to play with.

It was the redhead in the secretarial pool who introduced him to the first of the reenactment groups. She had been willing enough, and her reaction to the photograph of him on the college team had started it. She had almost bounced off the bed in her enthusiasm. He should start fencing again; he should make a costume and come to this and that event. She would introduce him . . .

She didn't, because he dropped her when she insisted on lecturing him about Celtic mythology and the correct pronunciation of Welsh names. Also she had the quaint notion that he should make his own costumes—patently ridiculous, that's what money was for, to avoid the need for even one pricked finger. Still he let her down gently, for him, after he'd found out which group she belonged to so that he could avoid it.

Because he wanted to appear like a knight out of legend—like that—he couldn't quite remember—who appeared in a flash of light in some fantasy movie. He roamed the Internet, looking up sites that introduced him to the many, many groups involved in what he called fantasy history.

And now here he was. Nominally a member of a mythical kingdom, he'd invested in new weapons and the best clothes he could find in the catalogs. Money was no object—he was going to do it right. He'd been to the announced fencing practices; he'd warmed to the praise that his correct form garnered. But the actual bouts were harder than he had expected.

His opponents didn't stay on the strip. They used defenses

illegal in college—batting his blade aside with a padded hand, or with stupid plywood circles with screen-door handles screwed on the back, which they called bucklers. They kept lecturing him about his form, about history, about outmoded handicrafts, as if they were experts on something important.

Most of the people in the group were, in Clyde's eyes, losers. Secretaries, receptionists, a junior high teacher, computer nerds. Not one of them had a clue about finances, and they thought money was vulgar. They wore unfashionable clothes even when they weren't in costume, and they persisted in calling each other by their fantasy names, or strange nicknames. He couldn't completely conceal his contempt for them, for their pretensions at expertise, and they repaid his contempt with a certain coolness that made him all the more eager to prove his superiority.

He knew there was another fencing practice somewhere. No one would admit to it, or tell him where or when, or who was going, but he couldn't mistake the signs of secrets withheld. "Ariana" had explained a bruise one day by saying she got it Wednesday at "Bord's." Another time he heard a reference to "That night Mike came to Bord's with his new blade." No one would admit to being Bord, or knowing who Bord was, not even "Ariana," who in real life was Stephanie Neill, a dental receptionist.

But the best fighters in the group had all mentioned Bord at least once, and they hung together. They had tricks no one else seemed to know. They exchanged knowing looks, which excluded him.

It wasn't fair. He could learn those tricks if only he had a chance. He could beat that stupid old man if he knew the tricks. There had to be a way.

It was then he remembered the Tsering process. Tsering was some kind of Asiatic mystical sort, and ordinarily he scoffed at all that, but—Wilhelm Wolfe was a solid businessman, a German. And the first reports had all been favorable. Expensive as hell, but so what?

He downed the rest of the beer and stalked out of the fake tavern. He would show them. He would come back next year and beat them all.

☐

His executive assistant did not turn a hair when he asked her to find out who the top fencing masters were in the sixteenth through nineteenth centuries. By the end of the day, he had a list, courtesy of a reference librarian at the state university. George Silver, Saviolo, de Grassi, and Angelo. A brief biography of each, with an equally brief commentary on which subsequent fencing masters had preferred which of these.

He chose Silver, because Silver was English. He wouldn't have to wrestle with a foreign language, and he was fairly sure that Silver (whose biography included the comment that he had scorned the Italian, French, and Spanish fencing instructors) was actually the best.

The staff at the Center didn't ask him why he wanted George Silver, and he didn't volunteer. It was none of their business anyway. It took them a while to locate the necessary biological bits, but the call came within the month. He rescheduled what he could, cancelled the rest, and checked into the facility.

☐

Clyde woke up abruptly, and before he'd realized it had swung his legs over the edge of the bed.

"How do you feel?"

"Fine. Quite well, actually—"

I do not. I feel like I've just waked up in a whore's bed—God's teeth, what a foul stench of perfumery!

Clyde blinked. It had to be the voice of his fencing master, but it didn't sound at all like the cultivated English voices he'd heard in PBS specials. And he himself could scarcely smell the faint floral scent of the room deodorizer.

What tomfoolery is this? This isn't my body! This gross giant—!

"There's nothing wrong with my body," Clyde muttered. The doctor cocked his head. "Just the . . . new inhabitant," Clyde said to him. "He seems to be surprised to find himself in a new body."

"Ah—you are aware of him as a separate personality. That's somewhat unusual, but not unknown. Well, that will change. You will integrate into one seamless self in a few days."

"And then," Clyde said, "I'll be the best fencer in the world . . ." He had just time to wonder why he'd said that, and not "—in the SCA—" when the strange voice spoke up again.

You want a fencing *master? You stole my bones for your foul sorcery, just to get a fencing master?*

Clyde told himself to ignore the voice and went on chatting with the doctors through the checkout procedure. In the passage outside, he suddenly whirled, in a dance step that ended with his right arm outflung toward the door.

You damn well need a fencing master—an unbreeched infant could turn faster. At least you chose the best, not one of those fantastical Italians, more fit to teach how to wound a friend than kill an enemy.

Clyde made it to the street, before Silver's voice intruded again.

God-a-mercy! What witchcraft is this?

Clyde opened his mouth, then realized he didn't have to talk aloud to Silver—he could, with a little concentration, talk directly to him mentally. He ran through a quick précis of the intervening four hundred years, which included everything he knew—history had never been his favorite subject—and was rewarded with silence almost all the way to the airport.

Then, in an ominously quiet tone: *This is not England?* No, Clyde thought. We were an English colony, but . . . *Rebellion! Treachery! Why—what wicked prince so misled you—*

Not me. I wasn't born yet.

Four hundred years . . . and yet Our Lord has not returned?

Clyde had no idea what that meant.

Or is this Hell, and have I been damned?

Religion. Silver was talking religion. Clyde sighed in relief. "Nobody cares about that anymore," he murmured. The taxi driver cocked an eye back.

"Whazzat?"

"Nothing," Clyde said. And to Silver: I mean, there are still churches, of course, but most people don't take them seriously. After all, we've been to the Moon . . .

Churches! What—has Rome then shattered, as men said it might, into the scintillant shards of heretical doctrines? And you care not? What have you for souls, then, if—

Science, Clyde thought firmly, as he paid the taxi driver, patted his jacket pocket to be sure of his passport, his plane tickets, his wallet. We have science. We don't have to worry about souls and Heaven and Hell. We don't need those musty old beliefs; we have knowledge.

Silence again, until he had passed the security booth and presented his ticket at the gate. You'll like this, he thought at Silver. Airplanes—ships of the air. Flying higher than birds, and much faster.

Witches fly to the Moon. There they commune with their foul master, Satanas, and dabble the bright orb God gave for the lamp of night with the blood of innocent babes. Surely I have waked to mine own damnation, to be locked in a witch's head and forced to take such flight.

We're not going to the Moon, Clyde tried to explain. Or to Hell; we're going to Houston. Before Silver could batter him with more Elizabethan hyperbole, he tried to explain, and discovered that he had really very little idea exactly where the city was, in terms of a gentleman of England in 1599, or how it had come to be what it was. I just live there, he defended himself. I don't study it.

You study not at all. I find nothing in your head but tradesmen's calculations, and—by God, sir, you are a usurer! Dirty Jew!

I'm not a Jew; my parents were Unitarians, when they went to church at all. And I'm not a usurer—

You have money lent at interest—that is usury—

No, it's quite legal. If I were to charge illegal rates—

Usury is legal in this realm? I say again, sir, you cannot cozen me; this is indeed Hell—and what is that hideous noise, the bawling of the demons of the air?

It's just the PA system. They give the announcements in several languages.

'Tis Babel, and this is Hell.

That remained Silver's opinion through the wait for the flight, boarding the plane—for which he had a description of such grossness that Clyde felt a blush crawl up his neck—and the flight itself. Though he was, to Clyde's surprise, intensely interested in everything he deplored. He expressed amazement that Clyde could not explain every detail that caught his attention.

I'm not a scientist, Clyde kept muttering internally. I'm not an engineer; I'm not a biologist . . .

You are not much, are you?

Then the flight attendant served his meal. Silver had been momentarily silent, allowing Clyde to choose the poached salmon, but his commentary returned full force when the food appeared. The fruit salad astounded him: the sliced kiwi he mistook for demons' apples, and the pineapple he would have made Clyde spit out if he could. On the rest of the food, he cast a cold eye and sharp tongue: it was not fit for human consumption, let alone sufficient in amount, and as for the utensils—where was a good trencher of honest bread? Why prick at bites with that Frenchified idiocy, that fork?

Silver's acid commentary didn't let up even when they reached Clyde's apartment. He disapproved of the elevator. *These devils' tools but soften the body—*

"I'm not soft—I'm much more fit than the average—"

If that be so, then the men of your world are like stalled kine fattening for slaughter. And the women—never saw I such a col-

lection of freaks and follies as you display here. Trollops, to say the best of them; not one honest dame among them. 'Tis no wonder you need someone like myself, but 'twill be a wonder if I can do aught but move your ignorance one hair sideways.

Silver finally quieted down as Clyde fell into bed, and into a sleep punctuated by dreams in disturbingly bright colors, sharp-edged dreams of thrust and parry, of stiff lace and gold embroidery.

▢

Clyde left for the office early—after that long weekend, he knew he'd have work stacked to the ceiling. Silver sulked below his conscious level, though an occasional twitch of a leg or theatrical turn of the hand betrayed his awareness of Clyde's doings. These came more often during international phone calls, especially the long one to Madrid and the shorter one to Naples. Clyde felt in himself a more than usual distrust of Sr. Ferraro, and a positive distaste for the accents of the receptionists who answered the phones.

By the end of the day, he felt edgy and tense, but he knew that was the natural result of dealing with business after a weekend away.

He had just settled into his hot tub for a nice relaxing water massage when his other ego snarled *Get your fat bum out of there, you lackadaisical heathen! Time to work!*

"I've been working all day—"

You call that work? Giving orders and sitting on your fat arse?

"I'm not fat—"

You're fatter than I ever was. And you eat enough for two, like a breeding wife. Such sugar'd stuff as you consumed today is child's meat. Wouldst be a fencer, shouldst eat like a man, not a boy.

Grumbling, Clyde pulled himself out of the hot tub, dried himself, and pulled on his fencing whites. They still fit; he threw a smug thought at Silver.

You a university graduate? You lie, sirrah. You have no Latin at all, and no Greek; you know less of theology than a paynim of the Africas—

Clyde didn't try to explain what modern universities taught instead of the Seven Arts. He just went to his salon.

Clyde's private fencing salon, fitted with mirrors when it had been his exercise suite with all the fashionable machines, reflected Silver's expression, grim determination.

Your legs, sirrah, are pitiful, mere sticks to hold your rancid flesh upright.

Clyde flushed. "They are not—"

They are. We can do nothing until you have springs where now those twigs slant crook-kneed . . . show me your footwork.

Clyde reached for his practice foil. Silver stopped him with a jerk.

No blade yet, twitterpate. Didst not hear me say footwork? It is the feet and legs we must train first, more's the pity.

Grimly, Clyde put his feet in the proper position, bent his knees, and advanced a step toward the mirror. He saw nothing wrong with his legs.

Sweet Jesus have mercy!

He advanced five steps and lunged.

More.

It was the first time Silver had been so brief, and Clyde backed away, to repeat the exercise.

Again.

Clyde did it again, and then again, and then again, until he was breathless and the quadriceps of his right thigh ached. Silver had made no criticism, beyond insisting that he do it again.

Change the leg, Silver said now.

"What?"

The leg, fool! As with a horse, change the leg to lead with the other. Oh . . . you have no horse? Clyde shook his head, a useless but habitual gesture, and felt Silver's scorn as a wash of acid in his belly. *No horse! And wouldst claim to be a gentleman!*

"We have cars," Clyde said. "They're a lot faster than horses."

And useless for conditioning you for fencing. Now—put forward your left leg. Repeat the exercise.

Clyde put forward his left leg, only to find himself unbalanced. Yes, his first instructors had had him learn to position himself with the blade in his left hand, yet he had never practiced much that way. Silver, he realized, didn't care. Silver's scorn drove him forward, back, forward, back, over and over, until his left leg cramped. He stopped, and bent to massage it.

His back twinged sharply. *And will you thus serve your opponent, bowing like a sheep before the butcher?*

"But my leg—"

Which would you, a trumpery cramp in the leg, which is only pain, or a stroke to the neck, which is life itself? Stand up, thou fool.

Silver drove him on, until Clyde was sweating, gasping, riven with cramps in legs and back. Only then would Silver allow him to use the hot tub, but not for as long as Clyde wanted. After that, he insisted on a cold shower "to revive the vital powers" and sent Clyde to bed without the bedtime snack Clyde's stomach wanted.

The next morning, Clyde woke to the sensation of someone prodding him with a bony finger. He rolled over sleepily, muttering to his presumed bed companion that she should cut it out. Silver cackled in his head, gleefully.

'Tis no strumpet, thou laggard. Up with thee, out into God's good morning, and brace thy slack limbs for war.

Clyde did his best to convince Silver that the old treadmill machine would do instead of a run in the park, but Silver railed at him. Clyde found himself jogging down the sidewalk toward the park through the early-morning gloom.

Once on the jogging path, Silver asked again why he'd been "waked to damnation" as he put it.

"Your reputation as a fencing master—I asked for a list of the best—"

You chose me not from knowledge of my work, but mere repute? And what is that, sir, these days?

Clyde could not lie to his coinhabitant, he quickly found, for Silver ferreted out everything Clyde knew about his reputation, from the decline of swords as weapons of war to their present popularity with groups like that he had joined.

And they still prefer de Grassi, do they? What say they of the Spaniards, then, and their great wheel?

They say it is too elaborate, and not practical enough.

In that, they say true. A long pause, during which Clyde could feel Silver rummaging in his brain, but couldn't tell what he was looking for.

Clyde took that opportunity to slow from a jog to a walk; he hoped Silver wouldn't notice.

Keep running. If I'm to be known through you, as my latest pupil, then you must prove me well.

His lungs burned; his heart pounded; sweat drenched him. He was sure Silver would kill him at this rate. But Silver didn't agree.

Naught's worse for young men than idleness. He who keepeth the body under discipline, shalt most readily meet danger.

Silver's advice changed his diet, too. Clyde had adhered, when convenient, to the current fad for low-fat, low-calorie meals, though supplemented with all his favorite treats. Silver insisted that only red meat would make a man brave; he urged Clyde to eat roast beef, steak, roast pork, venison, roast capons (Clyde gagged when he found out what a capon was), and when Clyde insisted venison could not be obtained without shooting it himself, he tried to talk Clyde into taking up hunting.

☐

For six months, Clyde struggled with Silver's unyielding regimen—walking, running, learning to ride that damnable horse, and, at last, fencing with a blade. Silver wouldn't let him use elevators, and grumbled when he rode in a car for any distance less than five miles. Those areas on which they agreed—that white men were naturally superior, that English was the only reasonable language in which to converse, that political correctness was the stupidest idea of the past two thousand years—hardly made up for the anguish of living up to Silver's standards for the student of fence.

Finally, Silver let him attend a weapons practice with the local group again. It was a moist, slightly cool day in February; Clyde wore his old sweats and carried the épée, whose guard Silver had made him weight with little slugs of lead.

"Hi, Clyde—where you been, man?" Darin didn't sound all that interested in where he'd been, Clyde thought.

"Business stuff," Clyde said. "Had to be on the road a lot—"

"That mess in India?" Darin asked. Clyde smiled. Darin always tried to sound as if he knew something about everything, but actually he was just another nerd.

The others looked him over speculatively. No real welcome—well, he hadn't really expected one. Silver, in his head, looked at them, and Clyde noticed him looking at Ariana and Moonsong more than the others.

Wenches in hose. Silver had finally grown accustomed to modern women, Clyde had thought—at least he'd quit commenting on them—but apparently not to modern women in tights with leather doublets, carrying swords. *That one with the long red braid has a sweet shape, methinks. She'd tumble well, I daresay. But that other—what does a gray-haired matron here? Those hips are fit to bear sons, not jiggle so in hosen while she pretends to fence.*

Wait and see, Clyde told his impatient teacher; she fences better than you might think. Slowly, with many delays and a lot of chatter, the group sorted itself into pairs. Clyde was matched against Paul, enthusiastic but not very skilled. He had beaten Paul even before. Now, with Silver inside, he was sure he could do it again.

Paul advanced in a rush, flailing wildly. Clyde caught his blade, trapped it in his guard, and yanked it away. Paul almost fell, then shook his head. "How'd you do that?"

"Easily enough," Silver said, out of Clyde's mouth. "Thou'rt not ready to meet opponents, with so weak a grip. Here—take thy blade—" Shut up! Clyde tried to say. This isn't how to talk to them! Silver had never taken over his mouth before; he had never imagined Silver could.

"You asshole," Paul said. He yanked his blade free and stalked off.

Clyde wrestled Silver for control of his tongue, and won, at least for the moment. "I'm sorry," he yelled after Paul. "I've been reading this book, and it just came out—"

"Yeah, right," Paul said, but he turned around. "What book? One of those fencing manuals? Sounds like that stuck-up idiot George Silver."

Clyde lost the next round, and Silver sprang forward. "Idiot, sayest thou? And what wouldst thou know, misbegotten offspring of apes and donkeys?" Clyde, struggling desperately to regain control, could have screamed. It was one thing for Silver to agree with him about the dark-skinned people of the world, but you just couldn't *say* things like that these days. Not out loud. Not in public.

"You!" That was Bjorn the Brave. "We knew you were a bad sport, Clyde, but we don't tolerate racism."

Silver had the same contempt for the concept as Clyde had had, and far less inhibition. "That black varlet call'd me an idiot!" he said.

"Go away," Bjorn said. "You aren't welcome here."

"No matter," Silver said. "Not one of you is fit to cross swords with me."

"You think not?" That was Ariana of the long red braid.

"Don't—" Bjorn said. But Ariana smiled, a wide toothy smile with no humor in it.

"I don't mind," she said. "In fact, it would please me to give him a lesson in courtesy as well as fencing—"

Silver chuckled unpleasantly. Clyde hadn't known his throat could make a sound like that. "Wench, 'tis you will be lessoned, as Petrucchio lessoned Kate—"

Clyde wished he could be anywhere else in the universe—even dead—which looked like a distinct possibility from the expressions of the others.

"Wait—" That was Moonsong. "Maybe he's playing a role." She turned to him. "Are you in character?" Clyde nodded. Though Silver had his tongue, he had left Clyde some control of his body. "Well—" She looked around at the others. "I didn't think he had it in him. And of course he would pick an unpleasant character—sorry, Clyde, but it's true. What's your name?"

"George," said Silver.

"You don't suppose he's trying to be George Silver?"

"No, probably George III," said Ariana, running her finger along her blade. "The crazy king."

Clyde felt the sweat running down his back. Silver had his tongue for the moment, and as soon as Ariana raised her blade, Silver had his whole body.

Ariana, though not the best fencer in the group, had quick reflexes, and her thrusts had always seemed, to Clyde, as clean-cut as diamond. But through Silver's eyes she seemed absurdly slow and clumsy, and he drove through her defenses again and again, until she stepped back, and said she was tired.

After that, in short order, Silver used Clyde's body to defeat all of the others, over and over, until they were panting and gasping and unwilling to meet him again. And he wasn't even winded . . . at last Clyde realized how much good those daily runs, those endless drills, had done him.

When the last bout was done, Silver went wherever he went at such times, and let Clyde have his tongue again. He could tell that the group was shocked by his new skill, and by Silver's scathing tongue. And yet they were impressed, as well, even by the abuse Silver had heaped on them.

"You're good, man," Paul said, clapping him on the shoulder. "Awful, but good, y'know?"

"I'm—sorry," Clyde said, surprising himself. How was it that when Silver said what he thought, it sounded so much worse? He himself disliked black people, but Paul wasn't exactly black—well, he was, but not the same way. He'd known Paul a couple of years, and—

"They were all racists back then," Hank said. It was an escape hatch Clyde was glad to take.

"Well—I'll bet we see you at the next tournament, huh?" Paul asked.

"Maybe," Clyde said. He wasn't entirely sure he wanted to enter a tournament, not if Silver could take over his mouth like that. What if he said something even more dreadful, and got him—them—attacked or arrested or something?

☐

He thought of going back to Tsering, to see if he could get the process reversed. But Silver, originally so horrified at the modern world, was now determined to save Clyde's soul.

If I be damn'd, and this be Hell, then naught I do will serve God. Yet I swear, I am still His man, though Satanas do give me the lie. And for that cause, I will obey our sweet Lord, and strive to save even a demon from Hell.

Clyde saw his world with new eyes, and discovered that he didn't much like it. He had expected Silver to be first amazed and then delighted with a chance to live in the future, but now that he had Silver's memories, he could understand why Houston, Texas, United States of America, did not satisfy George Silver, gentleman of England in the late 1500s. Silver dismissed all electrical and electronic devices as "mere sorcery," believed the exhalations of the petrochemical plants were the very chimneys of Hell, and considered mechanical contraptions (his term) as Devilish tools for making men weak. Worst of all, his deep-rooted belief in the existence of God, the Devil, witches, sorcerers, and the like began to fray Clyde's own rationalist conviction that there was nothing to worry about except the profit margin.

He found himself staring at the proposal his development team brought him with a vague distaste that the estimated return on investment could not dispel. Would God approve? He shuddered. He didn't believe in the supernatural, let alone Silver's version of God. But he had to believe in Silver—he had let them put Silver into his brain—and *Silver* believed in God. Bit by bit, phrase by phrase, Silver's beliefs moved in, took over spaces he had happily left vacant.

Was the love of money the root of all evil? Silver had certainly pursued patronage, and fees, as avidly as any other swordmaster of his day, but—there was something else he loved more, and it showed not only in his writing, but also in the very indignation with which he berated Clyde.

"Patriotism's old-fashioned," Clyde said late one night, when Silver's angry buzz wouldn't let him sleep.

'Tis inconvenient sometimes. A man intent on profit alone cannot at the same time serve his countrymen best—

"You don't understand," Clyde said. "We live in a different world, a world where the old rules don't matter."

Are you at last admitting you are demons, and not humans? Faugh! You eat and drink, and what enters your mouth passes out in the same form as in my day, with the same stench. You feel fear; your sinews harden with exercise; you laugh at bawdy jokes. Do I not see Christian and paynim at war, the dark Moor and the pale raider of the north eyeing one another askance? Do not your statesmen wench and wrangle even as ours? How then can God's rules, which are eternal, not matter? Fashions change, aye, and for the worse, but the unchangeable is always to be preferred, and that, sirrah, is Our Lord and His Law.

Day by day, week by week, Silver's certainties eroded Clyde's dogmatic uncertainties. He found himself going to church, hunting through the local congregations until he found one of the ultraconservative Episcopal churches that insisted on using the old prayer book. He read history, with Silver's acid commentary as a gloss on the English monarchy. He felt an unaccustomed awe when he saw the flag displayed. Silver nudged him in other, more dangerous directions. *If swords be obsolete, shouldst not an honest gentleman learn what arts and weapons are suitable for war?* Not me, Clyde tried to insist. But Silver was always there, night and day, sleeping and waking, with his granite certainty. He found himself looking up certain sites on the Internet, lingering in certain sections of bookstores, choosing movies and videos in very different categories than he had ever liked before.

☐

It came as a shock to everyone but the local fencing group when Clyde sold off his holdings and told everyone he was taking a long trip to the Middle East. It would have been a shock even to them if they'd known what he bought with his liquidated wealth. George Silver, English gentleman, was going on a pilgrimage . . . and incidentally, on his own somewhat fantastical version of a Crusade.

Shell Game

Margaret Ball

It was the time of the Long Rains—when gray-green mold covered everything that didn't move fast enough, when the ambient temperature dropped below seventy-five degrees Fahrenheit, and everyone put on sweaters and shivered. Murrundumali's other seasons were affectionately known as the Short Rains and, courtesy of the colonial government, Bloody Dry Time. The colonial government was gone now, had been gone for forty years. The mold was still with them. Amelia Thuwadi automatically swiped a damp rag over the top of her in basket. OK, she knew she wasn't getting through her paperwork fast enough, but having a gray-green film of mildew over the top of the stack of papers was insulting. Murrundumali was like that; it went out of its way to let you know it was boss. Quicksand on the coastal approaches, swamps on the southern border, desert all the way west to the border of the Lebitso Republic.

She loved it. And she hoped it was still there next Long Rains. She would even convince the gods that she loved the damned mildew, if that would persuade them to protect the country from a decimating tribal war, acquisition as a province of the Lebitso Republic, or occupation by the People's Democracy of Dumela. Any or all of which seemed all too likely in the chaos following the Old Man's sudden death in a helicopter crash. Unless the hastily recalled U.N. representative, Joseph Bagaay, her boss, managed somehow to pull the warring tribal factions together. This week.

Officially counted as an "emerging" country, Murrundumali consisted of a speck on the map, a representative in the United Nations, and three tribal factions who had been held in an uneasy peace by the personal power of the Old Man himself, Dominik Murundi, through the forty years since independence. Oh, there were rumors and problems and "facts" of an incendiary nature. Everybody "knew" that the Old Man's tribe, the Jurrkun, got first shot at all the government jobs; that the Baagan tribe was given preferential admission to the country's one secondary school; that the Kanunju were shopkeepers because they were so bloody clever they would cheat themselves unless they found somebody else to cheat first. No number of surveys and studies and census counts could convince the average member of any one tribe that he wasn't somehow being sneakily done down by the other two.

But somehow the Old Man, using all his native charisma and all the respect he'd won from all three tribes during the struggle for independence, had managed to keep things together for two generations. To young Murundans like Amelia, who had grown up with the picture of Murundi on the schoolhouse wall and the shrine to the Old Man tactfully concealed at home where the minister wouldn't see it and start ranting about pagan sacrifices, Murrundumali *was* the Old Man. Dominik Murundi, founder of a nation. OK, so maybe by the wider standards Amelia had been exposed to when Joseph Bagaay took her with him to New York as his administrative assistant, Murrundumali wasn't exactly a nation. More like a dirt-poor county somewhere in Alabama.

But it was home. Amelia took a deep breath of the warm, humid air and inhaled the familiar mixed scents of mildew, hot chilis, mojo-darra spice pot, and pungent jarra leaves. She mentally promised to burn a few jarra leaves on her personal shrine, just in case the Old Man was still around somewhere, watching out for the nation he had carved from a neglected corner of tropical Africa. As a matter of tact she kept the shrine at her apartment; unlike most Murundans, with their Sunday church membership and their collection of ancestor shrines, Joseph Bagaay was a devout and serious Christian, a deacon of his church, who had truly put aside the remnants of tribal paganism. He wouldn't forbid Amelia to burn jarra leaves to the Old Man's spirit, but he wouldn't *like* it; and after two years of working for Bagaay, she had come to revere him and respect his beliefs enough that she wouldn't for the world do anything to upset him.

Meanwhile, she had better get back to the usual—funny how after only a week it *had* become "usual"—balancing act of juggling half a dozen incipient crises and making promises that the Murrundumali treasury was totally unequipped to carry out. All of which needed Joseph Bagaay's signature before they could be sent out—and where *was* the Acting Minister this morning, anyway?

The office door swung open, and Amelia said, "Oh, good, Minister, we need . . . oh, it's you."

"Amelia, my love, you really must restrain these passionate exclamations of delight at my presence," said Gabundi, the Minister's other confidential aide. He slung a battered raincoat down over his desk chair and seated himself on a corner of Amelia's desk, pushing the papers in the in basket into a perilously teetering position. "Every day the same thing, or as good as. 'Oh, it's only Gabundi. . . . Oh, here comes Gabundi again. . . . No, Minister, it's nobody important, only Gabundi.' "

"It'll be, 'It *was* only Gabundi,' if you destroy my filing system," Amelia warned darkly, reaching to rescue the in basket before it toppled to the floor.

Gabundi caught her hand and gave her a dark, melting glance. At least, rumor said that it had melted the hearts of any number of silly little secretaries and receptionists around the U.N. Gabundi was reputed to have an excellent line involving dark secrets of Murrundumali love practices and jungle magic; upon success, this was followed by a second line about his six wives and seventeen children in Murrundumali and his passionate desire to find and take home with him a seventh wife who would carry out the traditional duties of maintaining the family dung heap and tending the family goats. The third part in the story was that the girl in question came and cried on Amelia's shoulder about her hopeless love for Gabundi and the impossibility of trading in her job at the U.N. for a lifetime of goats and goat dung.

"You could try, 'Oh, Gabundi, you brilliant man, you've solved all our problems,' " he suggested.

Amelia glanced up. "Have you?"

"Well, half of them at least." Gabundi stood, stretched, and made a show of massaging the small of his back. "Hell on the back muscles, sitting hunched over a computer all night. What a country! One road, two automobiles, three hundred television sets tuned to Nairobi, and a state-of-the-art networked computer system tracking and controlling the defense missiles and the national budget. The Old Man could have invested a little more in municipal plumbing systems and a little less in hi-tech, if you ask me . . . but then, nobody did, as I'm sure you are just dying to point out."

"The Americans paid for the defense system and the computers, remember?" Amelia said. "They like to buy fancy toys. Municipal plumbing systems aren't sexy. Which half of our problems have you solved?"

"I've hacked into the treasury code and got access to Murundi's personal stash, which happens to be about six times more than the official budget figures show—and mostly in Switzerland, but that doesn't matter; with the account number and authorizations, we can access it anytime we want. Finally figured it out around eleven last night. Told Joe B. then, but you'd gone home, lazy girl."

"You *did*?" Amelia regarded Gabundi with real, albeit unwilling, admiration. "Oh, I wish I'd been here! He's looked so worried ever since we got back—I'd have liked to see him happy for once."

"Don't worry, light of my life, you haven't missed anything," Gabundi told her. "He'd just gotten out of a meeting with Kristoferi Kamiirra. He just groaned and said money wouldn't save Murrundumali, only cooperation, and Jesus Christ himself probably wouldn't be able to get the Kanunjus and Jurrkuns to cooperate with a Baagan. Guess what Kamiirra's latest ploy is? He's been whining to the Dumelans about the terrible oppression of the Kanunju tribe in Murrundumali. Practically inviting them to invade and help him wipe out the Baagans and the Jurrkuns in the name of freedom."

Amelia groaned. "And yesterday afternoon we found out that Jaariji Pirinyarra is playing the same game with the Lebitso Republic."

Gabundi's eyes widened. "How? Surely the Lebitsan ambassador didn't tell you? And I know Jaariji wouldn't." The leader of the Jurrkun tribe had publicly refused to come to Joseph Bagaay, claiming any discussion would lend legitimacy to Bagaay's false claims of being the Old Man's chosen successor.

"I visited Jaariji's offices last week," Amelia said. "As a good little Jurrkun girl, wanting to keep contact with the Father of the Tribe. And I left a little present under his desk." Amelia grinned. "You think I didn't learn anything the two years we spent in New York? While you were playing computer games, I had some very interesting talks with the counterespionage and counterterrorism units of the American government. Found out exactly where to shop for their snoop gadgets." Her smile faded. "So, Gabundi, unless the Old Man socked away enough to pay for a whole new defense system, you'd better crack that code, too." The sophisticated electronic-controlled missile stations that guarded Murrundumali had been installed by American engineers, funded by American grants back in the days when the Americans thought every little Third World country was going to go Communist if they didn't pour money into it. And by the time the Berlin Wall crumbled and they realized their mistake, Murrundi had made sure all the American money had been transmuted into concrete and steel and electronic systems that they couldn't get back.

Unfortunately, he had also kept just as much tight personal control over the defense system as he had over the treasury. And Amelia noticed that Gabundi was looking distinctly less cheerful now that she'd brought up that little problem. In fact, he was sweating lightly, despite the fact that the Long Rains had brought the ambient temperature down to a mere seventy-five degrees Fahrenheit.

"That," he said slowly, "is a much more difficult nut to crack. Oh, I found out a few things last night—but they were almost too easy to find, almost laid out on the surface, as if Murrundi wanted the first hacker who looked at the system to find them and be warned off. There's a triple password system."

"So?"

"So if I run through likely password combinations, or try to give myself superuser authority, or any of the other basic tricks, and get one little thing wrong, the system doesn't just kick me out. It sets off the missiles . . . and the hidden bombs . . . and a few other things you don't even want to know about. Boom, boom, boom. No more Murrundumali. No more *Gabundi*. I'd be a little cloud of dust floating above a newly created crater that future archaeologists would ascribe to a meteorite crash."

"Mmmm." Amelia assimilated the information. "That would be very bad for your sex life."

"Not to mention yours—oh, I forgot. You don't do that sort of thing."

"No urge to be Wife Number Seventeen in charge of goat milking."

"Oh, come on. You know that was just a line I used to keep those silly little girls at the U.N. from getting too serious." Gabundi put his hand over hers. "With you it's different."

Amelia withdrew her hand. "Yes. The difference is, I don't know what lines you're going to use on me. Look, Gabundi. About the passwords for the defense system. Can't we just shut everything down manually and start over?"

"If you want to risk it," Gabundi said, "give me twenty-four hours' notice first so I can be on the first flight far, far away from here. You want to bet that wily old b—the Old Man didn't set up ways to deal with that, too? He wanted to make damn sure no one of our three tribes got control of the weapons system and used it to annihilate the other guys."

"Great. So we're going to put down two tribal insurrections and invasions from Dumela and Lebitso using pangas and hoes? Come on. Murrundi must have left *some* clue how to get into the system."

"He did," Gabundi said. "Joe B. already told me about the official way to get in. That's why I was up all night trying to hack around it."

"It's that bad?"

"It's *worse* than 'that bad.' As headman of the Bagaans, Joe's got one password."

"So great, your job is one-third done. All we have to do is find out who holds the other two. . . ."

"Let me give you a hint. Kristoferi Kamiirra has one of them. Now who do you think knows the third? Three guesses, first two don't count."

"Jaariji Pirinyarra?" At Gabundi's nod, Amelia slumped

down over her desk. "Oh, *galinggalii*! What do we do now? Burn some sheep's fat and try to call up Murundi's *wandabaa*?"

"Could try that," Gabundi said, "but not in the office. You know how Joe B. feels about pagan backsliding. We'll have to find some private place to set up a shrine. . . . You know, I've always longed to say this to you." He twisted his handsome features into a stage leer. "Your place or mine, thweetheart?"

"Just pucker up and blow," Amelia suggested, having benefited as Gabundi from American video rental stores. "No, really, what *are* we going to do?"

"Joe B. said he had an idea."

"Well, great! And just where is Joe B. when we need him?" Amelia glanced at her watch and had a sinking feeling in the pit of her stomach. "Gabundi, it's nearly nine o'clock. He's always in the office before seven. You don't suppose something happened to him?"

"I'd like to suppose he got lucky last night," Gabundi said, "but not Joe. He wouldn't. Would he?"

"He believes in the sanctity of marriage and chastity before marriage and he was always complaining to me how hard it is to meet good Baptist girls in New York."

"Well, he'd have a better chance in Murrundumali than in New York, that's for sure, but when's he had the *time* to meet any?"

"I don't know, but this morning was time for him to meet with the Secretary of Transport (acting), the Secretary of Agriculture (acting), and the Secretary of Defense (acting)." The three official holders of these posts had fled the country the day after Murrundi's death, leaving Joseph Bagaay scrambling to form some sort of interim administration.

Amelia's computer chimed and a deep, only slightly mechanical voice announced, "You have a priority one message."

Gabundi leaned over her shoulder and for once, as she

read the words that scrolled across the screen, Amelia did not object to his proximity. In fact, it was comforting—the slightly musky man-smell blended with the smell of a clean white shirt just back from Murrundumali's only laundry, the warmth of a large and muscular body behind her. And as they read the message, she felt in need of all the comfort she could get.

"*Galinggalii-yugal!*" Gabundi burst out. "Is that all he could tell us?"

"He's withdrawn nearly all the money in the Swiss account," Amelia said, "he's gone to Nairobi, he'll be back in twenty-four hours, we're not to worry, and if he doesn't return on schedule, we should contact this number."

"Oh, right," Gabundi said, "and what do you suppose we'll get when we do call? A prerecorded 'good-bye and sorry to leave you in this shit, my children'? *Guna-yugal!* I never thought Joe B. would run out on Murrundumali."

"He hasn't," Amelia said quickly. "He wouldn't." She was dialing the number he'd left as she spoke. A voice answered on the other end; she listened to the words through crackling static and hung up without speaking.

"I was right?"

"You were wrong, Gabundi. That's the main number for Nucore International's Nairobi office."

"Jesus H. Murrundi *Christ*!" Gabundi exploded. "He's blowing our entire operating budget to get somebody else's personality downloaded? Oh, I get it. He's going to download Murrundi."

"Can't," Amelia said. "That helicopter crash created a fireball that burned up everything in a half-kilometer radius, remember? No cells left to create a DNA model from."

"There must have been *something*. Nail clippings, hair strands in his bath . . ."

"Uh-uh." Amelia shook her head. "The Old Man may have been a nominal Christian, but he wasn't in the habit of leaving bits of his body around where anybody could use them. Did his own cleaning, his own personal care, had a little fire in a brazier every night to dispose of scraps. That time he got a cut on his foot from a broken bottle? He slapped a wad of Kleenex on the cut before it had time to drip onto the dirt, held it there till he got to the hospital, made the doctor give him the needle and leftover sutures, burned everything right there in the Emergency Room, burned the hospital bandage two days later when it came off, probably burned the stitches they took out. *Newsweek* heard about it from some flunky at the hospital and Joe B. had a *gunuu* of a time keeping it out of the news. He didn't want them to write us up as a bunch of ignorant savages who still believe in juju and spirits."

"Ignorant savages my left foot, *we* knew the spirit resides in every cell of a man's body centuries before those scientists at Nucore figured it out!" Gabundi said indignantly.

"Yes, well, in retrospect maybe that's too bad," Amelia pointed out. "There's no way we're going to get the Old Man back again, Gabundi."

"I wonder who we are going to get?"

"Somebody pretty far back, if it costs that much for the transfer." Amelia erased the message Joseph Bagaay had left and looked at the outer door. "Well, somebody's got to explain to the acting Secretaries of Transport, Agriculture, and Defense about Joe's sudden attack of the twenty-four-hour flu. That's your job, I think?"

"Why me?"

"Because," Amelia said demurely, "you've had so much more practice lying. Go on, Gabundi. Nothing to it. Just pretend they're a bunch of sweet young girls."

"Joe doesn't come back, I take over, I bloody *will* appoint a bunch of sweet young things to run this government," Gabundi threatened.

"Joe doesn't come back," Amelia said, "we better be on tomorrow's flight out of here."

□

The daily flight from Nairobi to Murrundumali City and back was late. It was always late. This time the delay was so long that Gabundi had more than enough time to purchase two nonrefundable, one-way tickets to Nairobi. "Just in case," he told Amelia, tucking the ticket folders into his breast pocket.

"We won't need them," Amelia said. "Joe wouldn't desert us. If he's not on this flight, it'll be because the sleep process took longer than he expected. I read up on Nucore last night. It can take as much as thirty-six hours of deep sleep for a recipient to assimilate the new personality."

"So if he's not on this flight, we'll go to Nairobi, go straight to Nucore, and check on him there," Gabundi insisted. "And if everything is as fine as you say, don't worry, there's no trouble getting seats back *into* Murrundumali City. It's the outgoing flights that are booked solid."

"So how'd you get those tickets?"

"Kanunju brotherhood," Gabundi said, "and a small bribe."

Amelia sniffed. "We Jurrkun don't take bribes."

"No? How do you think the Old Man amassed that fortune—oh, never mind. You're just lucky all the airport clerks are good Kanunju boys."

"Anyway, we won't need them. He'll be back."

"I wonder," Gabundi said slowly, "just *who* will be back."

"Joe B., of course—oh. I see what you mean. Well, we know he couldn't download Murundi."

"But he must have thought of *somebody* who would have what it takes to pull this country together."

"Shaka Zulu?"

"Machiavelli."

"Jomo Kenyatta."

"Attila the Hun," Gabundi suggested morosely.

"Attila we don't need. The three tribes can probably reduce Murrundumali to a desert without outside help. Besides, I bet even Nucore couldn't find any of Attila's DNA. No, it'll be a great peacemaker and leader. Someone like . . ."

The incomprehensible static of all airport communication systems crackled through the air, drowning out Amelia's last suggestion, and before the noise died away it was succeeded by the screaming whine of a plane coming in for a landing on Murrundumali's single, short, slightly waterlogged landing strip.

Before the wheels of the plane had stopped churning up muddy water Amelia and Gabundi were outside, watching the slightly damp passengers coming down the folding stairway. Amelia covered her head with a copy of the *Murrundumali Examiner*, then gave up and dropped the wet newspaper into a trash can. The flimsy paper was no protection against the steady downpour of the Long Rains, and the ink was running over her hands.

"There he is!" Gabundi announced.

There was a little space between the passengers before and after Joseph Bagaay, and it seemed to Amelia that there was less rain right over the Acting Minister's head. Almost as if the clouds had opened . . . no, that must be an optical illusion. But he certainly wasn't scuttling to get out of the rain like everybody else; he moved with a conscious, deliberate grace that was quite unlike the quick-stepping, wisecracking man Amelia had gone to work for.

"Bless you, my children," Joseph Bagaay said in his deep, resonant voice as he drew near to Amelia and Gabundi. "I knew that I could trust you to keep faith with me, for the seed that was sown has fallen upon fertile ground."

"Jesus H. Murundi *Christ*!" Gabundi exclaimed.

"Only the first and last of those," Joseph said, smiling beatifically. "Who but My Father's Son could bring peace to this troubled land?"

Amelia and Gabundi exchanged glances behind Joseph's back as he turned toward the parking area.

"You take him home," Gabundi whispered. "Tell him Nu-core called and emphasized the need of another twenty-four hours' complete rest. I'll go back to the office and say his flu is worse."

"We can't get away with it. All these people just saw him. . . ."

"All these people," Gabundi said, "are waiting to get on that plane out of Murrundumali. They're not going to stay around long enough to spread any rumors. And the airport workers are all my good Kanunju brothers. I'll appeal to tribal solidarity to keep a lid on this for another day."

"And then what?" Amelia whispered.

"We'll think of something. We have to. Jesus," Gabundi said, "is *not* what we need right now."

"Are you sure?"

" 'I bring not peace, but a sword,' " Gabundi quoted grimly. "Meet me at the Jarra Grill after you've got him settled."

"It may take a while."

"Four o'clock. That should give us time to think about what we're going to do next."

□

Gabundi was later than he'd hoped to be at the Jarra Grill. No Amelia. Had she given up on him and gone home? A word with the bartender—fortunately, another Kanunju—established that no, there hadn't been a tall, slender Jurrkun girl with a sharp New York hairstyle hanging around waiting for him, and Gabundi should only get that lucky in his dreams, and . . .

"Here she is now," Gabundi interrupted. He moved forward to meet Amelia, ignoring the bartender's whispered request to find out if she had any sisters who also didn't mind dating Kanunjus.

"You're not going to believe—" they both started at the same time.

"Oh, yes, I am," Gabundi said grimly. "I heard it, too."

"How?"

"You're not the only one around here who did a little shopping in the United States for specialty equipment," Gabundi said. He'd bugged the Minister's office last night, after Amelia revealed her little trick on Jaariji Pirinyarra's headquarters. But he hadn't heard anything worth mentioning until just before time to meet Amelia.

Amelia sank into the chair he pulled out for her and fanned her face. Droplets of rain sparkled among the close-cropped curls of her black hair, like diamonds adorning a Jurrkun princess of long ago. The tragic expression on her face suited that mythical princess, too.

"I can't *believe* he'd do something like that," she said, staring into the cold shandy the bartender had produced without waiting for an order. The man was hovering now, waiting for Amelia to express some desire: a different drink, something from the grill, the head of her worst enemy? His bearing suggested any of these might be obtained. Men did tend to do that around Amelia. It was obnoxious at the best of times; now, when they needed privacy, it made Gabundi think seriously about the penalties for killing a fellow Kanunju. He stared hard at the bartender, thinking about those penalties and whether it just might be worth it, until his fellow tribesman retreated and left them in privacy.

"It was a bit of a surprise," Gabundi allowed, sipping his own drink. "When he told us he'd had a download of Our Lord's earthly personality, I was afraid he'd give away everything . . . but not like this."

"No," Amelia agreed mournfully. "The Gospels don't mention anything about Jesus being sneaky or underhanded or devious or treacherous or . . ." She ran out of adjectives and swallowed half her shandy in one gulp.

"Something about the download must have driven him crazy," Gabundi suggested.

"Hah! Crazy like a fox! What does he think he's *doing*, conspiring with one tribe to wipe out another? Does he want to throw us back into the Killing Times?" Amelia finished her shandy and waggled a finger at the bartender. "Get me another of these, would you, and not so much ginger beer this time."

"Orange Fanta for me," Gabundi added. With Joe B. going crazy and trying to play one tribe off against another, a move almost guaranteed to revive the genocidal wars that had almost destroyed Murrundumali in the first decade after independence, one of them had better stay stone-cold sober. Still, it did seem a pity . . . for two years he'd fantasized about getting Amelia just slightly lit up, just enough to remove that top layer of inhibition that kept her so prim and proper, and now she had to take up serious drinking at a time when he didn't have *time* to take advantage of it.

Maybe it was the sense of personal betrayal that was breaking her heart. "Listen, Amelia," Gabundi said earnestly, as soon as their new drinks had been served, "I want you to know that I had nothing to do with it. It wasn't my idea."

"Of course not! Why would you conspire to destroy your own tribe?"

Gabriel checked the level of Amelia's glass. She hadn't even started on her second shandy. And whatever the mix of this one, the first had been the standard half ginger beer and half Simba beer. Half a Simba wasn't enough to get anybody, even a nondrinker like Amelia, seriously confused. It must have been the shock unhinging her.

"Amelia. Nobody's conspiring to destroy the Kanunjus. It's the other way around. Joe B. offered to deal with Kristoferi Kamiirra, to join the Bagaans and the Kanunjus against the Jurrkuns."

"Gabundi, how long have you been sitting here drinking? I know what *I* heard. As soon as I thought he was asleep and left him alone, he got up and went straight to Jaariji Pirinyarra's headquarters. . . ."

"No, he went to his office and called in Kristoferi Kamiirra. . . ."

"How would you know?"

"I bugged his office. Last night. When did you do it?"

"You dirty sneak! I never did. Only Jurrkun headquarters. So if you didn't have a bug in Jaariji Pirinyarra's office, you *couldn't* have heard him. . . ." Amelia tipped her head and poured the second drink straight down her throat. "Gabundi, I'm sorry. You'd better use one of those tickets and get out of the country on tomorrow's flight. It's going to be another Time of Killing, but the Kanunjus will go down first."

"Wait a minute." A faint light was beginning to dawn on Gabundi. "You heard him talking to Jaariji Pirinyarra. When?"

"About two o'clock. I'd just got home after leaving Joe B. safely asleep . . . I *thought*."

"Instead of which," Gabundi said, "he went straight to Jaariji Pirinyarra and convinced him that he wanted to make a deal to exterminate us Kanunjus, and as a token of good faith they exchanged their passwords to the defense system."

Amelia nodded. A tear slid down her cheek and splashed into the empty glass before her. "You heard it, too."

"Uh-uh," Gabundi said. "I didn't hear *that* conversation. I told you, I bugged *Joe's* office. He got there about three o'clock and Kristoferi Kamiirra showed up ten minutes later, and Joe told *him* he wanted to join up with the Kanunjus to exterminate you Jurrkuns. And as a token of good faith . . ."

". . . They exchanged their passwords to the defense system," Amelia and Gabundi chanted in chorus.

They stared at each other.

"It's such an obvious trick. How did he get them both to fall for it?"

"I don't know," Amelia said weakly, "but he's incredibly convincing. When I was eavesdropping on him and Jaariji Pirinyarra, he convinced *me*. He talked so fast and he sounded so sincere and somehow he didn't give Jaariji time to ask any inconvenient questions, and . . . I was absolutely sure he was betraying the Kanunjus."

"Joe B. wouldn't *do* that," Gabundi said. "But I felt the same way when I was listening in on him and Kristoferi Kamiirra. There wasn't a doubt in my mind that he meant to join his Bagaans with us Kanunjus and slaughter the Jurrkuns. I guess there wasn't a doubt in Kristoferi's mind either, or he wouldn't have swapped passwords."

"Well, I don't think Jesus would have been that sneaky, or underhanded, or, or . . ." The second drink was adversely affecting Amelia's ability to remember adjectives.

"So," Gabundi said slowly, "who *did* Joe B. download?"

□

The Acting Minister for Murrundumali was sitting comfortably in his office, looking with placid contentment at a computer screen, when Amelia and Gabundi burst in on him.

"*What* have you been up to, Joe B.?" Amelia demanded.

"Wait a minute." Gabundi dropped to his knees for a moment and removed a small, matte black button from the underside of the Minister's desk. "Wouldn't want anybody else tuning in on this," he explained to Amelia, dropping the button into his pocket.

Joseph Bagaay's black face turned a sort of dirty gray. "My office was bugged?"

"Only by me," Gabundi said. "I did a sweep for any other devices while I was at it. But *I* sure got an earful!"

"Thank Our Lord it was you," Joseph said sincerely. "It would have been terrible if a Jurrkun had heard that conversation before I got into the defense system." He shook his head. "You don't understand about modern technology," he said as if to himself, and then, "What do you mean, I should have *told* you? *I* didn't know you were planning . . ." He looked at Amelia and Gabundi again. "I guess I mean, I didn't *want* to know what my new personality was planning. He couldn't have done it without my cooperation."

"It doesn't sound," Amelia said severely, "like the kind of thing Our Lord would have done either."

"Hey . . ." Joseph spread his hands in a most uncharacteristic gesture. "It worked, didn't it? Kristoferi Kamiirra has two passwords, Jaariji Pirinyarra has two, and I," he said with gentle pride, "have three, all of which I have just changed, so the passwords they have are useless even if they get together and figure out my innocent little deception."

"Gabundi, what's *happened* to him?" Amelia appealed. "I went to work for an honorable decent man. Joe B. would never have used the words *innocent* and *deception* in the same sentence! What did Nucore *do* to him?"

"Nucore," Joseph Bagaay said serenely, "downloaded to my mind the personality reconstructed from the vial of True Blood of Our Lord Jesus Christ, a relic secretly kept in the Cathedral of Chartres for the last seven hundred years, and they didn't want to discuss how they got it. But I did see the provenance, and it was the authentic vial. Unfortunately," he said with a wicked grin, "the blood wasn't quite so authentic. I seem to have acquired the personality of Dagobert the Devious, a failed scholar and disgraced cleric of the fourteenth century, who turned to the trade in relics after he was run out of Paris on totally unfair charges of witchcraft—I assure you," he said earnestly, in a quicker and lighter voice than his normal one, "I used no black arts to conceal the pea under the nutshells, only my natural quickness of hand to deceive the eye and of tongue to distract the mind. And I never exactly told the Archbishop that the vial he purchased contained the true blood of Our Lord; I told him it was given me by a pilgrim from Jerusalem, which was true, and that the contents were so precious to me that I could not for my life set a price on it—I *am*, after all, very fond of my own blood and skin." He glanced down at his black hands, looking confused. "I suppose I should say, *was* . . . for this does not seem to be my own skin I now inhabit . . . but 'struth, I do feel very nearly as close to it as I did to my own. . . . Cheaters will cheat themselves, given a chance," said Dagobert/Joseph, "and as did the Archbishop in his time, paying me good golden louis d'or for two drops of my own blood, so did Kristoferi Kamiirra and Jaariji Pirinyarra in this time. The defense systems are fully armed now and I have fired demonstration missiles into uninhabited patches of the Lebitso Republic and the People's Democracy of Dumela. By fortunate coincidence, the Lebitsan demonstration site was quite close to a Kanunju village on our side of the border, and the explosion in Dumela happened within full view of a Jurrkun encampment. I expect Kristoferi and Jaariji will be getting the bad news quite soon. And now, if you don't mind," Dagobert/Joseph yawned, "I think I will take that long sleep you recommended, Amelia. Dagobert isn't quite up to speed on modern technology, and Joseph is having a hard time with Dagobert's, um . . ."

"Double-dealing?" Amelia suggested. "Sneakiness? Treachery?"

"I prefer to think of it as *craftiness*," Joseph/Dagobert said with dignity. "Oh, and by the way, while I'm resting, you might contact Nucore and explain why their access to Murundi's account was blocked before they could collect the second half of their payment. I certainly didn't get the personality I paid for, and Murrundumali can use the cash for other things. Tell them that if they refund the first half of the payment we probably won't sue them. . . . No, don't bother; I think we can make it perfectly clear to them when we wake up."

Renaissance Man

Jerry Oltion

Nathaniel Hoskins was in his basement laboratory, testing one of his designs for a perpetual motion machine, when the telephone rang. Without looking up from the slowly spinning plastic wheel, from which a dozen lead weights dangled on inch-long pendulum arms, he said, "Phone on. Hello?"

The flat video screen to his left flickered on, and his girlfriend, Elise, peered out at him. "Hi, Nathan," she said.

"Hi." He reached out with his index finger and stopped the wheel's motion, then frowned when it didn't start up again.

She frowned, too. "Are you still working on that thing? Perpetual motion is impossible, and you know it."

"That's what they said about cold fusion," he replied. He looked over at her, saw that her dark brown hair looked red in the picture, and reached toward the bottom of the display to adjust the color balance.

"What are you—oh. I wish you wouldn't do that. It looks like you're reaching for my boobs."

He gave the wheel a nudge. "Huh?" It spun half a turn,

the weights flopping over the top with a clatter like hail on a trailer-house roof, but it slowed to a stop again.

"I said when you do that, it looks like—oh, never mind. Look, the reason I called is because my dad just gave me two tickets to the play tonight. *A Midsummer Night's Dream*. It's playing down at the Center. You want to go?"

"To a play?" He looked back at her face on the screen. "Live theater? You've got to be kidding. The baud rate on something like that is even slower than movies."

She narrowed her eyes. "The baud rate?"

"Information transfer rate. Talk, talk, talk. Move around a little. Talk, talk, talk some more. Intermission while they change sets. And all the while the audience just sits there. With movies, I can at least keep working in my lab while I watch." He wiggled a sticky pendulum to loosen the joint.

"I know. Nathan, I'd like to do something fun with you for a change, not sit in your basement watching a television screen while you tinker with your gadgets. Besides, this is Shakespeare."

"I've seen *Midsummer Night's Dream* before."

"Not this performance you haven't. This is *Shakespeare*. The clone. All twenty-one of them." She peered out at him. "Hello, Earth to Nathan. You *have* heard of the Shakespeare clone, haven't you?"

He spun the wheel backward, but one of the weights whacked him on the finger, and he jerked it back. "No, actually, I haven't," he said. He looked up again. "Did someone actually clone Shakespeare?"

She rolled her eyes. "You've definitely got to get out more. I'll come by in forty-five minutes. And if you're still in that damned lab when I get there, I swear I'm going to . . ."

"Going to what?"

"I don't know. I'll think of something." She reached forward and blinked off.

Of course when she arrived he was still at it, tweaking the weights a little here, adjusting the lever arms there, convinced that the problem was just a matter of adjustment. It was so obvious how it should work: when the wheel turned, the weights on the ends of the little arms would flop outward at the top of their arc, adding weight to one side of the wheel and forcing it downward, while the weights on the other side would fold inward and rise up near the axle, not contributing nearly as much leverage or angular momentum. Once it started moving, the wheel should spin faster and faster, until centripetal force flung the levers outward all the way around, and they ceased to provide their differential force.

Leonardo da Vinci had described such a wheel over five hundred years ago, but he hadn't been able to get it to work. Nathan was convinced it was because he hadn't had access to the right materials. Just like Pons and Fleischmann much more recently with their cold fusion experiment, which Nathan had refined by trial and error until he found the right catalyst to trigger a continuous reaction. Now rich from his patent, Nathan had turned his mind to another "impossible" project, but this one was proving much more stubborn.

And to make things worse, he seemed to have attracted an equally stubborn girlfriend. It seemed like just a few minutes after she'd hung up when she entered his lab, said, "I warned you," and grabbed the wheel off its supporting armature. She cocked her arm back to throw it across the room, but she would have needed quite an arm to hit the far wall; Nathan had sunk a lot of his patent royalties into his lab.

And into his model. "Hey," he said, reaching for it. "Careful!"

"Why?" she asked. "It's a piece of junk."

"It could be the salvation of humanity," he said haughtily, scooting back his stool and stepping toward her.

She backed away. "You already did that. Isn't once enough?"

He shook his head. "Cold fusion only works with deuterium. Sure, I've ended our dependence on fossil fuels, but deuterium is just a tiny portion of the hydrogen in the oceans. It's an exhaustible resource, too. We need to have something like this ready to take its place when—" He lunged for the wheel, but he caught his left thigh on the edge of his workbench and tore a gash in his pants.

"Ow!"

Elise set the model down on the bench with a clatter of tiny weights, heedless of the levers, and bent to examine his leg. "Hold still," she commanded, when he reached for the wheel to set it back in its cradle. He sighed and relaxed; whatever damage she'd caused was already done. He could fix it later.

His leg, on the other hand, needed immediate attention. Blood welled up in the gouge that the countertop had taken out of his thigh.

"I'm sorry," Elise said as she dabbed at it with a gray shop towel.

"Oh, it's nothing," he told her, though it stung like crazy. If he made a big deal about it, she would feel guilty, and then she would want to look after him for days, maybe even pester him to see a doctor. He could lose a week of research to one little accident if he wasn't careful.

So he gently took the towel from her and held it tight to his leg to stanch the bleeding while he led her upstairs, where he let her dig around in his closet for a clean suit and tie while he squirted Bactine on the scratch and put a wide Band-Aid over it.

"Are you sure you're all right?" she asked.

"Fine. It was just a scrape. Is there time for dinner before the play?" As long as he was leaving the lab, he supposed he might as well make a night of it.

Her eyes widened in surprise. "Sure. Got anyplace special in mind?"

He shrugged. "Just calories. I think I skipped lunch to-day."

"You think? Don't you remember?"

"I was working."

He realized the moment he said it that he'd made a mistake. Sure enough, she sighed her deep, theatrical sigh, and said, "You work too much. You ought to enjoy being rich once in a while. You know, most people after they make their first billion dollars at least take weekends off."

"I'm not most people," he told her.

"I've noticed."

He couldn't tell how she meant that. He wondered sometimes why she stuck around. She might have been after his money, but she was second-generation Microsoft rich; she had no more need of his fortune than he did of hers. Maybe that was why. With him, at least, she always knew his interest was sincere.

When he showed any. He made himself forget the perpetual motion machine in the basement and concentrate on Elise instead. She was obviously trying to get him to spend a little more time with her; he should pay attention to her wishes. Who knows, it might even be fun.

He smiled at her as she tied his tie, but then something about her hair caught his attention. It had used to be light brown.

"What?" she asked, noticing his expression.

"You dyed your hair," he said.

"It's just a rinse. Don't you like it?"

"I—sure, but I adjusted the color on my phone to make it brown again, and now it's out of whack."

She shoved the knot up against his throat, nearly cutting off his air. "My hair messed up your phone, is that what you're saying? You're a real piece of work, you know that?" She turned away and stalked out of his bedroom, leaving him there clawing at the tie and gasping for breath.

☐

Dinner was a bit quiet, but at least the view from the top of the Space Needle filled the silence. The restaurant rotated all the way around while they ate, giving them a slow panorama of the Seattle skyline, Puget Sound, and Mount Rainier. Elise finally accepted his apology, and by the time they reached the theater she was holding his hand. He absently accepted a program from the usher, and after they sat down and their eyes adjusted to the light he held it so they could both read it.

"*A Midsummer Night's Dream*, the original play, the original playwright!" it proclaimed in thirty-six-point type.

"What's all this about cloning Shakespeare, anyway?" he asked.

She shook her head sadly. "You really haven't heard, have you? They've figured out how to extract memories from ancient DNA."

"MRNA," he corrected her. "That's where somatic memories are stored. DNA is the genetic blueprint."

"NBA, DNA, whatever. The point is, if they can find a tissue sample, they can use recombinant techniques to duplicate it, and then they can actually read those memories and play them into the actors' minds. So they learn everything Shakespeare ever knew, and they gain his aptitudes, his outlook, everything."

"But they aren't actually Shakespeare," he said, disappointed.

"Of course not. For one thing, it would take forever to grow an actual clone. But these guys are even better anyway. They're modern actors, *and* they're Shakespeare."

When the play started, Nathan was forced to agree with her. He had never seen *A Midsummer Night's Dream* performed so well, with such spontaneity and charm. Puck and Oberon and Titania seemed to function as one, and even the silly play-within-a-play that he had always disliked came alive with bawdy humor.

Theseus, on the other hand, seemed like an automaton

compared to the others. Nathan supposed he must be an ordinary, unenhanced actor, but during intermission he looked at the playbill and discovered that the actor was "hosting" an ancient personality as well; it just wasn't Shakespeare's. Because of an unfortunate mix-up in authenticating one of the original folios, the playbill explained, they had collected a few epidermal cells from Francis Bacon instead, and it was the Renaissance philosopher whom the unfortunate actor carried piggyback in his mind.

Even so, Nathan felt the tingling sensation of a new idea taking hold. If these actors could recall everything Shakespeare and Bacon knew, without losing their own individuality in the process, the possibilities could be endless.

One nice thing about being rich; the moment he and Elise expressed an interest in talking with the cast, they were ushered backstage, where the actors were busy removing costumes and makeup while chatting with their admirers.

Bacon had no admirers. He sat on a stool at the far end of the dressing table, staring into the mirror. He didn't turn around when Elise sat on the empty stool beside him, nor when Nathan said, "Sir Francis Bacon? The scientist?"

"I was just trying to decide that," he said into the mirror. "I am apparently no longer Douglas Peterson, the actor, no matter how generous the rest of the troupe is with their support." He sighed. "But I doubt if you came to talk about that. What may I do for you?"

"Actually, I did come to talk about that," Nathan said. "I'm interested in this process of reviving ancient minds. Shakespeare doesn't interest me, but Bacon does. Have you in fact inherited all his knowledge? And his thoughts? And what about your own? Are you two minds in one brain, or a mixture?"

The actor picked up a cloth and began wiping off stage makeup. "Answer that last one for yourself sometime. None of us are one mind all the time. I'm just a little more . . . variable than most. I still feel like me, but I have a lot more to think about now than I used to. Unfortunately, when I'm trying to be yet another person onstage, that untrained personality gets in the way." He looked at Nathan in the mirror, half of his face pale white again, the other half still darkened for his character. "If you've got questions for Bacon, ask them now. I'm having him removed tomorrow."

"You can do that?"

"So they say. I'm apparently the first to ask for it. It won't be complete, because I've hosted him long enough that his memories are becoming part of *my* body now, but this obviously isn't working."

Nathan licked his lips. "Maybe that's because you haven't applied yourself to the right project. Bacon wasn't an actor, but he was a hell of a scientist. I have a project that might interest him."

Peterson sighed, and when he spoke again his voice was subtly different. "Ah, another historian. I will tell you what I've told the others: there is still plenty of my vital essence left in the laboratory where I was revived. If you are truly interested in learning all I know, invite me into your mind as this poor soul has. You will learn more than you care to."

The hair stood up on the back of Nathan's neck. He looked over at Elise, who had shifted a little bit away on her stool. "I'm not a historian," he said. "I'm an inventor. I'm interested in your scientific knowledge."

Bacon nodded slowly. "For what project do you need the assistance of a sixteenth-century man of letters?"

"Perpetual motion."

There was a moment of silence, then the actor threw back his head and laughed. Everyone in the dressing room turned to look, and Nathan felt his cheeks grow red.

"The present has no shortage of fools, I see," said Bacon. "Perpetual motion! The only thing perpetual, it seems, is the search for it."

"It's not—"

"No, sir. I bid you good fortune in your folly. If you find

the secret, you may revive me again, and I will apologize handsomely, but I will not waste the life of this young man on a hopeless quest."

"It's not—" Nathan tried again.

"I bid you *adieu*," the actor said. "I grow weary, and tomorrow a part of me must die again. Leave me now, please."

Nathan looked in the mirror at the other people in the room. Nobody was laughing now. Nobody spoke. He felt the heat of embarrassment burning through his entire body, and he knew there was nothing he could say or do to redeem himself in their eyes.

Not now. But there was one thing he could do.

"Come on," he said, holding out his hand for Elise. "We've wasted enough time here."

☐

That night, back in his laboratory, he set his wheel model back in its cradle and pushed it slowly from side to side, watching the weighted arms swing back and forth. He was on the right track, he knew he was. He wasn't trying to get energy from nowhere; he was merely trying to tap an endless source of it. His machine wouldn't work in free fall; it required gravity to pull on the overbalanced wheel, so it stood to reason that the energy to power it came from gravity itself. And gravity was a force. You could measure it, even create it artificially in a centrifuge. There was nothing mysterious about it. Nothing foolish in trying to harness it.

Except for what it was doing to his personal life. He could still hear Elise's words as she dropped him off at his house, declining his invitation to come inside. "Get help," she had told him.

Get help. Those two simple words had damned iconoclasts for generations. As if anyone with an urge to push the boundaries of human experience was somehow deranged.

He stared at the weighted wheel, thinking about it, until well after dawn. Get help. Yes, perhaps he should.

☐

It took two weeks to get everything ready. Most of that time was spent tracking down and buying dozens of pages from the *Codex Madrid* and *Codex Atlanticus*, borrowing the *Mona Lisa* (it had taken a hefty donation to the Louvre for that), then examining them all microscopically for skin cells, blood cells, hair—anything that might contain the genetic material Nathan needed. Theoretically a single cell would do, but he wanted multiple redundant tissue samples so he could be sure he got the right memories. He didn't want to repeat the mistake the acting troupe had made with Bacon.

At last the tissue samples had been collected, authenticated, and duplicated, the memories decoded and enhanced. When everything was ready, Nathan found himself sitting in a comfortable chair in a windowless, pastel blue room, a shiny black virtual reality helmet resting on the table beside him while a technician taped his eyelids open to prevent him from blinking and missing a valuable moment in the life he was about to upload.

He asked the universal question everyone asks before a medical procedure: "Will it hurt?"

The technician looked like a high school student, and a scruffy one at that, but given young people's aptitude for computers and the like, Nathan supposed he had probably helped invent the memory transfer device. The kid grinned and said, "This will be the most painless learning experience you'll ever receive, trust me."

"Learning has never been painful for me," Nathan told him proudly.

The tech gave a little shrug. "Lucky you. Here, put this on." He handed Nathan the helmet. It fit snugly, like an expensive VR helmet should, but instead of a light-tight faceplate, this one had two laser projectors aimed directly at his eyes. He wanted to blink, but the tape held his eyes open.

He saw movement in his peripheral vision. "Okay, lean

back. Look directly into the projectors. Good." Something stung his left arm.

"Ow! You said it wouldn't hurt."

"That was just a little muscle relaxant to help you concentrate. Ready?"

Nathan took a deep breath, held it a moment, then said, "Let's do it."

"Okay. Showtime." He heard a click at the back of the helmet.

The projectors flashed on. He saw no image, just a rapidly flickering light. *The wrong frequency can induce epilepsy*, he thought. And the right frequency could induce memories. He settled back to see what he would remember.

☐

They had told him he would sleep. They hadn't told him he would dream. It made sense that he would; dreams are the brain's way of integrating new memories, and he had a lifetime of them to file away.

He felt the technician lift him from the chair and help him to a bed, but he was already in Renaissance Italy, flying an ultralight airplane along the course of the Arno River as he sketched a plan to divert it around the city of Pisa in order to complete the siege. His drawing paper flapped in the wind, the pen tearing holes in it, through which he could see the faces of Verrocchio, Salai, and Melzi, his mentor and two of his students. Salai twisted and became Machiavelli, the military genius with whom he had studied the nature of power under Cesare Borgia.

Now Machiavelli became the pilot, and Nathan watched helplessly as they dive-bombed his beloved Florence, raining incendiary bombs upon the helpless city. Rooftops erupted upward as buildings exploded, each one becoming a painting. *John the Baptist. Bacchus. Leda. The Last Supper*—all rose like moths from a shaken blanket, then burst into flame and tumbled back to the ground.

The dreams went on and on, immense crossbows of his own design skewering hundreds of men at a time; wooden assault vehicles blasting shrapnel at unprotected troops; catapults throwing entire cities at their enemies, leading to a deluge of objects—pots, rakes, television sets, bagpipes, old tires—that swept all of humanity before it.

He woke up screaming, "Wrong man! Wrong man! I am not a killer!"

The technician who had helped him earlier came running into the darkened recovery room. "Whoa," he said, holding his arms out, palms forward. "Hang on there. You're all right. It's just dreams."

"It was—" Nathan swallowed. "It was horrible. It felt like I was inventing every lethal weapon known to man. Even the stuff that wasn't designed to kill was deadly. Gah." He sat up and shook his head. New thoughts skittered for cover like mice in a granary. He took a few deep breaths, waiting for stability, but when it came it was not the familiar comfort of home. There was something new in his head. Some*one* new.

"He's here," he said softly. "I'm here." He held out his hands, touched his face. "I'm alive. And young!" The fear and horror began to recede, forced aside by wonder and excitement. "It worked! By God, it worked. We're both in here." He tapped his head lightly.

"Good." The technician consulted a notepad. "Do you remember Giacomo, your student?"

Nathan smiled. He did. He could recall the boy's curly hair and round, smooth face as if he were standing before him. "I called him 'Salai.' Means 'demon.' He was a handful."

"How about Elise?"

He laughed softly. "She's a handful as well. Is she here?" Then he remembered and answered himself. "Of course not—I haven't told her yet."

The technician laughed with him. "You won't be able to hide it. You're already glowing like a new father."

"I feel like father and son at once."

"And the dreams?"

"Already fading. I see what it was, now. I—Leonardo—often designed military machines for my patrons. Most of them were never built while I was alive, but eventually some of them were. And those led to even worse things. In our initial confusion, Nathan thought those were *his* inventions, and he wasn't ready for the shock of seeing his ideas carried to such extremes. He has apparently led a very sheltered life."

He felt an odd pang of regret at his own words. It was impossible to tell whose personality was feeling it; Leonardo from experience, or Nathan for the lack of it.

It didn't matter. He had experience now, however vicarious it might be, and his composite mind had nothing to repent.

He stood up. The technician hovered nearby, ready to grab him if he fell, but he took a few steps on his own, then nodded. "Oh, yes, I think we're going to like this."

☐

He headed straight for the laboratory the moment he got home, but he stopped in the doorway and marvelled at the lights, flipping the banks of incandescent tubes on and off one at a time and watching them flicker into brilliance half a dozen times before leaving them on and advancing on the computer and the racks of tools and test equipment. Voltmeters, signal generators, oscilloscopes, lathes, drill presses—every device an inventor could want waited within arm's reach.

"We're rich," he whispered. "My God, I never realized how rich I was."

The perpetual motion machine rested in its cradle. He sat down before it on his padded stool, propped an elbow on the workbench, and rested his chin on his hand. For long minutes he stared at the levers and weights, imagining them in motion but not touching the wheel. He visualized the forces acting on the axle, adding up the complex variables with the instinctive ability of any child throwing a snowball at a moving car. He closed his eyes and compared it to his drawing from five centuries ago, grunting with approval at the improvements he had made over the original design. Teflon bearings. Titanium armature. Polystyrene casing. Of course none of that would matter if the principle was false, but the more he looked at it, the more certain he grew that it *should* work.

He reached forward and gave it a slow spin. Watched it clatter to a stop.

To his left, a blinking red light caught his attention. He turned his head and realized it was the phone.

How did he—oh yes. "Phone on," he said. "List messages."

A dozen lines of text flashed onto the screen. Attorney, stockbroker, financial advisor . . . Elise. Nine days ago. He vaguely remembered that call. He hadn't wanted to answer it in the lab, and then in the rush of tracking down Leonardo's memories he had forgotten to return it.

"Play number seven," he said.

The list winked out and Elise peered out at him. "Nathan? I, um, I want to . . . well . . . are you all right? I'm sorry I yelled at you. Could you call me back?"

He was glad there weren't really two separate minds in his brain; the embarrassment would have been even more extreme. He sighed, slicked back his hair, and said, "Return call."

Her stored image winked out, to be replaced by a real-time one. "Hello? Nathan?"

"Yeah. Sorry I didn't call back right away. Are you doing anything important right now?"

She'd had time to stew a bit. Nobody likes being left hanging after they've made a peace overture. "It depends," she said. "What's on your mind?"

He shrugged. "I don't know. I need to get out and get some fresh air. I've also got some interesting news for you."

She looked past him. "You didn't actually get that stupid gadget to work, did you?"

"No." He gave it a spin. "I'll get it eventually, but in the meantime I'd rather spend the day with you."

She looked at him again. "Are you all right?"

☐

"I've never been better," he told her for perhaps the dozenth time. They were at the end of a pier in Waterfront Park, looking out over Elliott Bay and watching the gulls sweep past in search of handouts.

"But you're not even *you* anymore," she said. "You're some kind of hybrid."

He heard a buzzing sound overhead, looked toward the western flank of Queen Anne Hill, and saw an orange coast guard helicopter flying slowly toward them. "It works," he whispered.

She sighed. "That's what I'm talking about. Last time I saw you you were all zoned in on this perpetual motion thing, and now you're—"

"I want to ride in one."

"What?"

"A helicopter. Come on, let's go rent one. I'll fly."

"You'll *what*? Nathan, you don't know how to fly a helicopter. And Leonardo sure as hell doesn't know how, either."

She was right. But the urge was overpowering. To fly! He had wanted to fly all his life, and not in an airliner, either. And certainly not like that time off the roof of the Corte Vecchia in Milan. His leg still hurt from that. Then he realized it was the scrape he had gotten in his lab a couple weeks ago, but it certainly felt like the same ache he had lived with for the rest of his life.

"All right," he said, "we'll rent a pilot, too. But I want to do it. Come on!" He turned and started walking back up the pier.

A moment later Elise ran up beside him. "You're serious? You're going to just charter a helicopter?"

He held out his hand for her. "Sure. What good is all this money if I don't have fun with it?"

She shook her head, said, "I don't believe this is you talking. It *isn't* you talking." But she was smiling.

He didn't feel like driving in airport traffic, so they left his car in the parking garage and took a taxi. It turned out the driver knew someone who knew someone in the charter business, so he got on his dispatch radio and by the time they arrived, a little four-seat dragonfly was warming up on the concrete apron, its rotor swishing around slowly as the pilot went through his preflight check.

Nathan tipped the driver a hundred dollars, then whisked Elise away at a run for the helicopter.

There was paperwork to sign, more payment to make, but within a few minutes they were in the air, swooping out over Puget Sound to avoid the air traffic. The water glittered in the sunlight, ferries and sailboats carving long, steady wakes that crisscrossed it in slowly expanding vees of motion.

At first Nathan didn't recognize the sudden urge that filled him, but it hit so hard that he gasped for breath before he realized what it was. "I need a sketchbook."

"What?" Elise's voice came across full of static through the headphones they wore to dampen the engine and rotor noise.

"It's fantastic!" he said, holding out his hands and peering through the rectangle made by his thumbs and forefingers. "I tried to imagine what it would be like, but this . . . I must draw it. Do you have anything in your purse?"

She rummaged through it, came up with a pen, but no paper.

"How about you?" he asked the pilot.

The pilot was a thin, leathery man in his late fifties or so. Without taking his hands off the controls, he nodded toward the clipboard stowed between the seats and said, "I guess you can scribble on the back of the checklist. I can print out another one when we get back."

"Thanks!" Nathan took the clipboard, flipped the paper over, and drew a few bold strokes on it. He looked out the glass bubble and sketched a few more lines, roughing in the boat wakes and the shore of Vashon Island before he looked back down.

He couldn't have flinched worse if there had been a spider crawling on the page. His drawing sucked. A three-year-old could have sketched a better picture with a blunt crayon. "*Cazzo!*" he said.

"What's the matter, is the pen dry?" Elise asked.

"Worse than that—this cretin has never drawn anything in his life!"

"I wish you wouldn't refer to yourself in the third person," she said.

"Sorry. But the provocation! How can I live with these memories and not be able to draw? I painted the *Mona Lisa*! I remember every brushstroke. But this body has no skill." He slid the clipboard back between the seats and handed Elise's pen to her. "I will train it, but not today. Pilot, fly on!"

The pilot looked at him askance, but said nothing as he tilted the helicopter forward.

They circled the city, then coaxed the pilot into dropping them off on the end of the pier they had been standing on earlier in the day. They leaped to the wooden planks the moment he touched down, their hair and clothing whipping in the rotor blast, then the helicopter rose into the air again and sped away while they ran for shore before the police arrived. They giggled like children all the way to Pike Place Market, where they bought gyro sandwiches from a tiny booth and ate them while they strolled among the fresh seafood vendors.

Nathan noticed a woman examining a pile of silver-sided

halibut on a bed of crushed ice, and he couldn't resist saying in a loud voice, "Man, it smells like dead fish in here!"

"Nathan!" Elise said, punching him on the shoulder, but when she saw the woman bend down and sniff the fish, she burst out laughing. "You're terrible," she said.

"And you love it."

She said nothing, but the look in her eyes was reply enough. Nathan felt a twinge of alarm, but it was gone before he could examine it. Was he jealous of Leonardo? He *was* Leonardo. And Nathan, too. The best of both.

From the market they took the monorail to the Seattle Center and watched the fountain in action, its multiple jets shooting streams of water at random.

"I have designed fountains before," he said, "but none with such vigor."

"What *haven't* you done?" Elise asked.

He laughed. "Squared the circle. Discovered the secret of perpetual motion."

She looked at him with her head tilted a few degrees to the side. He expected her to harass him about his obsession again, but instead she said, "Have you ever gone skiing?"

He had to think a moment. The memory was very old, and it took him a second to realize it was from Nathan's childhood, rather than Leonardo's. "A couple of times when I was in junior high," he said.

"Want to do it again?"

"Today? It's the middle of the afternoon. The ski areas would be closed by the time we got there. Unless we called back the helicopter."

She shook her head. "No, I think I've had enough of that for one day. But how about tomorrow?"

He felt the struggle going on within himself, even started to say, "I really should get back to—" before his mouth closed seemingly of its own accord. Sure, he should get back to the lab, but he'd had more fun today than in recent memory. Why shouldn't he keep on enjoying life?

It was a totally foreign concept. So foreign, he was too shocked to stop his traitorous tongue when he heard himself say, "Skiing tomorrow sounds great. In the meantime, want to see a movie?"

☐

They watched the director's cut of *Ringworld*, newly released with extra footage of the crash landing and the escape through Fist-of-God crater. Nathan had a hard time staying in his seat. The special effects were designed to startle video-jaded teenagers; the modern-day half of his mind had trouble enough with them, but Leonardo kept ducking for cover.

When it was over they staggered out into the evening light, where Nathan leaned against the wall with his eyes closed while he tried to regain his equilibrium.

"Are you okay?" Elise asked him.

"Is there anyplace to get a good stiff drink within walking distance?" he replied.

"A drink? You?"

What was wrong with that? He shook his head, still stunned, then remembered. He didn't drink. It affected the mind.

And channeling a five-hundred-year-old painter didn't? He laughed, opening his eyes.

And saw the orange sky overhead. How long had it been since he'd simply stood on a hilltop and watched the sun sink into the west?

About five hundred years, apparently. "Drinks can wait," he said. "The sun never does. Let's watch this first."

They drove to the top of Queen Anne Hill, parked at the base of a huge red radio tower on Highland Drive, and walked to the stone wall to join the other couples looking out over the sound. The sun was an orange oval split by three or four lines of high clouds on the horizon. Bainbridge Island was a dark leviathan in the water, with occasional glints of reflected brilliance from the windows of moving cars.

"I think I prefer nature's light shows," Nathan said, knowing that this thought, at least, came from both his personalities. "They're slower, but they speak to a deeper part of the soul."

Elise leaned her head against his shoulder. He put his arm around her, feeling somehow awkward even though everyone else on the hilltop stood arm in arm as well. Maybe it was the whirlwind day he'd had. He was still trying to sort out his impressions. He had downloaded Leonardo to help him with his research, not to play around town, but at the same time he knew the things he had experienced today could prove just as valuable as anything he did in the lab.

Was that Leonardo's secret? He was easily distracted, but maybe that was how he learned so much.

Or maybe that was why he had left unfinished projects in his wake wherever he went. "Avoid excessive study," he had once said. "It will give rise to a work destined to die with the workman." But maybe that had merely been excuse-making. Maybe he would have been even greater if he'd had Nathan's focus and dedication.

It was hard to say. Especially when the sun was melting into the horizon and Elise was melting into his arms.

After the last blush of violet faded from the sky, they found a brew pub. A good porter helped matters considerably, though Nathan once again surprised himself by ordering the garden burger instead of a hamburger when Elise suggested some food to go along with the beer.

"Leonardo was vegetarian," he explained with a shrug.

She looked like she was about to protest, but she bit it back. He knew well enough what she had been about to say; he'd been thinking it all day himself. Why should he care what Leonardo *was* when he was still himself, still Nathaniel Hoskins?

And why hadn't she said so? Because she liked Leonardo. He was more fun.

It should have bothered him more, but he was also Leonardo now, and that part of him was flattered. Perhaps even a little smug, knowing he could hold his own in a world centuries beyond him.

He idly tore at his paper napkin, shredding it into little pieces as he and Elise talked about their day. He held them in his left palm, toying idly with them as they talked, waiting until she remarked once again how different he had become.

"The two personalities will integrate over time," he said offhandedly. "Unless, of course, one rejects the other."

She sat straight up in her chair. "What? One rejects the other? You never told me that could happen."

"I didn't want to worry you," he said. "Besides, the doctors said talking about it could trigger the process. It can happen at a moment's notice. If I relax, take the wrong drugs, get too drunk—there's a whole list of—" He stopped, rolled his eyes, then crossed them.

"Nathan?"

He coughed, then widened his eyes in panic. "It's . . . it's happening! Oh my God, it's—" He coughed again, bringing his left hand up to his mouth, the fingers curled into a tube. One last hard cough blew white fluff everywhere.

Elise shrieked and jerked backward, shaking the table. Nathan caught her glass before it could tip over.

"Gotcha," he said.

She had been inhaling for a really good scream, but she stopped short, her face twisting in the most amazing way. "Gotcha? *Gotcha?* Is that your idea of humor, you . . . you . . ." Their waiter peered around the kitchen door to see if they were all right, and she lowered her voice. "Don't you ever do that to me again."

Nathan grinned at her. "You're too smart to fall for it twice anyway."

"Is that supposed to be a compliment?"

"Yeah."

She took another deep breath, then said, "You sure know how to keep a person off-balance."

☐

That was apparently not all bad. She started smiling again when he sketched a caricature of her on a new napkin, drawing his lines with slow deliberation to compensate for his untrained hand. It wasn't beautiful, but it did capture her amusement in the set of her mouth and eyebrows. It must have been flattering enough, for she tucked it into her purse when it was time to go, and when he asked, "Where to next?" she took his hand, and said, "Your place."

They were quiet in the car on the way home. All the same, he felt awash in nervous energy, and he could see it in her, too. When he stepped inside from the garage he automatically turned toward the basement lab, but she said, "Oh no you don't. Not tonight. I have other plans for you."

He swallowed. "What, uh, what plans might those be?"

She leaned forward, murmured, "You're a certified genius now; you figure it out." Then she kissed him.

He shouldn't have been surprised. Part of him wasn't. Part of him had kissed her before, had even made grand plans for a slow seduction before he had become obsessed with discovering the secret of perpetual motion and nearly driven her away. But part of him hadn't seen it coming, had assumed that their relationship was merely close friendship. It had to be that way, because it had always been that way with women, and always would be.

He leaned back, his heart pounding.

She looked up at him with narrowed eyes. "What now?"

"He's gay."

"Oh, brother." She didn't stomp out. She just looked at him for a moment, then slowly reached up to her neck and began unbuttoning her shirt.

Leonardo had seen plenty of women disrobe. He had painted them nude, had drawn anatomical studies that would make most men blush. But he had never seen the look in their eyes that Elise fixed on him now.

"Time to fish or cut bait, sailor," she said as the crucial center button popped loose. She wasn't wearing a bra. The rounded curves of her breasts didn't quite touch in the middle.

Nathan had never seen that look in a woman's eyes, either. Not live. Not directed at him. He felt as if his brain might explode, but fortunately he didn't need his brain at the moment. Instinct took over. He reached out for Elise, hesitantly at first, then with growing eagerness.

They left a trail of clothing into the living room. The bedroom was too far away, at least for the first intense burst of passion. They used the couch, then the carpet, then they staggered into the bedroom when their skin began to cool, only to catch fire again under the covers.

"Well, I guess we've answered the old 'nature versus nurture' question, haven't we?" Elise murmured, as they drifted off to sleep.

Nathan wondered. He couldn't feel Leonardo's presence anywhere. Had he actually driven him out of his mind? Literally? He'd been kidding when he'd told Elise that one personality could reject the other, but now he began to wonder if he hadn't accidentally done just that to poor Leonardo. But sleep dragged him under before he could figure out how to search for him.

He woke briefly in the middle of the night, surprised to find himself in his brightly lit laboratory, but then he remembered that Leonardo often got up after only a few hours of sleep to continue his work by candlelight. Nothing flowed faster than the years, after all, and even though he had been granted more time than his due, there was apparently no sense in wasting any of it.

So Leonardo wasn't gone. And maybe he wasn't the wastrel Nathan had been afraid he was. All the same, he felt more of a sense of duality than ever before, as if the two minds in one body had separated like oil and water. Would this be temporary, he wondered, or had he driven Leonardo into his own realm? How could they function like that? Would he have to delete him and start over, like that poor actor who had hosted Francis Bacon by mistake?

He felt a rising tide of alarm, a tide that washed over him and sent him back into dreamland.

□

He was in bed again when he awoke. He looked out the window, but saw only blue sky from his angle. Milan? Florence? Or Seattle? Then he felt the warmth next to him, turned his head, and saw Elise looking at him, a soft smile on her lips.

Leonardo had crawled back into bed with her? Or had he dreamed the whole thing last night? He couldn't remember. But he remembered cold mornings in Italy, when that sluggard Salai wouldn't get up to stoke the fire, and he remembered equally cold mornings in his parents' house in Tacoma, slipping into damp clothing and running through the rain to catch the school bus. He was still his new self. But apparently part of him could sleep while part of him stayed awake.

"You look like you're thinking hard," Elise said.

He nodded. "It's been a busy night."

She laughed. "You ready for some more exercise?"

He felt a moment of panic, and it wasn't all coming from Leonardo. "Again?"

She tickled him in the ribs. "I meant skiing, silly."

"Yow! Oh. I—" Did he actually want to go? He was a bit surprised to realize that he did. "Sure."

She rolled over and looked at the clock on the nightstand. "Eight-thirty? 'Yow' is right! We'll miss half the day if we don't hurry."

They tumbled out of bed, showered, had bowls of cereal for breakfast, then gathered up all of Nathan's winter clothing they could find. He didn't have much, but a sudden thought hit him as he passed the basement stairs on the way to the garage, hat and coat in hand.

"What?" Elise asked when he paused.

"Goggles," he replied. "I've got to rent skis, but I can at least bring my own goggles." He handed her his coat. "Here, hold this. I'll just be a second."

"You'd better be," she said. "We've still got to go past my place for my stuff. I'm not waiting for you if you start tinkering around down there."

"I'll just get the goggles, swear to God."

He took the stairs two at a time, flipped on the lights, and went over to the tool rack, where his orange plastic safety goggles with the variably polarizing lenses hung beside the braising torch. He turned away with them in his hands, but stopped when he heard a familiar noise.

The perpetual motion wheel was spinning in its cradle, its weighted levers flopping over the tops of their arcs one after another and driving the wheel around and around. Tools and plastic shavings lay on the counter all around it.

"Leonardo?" he whispered aloud. Had he done this while Nathan was asleep? He stepped closer.

"Nathan?" Elise called from upstairs.

He felt a sharp sense of amusement from his alter ego. Dilemma! Behind door number one, perpetual motion. Behind door number two, the beautiful girl.

Leonardo *would* see the humor in this. In fact, he was jokester enough to set up the whole thing. Put an electric motor inside the wheel, for instance.

Except Leonardo alone didn't understand electricity.

The hair on the back of his neck began to prickle.

"Nathan, are you coming or not?"

"Coming." He stepped to the door, flipped off the lights, and climbed the stairs, listening to the soft clatter of overbalancing weights behind him. If it was truly perpetual motion, it would still be running when he got back.

Luck of the Draw

Thomas W. Knowles

It's always the same. I walk in out of the night, through the swinging doors into the saloon, a smoke-shrouded room trimmed in tired red velvet and faded gilt fixtures. Tinny music from the piano fades in and out like the song of a blue norther through telegraph wires. The carved ebony bar runs the length of the wall, stretching on forever beside a distorted, dusty mirror guarded by even ranks of gleaming bottles.

The room is filled with men and women who drink and shout and dance to the music, their bodies and their faces fading into a blur of joyless revelry. Their desperate laughter mixes with the tune, echoing back to me as cries of rage and pain. I know them. I've seen them or their like in a dozen saloons and gambling hells, and sometimes over the sights of my gun. A very few of those blank faces may once have belonged to my friends. In this place, they're neither friend nor foe, just faded shadows of memory.

It's always the same, the dream. I could figure it out if I cared to, but I don't give a damn. I've come to play. That's all that matters. That's all that ever mattered.

The dealer waits for me at the far table, his back to the wall. He's a stick-figure man, his gaunt, almost frail body swathed in a ragged old frock coat and a worn silk suit. The shadow of his black slouch hat hides most of his face. I can't see his eyes, the expression on his face, but I know that he's grinning. He always grins. I catch a glimpse of his ivory smile, which is like the flash of a hidden knife in the night.

"I came to play," I tell him.

"Table stakes," he says, "straight draw. Dollar ante."

"Fine by me." I put my money on the table, sit down and roll out a silver coin to meet the ante. "Bartender!"

A fresh bottle sits at my left hand, I don't even have to look to find it. I split the seal with my thumbnail, push the cork out, and pour a full glass. The whiskey burns on the way down, hits my throat like lye on a raw sore. The answering cough sprays my white lace handkerchief with bright red flecks. I tamp down the pain with another drink. I fill the second glass and push it across the table.

The dealer ignores it, opens a fresh pack of cards, and offers me the cut. I run the cards in a three-split and push them back to him. All the other sights and sounds of the place fade into the background as he deals, narrowing into the whisk and click of the new-minted cards.

The hand he deals me turns up aces and eights. Ever since the day that idiot, Jack McCall, shot Hickok in the back of the head, they've called it the Deadman's Hand. That's just a folktale, campfire talk, poker-house brag. Not even the people who actually saw that game remember exactly which cards made up the last hand Wild Bill ever drew.

Time for me to draw. I discard the eights. "Two cards," I say, and the dealer slips the pasteboards to me across the dark green felt. He stands pat. When I fan out my new hand, I see that the eights have come back to me—an impossible draw. I look up at the dealer, and even though I can't see his face, I know he's grinning. He always grins, that same old-ivory grin that mocks every smile made of flesh and blood. I grin back at him as I toss in two dollars to call.

The Deadman's Hand is a myth, but when you cut the deck with the grinning stranger who wears the black hat, every hand is a dead man's hand. It's whatever he wants it to be.

He lays down to my call. Card by card, he turns up four black cards—a ten, a king, a knave, and an ace. The ace of spades catches my eye. It glistens and spreads, a pure black hole that blots out the dream and pulls me into its darkness, up into the dying light of a cool afternoon. I open my eyes to the last rays of the Colorado sun filtering through the curtains of my sick room. The water stain on the ceiling looks like a distorted map of Texas.

"Here you are, sir," the orderly whispers from my bedside. "Just like I promised." The glass of the bottle he slips me is warm from his pocket. "Anything else?"

He makes his words polite, but I can see the fear and anger in the hunch of his shoulders, in the twist of his lips. He's afraid of being caught breaking the rules, but he's too greedy for my money to stop—and he's still too scared to cross me.

I wave him away, don't want him touching me. I have enough strength left to raise myself up on the pillows, to pull out the stopper, bring the bottle to my mouth. The whiskey burns like the cheap stuff it is. I keep my eyes on his even as I fight against fire in my chest.

"Just get out," I say as I pass him one of my last double eagles. It takes all I've got to keep the whiskey down, to hold back the cough.

He doesn't think I see him glance back at me, but I do. His look tells me that he'll be glad when I'm dead. He's not the only one.

Down beside my bed, my boots stand neglected. I haven't worn them for days, but the orderly hasn't stolen them yet. I guess he's waiting until I'm safely planted. Then he'll sell them to some penny-dreadful hack, some ghoul from the newspapers or a wax museum. He won't get my guns. I gave those to my last visitor, a kind of parting gift to the only man I ever called a friend.

A shiver starts up from the base of my spine to rattle my teeth. I take another drink and fall back against the bedstead, fighting the convulsion and twisting the covers until my bare feet poke out. They're cold, but I can barely feel them for the general numbness that has taken over my body. When I look down at them and wiggle my toes, the ludicrous nature of the situation strikes me. I've played so many games of chance, cleared so many high-stakes tables with a bluff or a pistol, only to die in bed. It's not what I wanted. I've never been a cheat, never let anyone else cheat me and get away with it. I guess there's a first time for everything, and a last.

The laughter is agony itself, tearing at the remnants of my lungs, but I can't hold it back. I look down at my bare toes again. "Damn, that's funny," I say, wishing I had someone there with whom I could share the joke. As my laughter redoubles into a choking rush of blood, the last of my strength evaporates. On the wall and the ceiling above, I see the last of the sunlight fade into evening.

I find myself back at the table in the saloon, back in the game. The dealer turns over his last card. It's a black queen—he's got a royal flush. He leans forward and pushes back his hat, no longer content to hide his hideous grin.

He wins.

□

It hit him the same way each time, the fear that turned his guts into water, his muscles into sawdust. Marcus Daniels tried to ignore the shriek of the wind as Shane Thorne slid back the old transport's cargo door, to ignore the terror it inspired. He adjusted his oxygen mask and leaned back against his parasail pack, his eyes shut tight as he silently repeated the mental exercise for serenity. The casual observer might think he'd fallen asleep, but sleep, like serenity, eluded him.

"Testing," Thorne said over the helmet radio. "Clear channel, everybody?"

Marcus listened as the other members of the jump team replied. He didn't have to open his eyes to see their faces, the gang of four who were his constant companions in their competition for the brass ring and the latest thrill. "Clear," he said.

"Okay, so everybody's got the drill down, right?" Thorne, who played with neutrons for a living and considered himself a "serious" scientist, became exceptionally cheerful when he found new ways to lead his friends astray. "On my mark, Marcus goes first, then Tina, Adam, Boone, and then me last. Let's see, we'd better calibrate our altimeters once more, just for safety's sake."

"Dammit, Shane," Adam Richards said, "you take all the fun out of it. We've checked, already. Give it a rest."

"It's fine with me if you want to go splat, old buddy. Just not when I'm leading the jump, okay?"

"C'mon, bro," Christina said, "cut us some slack. It's not like we haven't jumped before. Besides, these new 'sails do everything but fix your breakfast."

Thorne held up his hands in mock defeat. "Okay, okay, sis, just don't blame me when your boyfriend bounces off the prairie. This is a high-altitude jump, not some Saturday afternoon dive. If the automatic mechanism doesn't trigger the 'sail at the right altitude, you'll have to depend on the manual emergency chute. If you don't pull the ripcord before you hit the low ceiling, it won't slow you down enough."

Marcus gave up on the useless exercise, sat forward, and looked over to where Christina snuggled up against Richards. She used to sit close to him like that, back before she'd traded him in for his old college roommate. Perhaps Tina and Adam made a better match, a financial manager and a corporate attorney. She'd always been more interested in Marcus's net worth than in the bioengineering research that had made him that fortune. Richards, who would never have made partner in his firm without Marcus as a client, was interested mostly in himself. Christina enjoyed playing the role of a mirror, as long as the image she reflected was a shallow one.

"Enough of that," Marcus said. "Shane's not only right, he's jump captain. Everybody pay attention and check your readouts."

Boone Benavides's short bark of a laugh crackled through their earphones. "Not getting cold feet, are you, Marcus? You don't have to jump just because you're paying for the trip. I'll trade you, and you can pick up the tab for our next outing. Myself, I'm in the mood to ski some black diamond slopes this winter."

Marcus looked over to where his cousin sprawled against the bulkhead, his massive arms crossed over his chest. All he could see of Boone's face was the twinkle of his blue eyes over his mask, but Marcus could read contempt in every line of the big man's body. Boone enjoyed the show, and sometimes he didn't even pretend to be a part of it. If it weren't for the amusement factor he found in their little group, he'd probably rather hang out with his oil-patch buddies at the Petroleum Club.

Marcus just shook his head and turned to let Thorne recheck his instrument package against the final benchmark altitude relayed by the pilot. He knew it wouldn't do him any good to lock horns with Boone, any more than it would to argue with Thorne or to get angry with Christina and Richards. *Friends, lovers, and family*, he thought, *what would I ever do without 'em?*

A deep chime sounded over their radios. "That's the warning," Thorne said. "Time to get into position."

"No kidding, Shane," Richards said. "I never would have known it." Adam liked to hear himself talk, but he had little patience for listening to others.

Christina laughed, the sound of it reminding Marcus of her amusement the night she'd refused his marriage proposal. She said, "My big brother is nothing if not redundant," and then she looked over at Marcus. He snapped down his helmet visor so she couldn't see his eyes.

"Ready, Marcus?" Thorne's voice trembled with ill-disguised anger.

Marcus rose from the bench, turned to take his position at the cargo door, and grasped the hand ring at the aft side. Without really thinking about it, he let his free hand slide up to his throat. Through the thin fabric of his jumpsuit, he fingered the irregular lump of his good luck piece, the chunk of Lucite that hung on a leather strand about his neck. Preserved in plastic like a leaf in amber, the corroded metal shard within it was all that remained of an Apache arrowhead.

His great-great-grandfather had carried that arrowhead in his left lung for seven years, a reminder of a battle between his Texas Ranger company and a band of Victorio's warriors. The tough old bastard had coughed it up while he'd survived a bout of pneumonia, then had carried it in his pocket for thirty years more. It had been passed down through his family from father to eldest son. It should have come to Ben, Marcus's older brother, but Ben had gotten drunk after winning his last high school football game in his senior year. Ben had tried to beat a train at a county road crossing. They could have buried what was left of Ben and the five passengers in his car together in one box.

As he traced the outline of the encased arrowhead, Marcus remembered the day of Ben's funeral, his mother's grief and his own. At the graveside, his father had not shed a tear. Marcus had realized that day just how much he hated the man. Bass Daniels had prided himself as a hard man, and even though he'd pinned all of his hopes for the future on his oldest boy, he'd held back his emotions until afterward.

After the funeral, Bass stopped just inside the door to the ranch house and slapped Marcus to the floor. "Damned little crybaby," he said. "You should be in the ground instead of my real son." He turned on his wife. "This is your fault, coddling him and making him your pet. He's always got his nose in a book, can't ride, can't fight, can't take a little pain without sniveling. Look at him, crying in front of everybody—just like when he was four, when that milk-fed pony I bought him scared him to death. Hell, he's afraid of his own shadow. He'll never be a fraction of the man Ben would have been. Never."

Maria Daniels knelt by her surviving child, interposing herself between them. "And where did Ben learn to drink hard and drive fast, Bass? Who taught him what it took to be a man? He wasn't scared of anything except for you, except for maybe backing down from a dare. Everyone in town knows it, and they know that's why he got his girl and his friends killed. That's why we're not welcome there anymore, why people spit on the sidewalk behind your back."

His face suffused with red rage, Bass drew back his fist to strike. Suddenly, he dropped his arm back to his side and bared his teeth in a savage smile. "They're afraid to say it to my face . . . but you're not, are you? They all know that I could buy them and sell them, or break them if I decided to, but you don't give a damn for me. That's good, because I don't give a damn for you or the brat. Why don't you take him away for a while, go visit your mother until I get finished mourning my son? I don't want to have to look at either of you for a while."

Without another word, Bass Daniels turned away and walked into the den to the liquor cabinet. He took out a bottle and a glass, then walked past them to the stairs. He stopped on the landing, looked down at his wife and son. "I got an even better idea—when you get to your mother's house, just stay there. I can do without you or that poor excuse for a boy. Just call Ray Benavides and have him handle the legal details."

Marcus didn't see his father again until his senior year at Texas A&M, and that only as a waxy, unreal figure lying in a bronze casket. He came home for the funeral only because his mother and his uncle Ray insisted. The terms of his father's will turned the ranch over to the state of Texas as an addition to the adjacent park. Marcus used a portion of the trust fund to complete his education and start up BioGen, then donated the rest to charity.

The only item he'd kept from the bequest was the Apache arrowhead. He'd seen the cruel joke his father had made of the heirloom, intending it to serve as a reminder that his rejected son would never be worthy of the courage it represented. Instead, Marcus had taken it as a talisman, as the symbol of his defiance.

"To hell with you, old man," Marcus whispered, touching the arrowhead as he stared out into the abyss. "To hell with all of you."

The second chime sounded as the jump light over the cargo hatch flashed green. "Ready," Thorne said. "We're over the jump zone. Marcus, go on the count. One, two . . ."

Boone said, not laughing this time, "Sure you want to jump, Marcus?"

". . . three, go, go!" Thorne said.

Marcus closed his eyes, pushed back against the handholds, and launched himself into space. He drew his knees up against his chest and wrapped his arms around them, rolling his body into a tight ball. He held the cannonball position for ten seconds to make certain he was clear of the prop wash, then gradually spread himself out into a soaring position.

Despite the protection of his insulated suit, the thin air chilled him immediately. No clouds obscured the brown west Texas landscape that spread out below him. He could see everything in excellent detail—Del City and the foothills of the Davis Mountains to the west, the field with the landing target marked out just a bit to the east.

For that moment, falling through open sky, flying without wings, he found himself at peace with the fear. The parasail might not open, the emergency chute might fail, a thermal might catch him at final approach and toss him into a tree, a power line, or a barbed-wire fence. He could die any one of a number of ways.

But for the moment, he flew, alone and far away from the fear, insulated from what might have been and what might be. Laughter bubbled up from deep inside him, erupted to be ripped away by the talons of the unforgiving atmosphere. Under the oxygen mask, his lips pulled back into a defiant grin.

It was at that moment that he decided to go through with his plan to beard the Chimera in its den, to replace the fear he saw in his mirror with the grim-faced, black-clad messenger of Death. "I'm gonna do it! Do you hear me, Boone, I'm gonna do it!"

He was still laughing when the automatic release ejected the parasail, when the shock of the silk hitting the wind brought him up short. As he steered the 'sail down in a perfect spiral toward the hard-packed earth that rushed up to meet him, his mind had already moved on to the next step. He dumped air from the sail to bring him in close to the waiting truck, rolled with the impact, and hit the release snaps. Without looking up to see the others land, he stumbled to his feet and lurched into a run. Ignoring the champagne iced down in the cooler, he grabbed up the cellular phone and dialed the number from memory.

"This is Marcus Daniels of BioGen," he said, gasping for breath between words. "I'd like to confirm my appointment with Wilhelm Wolfe."

☐

"I'm still not satisfied," Wilhelm Wolfe said, frowning as he looked into his client's ice-blue eyes. He disliked the smug half grin Marcus Daniels wore under his dark blond mustache. He didn't like this particular client, didn't much care for his choice of subjects. "Why this particular person? He was a violent man, a gambler, a gunfighter, almost an outlaw.

He died a slow, wasting death of tuberculosis. Why not select a peace officer, a true lawman like your ancestor?"

"Because I'm something of an outlaw and a gambler, myself," Daniels said. "I built my company on my own, without my family's influence and money. I didn't succeed by ducking risks. I want a partner who can understand that, somebody who can keep up with me. Holliday lived for the challenge. I live an active life. Doc could stay up all night, drink like a fish, and still play cards like he was born with the deck in his hands."

Wolfe said, "Yes, and it killed him in the end."

Daniels looked away, his confident smile suddenly strained. He reached up and smoothed his mustache with thumb and forefinger. He hesitated for a moment, as if searching for the right words. "Maybe it did, but he made the most of the life he had. I've always admired him for that. I figure he deserves another chance, another go-round." He looked back at Wolfe and laughed. "Besides that, I'm betting that he'll help me show my high-rolling poker buddies a new trick or two. Doc will love Vegas and Atlantic City. Maybe I'll even take him to Monte Carlo, give 'em a taste of the real Wild West."

"This . . ." Wolfe shook his head. "I'm sorry, but I don't feel that I can recommend the procedure in this case. The subject of your request is unsuitable, unprecedented in our experience with the process. He was an addictive personality, an alcoholic. We've not, as yet, gathered enough data on the effect this might have on you. We couldn't guarantee that the process wouldn't allow his addictions to carry over into the new persona."

"Damn!" Daniels stood up and stretched out his arms. "Look at me, Wolfe. I don't do any drugs except for an occasional drink or cigar. I start every day with a five-mile run; I'm thirty-four years old, and I can outrun and outlast kids half my age. If I didn't have other income, I could make my living as a pro instructor in any one of half a dozen sports.

I've worked as hard to keep in shape as I have to succeed in business. Do I look like I'd let anything, anyone, change that?"

Wolfe looked up at the Texan and sighed. Marcus Daniels stood well over six feet in height. His tanned skin glowed with health. His face, unlined under a thick shock of curly blond hair, was blessed with the kind of sharp-planed features that one associated with the rugged cowboys who appeared in cigarette ads. The expensively tailored suit he wore required no padding to add breadth to his shoulders. As his long fingers curled into fists of frustration, Wolfe noted the unmistakable calluses that only came with regular practice in the martial arts.

At the peak of health and accomplishment, Daniels should be a prime candidate for the process. Still, there was something about the way he insisted on his choice of partners, a subtle note of desperation in his tone, that set Wolfe's teeth on edge.

"No," Wolfe said, "I don't think you'd intentionally destroy what you've made for yourself. But I do *not* wish to be responsible for allowing you to put yourself at risk. Perhaps, if you'd consider providing us with more detailed information from your family medical history . . ."

"My family has got nothing to do with this!" Daniels's shout filled the room with echoes, but he immediately restrained his anger. "Anyway, if what you've told me is true, you can reverse the procedure if it turns out to be a bad choice. I'll have a few weeks to decide, right? If you want, I'll sign a waiver that absolves you of any responsibility beyond that point."

He flopped back down into the chair almost as if his outburst had exhausted him. "Look, Mr. Wolfe, I've been thinking about this ever since Andrew told me about it. I know I'm not one of your original choices, but when I saw the doors it opened for him, I bugged him until he steered me your way. I'm determined to try it . . . hell, with my background in genetic engineering I'm one of the few people in the world who might be qualified to understand and appreciate it, at least the biological aspects. I'm not trying to pull some kind of industrial espionage. I don't have the slightest hint of how the optical phase of the process works—sounds like one of those Zen koans to me."

"Andrew McCallum selected a great writer because he wanted to write," Wolfe said. "Even if he did so on a whim, he made his choice with a positive intention in mind. I have no such confidence in your choice or your intention."

Daniels's eyes narrowed; his voice grew dangerously cold. "My intent is my business. I figure that having Doc Holliday as my partner will enhance my life. Are you going to work with me or not?"

Wolfe, even more convinced that he was correct in his assessment, started to reply. A quiet cough startled him. "Excuse me, Wilhelm," Dr. Chimera said as he closed the office door behind him. "We do not wish to interrupt, but we believe that the gentleman has a point. We specialize in assisting people to complete their destinies. If he is convinced that he has made the correct choice, we believe that we should give him the benefit of the doubt."

Wolfe's eyebrows arched in surprise. "You do? Don't you find his choice a bit reckless?"

"Not necessarily," Chimera said, punctuating the statement with a gentle smile. "The path to understanding is not always a broad highway. Sometimes it is a narrow trail."

Daniels stood up and held his hand out to the newcomer. "You must be Dr. Chimera. I'm . . ."

"Marcus Daniels, yes." Chimera grasped Daniels's hand for only a moment before moving to sit on the edge of the desk. "We have read some of your work on the bioengineering of staple grains for higher disease resistance and greater yield in arid climates. In particular, the methods by which your company developed that strain of maize for use in sub-Saharan regions interest us. Grains produced by those methods may one day feed nations."

"I certainly hope so," Daniels said. "And as I was telling your colleague here, I intend to be around to make that happen. I don't intend to drink myself to death, get shot in a gunfight, or gamble away all my money. I just want to show Doc a good time."

Wolfe gave his partner a questioning look, but Chimera's neutral expression gave him no clue. "Very well," he said. "If you truly believe it's best . . ."

"Yes," Chimera said, "one way or another, it will be for the best."

"Well, I've learned not to doubt your instinct for this." Wolfe looked up at Daniels, and what he saw in the man's eyes brought him up short. Now that he had what he wanted, why would Daniels suddenly look as if he'd been struck by lightning? As he watched the stricken expression creep across Daniels's face, Wolfe noticed that his hand reached up to touch a point just below the knot of his tie. For a moment, Daniels stood there, frozen in that pose.

"So . . . so, we can go ahead?" Daniels cleared his throat, then coughed. "How long? I mean, what do you need?"

Wolfe looked to Chimera, who stood in placid silence, then back to Daniels. "The agreed-upon fee, transferred as we discussed. Our recovery team has a lead on material, which if it is genuine, we can obtain and use without a great deal of time and trouble. You should arrange your business and personal affairs so that you can be ready for a sudden absence of at least forty-eight hours."

"And that's all there is to it?"

"Not quite," Chimera said. "You should prepare yourself for the path to understanding, Mr. Daniels. It should be all that you want, and more, but it may not be quite what you expect."

"What do you mean?" Daniels's earlier smugness had fled.

"Just that," Chimera said. A restrained smile tugged at the

corners of his mouth. "As your future partner might say, 'It's all in the luck of the draw.' Is that not what makes the game worth playing?"

Daniels stared at him for a moment, then nodded his head and smiled back. "Yes, you're right! That's exactly what he would say. Thanks." He turned to Wolfe. "The funds will be transferred to your account by this afternoon, sir. I'll be waiting for your call."

After the door closed behind the client, Wolfe said, "I hope you know what you're doing, old friend. This could lead to a lawsuit. I don't think that fellow is quite as stable as he appears to be on the surface."

"All the more reason to help him find the way, old friend."

"But Doc Holliday! What if he can't handle it? Where will we be then?"

Chimera smiled again, his face that strange but not unreasonable mixture of male and female, yin and yang, understanding and mystery. "What makes you think that Mr. Daniels will be the one who will be required to provide all of the solutions?"

□

When the receptionist ushered an eager, casually dressed Marcus into the quiet treatment room, he found both Wolfe and Dr. Chimera waiting for him. He could see that Wolfe, who looked tired and somewhat drawn, still had his doubts. "Caught me just about to head out for a parasail jump. Ahh . . . didn't expect to see you here, Mr. Wolfe. Do you usually observe the implantation process?"

"Sometimes," Wolfe said. "In this case, I will. I oversaw the acquisition myself. It took me all over the American West, from Arizona to Colorado to California. The particular source wasn't easy to find."

"What source." Marcus frowned. "Holliday was buried . . ."

"We didn't go there, Daniels." Wolfe ran his hand over

his eyes. "Sorry, jet lag. No, this particular source was a keepsake, a lock of hair preserved in a locket that had once been the property of a lady. It provided all of the physical material that we required."

"This," Chimera said, holding up a translucent vial and then plugging it into a slot in the apparatus beside him, "is one part of the process. The other we deliver with this." He rested his hand on the opaque visor and helmet attached to the mobile arm of the device. "If you would please take a seat, we may proceed. You will shortly go to sleep, then wake up thirty-six hours later with the new personality in place."

"Great!" Marcus said. "Just in time for the shoot and the poker game next weekend." He took off his leather bomber jacket and handed it to Wolfe, then settled back into the padded chair. He shifted into the cushions of the chair and managed not to flinch as Chimera deftly taped his eyelids back. The headpiece rotated down to fit over his face, blotting out the bright lights and muting the gentle drone of Chimera's voice.

"Please relax, Mr. Daniels. The introduction of the optical program takes only a moment. What you will see, what you feel, is the reflection of memory through the prism of the soul, so to speak. The light is shattered, scattered into the multitude of its parts, then retrieved from the spectrum to create a single image. It is your first step that begins a journey of a thousand steps. Afterward, you will sleep, and when you awaken you will find that you are no longer alone."

A sharp smell of antiseptic tickled his nose, then he felt the sting of an injection. Chimera's words echoed as if they'd come from a distance ". . . no longer alone." As his hand crept unconsciously up to touch the talisman at his throat, a many-hued light bloomed in the darkness, unfurled itself, and sped toward him. A flower of some kind, he thought, but then the light reversed itself. Like a kaleidoscopic image, it shifted and took on a new form, coalesced into a black, arrowhead-shaped symbol centered in a brilliant field of white.

A card, he said to himself. *The ace of spades.*

Then the darkness engulfed him.

□

"Feels different, somehow," Marcus muttered as the range safety officer checked the black powder loads in his replica Colt Pocket Model revolver. He hefted the gun, taking in the weight and feel of it, the sharp tang of the gun oil and powder. He automatically checked the location of the hammer to make certain it rested between chambers instead of on one of the live percussion caps, then slid the weapon smoothly into the pocket holster sewn into his vest.

"Talking to yourself again?" Boone reseated his twin Peacemakers in their holsters, one side-draw and one cross-draw, and stepped up beside Marcus at the competition firing line. He took off his hat and waved it toward the target stations scattered down Cowboy Action Shooting Range on the Benavides Number One Ranch. "You're a little distracted today. Want to call it quits and just concede the course?"

"No." Marcus took a deep breath of the warm Texas air, inhaled the scents of the Hill Country's cedar and limestone. It came to him that breathing shouldn't be so easy, that the pain, the fire in his chest was what he was missing. *Of course*, he thought. *My lungs are clear*. The simple act of breathing had been an agony for Doc. For years, his sense of smell had been deadened by booze and dust, disease and smoke.

For years, he'd lived with the smell of death. Marcus drew in another deep breath and reveled in it. *No more death, Doc. No more fear. We're going to beat the odds together.*

As he looked downrange, he noticed that something about Doc's experience had enhanced his own perfect vision, adding a new perception. He could almost sense the location of each of the steel targets hidden within the mockups of the Old West saloon, stage office, and bank. It was as if his hand, not his eye, could see them, could feel the invisible line drawn between his trigger finger and the marks.

"No," he said, this time with a smile. "I don't think so, cousin." He accepted the checked Army Colt .44 from the safety officer, drew back the tail of his long frock coat, and seated the gun in the belt holster. The officer handed him two loaded and primed cylinders, one for each gun; he put them in separate pockets of his vest. Turning to Boone, he tipped back his black hat, and said, "Do you feel like doubling the bet on this round?"

Boone cocked his head and smiled. "Sure, I don't mind taking your money. Is this a new attitude to go with the new character and duds?" Benavides, who wore more modern Western clothes and a town marshal's badge, shook his head as he looked over Marcus's black suit, coat, vest, and string tie.

"Something like that." As Marcus looked into his cousin's eyes, he thought of all the times that Boone had egged him on only to show him up. *Not this time.*

"Clear," the safety officer said. "Anytime you gentlemen are ready."

Boone and Marcus gave their assent. The announcer's voice blared out over the loudspeaker. "Ladies and gentlemen, please remember to remain in the safety zone while the range is hot. For the first round of the day, 'Marshal' Boone Benavides and Marcus 'Doc' Daniels will tame the streets of old Dodge City in a handgun-only match. They will advance, draw, and fire four rounds at the two targets at each station, then holster their weapons to advance to the next station. They will fire a total of twenty-four rounds each. The score is figured by the number of hits, time required to fire, and time required to reload. Gentlemen, you may begin!"

Marcus took the right, Boone the left. They stopped at the first station, Marcus across from the false-front saloon, Boone centered on the mockup of the livery stable.

"Sure you want to bet on those old cap-and-ball antiques, Marcus? Awful slow to reload, even with extra cylinders."

"I'm sure enough to double the bet again," Marcus said.

"Ready!" the announcer said.

"Ha!" Boone dropped his right hand to touch the butt of his revolver. "Done."

"Draw!" the announcer said. For safety's sake, Cowboy Action rules precluded the use of the fast draw. Marcus and Boone drew their weapons and held them straight up, waiting for the next command.

"Fire!"

As the two steel targets popped up in the windows of the saloon, Marcus felt a shiver. It passed, leaving an icy calm in its wake. Without thinking about it, he brought the .44 into line and squeezed off one shot and then another at the right-hand target. The steel rang as the soft lead balls impacted on it. Ignoring the smoke from his own shots and the quick reports of Boone's shots, he brought his gun down again toward the left-hand target. He fired twice more, stood still for a moment, then reholstered his gun.

The announcer said, "For the 'Marshal,' that's three solid hits and one miss at a time of 3.48 seconds. For 'Doc,' that's four solid hits in 4.03 seconds. Gentlemen, you may advance to the next station."

"Damn!" Boone said. "I beat your time but I dropped that last one."

"If that last one had been able to shoot back, he might have dropped you, old son," Marcus said. Boone started and almost stumbled. Even as the words left his mouth, Marcus realized that his slight Texas accent had drifted into a Georgia drawl. He couldn't hold back a quiet, dry little laugh. "Fast shooting does not replace accuracy. They would be looking for a new Marshal in Dodge about now."

Boone stared at him for a moment, then grinned. "Maybe so. Feel like doubling the bet again?"

"Love to."

The next station required the shooters to switch guns. At the command, Marcus drew the .44 and fired both remaining rounds so quickly that it almost sounded like one shot. Instead of firing at one target, he hit both targets with one shot each. He slipped the empty .44 back into its holster. As the announcer gave the command, he drew the Pocket Model. He fired, right and left, sending the targets spinning, then froze with the gun still aimed.

For just a moment, as he peered through the gunsmoke, the blurred outlines of the steel plates took on the likeness of faces. He shook his head to clear it, but the illusion persisted. The mock town faded into a dusty street where men jerked to the impact of bullets, then fell like puppets cut from their strings. In the very back of his mind, he heard a dry, cool voice say, *Shooting is easy, but forgetting is not. I always see the faces. They never do go away.*

"For the 'Marshal,' four hits, combined time 4.13 seconds; for 'Doc,' four hits, combined time 4.09 seconds."

Marcus blinked; the illusion faded. Still, he felt as if the air and the sunlight surrounding him had congealed into crystal. Everything became somehow sharper, more real, and yet unreal, from the smell of the gunsmoke to the cheers from the crowd. He could hear the blood singing through his veins, feel his heart pounding in his chest, but it also felt as if he were standing beside himself, watching. As if of its own volition, his hand moved to holster the Pocket Colt.

At the next station, he fired the four shots left in the Pocket Model, broke the gun down, slipped in the fresh cylinder and holstered it. He repeated the process with the .44. His heart was in his throat, but his hands remained steady, making the moves with practiced ease. He reloaded in less than half the time it took Boone to reload his cartridge revolvers.

The feeling of being caught in crystal shattered, leaving Marcus as abruptly as it had come. Its departure didn't change his performance—the skills that Doc Holliday had brought with him had imprinted themselves in nerve and muscle, in thought and eye. For the rest of the course, he drew and fired as if he'd never faltered, never doubted his ability. The targets rang and danced to his tune.

He found little joy in it. As he fired his last shot, he knew that he'd never bet on a shooting match again. In the eyes of a man who had lived by the gun, it was too much like betting his soul for a lark.

"Total hits for the 'Marshal,' twenty-two; combined time one minute, 21.32 seconds; total hits for 'Doc,' twenty-four; combined time one minute 02.46 seconds. 'Doc' Daniels takes the round with a new course record!"

Marcus stood in the wash of applause, oblivious to the announcer's call for the next round, until he felt a light punch on his shoulder. He looked up to see Boone smiling at him.

"Sneaky, cousin," Boone said, "very sneaky. You've been practicing! I know you'd like to stand here while everybody cheers, but we need to get out of the way to give the others their chance."

"Sure," Marcus said.

As they walked back to the starting line, Boone's booming laugh carried across the field. "I can't wait for the poker game tonight," he said, " 'cause I'm going to win back what I owe you. That is, if you haven't been practicing card tricks on the sly, too."

"You never know," Marcus said.

A serious expression dimmed Boone's smile for a moment, then he broke into laughter again. "Marcus, I've put up with your shit for years, just waiting to see if you could maybe surprise me. Twice in one day might just be too much for me, but it would be worth it."

Marcus had been trying to win Boone's approval for years, ever since they'd been kids, since long before Ben had died. More than that, he'd always wanted to beat Boone, to defeat him, then to rub his nose in it. Boone had always been faster, better, stronger, more sure of himself.

There had even been times when he'd wanted Boone to fail, to fall off a horse, to crash a race car, to tangle his 'chute.

Now that he'd finally won, he realized that Boone had been cheering for him to win all along. He had cheated Boone by bringing in Doc Holliday as a ringer, and yet Holliday's unflinching honesty wouldn't let him pretend that he hadn't. The taste of victory turned to ashes in his mouth, to a sulfur stink of gunsmoke.

☐

Marcus studied their faces across the table. "I fold," he said, tossing in his cards.

The post-shoot poker game at the Benavides Ranch was not going as planned. His first rush of confidence had burned off, leaving him open to Boone's careful raises and Adam's bluffs. He'd thought that Doc's skill would kick in as he played, but his game hadn't changed. He'd never been able to bluff successfully, or to see through a good poker face the way Doc could.

"Deal me out for now," he said. "I'm going to get some air."

Shane looked worried, as usual, but Boone limited himself to an annoyed grunt. Adam, who had the deal, said, "No problem, Marcus. Don't need a dummy for this game, and you've been playing like one all night." Tina just winked at him and smiled.

A cold rage washed over Marcus. He smiled and touched a finger to his lips. "You might want to rethink those words, my friend," he said in a low, careful voice. "Why, those are the kind of thoughtless words that might get a man into all sorts of trouble."

Oblivious to the tone in Marcus's voice, Adam laughed. "Hey," he said, "you're the one who's in trouble, Marcus."

He turned over his cards to show nothing better than a pair of twos. "You folded to my bluff, just like you always do."

A sudden sick fear replaced the anger as Marcus realized that his fingers had moved toward his shirt, searching for a vest-pocket gun that wasn't there. " 'Scuse me," he said roughly. He pushed away from the table, stumbled out of the study through the French windows and out into the moonlight. He managed to make it off the terrace into the grapevines before he threw up.

I would have killed him, shot him dead. As the spasm ended in a dry heave, he realized that he had to call Wolfe, to get rid of Holliday before it was too late. It had all been a dangerous mistake, another stupid risk. *What the hell was I thinking?*

Again, that quiet voice in the back of his mind said, *No, you wouldn't have killed any more than I would have. All we have to do, if we don't want to draw, is to remember their faces. All you have to remember is that you can never pull the trigger without paying a price for it.*

The moonlight writhed and stretched into shadowy figures that jerked to a lethal dance of lead, into the faces of nameless men who bled out their lives into the sawdust of saloon floors. Marcus twitched as if each killing, each murder committed in Holliday's search for death, was his own. He remembered them, every one of them.

"But we died in bed, alone," he said. "We never cheated death, never beat him. We worked for him instead. Fear not only rode with us, but inside us. We both wanted to escape from the fear, but now we share it." He couldn't stop the bubble of pain deep within his chest from bursting forth as a sob.

"Marcus," Boone said from behind him. "What the hell is wrong?" He felt Boone's strong hands pulling him to his feet, pushing him toward the pool house.

"What's wrong," he said, as Boone helped him sit down

in one of the cabana chairs, "is that I've screwed up, as usual."

Boone brought him a washrag and a beer from the wet bar. "No, you haven't," he said. "Adam is too stupid to notice, but I did. I've been waiting for years to see you push in his face for him."

Marcus sat silent for a moment, then cleared his throat with a swallow of beer. "Boone," he said, "why have you hung around with me all these years? Why do you put up with me, with this whole business?"

"Why?" Boone shook his head. "Lot of whys. Because you're my cousin, just about the only blood relative I have left in the world. Because Ben asked me to look out for you not long before he died. He knew what your old man was like even better than you did. He knew what was going on with you."

"I don't think you have any idea of what's going on with me," Marcus said, his hand moving to grasp the arrowhead.

"No?" Boone's lips thinned, his hard face grew dark. "Don't you think I know what that damned relic means to you? Your old man was a complete bastard. He left it to you like it was a white feather, but he was the coward, not you. I've seen you face your fears and defeat them, all but one. You think I haven't figured it all out? You take chances. You'll do almost anything on a dare. What are you trying to prove, Marcus?"

"Nothing!"

"Bull! You're trying to prove that the old bastard's wrong, even though you *know* he's wrong. You've just gotten into the habit, Marcus, and it's one you need to break before it breaks you. Let it go, cousin. It's time to grow up!"

"It's time for you to butt out, you mean!"

Marcus realized that they were both standing almost nose to nose, shouting at the top of their lungs.

He laughed. It welled up from deep inside, from the same spot that had generated his earlier sobs. At first, it was almost a giggle, then it built up into a guffaw. He couldn't control it, couldn't stop it. Boone, nonplussed, took a step back. Then his face divided in a broad smile. The smile opened into a roar of mirth.

By the time they finally had to stop for air, they were leaning on each other for support.

"Okay . . . okay," Marcus said, gasping. "I promise . . . to grow up if you butt out."

"Done!" Boone said. "I was getting tired of baby-sitting, anyway."

Shane's worried voice carried to them from the terrace. "Hey, what's going on out there? Are we going to play cards or not?"

Marcus and Boone looked at each other, then broke out into laughter again. "Damned straight we are!" Boone yelled. "Right, cousin?"

"Right," Marcus said. He could see the cards, the numbers and the suits, as if they lay on the table before him. *Right, we are, partner*, he said to Doc.

□

Marcus said good night to Boone and Shane, stumbled up to his room, and tucked his winnings into his travel case. *Always keep your winnings close, in case you have to leave in a hurry*. He knew he'd never cash Adam's IOU note—he intended to frame it, to remind himself of the bluff he'd run on nothing but a pair of jacks.

He pulled off his shirt and walked over to the window, where the moonlight spilled across the bare, hardwood floor of the old ranch house. As he looked out at the vineyards and the stock tanks, his hand moved automatically to the arrowhead. The Lucite was cool to the touch. The leather thong ruffled his hair as he pulled it over his head. He held it up into the moonlight so that he could see the scarred old sliver of metal.

True fear, he said to himself, *is not a jagged edge of metal, it's not the cold touch of death. It's the illusion of being alone.*

The talisman could pass on, to family or to a museum. Marcus knew that its original meaning had been restored to him, replenished by the laughter of brothers, revealed by the compassion of a man long dead. He tossed the arrowhead onto the bureau and fell into the bed, already turning his mind to the new adventures that lay ahead for him.

You're gonna love Monte Carlo, Doc. And if you think that's hot, wait till you see what we've done with medicine since your day.

☐

This time we dream together, my new partner and I. We're here to play the game, but we know it will never be the same again. We will never play alone.

As we step through the bat-wing into the saloon, the piano goes quiet, the indistinct revelers fall silent. They cease their meaningless dance and turn in place to stare at us. We can see their faces now, no longer blurred by the years and the pain of memory. Old friends, old enemies, they meet our eyes and do not look away from what they see.

Our spurs ring against the floorboards, the silver notes echoing like distant bells. The silence breaks as the people surround us, as welcoming voices envelop us.

"Hello, Doc," Wyatt says as he takes our hand. "Good to have you back." A laughing Morgan crowds in to slap us on the back as Virgil nods his quiet greeting. From the corner near the bar, Ringo lifts his drink and shoots us a wry smile.

They're all here, all except for one, but then we see her waiting by the table in the back. She's no great beauty, not like the actresses who have played her in the movies, nothing like the sleek, faithless Christina. But she is more real to us and dear to us than any image on film could ever be. As we draw near, she drops her carpetbag and gives us a kiss. The bar rings with cheers and good-natured jibes at our expense.

"Don't worry, Doc," Kate whispers in our ear. "I'm ready for trouble." She presses against us so we can feel the pocket pistol tucked into her sleeve. We remember the time she set a town on fire to save us from a lynching, and we smile.

The dealer at the back table hasn't changed; his grin hasn't dimmed a bit. He shuffles the deck and asks, in a voice as dry as dust, "Here to play again, Holliday? Table stakes, dollar ante."

We take out our money and drop it on the felt. "We're here to play," we say as we sit down. "Cut you, high card for the deal."

For but a moment, his smile falters in the shadow of his hat. Without another word, he points to a fresh deck. We break the seal, open the box, and draw out the fresh cards. They move stiffly at first, but it doesn't take long for us to warm them up. We fold in the deck a last time, then place it directly between us and our opponent, giving him the first cut.

He reaches out, divides the deck. He turns up the black queen, the queen of spades. He grins as we shuffle the deck, but then, he always grins. We return the deck to the center of the table, then look up into the shadows where he hides his eyes. "It's all in the luck of the draw," we say as we cut the deck.

"The ace of hearts," Kate says as she sits down beside us. "Your deal, Doc."

Ben touches our shoulder, and says, "Give 'em hell, little brother."

As we feel them crowd in around us, old friends, old enemies, and family, we look across the table at the man in black, who still grins, knowing that the game will not last forever. He's right, but we also know that, for as long as we can play, we will never again face him alone.

Divine Guidance

Sharan Newman

Alma May Willis slumped onto the stool in her dressing room, pulled off the heavy blond wig with a sigh of relief, and started removing the thick stage makeup. A few moments later she checked in the mirror to be certain that Alma was completely gone and she was plain Melanie Smith again. Lately, she had been having doubts.

"Joe, I can't do this anymore," Melanie said, still staring at her reflection. "There's nothing left in me."

Her manager, Joe Nichols, patted her on the shoulder.

"Now, Alma, honey," he began. "You say that after every revival tour. A week or two of rest at that spa in Costa Rica, and you'll be up there exhorting and singing and bringing souls to righteousness just like before."

Melanie shrugged his hand off her.

"Rest won't help this time, Joe," she said. "I'm not tired; I'm empty. I knew it tonight as I was on the eighth chorus of 'Jesus Was a Country Boy, Too.' That song always just made me sob with joy at knowing I was saved. But this time I felt like a sounding brass and out of tune to boot. It won't work, Joe. How can I make people open their hearts to the

Lord when mine is closed? I can't feel the energy anymore. I'm not sure that God wants me to go on with this."

A ripple of pure panic passed over Joe's face. He hid it quickly, though. He turned the stool around until she faced him and took both her hands in his.

"That's just nonsense, girl!" he insisted. "Why, I've never seen anyone in my whole life more filled with the spirit of the Lord than you. When you're up there pleading with those sinners, I come all over gooseflesh realizing how close you are to heaven."

"Alma may be, Joe." Melanie slid her hands free. "But I'm not. And I can't get into being Alma anymore. It doesn't feel right somehow. I tell you, God has abandoned me. I can sense it right down to my bones. Oh, Joe! I'm all alone."

She burst into tears.

"There, there," Joe said automatically. "It'll be all right. You just need a good night's sleep."

He called for her maid and chauffeur and told them to take her back to the hotel and see that she had dinner and a sedative. When they had left, he sat for a long time in the dressing room doing some serious worrying.

Melanie couldn't quit now. This Alma gig was the best thing that had ever happened to him. Joe had been doing the circuit for nearly twenty years, preaching in tents and strip-mall churches, just barely getting by, when one day this scrawny girl came up to him and asked him to baptize her, 'cause Jesus had told her to wash her sins away and spread His Word.

Joe was wrung out from an evening of hellfire that had netted him only $22.87, and he nearly said, "Sure, kid. For ten bucks I'll baptize you or your pet pig." But something about her made him think twice. Instead of telling her to come back for the next meeting, he sat the girl down and questioned her.

"Jesus told you?" he had asked. "What exactly did He say?"

She had heard the skepticism in his tone and hung her head.

"I know I'm not worthy," she had whispered. "But I heard Him just as clear as a bell. I was hanging clothes in the yard and this wonderful voice just came out of the sky and said, 'Melanie, my child.'"

She paused. "My mom and dad both passed away a long time ago, so I thought it might be one of them, but the voice went on to say that the world was a sad place because it had turned away from God and that I should go out there and tell everyone it was time to repent. So here I am."

Joe had looked over her washboard figure and limp brown hair and shaken his head.

"Honey, I don't think you could convert anyone looking like that. People won't believe God would waste His time on a skinny girl from the boonies. You need an image, a voice to pull 'em in. Now, why don't you just . . ."

And then, before he could send her out, this bit of a thing just opened her mouth and sang.

Joe had been blown away. She was a natural. Perfect pitch, with a richness and sincerity that could make a politician confess his sins in public on election eve. All she needed was a good manager. And right then, he knew it had been laid on him to make sure every sinner in the world heard her. Even with expenses, he was sure she would reel them in, every poor slob with a guilty conscience and a fat checkbook.

Alma May Willis was about to be born.

It had been wonderful, Joe thought. At first it was just her singing with him on his usual route; then offers started coming in for Alma to guest on the big televangelist shows. Then came the worldwide revival meetings, with thousands coming forward to have her bless and comfort them. She never claimed to be a healer, but now and then there was a cure onstage, and he wouldn't let her deny that she had caused it.

In ten years she had become one of the most adored ministers of the Gospel in the world. And Joe Nichols had become rich.

☐

But now she wanted to quit. Just walk away from her mission. She insisted that God didn't talk to her anymore and that could only mean He was angry with her work. Joe didn't know how he could stop her. All his urging and pleading had proved useless.

It was in his darkest hour that he remembered something he'd overheard at a reception at the White House, where Alma had sung the year before. Just a few words about some sort of mind meld or possession, only done in a lab. It had sounded like voodoo to him, but he knew the person they had been talking about, and it was true that he had changed dramatically. A Wall Street wizard on the brink of failure, he'd suddenly turned his finances around by investing in a painting found in a warehouse in France that had turned out to be a late da Vinci. Now the guy was making a fortune in Renaissance art.

Joe wasn't sure if there was anything in the rumor that the man really thought he was da Vinci or that it had cost him nearly all he had left to channel the artist or whatever he had done. The whole deal sounded crazy to Joe, but there was no denying that something had worked. Joe set about discovering what that something was. If there was a way to get Melanie/Alma right with her God again, he'd find it. The cost didn't matter. He'd pay almost anything to keep from losing his heavenly golden goose.

☐

It was a month later that he found himself sitting before Dr. Wolfe.

"Your proposal is an intriguing one," Dr. Wolfe admitted. "But it may be difficult. We haven't had much luck in getting samples from religious leaders. Those who have custody of the bodies are very leery of anyone taking bits of them."

"I don't want Billy Sunday or anyone really important like that," Joe explained. "I just want a saint. I don't care how old. Someone who had visions, for preference. Someone very sure in their faith and not very worldly in terms of money."

"Hmmm." Dr. Wolfe pursed his lips. "Pity we don't have anything of Ste. Perpetua's. She'd fit your specifications. Of course, she was a martyr, and I really don't know how much of the torture and violent death would be in the material. We might be able to get something from the tomb of St. Martin. He died naturally."

"No, I don't want a man." Joe was sure about that. "I saw that Dr. Chimera of yours. Doesn't know if he's male or female. Gives me the creeps. I can tell you that won't go over with the evangelicals. How about Ste. Bernadette? I saw that movie with Jennifer Jones. She had a lot of class."

"Mr. . . . . that is . . . Reverend Nichols," Dr. Wolfe explained. "I really don't think we can help you. Even if we had a sample from someone who came within the parameters of your need, we would still want to deal beforehand with the person who will be the subject of the joining. She would have to prepare for it and, of course, acquiesce to it, herself."

Joe chewed his lip. "You mean we can't slip her a mickey and, when she woke up, she'd hear voices again."

"Again?" Dr. Wolfe rose from his chair. "Reverend Nichols, we don't deal with people who have serious psychological problems. The consequences could be disastrous."

"Alma May Willis isn't a loony!" Joe insisted, standing as well. "She's only lost the faith a little. I want her to have the memories of someone else who believed. A live-in spine stiffener, kind of."

Dr. Wolfe had put his hand on the phone to call the guard to show Joe out. Instead he picked up a pencil and pad and wrote something Joe couldn't see.

"Alma May Willis, is it?" he said. "I heard her sing at a

gala once. She looks like a cheap doll, but when she sang, well, she almost made me believe in angels."

"She isn't singing now," Joe told him. "She sits in the house with the blinds down and prays all day for forgiveness. And she's done nothing to forgive. I know. I've been her manager for years, and she hasn't ever had a boyfriend, a drink, or a mean word for anyone."

Wolfe stood in thought for a moment. Then he hit the intercom button.

"Dr. Chimera, could you come in a moment?" he asked when the voice came through.

"Now, I draw the line at oriental saints," Joe said nervously. "It's gotta be a decent Christian one."

"Yes, I understand." Dr. Wolfe looked at him with distaste. "Normally, I don't think we'd take your case, but the idea intrigues me and, despite her gaudy appearance, Ms. Willis seemed to me to be a good woman. I'll consult with Dr. Chimera, and we'll let you know."

"When?" Joe asked.

"Very soon," Dr. Wolfe promised. "But I need to talk with her, myself. Nothing will be done without her permission."

"Don't worry." Joe was elated. "I'll get it."

☐

And so, a month later, Melanie sat in the same chair facing Dr. Wolfe and Dr. Chimera. It was decidedly Melanie, no makeup, hair combed back from her face and held in place with bobby pins, wearing a simple dress with no jewelry.

Looking at her, Dr. Wolfe began to have qualms about letting her into the program. Melanie was already two people; what would adding a third one do? He felt obliged to make this point.

Melanie leaned forward across the desk, her hands clasped like a pleading child.

"Alma is gone, Dr. Wolfe," she explained. "She was only

an invention of Joe's anyway. I need someone to take her place, someone who believes. Joe said you could help. Please, you have to help!"

"Yes, of course we'll try to." Dr. Wolfe was taken aback by her grief. "We have found genetic material from a woman who might do for you. Her name was Ste. Elspeth. She lived in northern England in the middle of the thirteenth century. Her bones were kept at a monastery until Henry VIII closed it down. The local people then took her relics and hid them in a cave until just last year, when they were rediscovered, along with evidence as to her identity."

Dr. Chimera picked up a thin file.

"We don't know much about her life," he admitted. "She seems to have been a local woman who decided to become an anchoress, a sort of hermit, rather late in life. She had a hut built next to the monastery and lived there for forty years, praying and giving advice based on visions of Jesus, that she averred came to her in dreams."

"Sounds perfect!" Joe exclaimed. "Doesn't it, honey?"

Melanie wasn't so sure. "But this Ste. Elspeth, she was a Catholic, wasn't she?"

"There wasn't anything else to be, back then," Joe reminded her. "I bet she'd have been a real Christian if she'd been born after Calvin."

"Yes, but I don't want to suddenly start saying beads or waiting to hear from the pope for permission," Melanie insisted.

"It doesn't work like that, Ms. Smith." Dr. Chimera gave her a gentle smile. "You don't lose yourself, you simply add the memories and knowledge of another. You can exercise your own judgment. And, according to my research, the rosary hadn't been invented when Elspeth lived. Nor did people like her have much contact with the pope, so you needn't worry on either count."

Melanie chewed on a strand of hair, thinking. Finally, she made a decision.

"OK. If it will help me find my faith again, I'll try it," she said. "Joe told me that if I don't like it, you can take her out of me, right?"

"Within a month or so, yes," Dr. Wolfe cautioned her. "But you'll know before then if you don't feel comfortable with the change."

And so that night, Melanie gingerly sat in the chair and let the technicians put the helmet and tape on her.

"Good-bye, Joe," she said in a small, nervous voice. "See you when I wake up."

Joe spent the time she was asleep in setting up a worldwide revival mission for the new Alma, to start in a week. No point in waiting; they had lost too much money already.

☐

"Joe," Melanie said a week later back in her dressing room. "Are you sure this silly wig and all these jewels are necessary? And this padded bra!"

She was looking at it with a horror she had never shown before.

"Of course it is," Joe told her. "Don't listen to that saint of yours on this. When she was around they didn't even have radio, much less wide-screen TV. For the media, you've gotta glitter! You just explain that to her."

Melanie laughed. "We can both hear you, Joe, and we know what TV is. It's only that now we're considering some things that we took for granted before. It does seem that one shouldn't appear to be so fond of worldly vanities while preaching the gospel of poverty."

"Hey, wait right there!" Joe interrupted. "No one said anything about poverty. Salvation, that's what you're preaching, and for that you need to shine like an angel, just the way you sing like one."

"Well, I suppose," she conceded. "But we think . . ."

Joe interrupted again. "And try to cut out that 'we' talk.

People are either gonna think you're nuts or the queen of England."

So, dressed as Alma, Melanie went out on the stage. The part of her that was Elspeth was astounded by the crowd that had come to see her.

Wundras! she thought. There weren't so many gathered to see King Edward go by!

She took a deep breath.

"Are you sinners?" Melanie shouted.

The crowd roared back. "Yes, yes sister!"

"Have you come to be saved?"

The roar grew even louder and more incoherent.

Melanie picked up the microphone, and the huge hall became silent. Without waiting for her cue, she began to sing.

> *"Stabat mater dolorosa,*
> *Iuxta crucem lacrimosa*
> *Dum pendebat filius"*

"What the hell is she doing?" Joe gestured frantically from the side of the stage.

The mournful tune rolled over the puzzled crowd. The band leader turned for guidance. This wasn't what they had rehearsed. Oblivious, Melanie sang on, her beautiful voice grieving along with the mother of Jesus.

The stage manager ran up to Joe.

"What gives?" she asked. "Is she singing in tongues, or what?"

"It's something new." Joe thought on his feet. "She's been working on it for a while. We weren't going to try it, yet. But, you know, when the spirit moves you, you've got to let it pour forth.

"Well, she'd better find a zippier spirit somewhere," the woman told him. "Or she's gonna put the audience to sleep."

Frantically, Joe tried to signal Melanie to switch back to "Even a Truck-stop Hooker Can Be Saved." But she had her eyes shut as she sang on, standing stiff and straight and not moving at all.

Joe waited for clatter as people got up from their folding chairs and left. He wondered if they'd throw things at her first. He tried to see over the lights into the crowd. They were ominously quiet.

Finally, Melanie came to the end of her song on a note that seemed to start from the pit of her stomach and work upward until it flew to the rafters. She opened her eyes.

Joe breathed a sigh of relief.

Then Melanie reached up and pulled off her wig.

"Brothers! Sisters!" she cried over the gasps. "My name isn't Alma May Willis; it's plain old Melanie Smith. I'm not beautiful, I'm not very smart. None of this," she jangled her bracelets and patted her chest, "*None* of this is real. I'm nobody special. But, you know what? God loves me anyway."

The audience went wild.

☐

Joe felt as if he'd been pulled around a field after a harrowing machine.

"All I'm saying, Melanie," he repeated, "is that if you're going to pull a switch in the program, you let me know first."

"I didn't know, Joe," Melanie explained. "I think it was Elspeth. She sang every day in her cell, you know. It seemed natural to us. And that was the song we remembered. I kinda liked it."

"Well, you're lucky that the believers did, too," Joe said. "But you can't expect them to every night. And all that nonsense with the wig and telling them your real name. That can only work once. What'll you do tomorrow night?"

Melanie smiled at him. He didn't like that smile. It had too much confidence. He'd always heard that those medieval nuns were subservient. No one locked up in a cell to pray all day should have a smile like that.

"Don't worry, Joe," she said, and patted his hand. "We

have some wonderful plans. Now, why don't you go on home. I have a few things to do."

Joe shuddered.

☐

Dr. Wolfe was sound asleep when the phone call came in. At first he couldn't understand the rapid speech at the other end of the line.

"Who is this?" he asked. "What do you want?"

"You gotta help me, Doctor!" Joe babbled. "She's crazy! This other woman is making her do terrible things!"

It was a few moments before Wolfe could wake up and Joe could slow down enough that Wolfe was able to understand what was happening.

"She gave up her stage persona?" Wolfe asked. "Well, in my mind, that's all to the good. I don't see what the problem is."

"But there's more," Joe went on. "She's bought these weird new clothes and won't wear her makeup and she's asking to see the books. She never did that before."

Privately, Wolfe rejoiced that the woman was taking an interest in the business side of her profession. He had suspected from the start that Joe might be taking a healthy cut of her earnings and even skimming the donations that were supposed to go to continue spreading the Word.

"I told you before we started this, Mr. Nichols, that we didn't know a lot about this Ste. Elspeth," Wolfe explained. "We know what she did, but not what she felt or how she thought. It sounds to me as though she was as devout as the legends say."

"Oh yeah?" Joe answered. "And where in your legend did it say she was a CPA? You've got to do something."

"I'm sorry, Mr. Nichols," Wolfe said. "We can only reverse the process at the request of the subject, herself. Unless Melanie is unhappy with the joining, I can't help you."

"But Dr. Wolfe!" Joe shouted.

"Mr. Nichols, it's four in the morning here," Wolfe interrupted. "Please let me go back to sleep. If Melanie wants to have Ste. Elspeth removed, have her call me during business hours."

He hung up. Then, as an afterthought, he shut off the ringer on the phone and went back to sleep.

☐

Joe had bit his fingernails to the quick. There must be a way out of this. Melanie had found her faith again, all right, with a vengeance. Oddly enough, the people seemed to be intrigued by her new self. The simple white gowns, the loose brown hair, just a touch of makeup to make her eyes seem larger and her skin more ethereal. Where the hell had she learned that? Anyway, it seemed to be working for now. Joe could let it rest for the time being.

It was this insistence on knowing the finances that was scaring him. He'd explained over and over about how much it cost to mount a revival and how it was necessary for her to live in comfort so that she could save her energy for her exhorting and singing. But that medieval cow wanted to know where every dollar went. And Melanie agreed.

It was enough to drive a man to drink.

"My life is in the toilet," Joe moaned. "It couldn't get worse."

He knew as soon as he said it that it was a mistake. He wasn't so sure about God, but he knew better than to tempt fate.

Sure enough, that afternoon Melanie called him to come over to the house. Neither she nor Elspeth was good with computers, but someone had given them readouts of all the financial statements, including a few that Joe thought he had hidden completely.

"Joe," Melanie began without a greeting. "We have way too much money for a Christian enterprise. It's obscene. And what am I doing with an investment in a gambling establishment in Atlantic City?"

"All the profits go to spreading the Gospel," Joe explained.

"All the profits should go to feeding the poor," Melanie answered sharply.

"Hey, we do that." Joe reached for one of the papers. "See, right here, we gave over a thousand dollars to a food bank in Dallas."

"Why just Dallas?" Melanie asked. "Why not everyplace we go?"

Joe thought. "Yeah, it would be good PR. Great idea, kid. Now, if that's all . . ." He reached for the rest of the papers.

Melanie stopped him, gathering them all up herself.

"No, Joe, that's just the beginning," she said. "We must divest ourselves of all worldly goods. We need to give alms to the poor, comfort the sick, and console the afflicted."

Joe felt his blood pressure rising.

"Then you can start with me, you ungrateful bitch," he sputtered. " 'Cause I'm feeling pretty damn afflicted right now!"

Melanie gave him another one of her scary smiles. He wondered if he could get an exorcist, since Wolfe refused to help him. There had to be a way to stop this before she bankrupted him. His eye caught the words at the top of one of the pages. Shit! She'd found the Cayman Island accounts, as well.

"Joe," she said soothingly, "right now you're only thinking of your body and its needs. I remember men like you. But I have to consider your soul and *its* needs. They didn't understand, either, when I entered the anchorage, but it was for the best then, and it is now, as well."

"Wait a minute!" Joe loosened his collar. "You mean you're not only gonna give away all our money; you're also gonna quit?"

"We don't need the stage and the sound system to preach the Truth," Melanie explained. "Just a bit of land, perhaps near a leprosarium." She paused, as if listening. "Oh, then a hospital will do. Perhaps we can found a hospice for those who might otherwise die alone."

"And how do you expect to survive?" Joe's voice was sarcastic.

"The way we did then," Melanie answered. "The way we do now. On the charity of the faithful."

Joe had had enough. He headed for the door, then turned around for one last volley.

"This is insane!" he shouted. "And so are you. I'll have you put away before you can do any more damage."

"I don't think so," she replied. "For a Christian to give away all their money is not insane; it's expected."

Joe slammed the door on her last words, but he feared she was right.

There was only one course open to him. It wasn't his fault. She had driven him to it.

☐

He bought the gun in Los Angeles from a guy in an alley. Cash money. There'd be no way to trace it to him. The silencer came from Denver. But it took him until the meeting in Cleveland to get his courage up. He'd told Melanie that she couldn't quit until she'd fulfilled all the contracts, and this was the next to the last one.

He had the disguise ready, hidden at the assembly hall. He began coughing two days before so that Melanie wasn't surprised when he told her he'd decided to stay at the hotel and get over his cold. When she had left he hurried down the stairs and out the back, shaking as if he really were ill.

It was all her fault. She'd driven him to this. He felt like Judas, but after all, if it hadn't been for Judas, Jesus would never have gotten into the Bible. The only way for Melanie to keep on bringing the sinners to God was to become a martyr. After all, who'd pay her any mind if she was stuck off in some hut in the sticks?

Joe was ready; he was psyched. He knew just where to stand so that he could ditch the gun quickly. Then he'd be just another horrified follower, lost in the crowd.

He took up his position as the show started. Melanie had made a lot of changes. The music now was acoustic, old stuff like dulcimers, lutes, recorders, bagpipelike things and weird drums that looked like hourglasses. Joe couldn't figure out why the people were still coming. The lighting was good, he admitted, lots of blues, with a gold spot on Melanie.

His hands were icy. It was hard to concentrate. He was pretty sure he was close enough for a clean shot, but what if she survived? Well, he'd just have to be sure she didn't.

The hall was completely dark except for a booth spot that flickered like a candle over Melanie. It was now or never.

He raised the gun.

The men on either side of him grabbed him swiftly, causing the gun to go off into the rafters. The people around them screamed in panic. Joe was one of them.

"Joseph Nichols," one of the men said. "J. Lynsky, Cleveland police. You're under arrest for embezzlement and attempted murder."

Joe was too shocked to resist. The police cuffed him and led him away in a daze. He couldn't understand it. He'd planned it perfectly. What had gone wrong?

The detective had wondered the same thing when Melanie had requested police protection because she feared her manager would attempt to kill her.

"What made you suspect him?" he had asked.

Melanie smiled. "A friend warned me in time," she said. "A very close friend."

☐

Sometime later, one of the researchers came into Dr. Wolfe's office.

"We've uncovered more information about that Ste. Elspeth," she told him. "It seems she was a martyr, after all.

She'd been an heiress and had just decided to deed all her property to a hospital for lepers when one of her relatives shot her through the window of her anchorage with a crossbow. Do you think we should warn Ms. Smith?"

Dr. Wolfe shook his head. He'd been reading the papers.

"I suspect," he told the researcher, "that she already knows."

Eye of the Day

Janet Berliner

"Mata Hari, 'eye of the day' in Malaysian, is symbolic of the sun."
—Nucore International Files

Eve Sunn led an idyllic life. At least that was what everyone thought. Everyone, that is, except Eve, who sat at Mission Ranch Bar, drinking single malt scotch and contemplating the downside.

She was nearly forty years old and what did she have? Raised in Carmel Valley, the product of private schools. She played a sound game of tennis and a reasonable game of golf. She had a membership to Pebble Beach Country Club, a psych degree from Golden Gate University, a shingle hanging outside her Skyline home-office, and a circle of friends who bored her to tears with their homogenized attitudes and lack of ability to focus on anything except the male-female ratio on the Peninsula, who drove which car, who did or didn't sleep with whose wife.

Carmel, she thought, taking some pride in the definition, was nothing but an empty chocolate box. The outer design was gorgeous; the inside contained nothing substantive.

What she needed was a change, some excitement in her life beyond staying home, doing her nails, and watching old, co-lorized Garbo movies. Not that she'd ever give up watching Garbo's *Mata Hari*, which she owned, but enough was enough. There had to be something else, and a way to gather the courage to take advantage of it.

The real truth was—she ordered another scotch—she was no different from the rest of them. She had spent her life too chicken to take risks that might perturb her comfortable little existence.

She hummed along with the bar pianist's lightweight ren-dition of "Jamaica Farewell." Harry Belafonte owns that song, she thought, remembering the concert she'd attended at a remote California winery. He had turned the stage into a beach, the hills into the tropics. Old or young, he was the sexiest man she'd ever seen.

"Would you look at who just walked in," the slightly over-weight but attractive woman on the stool next to Eve said. "I wouldn't mind getting into those britches." She sighed heavily. "Unfortunately, I'm not his type. He goes for tall, skinny, dirty blondes like you."

Automatically, Eve swiveled her barstool around, only to find herself staring into the craggy face of Carmel's celebrity ex-mayor. He smiled at her, and crooked his finger in a "Come on a my house" gesture. She made a half motion forward, then swiveled back to face the bottles that lined the mirrored bar. She watched him survey the room, shrug, turn on his heel, and leave.

"Are you crazy?" the woman next to her said. "You got something better to do?"

"Who needs Clint Eastwood?" Eve said. Inside her head, she answered herself. *You do, you fool. Minutes ago you were bemoaning your boring life. So what do you do when someone fas-cinating comes along and shows interest in you—all right, in your body—you act like a chicken-shit virgin.*

Irritated with herself, Eve went outside for a smoke. It was raining, as usual, not hard enough to send her back inside, just enough to dampen her hair and trickle down the neck of her dress. She ignored it and stood out there, chain-smoking, as if the defiance of weather and tobacco somehow compensated for her earlier behavior.

☐

The next morning, she woke up with a sore throat. The day was cold and blustery, typical of summer on the Peninsula, no matter what propaganda the city's Board of Tourism spread to unsuspecting tourists. She canceled her patients, made herself a hot cup of tea, which she drank while soaking in her bathtub, then gratefully crawled back into her warm bed.

She didn't stir again until noon, at which time she reached for the remote control and began to surf the channels on her TV.

Nothing held her attention. Television, she thought, feeling sorry for herself all over again, was only slightly less boring than her life. Forty years on this earth—almost—and her only claim to fame, for the precious little that was worth, was that she shared a birthday with the infamous Mata Hari. Outside of that, there was nothing. *Nada*. One ex-husband whose name she could hardly remember, a son who preferred not to remember her and was, she'd heard, roaming around the Australian outback in search of himself.

She glanced over at the mirror near her bed. She was tall, runway thin, reasonably attractive, an intelligent woman of independent means. In truth, she had a lot. What she didn't have was a life.

Feeling thoroughly sorry for herself, she stopped surfing to watch the Home Shopping Network. Not that she needed anything, she reminded herself. She wanted.

What?

Anything, anything at all that would make her feel better, she answered herself, as she made herself a mocha, added a healthy dash of brandy—for medicinal purposes—and settled down to an hour of Edgar Berebi and his newest collection of jewelry and artifacts, all of them copies, of course.

"Wait until you see the next piece," the host said, flashing a pendant and then a ring quickly on- and off-screen. "Just a minute." She stopped, pressed her earpiece into her ear, and appeared to concentrate deeply. "My producer is telling me something about a promotion." She smiled and released the earpiece. "Any of you who like what you're about to see and happen to have a birthday on August 7th, which happens also to be the infamous Mata Hari's birthday, call in quickly. The first one to get through will win a free pendant and ring."

She displayed the ring on her finger next to a velvet board which held an ornate pendant on a long silver chain. It had a large stone in its center and a dangling pearl at the end.

"These are exact duplicates of the pendant and ring Mata Hari wore in 1916, a year before her death at the hands of a French firing squad."

"Why not," Eve said to the TV host on-screen. "Why the fuck not. I want it. I deserve it." It was cheap enough, under a hundred bucks for the whole shebang even if she didn't win, she thought, picking up the phone.

She didn't win, but she placed the order anyway. The set arrived on her birthday. Wearing it, she watched *Mata Hari*. As usual, she cried when the beautiful, misunderstood courtesan was taken to her death. Thoroughly miserable now, she watched a documentary about the amazing work a company called Nucore was doing. If she ever found the courage, she thought, she would buy herself a new persona. Maybe even Mata Hari's.

The idea excited Eve so much that she called the telephone operator, asked for the number of Nucore, which had recently opened a branch in South San Francisco, and dialed.

She was put through to a man who identified himself as Dr. Chen. "Mata Hari, you say?" he asked.

"Yes," Eve said. "I need to be . . ." She searched for the right word. "Irresistible. And diabolical."

"An intriguing choice, if I might say so," Chen said. "Will you excuse me for a moment, please? I must check my data system."

Eve waited, tapping her painted nail against the telephone. Rat-a-tat-tat. Rat-a-tat-tat. Like a volley of gunfire.

"You are most fortunate," Dr. Chen said, coming back on the line. "It appears that the French government has been holding all documents to do with Margaretha Zell, better known as Mata Hari, in custody. You probably know that she died in October of 1917. They were not going to release anything for a hundred years. Since her personal effects are already part of a Dutch museum, my esteemed associate has been able to persuade both the museum and the French that eighty-one years was long enough to protect themselves from familial lawsuits. He is presently negotiating the purchase of what you want as part of a larger package which in-cludes—"

"Yes. Good," Eve interrupted, feeling an oncoming attack of cold feet. "Could we get on with this, please?"

"You understand, Ms.—"

"Miss. Miss Eve Sunn."

"You realize, Miss Sunn, that if this can be done at all it will not be inexpensive, and that once it's done, there will be a brief period for you to change your mind, but after that, there is no going back?"

Eve resisted the urge to ask how much. *Don't go there*, she thought. *Don't say it. This is one of those "if you have to ask the price, you can't afford it" events.* "How long before you will be ready for me?" she asked instead.

"I'm not sure," Chen said. "Perhaps as long as a few months. Time enough for you to think it over. If you will give me your telephone number, I'll call you when we are ready for you."

"Don't you need to send me a contract or something?"

Dr. Chen chuckled. "I don't think we're about to have a rush on Mata Hari," he said. "I'll be in touch."

With a mixture of relief and anticipation, Eve replaced the phone in its cradle. When her friend arrived to spend the evening with her, she said nothing about the call. She thanked her for the present she'd brought, a copy of *How Stella Got Her Groove Back*, the book. She also brought the movie, which they watched together. It was set in Jamaica.

Jamaica was seductive.

Eve's wanting began again.

It was a short step to the Internet, to Frommer's, and to booking an early December trip to Negril.

As September and October trickled by, Eve's wanting grew. She could feel it deep down in her gut, yet she could not define what it was. For a while, examining herself closely in her makeup mirror, she thought that what she wanted was a face-lift; by November, as her trip approached, she knew that what she wanted was much bigger than that.

What she wanted was a life-lift. A total transplant, in a manner of speaking.

In a moment of courage and supreme wanting, she called Dr. Chen.

"Yes, Miss Sunn, I recall our conversation. As a matter of fact, I was getting ready to call you and let you know that things are proceeding well at this end. If you have not changed your mind, fairly soon we should be able to take care of your needs."

My wants, Eve thought. "I'm going to Jamaica on vacation," she said. "Should I call you when I return?"

"We'll call you," he said. "When we're ready, we'll call you."

"I'll count on it." She felt far less sure of herself than she sounded.

Telling herself she'd think it through in Jamaica, she turned her thoughts to palm trees and piña coladas and packed for her vacation.

□

The rain came. It washed the sand under Eve's feet and sent steam rising between her toes, up her calves, into her groin, which was throbbing with the Calypso beat that poured from the loudspeakers above the bar behind her.

And then, as quickly as it had come, the rain was over. The sand dried, she dried, the throbbing softened. She lay on the sand and stared at the Caribbean and at Booby Cay, the small island Preserve—little more than a sandbar really—that lay a quarter of a mile away. What a perfect location for a casino, she thought, if Jamaica ever legalized gambling, or for a private villa. She wanted to see it, to walk around it pretending that it was hers. How to get there was the problem. She could try to swim it, but she wasn't much of a swimmer. If she survived the sharks, which were surely out there, she'd probably drown with the effort.

She reoiled her body. Slowly, she circled her navel with her finger, enjoying the intricacies of her hybrid Mata Hari–Lucrezia Borgia ring juxtaposed against her bare midriff and the coconut smell of the oil, slick beneath her touch. Unlike Mata—or Stella, for that matter—she hadn't quite gotten her groove back, but this was a pretty good-looking navel for a fortysomething psychologist. She stared at a gecko that sat on a rock a few feet away under a palm tree and envied its oblivion. It didn't care about the sign on the beach that warned of falling coconuts; it moved, breathed, ate, and eventually it died. Presumably, somewhere along the way, it copulated.

At the bar, speakers blared out a continuous round of mixed Bob Marley tapes. "Every little thing's gonna be all right." Yeah, sure it is, Eve thought, resenting the fact that she'd be spending her last night in Negril alone. She deserved better than that. Maybe it was the anticipation of the transformation she hoped to undergo upon her return to California; maybe it was wearing her Mata Hari jewelry. More likely, it was this beach and the locals, with their lilting speech patterns and *laissez-faire* attitudes. Whatever it was, she felt more positive about herself than she had in a long time. Not wonderful, mind you. Not empowered. Just better.

Part of it, she was sure, was the freedom everyone felt on vacation. Another was that she loved her hotel. The Mahogany Inn was exactly what she'd wanted—next door to one of the infamous all-inclusive, "what island is this?" resorts, yet filled with music and locals. Being next to Hedonism, the hotel shared the best part of Negril's long, white beach, where she spent most of her day, staring at the island, so close, and yet so inaccessible. She could rent a fishing boat for a day, buy any manner of drugs practically in the open, rent a Rasta from Renta-Rasta, but she had as yet been unable to find anyone willing simply to take her around the island and onto it, and she was too stubborn to pay for more than what she got.

"No problem."

The owner of the voice walked around to face her. He was young, nothing special, one of the beach boys she'd passed on her morning walks.

"I hear you want go to Booby Cay. I take you, no problem."

"Really?" Eve said. "When."

"Now."

"You have a boat?"

The young man pointed at a boat, hardly larger than a small canoe but sporting an engine aft. "Five dollah. American. I take you."

"Three," Eve said, knowing even that was highway robbery.

"Four."

"Deal," she said, standing up. "But once we're out on the water you don't say one word. I'm not looking for conversation. You can take me around the island a couple of times first so that I can enjoy being out there, but please no chitchat. Get it?"

He nodded. "Got it, lady."

"Good. Here's two dollars. You get the other two when we get back." She handed him two dollar bills. "I'm thirsty. Wait one moment while I get a soda."

He waited expectantly, apparently hoping she would offer to buy him a beer. She didn't. Though she normally didn't allow herself anything but diet sodas and all they had at the patio bar was straight, bottled Coke, she bought the soda and drained most of its warm contents. Instead of throwing the bottle into the trash can en route to the boat, she carried her towel, her sandals, and the bottle with her and maneuvered awkwardly on board.

True to his word, the young man said nothing. She trailed her hand in the water, marveling at how the blue zircon in her ring blended with the color of the sea. They had twice circled the island and were about to pull up at a makeshift wooden dock, when a powerboat zoomed across the water toward them. One man was at the wheel, another, tall body glistening in the sun, stood upright and steady on his feet. She recognized him as the Rasta who owned the jewelry stand on the beach where she'd admired several carved items, in particular a small, overpriced ebony totem which looked remarkably like one she had almost picked up years ago on a trip to the Sudan.

The powerboat slowed down as it came parallel. "Robber," the man yelled, taking a flying leap into the boat. "T'ief! Who you think you are, taking my boat?"

The leap was worthy of Scaramouche, but the dinghy had taken in water. His feet slid from under him, and he landed flat on his back. Furious and embarrassed, he stood up and, with one seemingly effortless movement, picked up the younger man and tossed him into the shallow water.

"Okay, lady," he said. "You wanna go island, we go island."

He stepped onto the dock and tied the boat to a short, wooden post. Eve slung the towel around her neck and slipped her Jellies onto her feet. Too shocked to protest, clutching her empty soda bottle, she allowed him to help her up and onto the dock. An elderly local couple sat at a wooden table, observing them impassively. Judging by their rods and tackle, they were fisherfolk.

"That way," the Rasta said, pushing her slightly toward a narrow footpath that led from a sandy beach into a cluster of bushes and palm trees.

"Hey. Slow down," Eve said, regaining some of her equilibrium. "Is the kid going to be all right?"

"He be fine. His friend come get him sooner or later. You give him money for my boat?"

"Two dollars, with two more to come. And who knew the boat was yours? He said it was his."

"I get that money from him," the man said. "Now you walk."

Trying not to show how terrified she felt, Eve walked. This kind of submission, she told herself, was definitely not a response worthy of Mata Hari, nor was this how Stella got her groove back. She had seen no people other than the two old folks at the dock, just a raggedy island dog, a couple of cats, and a few large, scuttling black things on the ground. As for the seabirds, the boobies she'd hoped to find, as far as she could tell she was the only booby around.

"I just want to walk around the island and then go back to the beach," she said, glancing back at the man and concentrating on keeping her voice steady.

"Yeah, right." He grinned at her.

"What's your name?" she asked, in as conversational a tone as she could muster.

"Marley," he said.

She had no reason not to believe him. This was Jamaica, where the Marleys were heroes.

"There," he said.

He was next to her now, leading the way toward a tiny grotto. It looked pleasant enough, but she didn't like this. Didn't like it at all. "No," she said. "I want to get back now."

"This good place to make love," he said.

She stopped in her tracks.

"I say—"

"I heard you. Thanks but no thanks."

He looked surprised, even hurt. He waved his hand. She noticed the coke fingernail, longer and whiter than the others. "That's what you come for. You buy, you get."

The sun was moving down into the horizon. The fisherfolk were out at sea. She could see them, a dot on the water.

"You made a mistake, Marley," she said. "That's not what I bought."

"All right," he said. "We find another place."

This time he walked ahead of her. She thought of turning tail and running, but he was bigger and faster. *Get this over with, Eve*, she thought. *Do something.*

"Here." He turned toward a small, sandy cove, bordered by many rocks and hidden by several large trees.

She followed him onto the cove. He sat down and patted the sand next to him. She balanced on the closest rock and took her cigarettes and lighter out of her shirt pocket.

"American cigarette?" He held out his hand.

"I have one left," she said, lighting it. She dragged at it then handed it to him, buying minutes. If he touched her, she thought, she'd threaten to set the bushes alight and burn down the island.

He smoked contentedly. When he was finished, he buried the butt. "We fuck now," he said.

She held the Coke bottle down near the rock, realizing now why instinct had driven her to bring it along. "Go ahead," she said, wondering where she was finding the bravado. "Rape me. But if you do, I'll cut off your pencil and burn down the island while you're bleeding."

Marley looked at her, at the bottle and the lighter. Whether he was afraid of her or of the conservationists, who would get him if she somehow made good her threat to set fire to the island, Eve didn't know or care. Whichever it was that convinced him, he gave up. Jumping to his feet, he led the way to the boat and returned her to the beach in front of Mahogany Inn.

"Two dollars." Marley held out his hand.

"Fu—" She stifled the urge to laugh. She'd already refused that invitation. *Don't pass Go, Eve*, she thought. *Don't collect $200. Just turn and walk away.*

She walked to her room, past trailing bougainvillea and yellow hibiscus. An hour later, after a long shower, she locked the door behind her, dropped the room key into one of the pockets of her black chiffon shirt-jacket, and headed for the patio bar. She ordered a rum something and, assailed by an island moon and the smell of jerk chicken, wandered to the railing and looked across the sand at Booby Cay. In the background, a local Calypso band started its first set, and she moved with the rhythm of the beat.

"Dance?" a familiar voice asked.

Marley placed himself possessively next to her at the railing. He, too, had changed his clothing. He wore white trousers and a red shirt, open to the waist. Around his neck he wore gold, too much of it. "I see you before time," he said. "You move like island woman."

Now what? Eve thought, shifting slightly away from him. Should she slap him, ignore him, scream, complain to the hotel management? Would she be accused of something awful, racism perhaps, if she simply said she didn't want to dance with him, or talk to him, or see him. She looked over at the bar and saw the younger man, the one who had taken her across to the island. By the looks of him, Marley had beaten him up to get the two dollars she had given him; he looked sorely bruised and more than a little stoned. If she said, "Get the hell away from me before I call the police and tell them you tried to rape me," would she, too, end up bruised and battered?

Marley reached into his pocket. "Here." He pulled out a doll similar to the elongated ebony carving she'd admired on the beach. This one was about three-and-a-half inches long and had a thin, visible crack across the middle. "Please take this. I'm sorry I frighten you. I thought you wanted to make love."

His voice was warm, sincere, his eyes inscrutable. Eve was tempted to take the doll and give in to the music and the tropical night. What difference did it make? She was leaving the next day. She'd never see the shithead again.

And he'd do the same thing to the next lonely lady who chanced across his path who might not be as lucky or think as fast as she had.

She pushed away his hand and his gift and turned her back on him. Taking anything from Marley was wrong. Plain and simple. She wasn't Stella or Mata Hari, this wasn't a movie or a piece of fiction, and she wasn't about to let hormones prevail over good sense.

☐

Eve returned home more tanned, less fulfilled, and more conscious than ever of the biting winds that were part of Peninsula life. During the plane ride, the top surface of both of her feet had begun to itch. She applied generous layers of calamine lotion, supplemented her tan from a bottle, and returned to work. At night, she scratched her feet until they bled; during the day, they were a continuous distraction, along with her palms, which had begun to itch with the same ferocity as her feet.

After a couple of days, she called her doctor, who was also an old friend. "It feels as if there's something alive under my skin. I can see these two, thin, squiggly red lines and . . ." She hesitated, not wanting to sound ridiculous. "I swear something's moving around in there, John." Her voice was edged with hysteria.

"Calm down, Eve. Have you been away, lately? To the islands, maybe?"

"I went to Jamaica for a week."

"That could be it," he said. "You could've picked up some kind of subcutaneous larvae on the beach. Island dogs carry them and pass them along via the sand. You probably didn't wear shoes, right?"

"Wrong, John. I wore Jellies." When he didn't say anything more, she said. "Look, I don't care how they got in there. I just want to get rid of them."

To Eve's relief, he didn't patronize her or make jokes about love in the tropics and ask her what else she might have picked up. Instead, he offered to make an appointment for her to see a tropical disease expert.

She had to wait a week for the appointment. A dozen times each day, she inspected the position of the worms; at night she dreamed that the larvae had started working their way into her heart or, worse yet, her brain.

The specialist confirmed her physician's telephone diagnosis. "John was right," he said. "Except they're not just larvae, they're *mutant* larvae."

Mutant. She rolled the word around in her mind. *Don't go there.* Without asking for a fuller explanation, she asked him to remove them. Now.

He shook his head. "Think about an earthworm and what happens when you cut one in half," he said. "If I leave behind the slightest trace—"

Eve held up her hand. "So what do I do?"

"These things generally die off after three weeks, at most six. No problem."

Right. No problem for him, Eve thought, accepting a sample tube of ointment which he told her should take care of the itch. "I suppose I should use this on my palms, too?"

"Palms? They both itch? The islanders call what you have right foot, left palm disease. I've never heard of both palms itching though."

"You have now," Eve said, scratching.

Three weeks later, the worms had reached her ankles. She was still scratching and she was sleep-deprived. He gave her another tube of ointment. In three months, she had lost twenty pounds. The magazines are wrong, she decided, seeing her emaciated image in a long mirror. There is such a thing as too thin.

She called the doctor and went back to see him. He was almost too solicitous, in the way of a physician who felt bad because he knew there were no real answers. He offered to send to the islands for a local remedy that had to be made up by hand with a mortar and pestle.

Ten days later, the paste arrived. She used every drop, though it burned her skin and left it red and raw, and still the little bastards thrived. Again, she called the doctor; he had no more answers. "Time and patience," he said. "They die eventually."

"Before or after me?" Eve asked, and hung up the phone. Her next call was to book a trip to Jamaica. There had to be a local physician, a shaman, someone, who would know how to help her.

She booked her flight with a connecting hop from Monterey, arranged for the Carey Bus to pick her up and take her to the airport, and made the largest decision of her life. "I hope you'll like your new body, Margarethe," she said. Then she dialed Nucore to arrange for her transformation.

"I know you said that you would call me—"

"It's perfectly all right, Miss Sunn," Chen said. "If you feel that you have had enough time to think this through and that you really want—"

"I really want, Dr. Chen," Eve said.

"Then we're ready for you," he said. "When would you like to come in?"

"How long does the . . . procedure . . . take?"

"Almost no time at all."

"I'm going to Jamaica in two days," she said.

"Again or still?" he asked.

"Again. I'll drive up tomorrow morning and see you."

They set a time for their appointment. She was there early.

The procedure was like having her eyes checked, something she had recently reminded herself she needed to do. There was absolutely no pain outside of the momentary stab beforehand when she saw the size of the check she was writing.

"I don't feel any different," she told Dr. Chen when it was all over.

"You will, dear lady," he said, shaking her hand and smiling. "I assure you, you will."

Driving home, Eve pushed her Porsche to its limits, enjoying the buttery feel of the road beneath her wheels. For the first time in her life, she was unafraid of the heavy fog that, as always, burdened 101 for the last ten or fifteen miles of the journey. She got home before dark, poured herself a vodka, straight up, threw her suitcase on the bed, and opened it to pack. Congratulating herself for her habit of leaving her Freedom Bag filled with medications and toiletries and always at the ready, she looked at the clothing items she'd left inside—those she inevitably took with her when she traveled, like her black chiffon big-shirt, the one she'd worn that last night in Negril.

She took it out, shook it, and noticed that there was something in the pocket. Reaching inside, she pulled out the ebony doll Marley had tried to give her. It fell apart in her hands, breaking along the crack she'd observed that evening.

Holding the pieces, she deliberated whether to glue them together or throw them away. Deciding she could always give the doll to someone else if owning it made her uncomfortable, she dropped one piece back in the shirt pocket and, fiddling with the other half, answered the door to a kid selling cookies. She shook her head, then, on impulse, pushed Marley's gift into the soil of the blooming geranium, as if burying it would erase the ugly memory.

She slept reasonably well that night, better than she had in a long time. The next morning, she saw why. Outside of the scars from her incessant scratching, the skin on her left foot was smooth and pink, and neither that foot nor her right palm was itching. She thought briefly about canceling her trip, but her right foot and left palm were itching as much as ever, and the larvae were there, feeding off her, growing, moving. Since she had no idea how to duplicate the cure, she dressed for the journey.

On her way next door to ask her neighbor to take care of the cat, Eve went over her mental checklist. Her stove was off, and she'd ask her neighbor to water her geranium. . . .

She stared at the plant. Yesterday it was gorgeous; today there wasn't a live petal left, and the edges of the leaves were brown and dry. That was one plant the neighbor wouldn't have to bother to water, she thought. Not unless the woman was into resuscitation. She bent over it to see if she could figure out what had happened. It wasn't until she fingered the leaves around the partially buried ebony doll that she saw the small, white larvae.

"*Merde!*" The French expletive emerged from the new part of her being, the Mata Hari part. She had not spoken a word of French in her life, yet the word curled around her tongue and burst forth like a familiar beast. "I'll get you, you son-of-a-bachelor," she yelled, throwing the last of her old what-will-the-neighbors think attitude to the winds as the realization of what had happened hit her.

She had never dabbled in the mantic arts, or even been particularly intrigued by them, but she'd never doubted, either, that there was more in heaven and earth than Horatio had dreamt of in his philosophy. Marley had cursed that doll before he'd put it in her pocket. She was sure of it—so sure that she would hoist him upon his own petard. There was going to be no canceling this trip.

Fully formed, the idea for revenge came to her.

Returning indoors, Eve placed her suitcase near the front door. Then she went into the kitchen and threw the second half of the ebony doll into the ice crusher. She filled her ring with some of the resulting charcoal powder, touched up her makeup, and, with exquisite timing, made it outside just as the Carey Bus pulled up in front of the house.

□

Finding Marley was easy. He was at his boat, ebony skin shining in the sunlight.

"You go to come back," he said, as if she looked the same and no time had passed since their last meeting.

"I've changed my mind," she said. "Tonight we dance. Tomorrow, we'll go to Booby Cay."

"No problem." Smiling easily, he placed an arm around her waist.

She let him leave it there for a moment before she stepped away. "Later," she said.

"Come soon," he answered.

"I will," she said, and meant it.

She dressed carefully for the evening. Cleaning the moisture off the mirror first, she placed her new necklace in her décolletage, admired her image, and went to the bar. She ordered a rum and Coke. After a couple of sips, she picked up the glass and wandered onto the beach. The moon traced a silver pathway across the sea, and a slight breeze played with her bare shoulders. The band, a different one playing the same Calypsos, stirred her blood with its steel-drum beat. Hidden from observers by a large palm tree, she flipped open her ring and, smiling, added its charcoal powder contents to what was left of her drink.

Marley was sauntering up to the bar when she returned. She handed him the glass. "Here, finish this," she said.

"What is it?"

"Rum and Coke."

He sniffed it, smiled, and drank.

They took a table in a dark corner near the railing and ordered dinner. Marley was a handsome escort and a great dancer. He knew all of the locals, and Eve enjoyed the attention they gave her as they stopped at the table to chat with him and appraise her. An hour went by, then a second.

"Another drink?" she asked, figuring her plan had not worked and deliberating how best to end the evening without mishap.

Marley shook his head. As he did so, his face caught the light and she saw the grey overlay on his skin. "I don't feel so good," he said, scratching his neck. "I go home now. Tomorrow we go Booby Cay."

Eve angled her right foot into the moonlight. The foot no longer itched, and the skin was clear. "Sure. Tomorrow." She hardly noticed when he left. Wondering why she hadn't realized before how attractive men looked in uniform, she smiled at a handsome Jamaican policeman who sat alone at the bar. He returned her smile, left his barstool, and headed toward her.

She wouldn't be spending her last night in Negril alone this time around, Eve thought, scratching her left palm. So what if it still itched, she told herself. That would stop, too, when she threw away the rest of the powder she'd left at home in the blender.

Then again, she could keep the powder. Fill the ring five or six more times if anyone hurt her. She wasn't going to be alone much anymore, and a girl needed protection, didn't she?

As Mata would say—and maybe even Stella—a *little* itch wasn't all that bad.

Voyage of Discovery

Nina Kiriki Hoffman

"Paige hasn't spoken since the accident," said the girl's mother, Linda Keynes.

Wolfe looked at the pale girl in the wheelchair. It was hard to guess her age; she was so thin she looked about twelve, but she might be older. Her brown eyes stared at the floor. Shoulder-length blond hair, carefully combed, was held back from her face with a blue ribbon. Thin hands rested unmoving on the chair's arms. The pleats of her powder blue skirt lay in perfect formation. She had been placed in the chair and hadn't moved since.

"She's been like this for nine months," her mother said. "I've had every test run, tried every treatment. The doctors say her brain still functions, and they don't know why she doesn't move or respond, but—" She turned away a moment, bit her lower lip, blinked rapidly. "You're my last hope."

"Mrs. Keynes," Wolfe said gently. "We work miracles here, but this may not be one we can give you."

"You can try." Her eyes, when she turned back to him, were full of fury.

"We can try," he said. "We can't guarantee anything." He watched the pale girl for half a minute. She blinked once.

Wolfe hesitated, then added, "You understand we've never done a transfer like this before? We have no data. We can't make any predictions about what will come of this. There's no way of knowing whether this is a mistake. A number of things may happen, and you might not be happy with them."

"I understand," murmured Mrs. Keynes.

"Have your doctors suggested that Paige might recover on her own? This process could interfere with that."

"The longer I wait, the less chance of recovery there is," said Mrs. Keynes. She glared at her daughter. "My daughter is sixteen years old. She is wasting away. I've almost run out of hope. I need to act. I want your process."

Her intensity battered Wolfe. He wanted willing clients, but who could tell if the girl was willing? What were the legal ramifications here? He needed to get his legal team on it. "Have you selected a donor?"

"Meriwether Lewis."

Wolfe straightened.

"Before the accident," said Mrs. Keynes, "Paige wanted to go to Mars. She knew the first manned expedition was years in the future, but she planned to be ready. She was always taking courses and doing exercises that would prepare her to go where no one had gone before. She studied explorers. Lewis was her favorite." She twisted the handle of her purse. "He knew how to find things. Maybe he can find . . ." Her voice faded.

"Didn't Lewis commit suicide?" Wolfe vaguely remembered a rumor about it. Suicide or murder, and at an early age. In either case, an ugly way to die. "This process offers the client memories, personality traits, intelligence, and skills of the donor. Lewis might be risky. Why not Clark? I believe he led a more normal life following the expedition."

"I have your fee. I have the legal right to take heroic medical measures on my daughter's behalf. I have made up my mind," said Mrs. Keynes.

☐

Paige sat up.

Linda Keynes set down the thriller she had been reading and stared at her daughter. She had been in the sleep chamber with Paige for a day and a half already, a day and a half of watching her daughter sleep, as though that were something she couldn't do at home.

At home they had a routine: Paige slept. Paige woke. Both states were similar. Linda or the hired skilled-care nurse attended to Paige's body's needs, washed her, fed her, propelled her in the wheelchair, tried to stimulate her with television, walks in the park or the mall, music, tastes of strange food touched to her tongue, massage. In all the time since the accident, Paige hadn't responded to anything.

Now she was sitting up.

A small flame of hope bloomed.

"Where . . . who . . . ?" The words came out as puffs of air.

Linda hugged herself. First words.

"Mother?"

Linda ran to the bed, sat beside her daughter, took her hands. Paige stared at her in the diffuse light of the sleep chamber.

"You are not . . . my mother," Paige said. She tugged one hand loose of Linda's grip and put it to her temple, then touched her chest. She shook her head and looked around the room. "This is no heaven nor hell I ever imagined." For a moment she stared at her own hand, and then said in a toneless voice, "This hand is too small. This is not my body."

"Paige," whispered Linda.

A stranger's eyes stared into hers.

Linda rose and ran from the room.

☐

"I believe," Chimera told Linda, handing her a teacup, "that the donor personality is usually secondary, indeed, almost unconscious initially, especially when the donor and the recipient do not know each other. In general the recipient is already occupying the mind, and the donor fits in around the existing structures. In our own case it was different; we knew we wanted to be equal partners, and had practiced working together beforehand. But a situation like ours rarely arises in the cases we have attended so far.

"In your daughter's case, the donor appears primary because your daughter's personality still sleeps, if she has not already left her body. It is still possible to reverse the process at this early stage. What is your wish?"

Linda sipped black currant tea and tried to slow her heart. Paige had sat up. Paige had spoken.

It wasn't Paige.

But it looked like Paige, and it was someone Linda could talk to.

"How long before the transfer is irreversible?" she asked.

"We speculate three to six weeks. No one has asked for a reversal so far, so we do not have hard data. You may wish to make up your mind about this soon."

Linda drank more tea and tried to calm herself. She would have to go back, see the person who wasn't Paige. She had imagined this differently: with this excitement to entice her, Paige would wake up. She would have the new personality to fascinate her and keep her occupied, bright and shiny as any new toy, and Linda would have Paige back.

Life was far too lonely without her daughter in it. Paige and Linda had had only each other in the four years following Mr. Keynes's disappearance, and they had built lives intertwined.

Since the accident, Linda had experienced life without Paige. She couldn't stand it.

Chimera put a warm hand on top of Linda's. "You do not have to decide right away," Chimera said gently. "But someone should be with her now, since she and her donor did not make a conscious decision to blend. The donor is alone and probably confused."

Linda set her teacup down with a clatter. "You're right. Excuse me, please."

☐

She opened the door to the sleep chamber, not knowing what to expect. What she found was Paige, wrapped in a robe, sitting on the edge of the bed and reading the thriller Linda had left behind.

At Linda's entrance, Paige looked up, and said, "Is it truly two hundred years since I was last alive?"

"How did you know?" Linda sat down on the bed beside Paige, not touching her, but near.

Paige flipped the book to the copyright page and pointed to the date. "We are in the new millennium? Everything I see is new." She pinched the blanket between her fingers. "What fiber is this? Of what substance are these walls composed? What are all these vehicles and objects the book speaks of? How does this clock show numbers on its face that change? What produces light of this cold color, without flame?" Her accent was strange, slightly shifted, but not in a direction Linda recognized, and her tone was lower than Paige's had been.

"How is it," Paige went on in a softer voice, "that I find myself in the body of a girl?"

Staring at her clasped hands in her lap, Linda spoke of the process she had put Paige through and why. "Paige has been so sick," Linda concluded. "I was ready to do anything to bring her back."

For a long time Paige sat silent. "It is indeed curious to be thought of as a commodity," she said. After a moment, she continued, "Well, I shall be reconciled to this presently. I find an abundance of objects here to interest and amuse me. At present I cannot determine whether your daughter's spirit still exists. I presume that you and I shall continue our association. What do you wish me to call you?"

"You may call me Linda," Linda said, a pang in her heart because even though it was not Paige's accent asking this distancing question, it was Paige's voice. "What do you wish me to call you?"

Paige considered. "Are we engaged in a deception? Will we go among those who know your daughter? Is it necessary for others to believe it is your daughter who speaks when I speak?"

Linda smiled. "I'm not allowed to discuss this procedure with anyone outside these walls, so I guess you could say we're engaged in a deception. At least, *I'm* not telling anyone who you are."

"Then you may call me Paige," said Paige. She frowned. "Does this deception require me to call you Mother?"

"I don't think I could bear that," Linda said.

"Then I shall call you Linda." Paige stood up, took a couple steps. "I find myself unwell, or at least lacking in spirits."

"Paige has been motionless for some months," Linda said. "Her muscle tone has deteriorated."

"I will restore it." Paige strode around the room, then collapsed on the bed. "But it will take time and exercise and adequate food, possibly medicine. You have not answered my previous questions."

"What? About the bed, the wall, the clock? The blanket is synthetic fiber. I don't know what the wall is made of. The light and the clock work by electricity, but I don't know how."

"Electricity? So Franklin's experiments had merit! Perhaps you can answer other questions for me? The book says it is printed in the United States of America, and lists Boston and New York. Are we then in the United States? How many states are there now?" Paige sat up and gripped Linda's arm. "Do the United States stretch from the Atlantic to the Pacific? Do any now remember what Captain Clark and I accomplished?"

"Oh, yes," Linda said. "The U.S. goes from Atlantic to Pacific and includes a number of other places. There are fifty-one states. People are still studying your journals and papers. Towns and rivers and plants and animals are named after you and Clark, and your trail is marked so that people can follow in your footsteps. At home I have a computer that can answer all your questions, including ones about what things are made of."

"A computer? A mathematician?"

"It's a thinking machine. I don't know how to explain this. Just come home with me, and you can see for yourself."

"I shall." Paige dropped her feet over the edge of the bed and stood up again. "This unaccustomed fatigue," she muttered, glaring at her legs, which shook.

"Wait a minute." Linda got up and went outside into the hallway, where Paige's wheelchair had been left following the transfer—an orderly had carried Paige from the laboratory to the sleep chamber. "It's all right," Linda said, wheeling it in. "You can use this until you're ready to walk again."

"Oh! Remarkable!" Paige rushed over and bent to examine the wheelchair. "Handsome. Fine craftsmanship." She touched the spokes of a wheel, felt the tires, examined the armrests and footplates, moved the chair and watched its wheels work in concert.

"Sit," said Linda.

Paige straightened and stared at her. After a moment, Paige sat in the chair. Linda wheeled the chair to the door, opened the door, and pushed the chair through it.

"Wait," called one of the project scientists from the doorway of the laboratory down the hall. "We need to do a checkup and debriefing."

"Later," Linda said, pushing the chair swiftly in the other direction.

"Debriefing?" Paige gripped the push rims on the wheels and braked the wheelchair, looking back over her shoulder.

The scientist dashed up to them. "We need to collect data on how the transfer went."

"We don't have time for this," Linda said.

"Linda, I find this a rational and sensible request. I will speak with you," Paige said to the scientist. She straightened in the chair.

Linda wanted to argue. Paige looked at her with clear brown eyes and waited.

No, thought Linda. *Not this again. Will she still fight me every step?* She sighed, and said, "All right."

☐

Chimera conducted the interview while Linda sat to the side, her hands closed into tight fists on the handle of her purse. She felt the fear and fury burning inside, a tiny hard hot flame somewhere down below her stomach.

"I have not experienced any blending in the mind. I find myself wholly myself, save for this body," Paige said, staring down at her arms, her lap. "I recall extremely troublesome things from my former life. I find much of what I see mysterious. I have innumerable questions."

"Patience. I am certain you will have time and space to explore."

Paige smiled. She looked so much like her old self that Linda's heart hurt. "I am considerably excited by the prospect," Paige said.

☐

On the way home in the Mercedes, Paige peppered Linda with questions. Where were the horses? How did cars work? This mingling of races on the sidewalks, what did it betoken? Paige was astonished and thoughtful when she learned that slavery had been abolished.

She was hungry for every morsel of information Linda could give her, but she made Linda feel stupid.

Why should I know how metal is formed into sheets and then made into cars? Why should I know how neon works, or internal combustion engines? Why should I know how architecture makes such tall buildings possible? "Give me a break," she muttered.

Paige stared at her for a long moment, then subsided in the passenger seat and asked no more questions.

In a strange way, Linda felt that the worst parts of her daughter had returned. In another way she feared the stranger beside her. Who was she bringing into her home?

☐

"I'm sure you're tired," Linda said, after she had wheeled Paige into the kitchen from the garage. The kitchen felt huge without the cook in it, but Linda had called earlier and told the household staff to take a week off. She wanted to give Paige, whoever Paige was now, time to adjust.

Paige viewed her without expression.

"Are you hungry?" asked Linda.

"Yes." At this Paige showed animation. She looked around at hanging pots and pans, the teakettle sitting on the stove. Gleaming white and steel kitchen technology stood on broad, pale, spotless counters: the latest coffeemaker, can opener, mixer, blender, food processor, bread machine, microwave oven. By the stove stood a wood block of the finest knives. "This is surely a kitchen?" Paige said. "Where is the hearth? What is that yellow vegetable called?" She pointed to a bowl heaped with fruit.

"Bananas," Linda said. "I don't know what you're used to eating."

"A great variety of things."

"I'll just throw something in the microwave, then. You let me know if you like it."

Linda opened the freezer, and an instant later Paige stood beside her, slipped a hand into the cold compartment, and exclaimed in surprise. "Winter in such a small place, without ice? How is this accomplished?" At Linda's glare, Paige stepped back. "Pardon me. I forgot myself."

"Maybe you're not tired, but I am," Linda said. She took a deep breath, let it out slowly. "I'm sorry to be so abrupt. It's been a long and strange day."

"For both of us." Paige's voice was quiet, reasonable.

"This is a freezer. It preserves food. It works by electricity, and I don't know how. Below that is a refrigerator, which preserves food at a warmer temperature, but still cold." Linda opened the fridge door and let Paige feel the temperature inside.

"What is in all these boxes, if I may ask?"

"Food."

"Milk," Paige read. She touched the carton. She fingered a plastic container full of leftover potatoes. "This material . . ."

"Plastic. I can't tell you more. You'll have to ask the computer about this." Linda's voice came out sharper than she meant it to. She got along perfectly well in life. Why did this new Paige make her feel so . . . inadequate?

"Assuredly, I also employed things I could not manufacture," Paige said after a minute. "Just not so many of them."

"Things have changed a lot." Linda opened two microwave meal boxes and took the food out. She let Paige touch the frozen food under its plastic film. She poked holes in the film over the entrées to vent them, then thrust the meals into the microwave and hit the minute button eight times. "Have a seat."

"But—" Paige stared into the microwave's window. The meals rotated, and the microwave made strange huffing noises. "What a curious process."

"Cooking," said Linda.

Paige glanced at her, one eyebrow up, eyes sparkling.

Linda gave her a reluctant smile. "Wait and see." She set the table and urged this new Paige to sit at the place where the old Paige used to sit. "How about water to drink?" she asked. Paige nodded. Linda filled two cups with tap water, glanced over to see Paige staring at the sink and faucets, visibly restraining herself from jumping up to investigate.

Linda got the salt and pepper shakers and placed them on the table.

Paige stared. "May I?"

"May you what?"

Paige lifted the shakers and sprinkled a little salt in the palm of her hand. She touched her tongue to the salt. "Oh. Good! This, at least, has not changed." She sighed and smiled.

The microwave dinged, and Linda got the dinners out, stripped the film off them, and set them on plates. She didn't have the energy to dish things out of the microwave containers and onto a plate, and wondered if Paige would understand that sort of thing anyway. Who knew about table manners of the past?

Apparently, though, Paige knew how to use a fork, knife, and spoon. Not exactly the way Linda used them. But she did manage to eat, sometimes biting things off the point of her knife. "Interesting," Paige said after tasting each dish. She salted everything, even the apple crumble dessert.

Linda ate without paying attention, feeling twitchy. What was Paige going to ask her next? Just the thought of that bombardment continuing was enough to sour her stomach. But they finished eating in silence. Maybe they could watch a movie, something soothing, and go to bed without any more problems.

Paige set down her knife and fork.

Linda sighed.

"Would you introduce me to the computer now?" Paige asked.

It was much more work than Linda had imagined. Paige had never seen a keyboard before, didn't know that if you pushed the power button by mistake the whole system would shut down and have to be rebooted, didn't understand about monitors, how the screen glowed without fire, how letters could appear and disappear at will without being touched, or why you could move the cursor by using the mouse. (Why call it a mouse when it bore no resemblance to the biological sort?) Two hours later, Linda wanted to scream. She was tired of exclamations of wonder, endless questions, teaching. She had wanted her daughter back, and what she had gotten instead was some kind of fiend of curiosity.

The CD-ROM multimedia encyclopedia totally entranced this new Paige. She got lost in it.

"I'm going to bed," Linda said at length. "If you crash the computer again, you'll just have to wait until morning before I reboot, all right?"

"Very well," said Paige. "Thank you for your many kindnesses."

Linda kissed Paige's cheek, forgetting for an instant that this was a stranger. She left Paige's study, accompanied by a symphony of hunt-and-peck typing clicks. At the doorway she glanced back. Paige's head, outlined by a halo of monitor light. How many times had she seen that image? Tears rose in her eyes, but did not spill over.

☐

The hands remembered.

Sometime in the smallest hours of the morning, when Lewis had been amusing himself with the computer for a long time, fatigue settled over him. His head drooped. His fingers rested on the keyboard. He closed his eyes.

The deep melancholy he had been holding at bay all day with determined curiosity finally engulfed him.

He was alive, weak, female, little better than a slave, in the midst of a world he did not comprehend, in the care of a woman he could only characterize as hostile. For a short while he allowed these gloomy reflections to overcome him. At last he drew in breath and banished them. What were his resources? What were his immediate goals? What was his best next action?

After all, he had tools to hand, much to interest him despite his straitened circumstances, and plenty to eat, though it all tasted strange.

His fingers twitched.

He opened his eyes and saw his hand reach for the mouse, scroll through directories, select one, and click. A box asking for a password appeared. Both his hands dropped to the keyboard and typed, using more fingers than he had yet used to form words, unaccustomed to the placement of the letters as he was.

Paige's private journal opened to him.

He came wide-awake, then, and read.

He found a map full of landmarks. He studied it as ardently as he had celestial observation, medicine, botany, zoology, taxidermy, and anatomy before his last expedition.

Much of what Paige had written defied understanding, couched as it was in the dialect of the present, full of inventions and attitudes Lewis did not yet understand. But he could grasp a lot of it, if not by definition, by context.

Paige had started the journal as soon as she learned to write. It was full of adventures, mostly trips she had gone on with her father: to the beach, to the mountains, to glaciers and zoos, buildings and craters, badlands and painted deserts and petrified forests: descriptions, events, questions, guesses, colors, textures, sky, and things her father taught her. The journal started simply, but Paige honed her writing skills as she went.

She didn't write every day, only when she had something exciting to relate.

In the summer of her twelfth year, her father disappeared. "Mom says he left us, but I think someone stole him. Someone killed him or kidnapped him. He would never leave me, never," she wrote, and let two years slip by in silence.

In the midst of her fourteenth year she began to write

again. She had participated in a school project about Mars. She had been excited by pictures of a place where humans had never been, and her longing to explore resurrected itself. She made lists and plans. She researched astronaut training programs. She took classes that would lead her toward a college major in extraterrestrial science, and began rigorous physical training.

He stopped reading and glanced down at Paige's pale arms, his arms now. Thin by atrophy. He knew from her reports that she had conditioned herself well. All lost now, but not irrevocably.

"Mom keeps zoning out whenever I talk about my plans," Paige wrote on her sixteenth birthday. "My friends think I'm nuts, too. Journal, you're the only one I can talk to about this anymore. Well, the only one who listens, anyway. Mom won't listen to what she doesn't want to hear. She definitely doesn't want to hear about my plans to leave, even just to go away to college. I guess I'll just shut up to everybody but you."

Nine months ago, in the second-to-the-last entry in the file, Paige wrote about a prospective school field trip to Mount Hood, and how excited she was by the prospect of snow camping, something she hadn't done since her father left. "Mom doesn't want me to go on this trip," she wrote, "but I've got to. If I stay cooped up here any longer, I'll go crazy."

The final entry startled him. It was only six months old. It read: "I'm better off dead."

Armed with information, he lay on the bed, closed his eyes, and went exploring.

□

"So, did you crash the computer again after I left last night?" Linda asked Paige at breakfast the next morning. Morning? Well, it was almost afternoon, actually; Linda had been awake for four nerve-racking hours by the time Paige struggled out of bed and came downstairs. Paige's hair was tousled. She had dressed in green Levi's and a purple shirt, clothes Linda had thought she had thrown out soon after the accident, when she had gone through all Paige's things and gotten rid of the clothes she had always hated.

Paige looked nothing like a doll anymore.

"Indeed I did." Paige drank the juice of oranges, ate the eggs of chickens.

"But before you did that, did you find answers to your questions?"

"To some of them." Paige straightened and wiped her mouth on her sleeve. "It is strange to read what history has written of one. All our endeavors of twenty-eight months, our hardships, the majestically grand scenery we beheld, the flora and fauna and peoples we described, the rivers and lands we charted, discharged in a few small paragraphs. Having read those, I explored the accomplishments of others in recent history. The years since I died have been astonishing ones."

Linda hadn't even introduced this Paige to the Internet yet. Just showing Paige the encyclopedia had driven Linda nuts. How could music and voices come from a small machine? Where were the musicians, the speechmakers? How were these images created, so close to life as to imitate it exactly, better even than one could create using a camera obscura? How could such pictures move? And the events described and pictured beggared the imagination. The moon walk, the Civil Rights March on Washington, the *Hindenburg* going down in flames, two world wars and countless smaller ones, bombs, warships, airplanes, Charles Lindbergh's solo flight across the Atlantic, Amelia Earhart . . .

"No kidding," said Linda.

Paige glanced at her with raised eyebrows, then sampled buttered toast.

Linda drank coffee and tried to get her mind to work. Just

thinking about her session last night with Paige and the computer made her head pound.

If this Paige, who was not her Paige, continued being this curious and demanding, Linda wasn't sure what she would do.

She still had time to ask Nucore for a reversal.

And go back to a motionless daughter, a doll she had to care for? Days and nights of despair and ultimate loneliness?

Besides, she was getting to know this Paige, if not to like her. Reversing the process would feel like murder.

Maybe she was justified in murdering a rapacious information demon.

Meriwether Lewis. What had she been thinking?

Lewis was the one Paige had talked about most often, and Linda had some idea of who he had been and what he had done. He was not supposed to bother Linda. He was only supposed to play with Paige and keep her happy, if things had gone according to plan.

Really, would any other explorer have been easier to deal with? At least she and Lewis shared a common language. Sort of. Balboa, Cortés, Columbus would have been even worse.

She looked up as Paige, standing at the counter, poured herself a mug of coffee and added three sugar cubes. "Don't drink that!"

Paige checked, glanced at her. "Why not?"

"It's not for children."

"I am not a child."

They stared at each other, unmoving, for a long moment. Then Paige lifted the mug and sipped from it.

A hand closed around Linda's heart and squeezed. This was too much like her last conversation with Paige before the accident. "You can't keep me caged up forever, Mom, not when all my life, all I've wanted is to get my wings working and take off."

Linda had told Paige she was too young. She was only sixteen. She owed Linda at least two more years at home before she did anything dangerous like camping on Mount Hood, where people died every year, even people who had lots of wilderness skills and should have known how to handle sudden weather.

Linda stood up and strode across the room. She loomed over Paige. Paige had spent the last nine months nearly motionless. Linda had total confidence that she had physical strength on her side. She could force Paige to put down that coffee cup.

Paige studied her for a moment and took another sip.

"Don't," Linda said in a low, harsh voice.

"Madam, I may be only a commodity to you, but I was taught the most valuable lessons of my life by the man who wrote the Declaration of Independence."

Independence. Linda's hands closed into tight fists. She turned and paced across the kitchen.

Just like Paige. Wouldn't listen to someone who knew what was best for her. Just like Paige, resisting her every step of the way.

Why had she ever wanted Paige back?

She loved Paige above everything else in life. She only wanted to keep her safe from the menacing world out there. Everywhere you looked, something else waited to hurt you. Something waited to snatch you from those you loved. You were never heard from again.

"You're not doing this to me again," Linda said, turning around.

Paige set the mug on the counter and crossed her arms over her chest. "You're not doing this to me again," she said. Gone now was the strange accent, the deepened tone of the stranger. This was the voice of her daughter.

"Paige," Linda cried.

"Oh, shit," said Paige.

"Paige." Linda felt the heat of tears in her eyes. "How long have you been back?"

Paige turned her head sideways. Linda stared at her profile, at the clean line of jaw, the perfect frowning mouth, the clear brown eye. "I'm not ready for this," Paige muttered. "We had a lot more prep work planned before I came back, strength and stamina to build, supplies to pack."

"Paige," Linda whispered. Wet streaked her cheek. "Oh, Paige."

"Mom. You took heroic measures. For that I have to thank you." Paige turned back. She stared into her mother's eyes. Her arms uncrossed and lowered to her sides. "Now I've got what I really need—somebody who knows how to lead an expedition. I'm my own native guide. I'm finally ready to head out, or I will be as soon as I get my health back. There's lots to explore right here on the planet."

"Don't leave me." Linda's hands gripped each other, squeezed till it hurt.

"I'll die again if you confine me," Paige said, her voice a mixture of her own and Lewis's, strong and sad, dense with conviction.

Linda stared and stared at her, then went to the table and sat in her chair. She dropped her head into her hands, rubbed at her pounding temples. "But I—if you go out—" Wearily Linda lifted her head. If only Paige were eight years old. Curious, but too small to run around by herself. Beautiful, smart, perfect. And containable.

She stared at her daughter, focused on that determined chin.

This was not an eight-year-old Paige.

And she wasn't the Paige who had stood at the top of the stairs, her backpack and sleeping bag on her back, yelling that she was going on this camping trip whether Linda wanted her to or not. Not the Paige Linda had grabbed, had shook. How could she leave? How could she defy Linda? Didn't she know she was acting just like her father had?

This was not the Paige who had slid out of Linda's grip and fallen down the stairs, skidded down on her backpack as though on a toboggan, horribly quick and horribly slow, stopped with a thump as her head cracked against the banister at the bottom.

And this was not the Paige of the past nine months, more dead than alive, a doll daughter without movement, will, or response. Linda had been able to do anything she wanted with that Paige, but it hadn't made her happy.

Linda stared at her daughter and saw resolution in her face, beautiful, threatening awareness.

"You can knock me down and paralyze me again," Paige said in a low voice. "This time it will kill both of us. Is that what you want?"

"No," Linda whispered.

"I have to go out and look around. It's what I was born to do."

"What if it kills you?"

Paige's brown eyes stared into Linda's for a long moment. "I'll die happy."

"If you go out and the world claims you . . . what if you never come back? What if you disappear the way your father did?"

Paige sighed and drank more coffee. "I won't disappear," she said slowly, "if you'll stop trying to chain me up."

How can you tell? How can anyone ever tell? People disappear whether you want them to or not.

Sometimes people disappear even when they're with you.

Linda buried her face in her hands, hid her vision. Yesterday's headaches, today's brief joy drowned in pain; she held those things inside.

She heard Paige breathing, waiting.

The stranger's voice spoke. "By the time we returned, they had given us up for lost and begun to forget us," it said. "But we returned."

Linda pressed the tears from her eyes with her index fingers and looked up. Her hands tightened into fists in her lap, and she felt tension in her shoulders.

Paige studied her with the polite expression of a stranger.

I've already lost her.

I gave her to him. The king of questions.

He saved her life.

Linda stared down at her fisted hands. She opened them. Tension seeped away.

She couldn't hold on to everything forever.

"Take care of yourself," she said to both of them, hoping they each understood.

Relics

Kristine Kathryn Rusch

Scott's earliest memories were of being carried. His mother held him close to her, like a baby, and he used to fight it. *Put me down, Mommy*, he'd say, sometimes loud enough for strangers to look, and his mother would hold him closer, placing one hand on his back as if to protect him. *No, baby. It's not safe here. Wait until we stop.*

And stop they always did, sometimes in a church basement, where there were cots and thin soup that somehow tasted better than anything he ate now. But mostly they stopped in alleys and slept in boxes, or under stairs, huddled together to keep warm.

The nuns always said that he had been fortunate: his mother had died in the basement of St. Mary's on a cold December night. They had whisked him away from her—always using that hated language of death: *she's with God now.*

God don't need her, he'd say. *I do.* But that didn't seem to matter to them. It didn't seem to matter to anyone. He had found his way into the system, and the system had placed him in the Catholic orphanage, one of the few left in the country, because he had been left in a Catholic church, and therefore had to be one of "theirs."

He'd been four at the time, a big boy in his mind, little in theirs, and the nuns had taken to him. "Sweet," "angelic," "cherubic," were all words they used to describe him, and soon the other children began to resent him. He started to learn the cost of being the favorite.

He was an observer, even then, and what he learned in his observations was that other children who were marginalized had made choices: either to become something their peers accepted or to spend time alone. He didn't want to change to become accepted. His mother had loved him as he was, and so he spent most of his time alone, with books and computers and studies. The nuns continued to approve, and the other children continued to pinch him, or accidentally trip him, or punch him hard in the stomach when no one was looking. He never reported these incidents. He never said much of anything.

His demeanor, his looks, and his IQ got him the interview with Mr. Fitzgerald. His willingness to try something new got Fitzgerald to pay attention to him. His desire to have someone care for him gave him the courage to leave the sisters.

He had hopes. But he also had a horrible fear that somehow, they were going to be dashed.

☐

Rory Fitzgerald tugged on his diamond cuff links, and then shook his arms ever so slightly, making certain that the sleeves on his silk suit fell into place. He stared at the boy through the one-way glass. This room was cold, and the metal chairs were sterile. The air smelled of disinfectant. He clasped his hands behind his back, wishing he were somewhere else.

The boy didn't seem to notice anything amiss. The boy never did. He was sitting in the waiting area, as Dr. Wilhelm

Wolfe had called it on Fitzgerald's first visit. If the boy had already undergone the process, the scientists could watch him from here, should they deem such action necessary. Wolfe had reassured Fitzgerald that such action was rarely necessary.

Right now, though, the scientists had wanted to observe Scott. Not that there was much to see. The waiting area consisted of some brown couches, some children's puzzles, and a table in the center of the room. There was no computer. There was, however, a television set, currently unplugged, and a phone against the wall. Scott had ignored both items, going instead for the reading material in the center of the table—a few tawdry paperback novels, several coffee table books, mostly about the art of Europe, and a downloaded copy of that day's newspaper. Scott glanced at the newspaper, then thumbed through the art books. He was on his second now, and Fitzgerald was growing impatient.

The scientists were supposed to be observing the boy, but Fitzgerald was in this room alone. He was beginning to wonder if people were observing him instead. He didn't like the feeling.

At that thought, a door opened and a woman entered. She was petite, her dark hair in perfect cornrows with matching orange beads that encircled her head like a veil.

She extended her hand. "Mr. Fitzgerald," she said. "I'm Lucienne DeVore. Dr. Wolfe sends his regrets. He was called out of town on some urgent business. I'm to be the one in charge of your case."

He didn't take her hand, staring at it until she withdrew it. "I would prefer to work with Dr. Wolfe."

"I'm afraid that's not possible." She smiled, even though he could see in her eyes that the expression cost her a bit. "I'm the one who would have been in charge of the case anyway. Dr. Wolfe would have been handling the P.R. You're actually going closer to the source."

He kept his hands clasped behind his back. "You know what I want."

"Yes." She glanced at the boy sitting in the waiting room, and her eyes softened. "I think it's highly irregular."

"This entire procedure is irregular," Fitzgerald said. It wasn't something he would subject himself to. Merging his own personality with another, no matter how brilliant. The scientific process, which had been explained to him a dozen times now, did not reassure him. So DNA codes constantly reencoded, storing an individual's personality, character, and memory in each DNA molecule. So that could be removed, and, with a simple procedure, "downloaded" into a form that could be scanned into the retinas and then into the brain of a new host. So what that the personalities blended, "improving," or so Wolfe claimed, on the personality that was already there. It all sounded horrifying to Fitzgerald.

He did not believe he needed improving, and he was not about to share his body with anyone, even though, his friends who had gone through the procedure assured him, it wasn't like two souls sharing the same brain. It was more like an augmentation.

Fitzgerald didn't need to be augmented, improved, or blended. And he had already had his lawyers draw up papers that prevented others from downloading his own DNA encoding after his death. When he died, he would be well and truly dead. No tampering allowed.

Still, that didn't stop him from wanting to make use of this procedure in other ways.

Lucienne DeVore was staring at him. Apparently she hadn't liked his last comment. "I was referring to the irregularity of your source, Mr. Fitzgerald. We can't guarantee that the DNA is the one you're looking for. We can't verify anything."

"Nonsense," Fitzgerald said. "The Catholic Church has verified that the DNA in the bloodstains is from a male human."

DeVore sighed. "Forgive me, Mr. Fitzgerald, I wouldn't trust the Catholic Church's scientific methodology."

Fitzgerald tilted his head, so that he seemed even taller. "I assume you have the Shroud."

"We have gotten access to it, yes."

"And I assume you've tested it, or the boy and I wouldn't be here."

A slight rose color dusted her dark cheeks. "Yes."

"And what have your tests confirmed?"

"The Shroud of Turin is highly contaminated, Mr. Fitzgerald. Not just from its examinations in 1978, but also from its long history. It's gone from hand to hand for centuries— and that's only its documented history, the history the Church considers accurate. Its unofficial history is even more complex, with thefts and secret rooms, and that doesn't even address the fact that no one knows where the Shroud was from the death of Christ until it turned up in Constantinople in the thirteenth century. There's even a dispute as to whether the image on the Shroud is an idealized version of Christ or what a man from his background in that part of the world would have looked like."

Fitzgerald knew the history of the Shroud. He knew the controversies. He knew it all. "What do your tests confirm, Ms. DeVore?"

She closed her eyes. He could feel her exasperation.

"Ms. DeVore? The bloodstains?"

"They are unusually red," she said. "Dried blood is black. Dried blood that old is very black."

"I know what dried blood looks like," he said, lowering his voice. His staff would be ducking for cover by now. When Fitzgerald lowered his voice, he was getting angry. "What have your tests shown?"

"That the stains are mostly red ocher and vermilion tempera paint."

"Mostly?" he asked.

She opened her eyes and raised her head toward him. She

was as angry as he was, but didn't dare show it. He was a client, after all. "There is the blood of a human male mixed in with the paint."

"Thank you, Ms. DeVore."

"It's Dr. DeVore," she snapped. "And you knew about the blood already."

"Yes," he said. "I did. Is the DNA good enough for you to use?"

"Yes," she said.

He nodded. "Then go ahead. Do the procedure."

"Forgive me, Mr. Fitzgerald," she said, "but I don't advise this. You believe that the blood in this Shroud belongs to the son of God, but there's no proof of this. For all we know, that blood could be from a common criminal who died on the cross in the first century A.D. Or it could be from a grimy pilgrim who touched the cloth with bloody fingers when it was displayed in the Middle Ages."

"True enough," Fitzgerald said. "But in all matters of faith, there needs to be a certain level of belief. I happen to believe that the blood belongs to the son of God."

"Then why aren't you undergoing the procedure yourself?" DeVore asked.

Fitzgerald smiled. "Successful men, Dr. DeVore, always hedge their bets."

☐

He was lying to her. Lucienne walked down the hall, feeling frustrated but unable to do anything about it. Fitzgerald was lying to her. There was another reason he was subjecting the boy to this procedure, and it had nothing to do with worrying that the blood on the Shroud did not belong to the son of God. The man had a scheme, she was sure of it. She had said as much to Dr. Wolfe, who had nodded, and said, "It's none of our business what our clients do with our gift."

But she disagreed. And so, apparently, did Dr. Wolfe. There was no emergency, at least not something that someone else couldn't handle. He had left because he had known that Fitzgerald would want to work with him, and Wolfe was afraid this whole procedure would go awry. The scientists wanted Wolfe to turn down Fitzgerald—and he had, at first. But Fitzgerald had kept coming back, offering more and more money for the procedure, until he was paying ten times what all the others had paid. And he hadn't balked at that. Wolfe had thought that Fitzgerald had been prepared to go even higher.

A man did not do that when he was trying to hedge his bets.

Lucienne pushed open a door and entered the research wing. The Shroud wasn't there—a group of their people (and she was thankful she didn't know who) had managed to get the sample on-site. She didn't know if they had sneaked into the Cathedral at Turin and violated the holy relic, or if they had had official permission. She doubted the latter, but she didn't ask. She was learning there were many things she couldn't ask at this job.

Still, she went to her computer and looked up more information on the Shroud. So many hands had touched it. So many people had violated it. That would have created a problem right there, even if the DNA on the material was known to be that of the historical Jesus. But no one could even prove that. The scientific studies she had read were in two types: the ones done by believers and the ones done by skeptics.

Both had an agenda. Both started knowing how they wanted the evidence to turn out. So believers started with the premise that the image on the Shroud was that of the historical Jesus, and tried to use science to prove it. Skeptics started with the premise that the image on the Shroud was faked, probably in the Middle Ages, when religious "relics" commanded a high price, and set out to prove that. No one had approached the Shroud with an open mind. No one had conducted a strictly scientific study on the thing. She wasn't sure if it was possible.

Still, the skeptics' evidence was the most convincing to her. The Shroud was one of forty reputed burial cloths of Jesus, although it was the only one to have the apparent imprints and bloodstains of a crucified man. The relic first appeared in the mid–fourteenth century in the tiny village of Lirey, France, and was declared a painted "representation" by Pope Clement VII. Religious critics of the Shroud said that it contradicted the biblical record, which described multiple burial wrappings and included a separate napkin for Christ's face. In modern times, the Shroud had been radiocarbon-dated by three independent labs. They all found that the age span of the cloth fell somewhere between A.D. 1260 and 1390.

The believers, on the other hand, claimed that microbial contamination on the Shroud probably skewed the radiocarbon-dating results. In the mid-1990s, researchers from Texas found a blood glob that contained three different human genes, and the testing continued. The debate raged, just as it had, throughout the centuries.

And now Lucienne was in the middle of it.

Frankly, she wouldn't have cared if Fitzgerald were going to insert the mystery DNA into his own brain. But he had adopted a child specifically for this purpose. What would he do if the child proved to inherit the memories of a pope or of a pilgrim? Remove the memories within the allotted time period? Or kill the boy and start again?

Could she live with that?

And what would Fitzgerald do if the DNA turned out to be that of the historical Jesus? Download some into himself? Then what? Pretend he was the Second Coming? But how could he be if the boy already had the DNA? And how would the son of God get along inside the body of a man as ruthless as Fitzgerald? Who would win?

All she knew was that the boy would lose. And she didn't know how to warn him away, any more than she knew how to warn herself away. She was already in way too deep.

For if word of this got out, if word of any of it got out, it wouldn't be Wolfe's head that would fall, or the corporation that would suffer. It would be hers.

She put her head in her hands. She used to love her work, before it had ethics and politics and money mixed in. Now she found herself wishing she could be someplace else.

□

Scott ran his fingers across the glossy pages of the book. The dense ceiling painting, with its sybils and prophets, its images of God, and its nine Old Testament subjects held his attention. That Michelangelo had lain on his back for years painting this masterpiece on the ceiling of a chapel fascinated him. That this painting still remained fascinated him more.

He had never seen art books like this one before. For the last few moments, he had been studying the in-depth photograph, the one that showed Michelangelo's depiction of the Creation. The angel in the center, the beasts of the field, the thinking man, probably representing God, all entranced him. Scott loved to draw, but the images he turned out were crude and ugly. Even his stick figures needed work.

A door opened, and he turned. A man in a white lab coat stood there, smiling at him. "It's time," he said.

More than time, Scott thought. Mr. Fitzgerald had gone to talk with the doctors, and had been gone almost the entire time.

"Will Mr. Fitzgerald know where I am?" Scott asked, trying not to sound needy.

"Yes," the man said with a gentle smile. "You ready? This won't hurt."

Scott nodded. He knew it wouldn't hurt. He'd had eye examinations before, and that's what Mr. Fitzgerald had said this would be like. Scott wasn't sure why Mr. Fitzgerald had wanted him to have another personality added to his own. Scott wasn't sure he wanted one, but Mr. Fitzgerald had told him it would be the best personality in the entire world.

Scott had overheard one of the assistants talking about the

whole thing. Mr. Fitzgerald thought he had found the remains of Jesus, and it was Jesus that Scott was going to house. Scott wasn't sure if he was frightened or excited.

All he knew was that he would never again be alone. And for that, he was willing to do anything.

Scott carefully closed the book and stood, brushing the lint off his new pants. Then he followed the man in the lab coat out of the nicely decorated waiting room and into the cold hallway.

The change in temperature was what made him shiver; he was sure of that. He just wished that the shivering would stop.

☐

"The boy's been asleep for six hours," Fitzgerald said as he entered the conference room. "They assure me he'll sleep at least thirty more. I do want to be there when he awakens, however. We'll see if this thing takes."

The conference room was small. This was one of his many branch offices, and the room reflected that. It had a single teak table in the middle, matching teak furniture on the sides, and brass fixtures throughout. A wet bar stood in one corner, a small serving area in another so that the area could double as a place for social gatherings. Its far wall was all glass, although he had the curtains closed so that there wouldn't be any distractions.

This meeting was with his secondary staff. His main staff had known about his plans since he had started looking for the boy. The main staff were still on-site, making sure everything went as advertised.

"Forgive me, sir," said Annabella Martinez, the youngest and fastest rising of this important group, "but I don't understand the point of this. If the boy does channel—or whatever you call it—the historical Christ, what do we get out of it?"

"Nothing except press attention for a while," Fitzgerald said. "And maybe not even that."

"He's twelve years old," mused Roberto DePalma, the middle-aged thinker who would one day replace Fitzgerald's main advisor. "You expect him to talk to the leaders of the temple?"

Fitzgerald turned and poured himself some of the fresh coffee that he'd ordered made for this meeting. "If the spirit moves him."

"You sound like you're a believer," Martinez said.

Fitzgerald shrugged.

"How do we fit in?" asked Marcus Napier, the newest member of this team. Napier was a former college football great with a ruined knee, and he still looked as if he were going to burst out of his suits.

"When he gets old enough, he'll need a ministry," Fitzgerald said. "And need someone to sponsor that ministry."

"Knowing you, boss," said Betty Camden, who had been with him from the beginning and who had set up the secondary team, "you'll make a profit off this ministry."

"Yes," said Martinez, "and didn't Jesus throw the money changers out of the temple?"

"Out of the temple, yes," Fitzgerald said. "But not out of the streets."

"But the idea's the same," Martinez said. "He didn't want anyone making money off religion."

"Hmmm," Fitzgerald said. "That's only one interpretation. And don't forget. Young Scott'll still be a part of this. He'll understand the need to reach a worldwide audience."

"Young Scott'll know that you make news, and you get the audience without paying for it," Napier said.

"Really?" asked Fitzgerald. "A boy of twelve?"

"Hell, a boy of five should know that, in this culture anyway."

The entire group laughed. Fitzgerald waited until they were done. "Just be ready," he said. "We don't want to pamper the boy, but we don't want him to miss opportunities either."

"Opportunities?" asked DePalma.

"If he thinks he needs to minister to the homeless, for example, let him," Fitzgerald said. "Philanthropy will only help our image. In the meantime, we'll make sure he has a proper education—religious and otherwise—and we'll make sure that he's well taken care of."

"I never expected the Second Coming to be like this," Napier said.

"I never said this was the Second Coming, now did I?" Fitzgerald said.

"What else would you call it?" Camden asked.

Before Fitzgerald could reply, Martinez said, "That brings up another problem."

Fitzgerald turned slowly toward her. "Yes?"

"If this DNA truly does come from the son of God, aren't you afraid of incurring God's wrath?"

Laughter again broke out at the table, but Fitzgerald stalled it with the movement of a hand. "Do you believe God would allow such a thing?" he asked.

"That His son gets brought back against God's will?"

"Yes."

Martinez looked confused. "I guess it seems unlikely."

"Yes," Fitzgerald said.

Napier frowned. "If you believe that God won't let His son come back, then why are you doing this? Do you believe this is God's will?"

Fitzgerald shook his head. "I believe that Jesus Christ, the man the New Testament is about, was the greatest con artist of His day. He was, I think, a very religious man with a message, who sincerely believed what He said. I also think that He had no more special powers than you or I."

"If that's the case, then why the Gospels? The apostles? The impact?" Martinez asked, a bit of an edge to her voice.

"All religious figures have their disciples," Fitzgerald said.

"For that matter, all politicians and entertainers do as well. Most have things written about them. Most can point to an impact. I could be trite and make the same argument about our old friend Elvis. Or I could be sincere, and point to Dr. Martin Luther King, a charismatic man with disciples who might in turn be called apostles. King has had books written about him and his martyrdom, many of those books by his disciples, and he had a tremendous impact on our generation and generations to come."

"It's not the same," Martinez said.

"Oh?" Fitzgerald asked. "I think it is."

"Then how do you know that Scott will speak for our time?" Napier asked.

"How can he not?" Fitzgerald asked. "With that personality inside him, he'll have to speak out. He'll have to re-form."

"He'll reform you," Martinez said.

Fitzgerald studied her for a moment. Her cheeks were red, and her eyes were flashing. "Would you like to be off this project?"

"It would require a demotion, wouldn't it?" she asked.

He shrugged.

She shook her head. "I would rather stay and watch."

"It's your call," he said. "As long as you don't interfere."

She didn't respond. Napier leaned back in his chair. It creaked under his considerable weight. "So we get what from this? Money?"

"Tax-free," Fitzgerald said.

"There's got to be easier ways to make money," Camden said.

"Power." Martinez got up to pour herself some coffee. She took a mug instead of a cup, and gripped it by the top as she brought it back to the table. The steam formed water beads on her palm, beads that dripped onto the teak surface. Camden nervously wiped the stain away. Martinez didn't seem to notice. "Mr. Fitzgerald is after more power."

"It would seem to me," Napier said, "that the power would belong to Scott and his historical friend."

"And, if you read the written record," Martinez said, "they won't want it. So, by default, it'll belong to our boss here."

Fitzgerald smiled at her. Maybe she would be an asset after all.

"I've read the New Testament," Napier said. "Studied it every Sunday in fact. Had to memorize large parts of it in the sixth grade. And I know that the historical Jesus won't stand for the misuse of power."

"Who said we were going to misuse it," Fitzgerald said.

"Then what will you do with it?"

He put his hands on the table. "Imagine how it'll feel for Jesus to come back, to see what's been done in His name. Imagine how He'll work to set things right."

"And you'll make that possible for Him?"

"Of course," Fitzgerald said. "One of us has to manipulate the system."

"I'd teach Him how to do that myself," Martinez said.

"He won't let you manipulate the system," Napier said.

Fitzgerald smiled. "Oh, He just might."

The group erupted into argument. Fitzgerald's smile grew. Now he had them where he wanted them. Debating the issues he wanted. Thinking the way he wanted. There wasn't any more to be said at least, not by him.

He excused himself and walked to his own office, with a view of the city skyline. Lights everywhere. Perhaps this was what God saw when He looked down from the heavens, lights and evidence of life being lived. Not necessarily well. But lived.

Fitzgerald took a cigar out of its box and ran his fingers along the wrapping, not quite willing to smoke it. There were better ways to make money, yes, and he'd done many of them during his lifetime. He was a self-made man, born to a poor Catholic family, made poor in the name of religion. Too many children, not enough money, his father old before his time trying to work and raise a family and keep them all in food and clothes. Eleven children, no birth control, his mother dying along with the twelfth because it was God's will. God's will, as interpreted by the Church. The Church, which had told Fitzgerald he could not marry his Lutheran girlfriend and the love of his life if she did not convert. The Church, which claimed that a woman was merely a host for the precious new life that grew within her, a host that could be discarded before the new life was. A life that was discarded—first his mother, then his wife, his wife who had not been recognized by the Church that raised him.

What kind of power was he seeking? Only the greatest kind, the most lasting kind. He had the money. He could buy a senator, or even a president, but that sort of influence had a four-year or, at best, an eight-year limitation on it. No. He wanted influence that would last centuries. That would cure wrong-thinking, and restore the religion to its pre-interpretation days.

For that he needed the historical Jesus, not necessarily the son of God. He needed the man who made the pronouncements recorded in the Gospels, the man who admonished His followers to love one another. The man who forgave adulterers and told those without sin to cast the first stone.

Such a man could not be created. Only revived. And Fitzgerald did not have the courage to host such a man himself. The boy was as pure as they came, and he had no real personality. He wouldn't contaminate the soul that Fitzgerald was trying to give him. The boy wouldn't interfere with it either.

Let the second team—and the first—believe that Fitzgerald was in this to create a new religion, to have tax-free money, to found an international religious scam. Let them believe what they would.

He was in this for his own reasons, and he would confess them to no one. They were between him and his elusive God.

☐

For the last three hours, Lucienne had watched the boy sleep. He lay on his side, under a heavy quilt that she had made especially for her patients, believing that, in this time of change, they needed something with a bit of personality to sustain them. His eyes moved rapidly in REM as he absorbed the information they had downloaded into him, the unknown personality that was now merging with his.

She had never felt such qualms before, not even when Tsering conducted the first test on himself. She had been an observer then, and a believer in the process as well. Her beliefs went like this: humans lived an entire lifetime, accumulating knowledge, and for what? To abandon it like a well-thumbed book when they died? Such knowledge needed to be preserved, passed on, and the best, the strongest personalities, they too needed to be preserved and passed on. Most died well before they had finished their contributions to the world.

Lucienne wasn't sure she believed that anymore. She'd seen too many transfers already, watched personalities clash or worse, seen the ones that were misinterpreted by their peers and turned out to be something other than expected.

She wasn't sure what frightened her most about this case: the fact that the blood sample might be from an unknown source, or the fact that it might be Christ's. What if his disciples had misinterpreted his nature? What if he were an entirely different man than the one remembered in the Bible?

How would she be able to tell what she had done? How would she be able to tell if the transfer had been successful or not? How would she know if she had destroyed all that was good in this boy or merely augmented it? How would she know?

Watching someone sleep was such an intimate thing. The sleeper looked so vulnerable, and in this case, he was. She had made him even more so.

She stood and left the sleep chamber. Her assistant stood outside, as if he had been uncertain whether or not to go in.

"Mr. Fitzgerald is here," her assistant said. "He insists on going into the sleep chamber."

Lucienne shook her head. No matter how much money Fitzgerald paid, he wouldn't violate this rule. Scott got to wake up, and incorporate his new self, without the help of the man who paid for the procedure.

"Tell him he'll have to wait to see how the procedure turns out, just like the rest of us."

Her assistant sighed. "He's not the easiest man to deal with."

"You'll manage," Lucienne said.

"He wants to know when you'll wake Scott up."

"I won't," Lucienne said. "He'll wake up when he's ready. You should know that."

Her assistant nodded. "I just wanted to be able to quote you."

"Make Mr. Fitzgerald comfortable," Lucienne said. And then she smiled. "Tell him it's necessary. The boy might wake up in fifteen minutes. It might be an hour. It might be eight hours. I will not rush the process, not for Mr. Fitzgerald, not for anyone. He wants this done right, and that's what we'll do. Is that clear?"

"Sure wish you were telling him," her assistant said, and left.

"I'm glad I'm not," Lucienne muttered, and then went back to her office. She would let Scott come to his own in peace.

☐

He woke slowly. He knew he had slept a long time, but he was exhausted, as if he had run a thousand miles in his dreams. Scott rubbed his eyes. He had never fallen asleep in a doctor's office before.

He didn't sit up; nor did he open his eyes. Not yet. He

was assessing this difference that he felt. He felt older and younger at the same time. His body felt strange and normal. He had a confidence he'd never had, knowledge he didn't know how he had gained, and a sense of the past that he wished he could attribute to all those paintings he'd looked at in the waiting room, but somehow he knew that that attribution would be wrong.

A chime sounded above him. Part of him accepted that as a normal sound, and another part was startled.

Slowly he opened his eyes, his hand falling on the quilt. He had never been here before, in this comfortable place with all the metal on the walls, the blinking lights. Part of him was startled, almost frightened, at the difference, and he worked to calm himself. This was not his room at Mr. Fitzgerald's place, nor was it his dorm room at the orphanage. It was not a hotel room. It had to be a place where the doctors let their patients recover from this procedure.

He sat up. He still felt like himself, only stronger. Better. More confident. But he couldn't feel another presence inside himself. He couldn't feel anyone at all. But there were memories inside him that hadn't been there before. And ideas. And a willingness to wait and see. A calmness that went beyond anything he had felt before.

He leaned against the wall and absorbed the newness of this place, taking extra time to think. And as he did, he felt those new opinions, those new ideas, overtake him, and he was glad.

□

The wake-up chime sounded. Lucienne swore softly under her breath. She hadn't been gone from the sleep chamber that long. Perhaps he had already been waking when she left. She should have waited, even though it made her uncomfortable.

He shouldn't have opened his eyes and discovered himself to be alone.

She hurried down the hallway and back into the sleep chamber. She opened the door slowly, so as not to startle Scott.

He was sitting on the bed, one hand on the quilt, staring into the distance. When he saw her, he smiled.

"Dr. DeVore," he said, his voice sounding older, more mature. She found she missed that younger voice, the hesitation, the poorly disguised need to please.

She grabbed a chair and pulled it toward his bedside. "How're you feeling?"

"Different," he said as if that were expected. "Calmer."

She waited.

"How am I supposed to feel?" That question, she knew, was from Scott.

"I don't know," she said. "Experiences vary."

"Tampering," he said in that older, more secure voice, "with God's law."

She felt a shiver run down her back. "I don't think so," she said. "If God hadn't wanted mankind to discover the secrets of the universe, He wouldn't have given us a brain."

Scott smiled. It was an adult, approving look, as if she had been given a test and passed. "You're very astute, Dr. DeVore."

"What do you remember?" she asked.

"Everything," he said. "And nothing. Part of me believes you should be wearing a robe instead of that lab coat. Another part can hear voices, the bray of a donkey."

A shiver ran through her. Why would he say that? "Your English is very good."

"Scott's English is very good. I would speak my native tongue, but I'm to understand you're not familiar with Aramaic."

"Only Greek," she said.

He blinked, and she thought she saw something—calculation? confusion?—cross his eyes. "Why would I speak Greek?"

Confusion then. It would take her a while to get used to this new personality. It seemed dominant. But then, of course, it would be. Anytime you combined an adult with a child, the adult would dominate. But she hadn't expected this kind of power. The man, whoever he had been, had had charisma.

Fitzgerald had instructed her not to ask any questions about the downloaded personality. She wasn't to put any ideas into the boy's head as well. The boy had known what they were doing, but not, Fitzgerald said, who they were downloading; that would be enough. Fitzgerald's psychologists and her own people had seen that the boy had no duplicity in him. He wouldn't lie if he had received the wrong personality.

He wouldn't lie about being able to speak Aramaic, for example.

He took her hand, and stroked it, finding the pressure points and relieving the stress. Calming her. To a person two thousand years ago, such an action would have felt like magic. Like the hand of God.

She looked into his eyes and saw no malevolence there. Only a goodness and a willingness to please.

"Scott?" she asked, partly because she wanted to hear from him, and partly because she wanted a moment to think about the personality she'd seen looking out his eyes. "Are you all right?"

"Yeah," he said, sounding like himself, sounding confused. "But I thought there'd be somebody in here with me."

"No," she said. "You share a personality now. It's like I've given you a superpower, you know, like Spider-Man or Superman. Something you hadn't had before, something that makes you more than you were."

"Oh," he said, and he sounded faintly disappointed. "I thought I wasn't going to be alone anymore."

She put her other hand on his, feeling drawn to him like

she had never felt drawn before. "It's part of the human condition to be lonely," she said.

He sighed. "I'm beginning to understand that." And the gaze he turned on her was haunted, it seemed, with images of a life long gone. A life lived in public, and yet lived so very, very alone.

☐

Fitzgerald finally got past the security people. Damn them for all their regulations, and damn DeVore for keeping Scott in the sleeping chamber when she knew that Fitzgerald was waiting. He'd been watching the clock since the boy went under, and he'd had a security guard report when the boy woke up. It had been nearly a half hour, and he hadn't been contacted. A half an hour was too long to leave DeVore alone with the boy. That thought sent Fitzgerald scurrying down the hallway, talking his way past the security people, threatening them with loss of their jobs, and their families' livelihoods if they interfered with him again.

He opened the door to the sleep chamber to see Scott and DeVore holding hands.

He stopped, uncertain how to approach this boy, now that everything was complete.

The boy turned to him. Scott was there, in the face, in the eyes, but someone else was as well. Someone else who had a lot of personal power, charisma, and intelligence. Someone else who seemed to be able to see Fitzgerald for exactly what he was.

"I am stunned at your lack of compassion, Fitzgerald," Scott said in a voice that wasn't Scott's at all, but belonged to an older, wiser man. DeVore looked up in surprise. "You find a boy who wants nothing more than to reexperience the love he'd had with his mother, a boy who needs affection and hugs, and you send him here, where you lead him to believe that he'll have his own companion inside him for the rest of his life. You offer no comfort, you give no hint at what you're really trying to do—except that you won't visit with the boy. You won't touch him, even in reassurance, and you see him only as a thing. What are we to do for you? Make more money? Hmm? Or expiate the guilt you've acquired in all your cold, ruthless dealings with people who never quite seemed real to you?"

The moral authority in that voice took Fitzgerald's breath away. In spite of himself, he smiled. It had worked then. It had worked.

"I'm sorry," he said, and wondered how long it had been since he'd uttered those words. He suspected he'd be saying them a lot more now.

"Sorry is such an inadequate word," the boy said. "You must desire forgiveness within your own heart, act upon that, and make things right. You must never harm people again."

Fitzgerald bowed his head, keeping his expression from the boy and DeVore. It had gone even better than he had hoped. Even now the boy had strength to lead.

"Forgive me," Fitzgerald whispered, and the boy's hand reached up and touched Fitzgerald's forehead, like a benediction.

□

It was all new and strange. He had only a child's perceptions to guide him, a child's perceptions and his own cunning. He didn't dare play this too far, didn't dare admit too much. He had done that the last time. He had had the perfect scam going, and then the pope's guards had gotten him to confess. He could still feel the sting of the lash against his back, remember how the words tore out of his throat.

Yes, he had cried. *Yes. I faked the Shroud. It is a painting.*

And he told them how he had done the work, in the style of the Coptics, and how he had even added some of his own blood to the red ocher so that the shroud would have a slight, subtle odor of decay.

He had made a small fortune from his relic, only to lose

it and his reputation, slowly over the years. And then Pope Clement VII discovering him, getting the confession from him, and ruining the rest of his livelihood. He remembered being a broken man.

He would not break here. The woman was easy enough—women had always been easy—and this child, this Scott, he with the brilliant mind and the command of this silly language and a great knowledge of the Bible, knowledge denied one such as him in the past—had the face of an angel.

The test had been Fitzgerald, and it had been easier than he had thought it would be. Fitzgerald believed, beneath his bluster. And within that belief was the key to his control.

But he needed to go lightly. A scam played best when it was underplayed. He had learned that all too well the last time.

Fitzgerald's head was still bowed. Dr. DeVore was watching Luc—no, Scott. He had to think of himself as Scott—with curious eyes, eyes that held doubt that was fading by the minute.

Luc closed his eyes and leaned his head back. He needed a moment to collect himself, to think.

He had the time to learn. Fitzgerald had even given him that. The boy was only twelve. Luc would bide his time. He would calm Scott, whom he could feel within him, frightened and sad and worried that this new confidence of his, this new knowledge, would destroy them all.

But the boy was wrong. If all went the way Luc planned—and it would go that way. How could it not, with a rich sponsor, and a public willing to believe, all waiting for a Second Coming?—then Scott would get his wish as well.

He would be loved beyond his fondest dreams.

He felt hope within the boyish part of himself. The Scott part. The part that formed the anchor for them. *Yes*, he thought. *Love*. He could guarantee that. He'd never had a shortage of it. He could always sway people to his side. He'd nearly had those guards at the end. If only the pope hadn't entered that filthy cell and spoiled everything.

But "if onlys" were long past. He was getting a second chance. And so was the boy.

And together they would get everything they wanted. Riches beyond their wildest dreams. The affection of millions. The power to change history.

But what of God? The question came from the boy-self, the well-schooled boy, the boy raised by nuns.

Luc had to fight the urge to smile. *The good doctor is right*, he thought. *If God had not wanted us to use this technique, He would not have allowed us to understand it.*

It is temptation from the devil.

The urge to smile was almost overwhelming. *You'll keep us humble, boy*, he thought, and liked that. It was the missing detail. He sighed and let himself sink back into sleep. He wouldn't hold himself apart from the boy any longer. Together they would make a perfect team.

Together, they would conquer the world and all its minions.

Together, they would convince the multitude that they were the son of God.

Night Owl

Carole Nelson Douglas

I should not be such a fool as to pray that one little bit of hell should be remitted, one consequence altered either of others' mistakes or of our own

—Athens, June 1850

"They say she mesmerized the owl, but that was quite impossible, of course."

"Mesmerized?" Dr. Chimera repeated the word in that unnerving vocal blend of tenor and contralto that sounded vaguely computer-generated. Yet there was nothing of the automaton about the slight Asian figure who sat as graceful as a Quan-Yin carving in a chair in Wilhelm Wolfe's ultra-modern office at Nucore.

The woman from social services frowned, as if gathering thoughts that kept unraveling. "It was a very young owl. An owlet, I suppose. She picked it up after it fell from its nest in the Parthenon, calmed it, and put it in her pocket. Very unlike her, but it went home with her to England, became a pet. She wept when it died on the eve of her fateful departure for Scutari. And, much later, she kept cats."

"So she called it Athena because she found it in Athens?" Dr. Chimera's facial expression of polite interest had smoothed into a mask of meditation.

"She called it Athena, I imagine, because she had been named after a city herself, and she also had been given quite an extensive classical education, for a woman of her time."

"That was the point, wasn't it?" Dr. Chimera sounded melancholy, and perhaps a bit rebuking. "She was a woman far ahead of her time."

"So far ahead that she nearly had a breakdown in Athens. She feared she was 'rapidly approaching the state of madness when dreams become realities.' That was before she found her special place in life and the world three years later. She suffered before she succeeded."

The social services woman sighed. Her name was Mavis Rankin, and the last time she had come here she had been passionate rather than distracted. Like so many social service workers she was in her middle years, well groomed but simply attired, not unlike the dead woman she discussed. Except that Mavis Rankin would never have kept an owl. Or have named it Athena.

Chimera sighed in turn. This was the first postmortem their procedure had required. A melancholy matter, and one that shook the project to its secret foundations.

Not only an owl had died, long ago. Or a woman, a good long while after that, but still long ago. A child had also died, not long ago. And that was a problem.

> *Her influence on people's minds and her curiosity in getting into varieties of minds is insatiable. After she has got inside, they generally cease to have any interest for her*
> —Parthenope, England, 1853

Only a few weeks ago Mavis Rankin had sat in this same chair, facing Wolfe's intimidating desk and the banks of windows at his back.

She had been just as nervous and a little angry.

Righteous anger, some would have called it. Dr. Chimera, after long study of all things Zen, had concluded that anger— in any of its one hundred and one variations—was a wrongful waste.

Wilhelm Wolfe had become angry too. "Blackmail." He had thrown the word out like a crumpled ball of wastepaper.

Blessed are the righteous, for they shall never retreat.

"I prefer to think of it as . . . tithing." Mavis Rankin firmly balanced her bulky purse on her thighs like a renegade toddler.

"Tithing?" As a successful businessman, Wolfe was a master of succinct dismissal via scathing repetition.

The echo only straightened Mavis Rankin's spine, already erect. This woman who had not bothered to reverse the inroads of aging had the appearance of a shopworn fairy godmother.

"Tithing," she repeated as sharply. "Look at this place! Everything sleek, ordered, reeking of technology and profitability. You offer a . . . discreet service, Mr. Wolfe. Nucore is merely a cutting-edge Make-a-Wish Foundation, only you charge for your transformations. I'm simply suggesting that you offer the world that knows so little of your advances some small benefit. A charity case, you could call it. One child."

"There is more at stake than donating what you call our 'services,' " Wolfe said.

At that point, Dr. Chimera's serene attention had seemed to sharpen. The blended souls sharing one pair of ageless dark eyes looked long into Mavis Rankin's angry, pleading gaze. She was used to fighting impossible odds, and that often made her impossible to deal with.

"The point Wilhelm is making is that your . . . client cannot make a choice on her own. We risk violating a soul."

"A soul that is locked into a tormenting solitary confinement beyond the ken of all your 'advanced' scientific minds!"

Mavis clutched the purse's latch and clicked it open. Then shut. Then open again, unaware that the catch was chattering like an old-time telegraph.

"You interpret this child's actions as torment," Chimera went on thoughtfully. "You cannot be sure how she herself perceives the state of her soul or of the world around her."

"I can be sure how her perceptions manifest themselves."

The brass latch stopped stuttering as it was wrenched open. Mavis Rankin drew out a portfolio of slippery color photographs of exquisite clarity and detail, and leaned forward to fan them on the desk's empty surface like a deck of gigantic, graphic playing cards.

The man winced away from the images revealed, but Dr. Chimera, that unearthly meld of man and woman, remained unflinching. "I do not see how another personality could repair what even today our best diagnosticians don't know how to define."

"She is verbal. And shows streaks of genius. We have had some luck with overstimulating those of her senses that seem dampened; that's where the self-multilation comes from. An urge to feel at any cost. She is obsessively fascinated by order, of course, but her musical and mathematical abilities often show a remarkable clarity."

"I can't see it." Wolfe spun his chair to face the jagged skyline of rooftops beyond his windows. "What would such a blending do to a resurrected personality? You are condemning it to that same 'solitary confinement' your client faces. Sanity sequestered in a living shell of unreason."

"No." Mavis Rankin's fierce conviction made Wolfe's chair spin back to the room as if automated. "I am proposing to send in a teacher. An interior Annie Sullivan."

"Helen Keller was deaf and blind and therefore mute, but her mind was normal, even extraordinary."

"But the young Helen Keller, unable to communicate, didn't act like what she was. She acted like a wild animal. Annie Sullivan had to tame her."

"And it nearly killed Sullivan," Dr. Chimera said.

"*This* Annie Sullivan is already dead! And you said there was a brief time to reverse the . . . importation. Three weeks, no?"

"Can you imagine what mayhem can be done to a mind in three weeks, or to two minds?" Wolfe shook his head.

But Dr. Chimera frowned. The expression was not so much a furrow as a slight tensing of the smooth skin above the bridge of the nose, the site where the third eye was said to reside. "Most of our clients are enhanced by the blending. They describe higher energy, clearer visions."

"Exactly!" Mavis swept the photos of the mutilated hands back into the folder in her purse. "It is not enough to try to reach these children from the outside. We must begin within. This girl is twelve, prepubescent. She is able to communicate well for an autistic person. She speaks in sentences. She draws."

"And the obsessions? The rages?"

She regarded Wilhelm Wolfe wearily. "They are there. The frustrated symptoms of a mind trying to tell the deaf, blind, and senseless beings we 'normals' all are how to reach it." She sat back, her arguments, even her anger, exhausted at last. "And then there's the child's name."

Dr. Chimera nodded, noncommittal. They always seemed that way because conflicting emotions so seldom ruffled their placid surface. "Athena. Greek goddess of wisdom and war. Birthed from her father Zeus's head after a colossal headache. Symbolized by the owl."

"Since we are talking about the ancients," Wilhelm Wolfe conceded with a trace of humor, "I suppose we could consider that an omen."

"An omen of good fortune," Mavis Rankin corrected, aware she had won, at last.

Dr. Chimera said nothing, but then, they never spoke unnecessarily.

I never saw a mind so continuously concen-
trated on her work. Is it a mind that belonged
to some other planet? . . . For it does not seem
adapted to the human frame, though it has
forced that frame to obedience.
    —Mai Smith, Scutari, 1853

Athena was thin, with underdeveloped muscles, but walked without aid. She reminded Wilhelm Wolfe of an owl, with her eyes behind enormous magnifying lenses, her thin white face fading into a passive chin. She spoke her greetings quite clearly, though with an even, mechanical emphasis on each word that betrayed her many mental and physical challenges.

She wore loose slacks, rather like Chimera, and a knit shirt, both pale gray.

"She is used to being examined for the glasses," Mavis Rankin explained.

Wolfe nodded, hoping the procedure would not distress the subject. He still had reservations, even though Athena had been an abandoned child and had no known family to approve or disapprove of what they were about to do.

"You have the . . . material?" Mavis still clutched the same large awkward brown purse. At his nod, she added, "May I ask how—?"

"We are well-financed international tomb-robbers and museum knock-off artists," Wolfe answered wryly. "DNA of even long-deceased persons can linger on intimate possessions. Glasses, for instance." He nodded at Athena, who was staring past him, past his desk, past her own scarred fingers, to a mutating rainbow in a bottle, some executive toy he had been given by some forgotten client long before Nucore existed.

"The autistic child is isolated, utterly alone, asocial." Mavis recited the pathology almost as mechanically as Athena spoke. "This woman was recognized the world over for her compassion, her driving need to minister to thousands, to affect the well-being of millions, of so many in her own century and many more beyond it."

"You think she can light the lamp of reason in one grievously disordered mind?"

"I hope so, Mr. Wolfe. That is all we can do in our field: hope."

"In this case, that's all we can do in our field too. Come. Dr. Chimera is waiting for us."

> *She is much of an enigma, perhaps a creature of another race, so high, mighty and angelic, doing things by impulse and some divine inspiration. . . .*
>
> —Mrs. Elizabeth Gaskell,
> author of *Cranford*, 1854

They had feared an explosion during the procedure. New experiences fanned the outbreaks of fear and rage. But the procedure room was quiet, carpeted, and the client was unrestrained. They tensed when Dr. Chimera bent near Athena's face and said that her glasses would have to be removed, gently doing so. The doctor's voice was smoother than any media announcer's. Its odd blend of tenor and contralto seemed to soothe the savage beast that prowled the autistic soul.

Taping her eyelids open took only an instant, then the helmet was lowered over her thin, pale face. The machine hummed, and clicked; the bizarre helmet obscured the girl's head as thoroughly as a mask of Greek tragedy.

Mavis Rankin's hoarded breath finally leaked from her lungs like a silent whistle, taking so long she thought she might faint.

Then the contraption was lifted away. Athena's head drooped on her neck, a white peony blossom weighted down by rain. Chimera led her to the sleep chamber for the many hours of rest required while the alien DNA reconstituted the memories and personality of another person within the enigmatic chambered nautilus of Athena's brain.

Back in his office, Wolfe offered Mavis a glass of wine.

"White," she answered his question, thinking of Athena's papery skin. Athena was the institute's prize pupil. No autistic child had accomplished so much. If this union proved disastrous, the ground lost might prove unrecoverable. "What do I do now?"

"Wait until she wakes, observe, then take her . . . home—?"

"We have a combination residence and school."

"Take her there and observe some more."

"Will . . . the new personality manifest itself immediately? Directly?"

"It depends on how easily that personality can work through the medium of a disordered, or rather, overordered brain. It's not as if the person is actually there, inside Athena, in miniature. This process is a recombination of sorts. The two minds will twine in a symbiotic relationship, and we may never quite be sure which vine is in a growth spurt at the moment. Ideally, the combination should be seamless, as you see in Dr. Chimera."

"But . . . they . . . were a long and happily married couple. Surely some symbiosis was already in place."

"You're right about that!" Wolfe smiled and leaned back in his executive chair, which did all sorts of contortions to accommodate his restless body. He stared into his goblet of red wine. "I must admit that Dr. Chimera themselves are our most successful operation. And, of course, we don't often have clients who mix genders. Most are too leery to add the battle of the sexes to their already challenged psyches."

"That's why I picked Athena's . . . mentor so carefully. A mature woman who lived to a great age, who saw the carnage of her violent century, but also eased its effects."

"Are you sure that a person exposed to such conditions is the best blend for Athena?"

Mavis frowned. "I believe the autistic person sees and feels more horror than we can imagine. I'm hoping that introducing Athena to someone who has seen similar desolation and not only survived it, but acted to end it, will be the perfect partnership."

Wolfe sipped the bloody wine.

"I hope you're right. In this case, you're the doctor."

> *I have felt here the suspension of all my faculties, I could not write, could not read. . . .*
> —Karnak, on the Nile, March 1850

Mavis took the sleepy, docile child back to the institute in a closed car driven by a staff assistant. Treating autistic children involved total environmental stimulus control. Too much was happening, or not happening inside them; the trick was to tease them into responding to the external world.

Now, who-knows-what was happening inside Athena. Mavis admitted to herself that this blended DNA scheme could be the worst thing that could happen to the child.

Because the young girl had progressed so well for her condition, no signs of dawning "normalcy" showed themselves in the first twenty-four hours.

But the twenty-fifth hour . . .

"Miss Rankin, come quickly!"

She had taken a room in the institute, sleeping on-site, expecting whatever might happen. "Is it Athena?" she asked the young therapist who summoned her from breakfast. "Is she all right?"

"Quite right. Still drawing those endless symbols. But they've changed suddenly." The young woman walked ahead, almost running, the long brown tail down her lab-coated back undulating like a braided serpent. "Maybe it's a result of the off-site treatment."

That was what Mavis had told the staff: Athena had been taken off-site for a new treatment.

The institute offered day rooms with complete temperature, light, sound, odor, and textural control. Any autistic client, whether hypo- or hypersensitive in any of the five senses, or even if one of the "white noise" cases that fell in between the two extremes, could live and work in a hothouse environment designed to under- or overstimulate each one's uniquely isolated brain and body.

Athena sat alone in a twilight room, her head in its short, unstylish institutional haircut bent over the long rolls of butcher paper she favored, her right hand drawing rank after rank of arcane symbols.

This was nothing new, and Mavis told the staff member that.

"But . . . it's *what* she's drawing." The aide squatted excitedly beside the table, where the already used paper curled into a pile, and pulled up a handful.

Athena worked on, in the utter, unrelieved oblivion of autism.

Mavis blinked at the symbols on the paper. They were no longer nonsensical, but they weren't ordinary writing or drawing either. "I've seen the like before."

Mavis found her eyes dwelling on the crude stick figure of a bird, an outline of an eye, and found herself becoming excited. As arcane as these pictographs were, several repeated, like words in a sentence.

"Or course you have," said the therapist, who lacked Mavis's forbidden knowledge and thus was not blinded by the obvious. "They're Egyptian whatchamacallits. You know, monument writing."

"Hieroglyphs. But . . . how?"

"You mean that we don't let the patients see anything unusual that might frighten or obsess them. Perhaps something she saw at the off-site treatment. They might not be as careful as the institute. A print of a pyramid mural or something?"

Mavis found her hand crushing paper until it crackled. "Did they mix up the material, the fools?"

"Material?"

Mavis shook her attention back to Athena. They were tomb-raiders, Wolfe had said quite blithely. Had the DNA been mislabeled? Was Athena . . . infected by some ancient royal ninny?

First she would call Nucore. Then she would call the science museum to find someone who could read hieroglyphs. And then she would order more detailed biographies. It was always possible that *she* had seen Egypt as well as Europe.

> *She takes up one thing at a time and bends her whole soul to that. Music it was once . . . the scientific part. Then again the study of the truth as disguised in the myths and hieroglyphics of the Egyptian religion took hold of her . . . for a year and a half in Egypt and Athens she was absorbed in this.*
>
> —Mrs. Gaskell, 1854

"*The Egyptian Book of the Dead*?" Wilhelm Wolfe sounded flabbergasted over the comline, but he wore the same urbane businessman guise he always presented on the vid. "No, there's been no mistake in collecting the material. Besides, none of our clients has quite dared to delve such an ancient mind . . . yet. I would suggest you investigate your subject further."

Mavis snapped off the communicator. She had already done so, first relying on Disney InfoEnterNet, the dominant Web merchant. She had found only the same biographical material she had already accessed, and had grown so disturbed, and desperate, that she had ordered actual books: outdated, worn, yellowing, dingy books. They sat in stacks at the foot of her bed like dirty laundry.

Some books had broken spines, the aged, frail cheesecloth

bindings showing through like bits of the crinoline that supported the long, bell-shaped skirts the women of that time wore. It was hard to imagine *her* doing what she had done in that impeding getup. Engravings and photographs (Mavis was amazed that photography was available then) were all black and white, or shades of gray, rather.

She surprised herself. Mavis had gathered biographical data illustrated by photographs taken near the end of the woman's long, even interminable lifeline, in which she looked like a White Widow of Windsor with her perpetually present ivory-colored scarf framing wings of still-dark hair parted severely in the middle, a fashion retained from her early-nineteenth-century girlhood. Her plump face was almost orientally inscrutable in its deceptive youthfulness, reminding Mavis of Dr. Chimera's androgynous serenity. Yet she had made her most dramatic mark in mid-life.

The books dwelled more on her early experiences than the information Mavis had found on the D'Net, and the photographs and sketches of her even then revealed a remarkably attractive woman. Mavis was shocked to see this elderly Queen Victoria doppelganger depicted as a lovely, delicate creature of leisure in her first three decades, a woman who had refused three impressive suitors to remain single and thus change history.

Perhaps one defining engraving had fixed her in the popular mind: a lone woman, among all those ragged and suffering men, making her rounds of four miles of corridor, bearing an odd glowing artifact like the bellows of a small, upended concertina.

By the light of that primitive flare, her shadow had fallen upon the fallen, and her legend had begun, inspiring the lines of Longfellow:

> *And slow, as in a dream of bliss*
> *The speechless sufferer turns to kiss*

Her shadow, as it falls
Upon the darkening walls.

– – – –

Theirs not to reason why,
Theirs but to do and die . . .
—Alfred, Lord Tennyson, 1854
The Charge of the Light Brigade at Balaclave

"Quick! Outside!"

The aide's hysterical call preceded her apparition in the doorway.

Mavis let the seductive book fall shut on the old-fashioned words. "Athena?"

The sharp, strong nod of the aide's pigtailed head said it all.

They reached the activity yard, finding the other residents flocking together in shock under the shade of an arbor.

Sunlight fell on the gravel walks and plantings, the sand-box and the bright geography of children's swing sets. Repetitive motion could soothe their restless, sequestered minds, and inexpensive musical instruments lay everywhere, another toy that acted as therapy.

Athena alone moved, her arm swinging up and down, her hand clutching a plastic flute.

Mavis paused, like the rest of them, confused.

"At least it's not head-banging. The motion, the repetitiveness—"

"Not how . . . what!" the aide answered with a shudder in the bright sunlight.

Mavis approached her charge, seeing how the sun's rays glinted off the short thick strands of her red-gold hair, making it into a corona.

The flute's end had shattered on the concrete of the sidewalk, but still it rose and fell like a hammer, in meticulous rhythm, not musical but mechanical.

And as Mavis neared the scene, she saw the purpose of the purposeless movement.

Ants. Dozens and hundreds of ants. Smashed. Crushed into powder, in such numbers that their brown corpses formed a thick rivulet like long-dried blood across the sidewalk.

A few straggler ants lurched around the shambles of their sandy hill, but the battered red plastic piston crushed even them, every one, in its relentless beat. Mavis had never seen such a slaughter.

Athena's enormous eyes looked up, through the magnifying lenses of her glasses. She said but one word.

"Vermin."

> *I will send you a picture of my caravanserai, into which beasts come in and out. Indeed the vermin might, if they had but "unity of purpose," carry off the four miles of beds on their back.*
>
> —Florence at Scutari, 1855

Here at last was a manifestation of the added personality, if an unpleasant one.

Mavis Rankin had never thought of her heroine as a pest exterminator, but a closer study of her life and work revealed that the humanitarian mercies the world celebrated were, in fact, a minor if dramatic highlight of her ninety years.

Mavis was forced to report to Dr. Chimera and Wilhelm Wolfe.

"History has misrepresented her," she told them.

"History has misrepresented everyone," Wolfe responded. "That is what makes this project so fascinating, and dangerous."

"I'm puzzled that so little of the added personality has shown itself." Mavis adjusted her large purse on her lap.

"And you are worried," Dr. Chimera added.

"Worried? How?"

The slender shoulders shrugged. "The first outward man-ifestation was violence of a sort. An approved violence in our society, true, but our fear of the non-'normal' mind has al-ways been that it might direct its disorder in our direction someday. Autistic people may frighten us, but they harm themselves."

"Exactly! I wanted Athena to see beyond her imprisoned self, to know compassion, to learn empathy for others."

"Perhaps she has." Wolfe had templed his hands beneath his chin, an oddly Asian posture for one of his temperament. "Perhaps passion precedes compassion. What else have you learned about the imported personality?"

"She really wasn't anything like I expected her to be. Her time in the war zone was the shortest period of her life, though it redirected everything that came after. I had no idea that Crimean fever nearly killed her, and she became bedrid-den afterward, literally lived, worked, and wrote from her bed for the last fifty years of her life. She had great influence, of course, thanks to her sanctified position in the popular mind and her innate gifts as a statistician and politician. She rev-olutionized contemporary thinking, was considered one of the three people to most benefit humanity in the nineteenth century. But this sequestered life was an odd resolution for a woman who had taken such an active and previously unheard-of role in the war. She was tireless. Barely slept for month after month, year after year, mostly writing letters outlining needs and seeking support. She found the situation in the Bosporus 'calamity unparalleled,' and she had injected herself into it, having no idea what kind of hell to expect. It was worse than hell itself. Four miles of men in beds, sur-rounded by filth, often dying within ten minutes of having a limb amputated.

"And even before the war, before she was finally allowed—

or finally forced her family to allow her—to do at age thirty-three what she had always yearned to do . . ."

"Yes?" Dr. Chimera urged, as if he/she expected her next conclusions.

"She was . . . quite obsessive. Repeatedly mentioned a secret 'vice' of daydreaming to escape the strictures of her comfortable aristocratic family's life: dinner parties and teas, the London social season, genteel sight-seeing abroad, changing one gracious residence for another with the various seasons, and always being 'in season' for the marriage market. She was educated by her father in three languages, mathematics, and music. She even had a literary bent, once started a novel before she was permitted to work in her true calling. The three exceptional and prominent suitors she turned down remained her lifelong devotees. Yet she was always tormented by her frantic ambitions to do something more, something almost a religious calling."

Mavis paused and gathered the leather straps of her handbag into her hands, as if using the reins on some invisible horse that was trying to carry her where she didn't want to go. "And . . . and her letters and diary mentioned thoughts of suicide. Despair. Often."

Wolfe nodded. "Dark undercurrents ripple through every success story. So the public image is often a gloss."

"What does this mean for Athena? Will this unilluminated side of the sainted 'Lady with the Lamp' worsen her condition? Should we . . . extract . . . Florence Nightingale from her psyche? Have I made a terrible mistake?"

"You could have." Dr. Chimera's voice was calm and soothing, which did nothing to undercut his diagnosis.

"Those dead ants." Mavis shuddered. "Those slaughtered ants."

"Sacrificed to the necessity of sanitation," Wilhelm Wolfe, the pragmatist, corrected her. "Didn't Florence Nightingale have to fight filth as well as disease?"

"Yes, as a matter of fact." Mavis nodded as she went on. "We think of her with her lamp and that damned shadow passing like an Angel of Life through the vast and miserable battlefield hospital, the world's first nurse who was not considered a debased drab or a drudge because she would tend men's wounded bodies.

"But nursing was the least of it. The filth, the infestation . . . first she had to organize her nurses into cleaning women and laundresses, become a supply sergeant and a hospital kitchen impresario. The real lamp that drove her was not the Turkish one she carried through the wards, but the one in the room that never went out night after night while she bullied and begged her supporters in England for assistance. Her ink often froze in the well that cold winter. But what she achieved . . . she anticipated the breakthrough move in medicine to sterile surgery conditions; she wrote the book on preventative medicine and sanitary care; she, with no medical training."

Dr. Chimera smiled without comment as she paused for breath, and Mavis realized she was beginning to sound like a disciple. She unleashed her anxieties again.

"The conditions of the war in the Crimea, the constant contention with a dubious male command more interested in victory, promotion, and politics than the lives of its soldiers, they are more than any Victorian lady was reared to face, much less conquer. I didn't realize that it would take such a fierce personality to achieve it. Athena's condition makes her fierce enough. We must end the experiment."

"There is time yet." Dr. Chimera focused on the view beyond the windows. "All personalities have their surprises. Why shouldn't a melding of personalities be as unpredictable."

"But Athena was unpredictably predictable before! The hopeless spell of autism we know how to deal with."

"The benign neglect of the military hospital at Scutari, you mean," Wolfe put in.

"Better than a truly unpredictable outcome!"

"Perhaps not." Dr. Chimera rose and came to Mavis's side. "May we?"

Despite the politeness, the doctor's communal identity still shocked Mavis. Dr. Chimera gestured to the capacious bag on her lap, and she mutely surrendered its contents: the books on the life of Florence Nightingale. "Leave these with us for study. Perhaps you should go and confront your battlefield. Your patient may need you."

She opened her mouth to object, but said nothing. There was time yet, after all, to reverse everything. And no real harm had been done. Except to ants.

> *This want of love for individuals becomes a gift and a very rare one, if one take it in conjunction with her intense love for the race, her utter unselfishness in serving and ministering. . . .*
>
> —Mrs. Gaskell, 1854

"How is she doing?" Mavis asked the aide.

Athena was again in the recreational area, off by herself, bent over something.

"She isn't sleeping. She writes those hieroglyphics constantly."

"Nothing different in the pattern?"

"Well . . ." The aide opened her case file and extracted a single sheet of paper. "There was suddenly a sentence."

Mavis read the words, "I would like to see Athens again," sandwiched between the glyphs of a bird and an eye.

"This is pretty significant!"

"But it doesn't mean anything."

"Not to you. It might mean something to . . . other people." She glanced to the young girl in her blue jeans and plain blue T-shirt. What catchphrases would the autistic personality flaunt? "What is she doing? That concentration . . . she's not mutilating her hands again?"

"It's been so long—" The aide's face went white. "Oh, no!"

Mavis was already running toward Athena. If Florence Nightingale, sheltered Victorian lady, could face men whose skin had worn off their backs, she could handle superficial cuts.

"Athena?"

The girl looked up, wide-eyed as always.

Mavis spotted a blotch of red on her hand, and her heart seized. The self-mutilation had stopped before the experiment. Now it was back. No time to be lost. Back to Nucore.

"What is it?"

Athena's hands opened, slowly, like a time-lapse blossom on film.

"It snapped at me," she said. "Sometimes I snap at people, but it snapped at me."

Feathers as fine as dandelion thistle filled Athena's hands. A baby bird, looking bald, blinked eyes as black as onyx. It pecked Athena's thumb.

"It's just hungry," Mavis said. "It didn't mean to hurt you."

Athena looked up again. "I know. Can I feed it?" She frowned, the expression that usually signaled exit into an autistic trance. Instead she asked another question. "Do you think it would eat ants?"

> *My present life is a suicide. Slowly, I have opened my eyes to the fact that I cannot now deliver myself from the habit of dreaming, which, like gin drinking, is eating out my vital strength . . . Why, oh my God, can I not*

*be satisfied with the life that satisfies so many
people?*

—Florence at Embley,
December 31, 1850

"It's incredible." Mavis set her purse on the floor beside her chair and glanced from Wilhelm Wolfe to Dr. Chimera.

"Athena?" they asked in unison.

"Maybe. Maybe not. She is devoted to nursing the bird. A baby robin she found. She wants to visit foreign lands, she says. She has embraced the music therapy for the first time, and shows talent verging on genius. She's equally obsessed with numbers."

Dr. Chimera nodded. "Music and mathematics. The left brain will not be denied, no matter the circumstances. These are the fields in which the severely mentally challenged excel. The so-called idiot savants."

"Maybe we are all idiot savants," Mavis said grimly. "I sense that Athena as I knew her has . . . died, yet I think that Athena has a chance at a normal life now. An abnormal normal life, but—"

"Don't we all have that?" Dr. Chimera suggested with an oh-so-inscrutable smile.

"And you know what part of Florence Nightingale is manifesting itself in her?"

"No, tell us," Dr. Chimera urged.

"It's the predictable life she would have, could have, lived. Devoted to study, compassionate only on the individual level. Unlikely to change the world. It's as if Florence had a chance to be ordinary, no longer driven by her need to minister to the world."

Wilhelm Wolfe cleared his throat. "And as if Athena has a chance to be ordinarily extraordinary. No longer driven by her need to escape the world."

"For her condition, yes. For Florence, the ordinary was death. For Athena, the ordinary is life." Mavis sighed. "It wasn't what I expected."

"Neither was Florence Nightingale." Dr. Chimera looked pleased.

"Neither," Mavis admitted, "was Athena."

"Perhaps," Dr. Chimera said, "that is the point."

> *How one feels that the more real presence in the room is the invisible presence which hovers around the death-bed and that we are only ghosts, who have put on form for a moment, and shall put it off, almost before we have time to wind up our watch.*
>
> —Florence's letter to
> Hilary Bonham Carter, 1845

Who Am a Passer By

Gary A. Braunbeck

I mourn not that the desolate
Are happier, sweet, than I,
But that you sorrow for my fate
Who am a passer by.
> —Edgar Allan Poe, "To ——"

1

We are in Richmond, Virginia, and we can't remember your mother. She was an actress. She was beautiful, they say. No one remembers your father. Of him nothing is written, spoken, chiseled into stone, and so, we believe, it is "natural" that you do not remember him. But your mother carried you here to the city of Richmond in her arms. She languished through the sweltering months of summer. The play moved on to Charleston without her. Her pain increased daily. The coughing from the attic room, the groans, the sudden shrieks. The women muffled your ears against them. You were bad, a bad boy, bad little boy. She died. You can't remember her face, her touch, her smell, her voice, all of which were beautiful, they say. They tell you/us this even today, the few whose descendants knew her those last months. Women, young women once, not even children then, old women now. You remind them of her, for they have photographs of her, her beauty and radiance, kept all these years in dusty, aged frames, the glass now discolored with time. If only they could remind you of her. We are Edgar Poe the poet, author of "The Raven." In a few minutes we will recite that beloved, that "magnificent and profound" poem to the literary citizens of Richmond, Virginia. Afterward, we will describe how you actually composed the poem, the rational procedures by which you constructed it, and they will be amazed. You too will be amazed at this new account of your ingenuity and self-sufficiency, your mastery of the intricacies and logic of language and emotion. And your mother would be amazed too, had she lived to see it, hear it, watch you mystify them by the comical means of demystification, enchant them by means of disenchantment, bewilder them with your clarity. They will feel privileged and released, for you will have demonstrated how any one of them could have written your beloved poem himself, had he merely been willing to apply himself to the task. But you, of course, have been the only one willing to apply himself to the task, and that is the reason the poem is yours, you are its author, you are Edgar Poe the poet. Anyone could be Edgar Poe the poet, anyone, were he merely willing to apply himself to the task. (That is one of the reasons why you are now we.) You believe that, and when you politely excuse yourself and depart from the company of these literary ladies and gentlemen of Richmond, Virginia, they will believe it too. It will give them a certain relief. How wonderful, they will each separately think, to know that you could be Edgar Poe the poet if you merely applied yourself to the task. And how wonderful, they will each separately think, to be free not to apply yourself to the task! They will each accept one more glass of sherry and, in your absence, will admire your elegant yet forceful presence upon the stage, your charm and lucidity in private conversation, your erudition, your "profound and tender" eyes, your "musical" voice, all quite as if each person in the room were separately admiring his own presence upon the stage, his own charm, lucidity, erudition, eyes, voice. They will each separately admire your irresistibly beautiful mind. Your fame. Your position among men. Your role with women. Your exotic past. Your miraculous resurrection in our new body. Then we will read to them a new poem, this one even more profound (in our eyes) than "The Raven." And again that part of us that is you will mourn your dead mother, and that part of us which is me will mourn the fate of my mother who, though not dead, seems nonetheless lost to me/us.

An image comes to our mind: that of a man no longer young but far from old, who walks the halls of one of the astoundingly large, shiny buildings you have seen since your rebirth. He is dressed in grey coveralls. He wears heavy work boots. He pushes a cleaning cart which holds, among other items, a mop and bucket.

And now, as we look upon that still figure, the me of twenty days past, as we look down through the darkening tunnel of four-hundred-and-eighty hours, we cannot smile. He fills us with regret. He embarrasses me/us. I/we regret the things he did, and the things he did not do. I/we blush at his desires; I/we cannot share his dreams. The child may be father to the man, but who is to insist that we must love the children we/I/you once were? And do we wish to remain as one within his body? That decision must be made soon.

How to describe him?

His name was Peter Krantz. He was thirty-six years old, a high school graduate who never made it into college, despite being dubbed "extremely bright" by many of his teachers. He wanted to be several things in his short life—musician, actor, artist, writer—but his desire to be creative far exceeded his talent for creation. So he worked as a janitor, dreaming of the day he might do something worthwhile with his life, create something fine and true and majestic for which the world would remember him, and then, perhaps, he might be able to take his mother from that depressing nursing home where she was now living out the remainder of her days, sometimes lucid, sometimes not.

And then came that afternoon he was approached by a pair of security guards and asked to accompany them to one of the upstairs offices. The man whose name was written on the gold plaque on the front of the building wished to speak with him.

"Have I done something wrong?" he asked the guards.

"No, no, not at all, Peter. It's just that Mr. Blackmore wants to ask you something."

So he went along with them, riding the private elevator to the very, very top floor, where all the carpeting was plush and the doors were glass and the walls hand-rubbed polished oak. It was a world where he felt he had no place—beyond his cleaning duties. He was escorted into a magnificent office by a lovely younger red-haired woman who introduced her-self to him as Antonia and inquired if he would like anything to drink. He thanked her, excited by the smell of her perfume and embarrassed by that excitement (he'd never been very good with women, let alone ones this lovely and alluring) and asked her for a soft drink. She smiled at him a smile of pearls and said she'd be right back.

He sat down on the thick cushion of a leather wing-backed chair and waited for Mr. Blackmore to speak with him.

The soft drink arrived. Antonia smiled at him again as if he might come to mean something to her (though he knew he was only fantasizing), then Mr. Blackmore entered and Peter's life was mere hours away from no longer being mine but being ours.

2

We have been seated on a straight-backed chair in the center of the stage. A few feet in front of us, Dr. Woolsey, dean of

the university, reads at the lectern from his prepared intro-
ductory speech. We watch his broad back, his speckled hands,
his rising fluff of white hair. The thick tube of fat at the base
of his skull contracts and hardens, and he lifts his gaze to the
heavens so as more adequately to praise the poet Edgar Poe
author of "The Raven." You. Me. Us. Who cannot remember your mother. In your/our dreams she appears with her
back to you, her arms outstretched before her. She ignores
your call of *Mother! Mother! It is I, Edgar Poe the poet!* But
she does not flee or otherwise remove herself from you. She
stands there in a white dress, as if at a lectern, with her arms
outstretched, her gaze lifted heavenward, as if more adequately to praise her son, or as if to pray for permission for
him to join her. For without permission you/we cannot join
her; you may not move your feet, you may not take a single
step toward her. It is as if you are bad, a bad boy, bad little
boy. That is how she appears in your dreams of her and how
you also appear there. A moribund tableau vivant, a frieze cut
in a wall of darkness. Not a conscious memory, though. For
when, awake, you/we try to remember your mother, as you/
we do now, you remember nothing, and no mind can picture
nothing, and so you remember Mr. Allan and the tobacco
warehouses, the canal alongside the James River, your cousin
Virginia and her mother. You recall your room at the college
in Charlottesville, the parade ground at West Point, and then
your half-empty bottle of Madeira on the spindly table off-
stage right. You remember your/our white handkerchief,
slightly spotted with the wine wiped from your/our chin, now
tucked neatly into our breast pocket to hide the purple stains
from view of the audience, who can see us clearly up here
stage center. Someone in that audience is coughing, nervous,
repeated coughs coming from her throat, habitual and not
the consequence or sign of illness. It will have a slight negative effect on our recitation, for, unless we can pick up the
rhythm, her pattern of coughing will succeed in filling the
spaces while we are silent between stanzas or when we pause
momentarily for dramatic effect, and it may have the effect

of silencing us completely. We listen closely for the pattern of her coughs, and, surreptitiously, we hope, slip our watch from our vest pocket and study its face, while Dean Woolsey continues his lengthy introduction of the poet Edgar Poe and the unseen woman coughs, then coughs again, and, after thirty-two seconds, yet again. We calculate that if we commence reciting the poem seventeen seconds after a given cough, she will cough again in the middle of the third line and after that at the middle of every twelfth line (the fifteenth, twenty-seventh, thirty-ninth, etc.) and at the end of every twelfth line from the beginning (the twelfth, twenty-fourth, thirty-sixth, etc.). This particular spacing will minimize the effect of her coughing, will make it only slightly negative. But negative just the same, for it means that we will have to run each of those twelfth end-stopped lines rapidly into the following line, which will blur our every sixth rhyme and somewhat diminish the dramatic structure of the poem. As for its effect on the raven's harsh refrain, we can only hope that the audience is sufficiently familiar with the poem to hear with its collective ear the croak of Nevermore in the very coughing of the woman, as it were, as if you/we Edgar Poe the poet said nothing, as if we merely mouthed the words for the raven, for the unseen woman in the audience coughing, for the woman in your dream, for your/our mother dying in an attic room in Richmond, Virginia, for our/my mother, languishing in a nursing home in Cedar Hill, Ohio, and yet again for your/our mother, whose consumptive cough and groans and finally her very shrieks are muffled into silence by the women in the kitchen wrapping your head with a scarf so that you cannot hear your mother dying, will not remember this awful time in your life, and will not remember your mother.

And yet again, we find ourselves staring at the man I was before there was a we.

3

The first thing Mr. Blackmore did after entering the office was shake Peter's hand and assure him that his job was not in jeopardy. The second thing he did was reach into his desk drawer and remove a small stack of papers, which he then handed to Peter.

Peter stared at them. "What's this?"

"It's a security agreement. The language is very complicated but the essence of it is this: Nothing that we discuss in this office can ever be repeated to anyone, ever. There would be dire consequences for everyone involved if you were to talk about this."

"I . . . I don't know, sir, I mean, it's not that I don't trust you or anything like that—"

Blackmore held up a hand, silencing Peter. "I know it all seems rather melodramatic, and for that I apologize, but the fact of the matter is that both of us—and perhaps even humankind itself—stand to gain a great deal. I can't say anything more specific until you sign that document Peter, but I can add this: Even if you refuse to participate in what I will tell you about, I will pay you fifty thousand dollars simply for listening to the offer." He sat down, folded his hands, and leaned toward Peter, lowering his voice so that it resembled that of a concerned friend. "I know that your financial situation is a bit shaky, Peter, with what you're paid as a member of the janitorial staff, and I also know that you're personally covering the expenses that Medicare doesn't pay for your mother's care at the nursing home."

Peter started to say something, but once again there was Blackmore's hand. "I know, I know, believe me. Yes, I've had you thoroughly checked out. A man in my position has the means to do that. For the record, what was handed to me was an in-depth report on a man with solid, decent character; a bit of a loner, perhaps—or maybe just lonely—but a good man. One who can be trusted. One who spends perhaps a bit too much time in solitary pursuits—reading, listening to music, going to movies—but also a man of above-average intelligence . . . Which is a bit confusing, considering the line of work you've chosen for yourself."

"Mom always said that I never really realized my potential."

"That doesn't make you a failure, Peter."

"It'd be nice to believe that, sir."

"Believe it. Look, you've got nothing to lose here. Say no, and you still keep your job and will have fifty thousand dollars deposited in your bank account by the end of the day. Say yes, and I will pay you one million dollars."

One million dollars.

Peter couldn't believe what he was hearing. He asked Blackmore to repeat what he just said, and the man did.

"I'm not screwing around here, Peter. You'll understand more if and when you sign the security agreement, but until then there's not a lot more we can say to each other."

Peter thought about his rapidly dwindling savings and checking accounts. Fifty thousand would sure take a lot of pressure off.

A million dollars would . . . would . . .

He was so used to having to scrape by he couldn't even begin to imagine what he could do with that kind of money. He never was very good with his imagination—hence the boxfuls of bad novels and short stories and poetry that he never sold.

He signed the agreement and handed it to Blackmore, who looked so happy he seemed on the verge of tears.

"Thank you, Peter, thank you so much."

He looked at a photograph on his desk. Peter knew—as did everyone employed by Blackmore Industries—that the photo was of Blackmore's wife, Stephanie, who had died last year from stomach cancer.

"A few days ago," said Blackmore, setting the photo back

in its place, "I was witness to something quite remarkable, Peter—no, scratch that. *Revolutionary.*" Then Blackmore laughed. "My God, even that doesn't begin to describe what I saw and heard. Do you know who Wilhelm Wolfe is?"

"Um, yeah, I've read some things about him—he's like a geneticist or something, right? DNA research?"

"Yes—but not just any DNA research, Peter—oh, no. What has happened at Wolfe's laboratories could very well change the course of human events."

And then he began to describe, in great detail, what he had witnessed.

A scientist named Tsering had discovered that everything which made an individual unique was encoded in their basic DNA—life memories, both inherited and acquired, nature and nurture, as well as memories of the shape and health of one's ancestors, were encoded there. Tsering had created a process wherein this code could be drawn from the DNA of someone who had died—providing there was enough material remaining from which to draw the DNA—and made transmittable.

"Tsering himself was the first subject. He gave to himself the codes of his late wife, Chime, the two of them becoming one, a new person, a new being: Chimera. I saw how this was done and it is absolutely astounding. But it is illegal, Peter— something as revolutionary as this could be tied up for decades in governmental red tape, so Wolfe and Chimera have asked a handful of people to invest in this process, even participate in it." Blackmore once again looked at the picture of his late wife.

"I want what Tsering has. I wish to be reunited with my Stephanie. But I've a confession to make to you, Peter: I am something of a coward. Yes, I saw the film of Tsering's transformation, his *merging*, if you will, and I saw the person he . . . she . . . *they* have become, but still I fear it. I want to see the process for myself. I want to be there at Nucore, in the lab, when they perform a transmission."

"How dangerous is it?" asked Peter.

"According to both Wolfe and Chimera, there's no danger at all. But I'm a born skeptic—I was, after all, born in Missouri, the 'Show Me' state." He shrugged. "I want them to show me before I submit to it myself. I would like you to be the person who agrees to be my test subject."

Peter was stunned. "Why me? I mean, wouldn't I be stuck with that for the rest of my life? Jesus Christ! With all due respect, sir, you're asking—"

"The process is reversible, providing it is done in the first thirty days after the initial merging. You wouldn't have to remain merged, Peter. I simply need to see it work for myself."

"I don't know, I really don't."

"Two million, then."

"It's not the money, sir. It's—"

"Then I'll make it three."

Peter sat in stunned silence. Three million dollars. Three million dollars was Up-Yours money. He could pursue other interests—traveling, painting, maybe music or writing again, and have all the time in the world to do so.

Three million dollars. Up-Yours money. And it was safe, after all, wasn't it?

When he next spoke to Blackmore, his voice was soft, hesitant. "Who would I . . . I mean, how would they go about choosing whose code would be transferred to me?"

Blackmore smiled. "They wouldn't, not exactly." He produced a single sheet of paper from his desk drawer. "This is a list of the DNA they acquired prior to revealing the existence of this procedure. They wouldn't say *how* it was acquired, but it wouldn't surprise me to find that a little . . . for lack of a more sensitive term . . . *grave robbing* was involved."

"Jesus."

"So you can see why this must be kept secret?"

"Oh, yeah . . ."

"Take a look at the list, Peter. You choose your . . . partner."

The list contained the names of great world leaders, philosophers, actors and actresses, composers, writers, artists.

Peter suddenly felt more a failure than ever as he read down the list.

He wasn't even aware that he'd begun crying until he saw a few of his own tears splash upon the page.

Blackmore came around from behind his desk and put a hand on Peter's shoulder. "It's all right, son. It must be humbling as hell, to see those names, realize what they accomplished . . ."

". . . And how little I've done with my own life," croaked Peter. "Look at me—I'm a *fucking janitor*. I had such dreams when I was younger—to be a great artist, or musician, or writer. Somewhere along the line I realized that things like that don't happen for people like me. Oh, sure, I might be 'above average' but what the hell does that mean in the end? I don't have the makings of a great leader of men, I don't have the insight to be a 'great thinker,' and what little talent I possess is just acceptable enough to pass as ordinary—pleasant enough, but nothing special. And what . . . what will I leave behind when I die? The cleanest bathrooms in the downtown area? Big-goddamn-whoop."

"Perhaps *this* is what you could be remembered for."

Peter shook his head. "I don't think so. I don't know. Maybe." He wiped his eyes and blew his nose. "I'm sorry, Mr. Blackmore, but I . . . I can't give you an answer right now. Could I have a little time to think about it?"

"Of course. I only ask that you make your decision before the end of the week. The process takes nearly two days to complete—but for thirty-six hours of that you'll be asleep. I have everything arranged to fly us to Nucore this weekend, if you agree."

"I'll let you know in a day or two, then."

"Good, very good." Blackmore squeezed Peter's shoulders. "I can't tell you what it means to me that you didn't say no."

"I do have one more question, sir."

"What's that?"

"What made you pick me? I mean, I'm guessing that you checked out dozens, maybe even hundreds of possible subjects. What made you pick me?"

Blackmore stared directly into Peter's eyes. For a moment he didn't speak, as if he were struggling with how to tell the truth—or if to tell it at all. Finally, he drew in a deep breath and said, "Your intelligence and character *were* truly contributing factors, but neither was the deciding one."

"So what was the deciding factor?"

"Please don't be insulted by this—"

"My pride and I parted company a long time ago."

Blackmore smiled somewhat sadly. "I needed someone who, while not quite at the end of their rope—"

"—could see it from here?"

"Yes."

Peter thought about that for a moment, then nodded. "Yeah, I can understand that. It's not a matter of pity, and it's not a matter of feeling superior to some lower life-form. It's a simple business matter, one of supply and demand. You find a consumer to fit your product. Or something like that."

"You're a good man, Peter Krantz."

Peter nodded and walked to the door, then paused with his hand on the doorknob. "I don't know if I'm a good man, Mr. Blackmore, but maybe I'm a man who'll finally be good *for something*. That's not self-pity talking, either. I realized long ago that whatever it is that makes a human being genuinely extraordinary, I don't have it. But that's okay. The world needs mediocrity to balance the brilliance. Thank you for respecting me enough to tell me the truth."

And with that he left the office.

At her desk, Antonia said good-bye to him without looking up.

He wished he could have seen her smile one more time.

4

We return to the hotel, sober and alone, exchange greetings and complaints about the midsummer heat with the desk clerk, and climb the carpeted stairs to our room on the second floor. The recitation went well. We overcame the woman's coughing interruptions just as we'd planned, and at the end the audience rose and applauded with gratitude. Near the back, Dr. Wolfe and Mr. Blackmore beamed with triumph. They were here to observe how successful the procedure had been. They have promised us time to be alone this evening, to reach our decision. A few women near the front, when they rose from their seats to thank us for reciting our "magnificent and profound" poem, could be seen with tears washing their cheeks. Afterward, when we departed the stage, we discovered that someone, a janitor, probably (how oddly appropriate), had removed our half-emptied bottle of Madeira. At the time, we took the disappearance of the bottle as a blessing and a sign, and later, at the dean's gathering for the literary ladies and gentlemen of Richmond, Virginia, we declined the sherry and asked for water, a glass of cool, clear water with a bruised leaf of mint dropped into it. And so now we arrive at our hotel room sober. But late, past midnight, for, because tonight we were sober, we spoke to the ladies and gentlemen with a lucidity driven by logic that astonished them, made them beg us to stay and continue to mystify, enchant, and bewilder them with our demystification, our disenchantment, and our clarity. Man is always amazed by what is most rational, we muse to ourself as we enter our darkened room. The irrational, though it makes him feel helpless, out of control, childlike, seems more "natural" to him. We light the lamp, sit on the bed, and slowly remove our shoes. We think: *And man is right to believe in the "naturalness" of un-reason. And right to be amazed by what is most rational, to be simultaneously shocked and relieved by one who presents himself as demystification, disenchantment, and clarity person-*

ified. Both right and good—for those are the modern vices we set against the ancient virtues of faith, hope, and charity!

We hold our head in our cool palms. Oh my! Oh my! To aspire to purge one's mind and all its manifestations of every taint of un-reason—such an aspiration must be blasphemy! For to be pure reason, to be self-generating, to be unable to remember your mother, is to be a god! Is that why we can't remember your/our mother's face, her smell, her touch, her voice? Is this painful absence the necessary consequence of our o'er-vaunting ambition? Evil. Evil. We say the words aloud, over and over. "Evil. Evil." We draw off our socks and our trousers, our jacket, vest, shirt, and necktie, our underclothes, all the while murmuring, "Evil, evil, evil." Until at last we are naked, the poet Edgar Poe author of "The Raven," naked in the dim light of a hotel room in Richmond, Virginia. We peer down at our toes, bent and battered, each toe topped with a thin wad of black hairs. Our knees, knobbed, the skin gray and crackled, and our gaunt thighs, our genitals, dry, puckered, and soft, half-covered with a smoky patch of hair. We look at our drooping belly and our navel, that primeval scar. We study our hands, twin nests of spiders, and our thin arms, the moles, freckles, discolorations, fissures, hairs, and blemishes, and our pale skin.

Suddenly we try to look at our face but cannot. There is a dresser mirror across from us to our right a few paces, but that will not do. We want to look upon our face directly. And cannot. We know that if we can look directly at our own face, we will be able to remember your/our mother's face. And then her touch, her smell, her voice. We touch our face with our fingertips, rubbing them across nose, lips, eyes, ears, and cheeks. We can get the facts of our face, but cannot look upon it directly. Just as we can get the facts of your/our mother's life, but cannot remember her directly. Is that why we have aspired to what is evil? Because it was easier than to become a "natural" human being, easier than remembering your/our mother? Easier to be evil than good? We are weeping silently. Which is it? Are we unable to remember your/ our mother because we are evil and persist in blasphemy, or are we evil and persist in blasphemy because we cannot remember your/our mother? Which? For one must be a cause, the other the effect. Which the cause? Which the effect? Why are we weeping? Why are we naked? Why are we the poet Edgar Poe author of "The Raven"? And why also are we the janitor once called Peter Krantz, lately of Cedar Hill, Ohio, whose mother lies in a nursing home, waiting alone for her faculties to abandon her altogether? Why are we not a particular, remembered, and memorialized mother's son?

Without meaning to, we glance in the mirror and see Peter Krantz's face, and once again we remember.

5

Nurses with dark circles under their eyes, their shoes softly squeaking against the polished tile, moved briskly along toward some pressing task, hastened not so much by urgency as the need to keep themselves awake; a middle-aged orderly who looked as if there were 2,341 other things he'd rather be doing at this moment whisked by with a snack cart full of chocolate chip cookies and tea—"Some goodies for us late-night folks," he said to Peter on his way past; one of the restless ambulatory patients, his tattered robe hanging open, shuffled toward the front desk, a small globule of saliva creeping from the crusty corner of his mouth, bursting, then streaming down his chin; and, nonplussed by it all, the head nurse sat behind her desk, making notations on various charts.

One-forty-five A.M. on the Alzheimer's Unit and all was well.

As well as could be expected, anyway.

Peter turned back toward his mother's room. She was awake now and staring at him. He wondered if this were one of her lucid periods or not.

"Well, don't just stand there, Petey," she said, parting an area of her bed. "Come sit here and talk to me."

Petey. She had called him Petey.

Which meant that she was lucid for the time being.

He sat on the edge of the bed and held one of her hands in his own. "How are you feeling?"

"Like the belle of the ball—what do you think? It's almost two in the morning and I can't seem to get back to sleep."

Peter smiled. "I remember how you used to read stories to me when I couldn't sleep."

Something sparkled in her eyes. "Hey, that's a good idea. Why don't you tell me one of your stories? I know how much you used to love writing stories and such." She lay back on her pillows, getting comfortable. "Tell me one of your stories."

Peter stared at her as he searched his mind for a tale to tell, but all of his remembered stories were so mundane, so extraordinarily *average* that they all blended together in his mind to form one massive tome of mediocrity. It had been so long since he'd tried to come up with something new he didn't know if he even had it in him anymore.

He tried

He really did.

God knew he tried to come up with something new to tell her, his mother who was now wholly with him but who knew for how long, and shouldn't this woman who'd cared for and loved him all his life be entitled to a story at two in the morning if she wanted one? She didn't have that long left, no matter how you looked at it, and Peter felt diminished, useless, pointless and purposeless as he fumbled for the words to begin the tale he didn't have at the ready, anyway.

He saw it register in her eyes: disappointment.

And he suddenly hated himself for this impotence. But she would understand, she always did, that was Mom's way. It would be okay with her that she couldn't get her son to tell her a story—"You can't miss what you never had," she used to say when things weren't going well—but she should have some measure of peace and joy in these last years/months/ days of her life, one spent working so long and hard and never getting so much as a "Thanks" for her efforts, but that was okay with her, as well, because a person did what they had to do to care for their family, and the safety and comfort of their children was their greatest reward, that, and the promise of the day when they could look back over the arc of their life and see their children having all the things they never could—and what did she see in Peter? A janitor, a mediocre man who never realized his potential, a disappoint- ment who was here to disappoint her yet again . . . but that was okay, it had been a good life . . . *good enough*, anyway, but that wasn't enough for her as far as Peter was concerned. Dear God, there should be a chance to make up for all the hardships and heartbreaks, shouldn't there? And if he were more than he was he could do that, he could make these last days rich and full and joyous and—

—and still there was no story.

He pulled her close to him and wept on her shoulder.

"It's all right, hon," she whispered. "I understand. It's been a long day for you, you're tired. Go on home now and get yourself some sleep. You can maybe tell me a story to- morrow, okay?"

Ten minutes later he was at a pay phone calling Black- more.

". . . 'lo?" said Blackmore in a groggy voice.

"Mr. Blackmore? It's Peter Krantz."

"*Peter*," replied Blackmore, sounding suddenly alert.

"I'll do it, sir."

"That's *wonderful*, son, just wonderful. I'll call Wolfe right away and tell him. Have you made your choice?"

"Yes."

Then he spoke the name, and the world he knew changed forever.

6

A small throbbing behind the eyes, not quite painful but the threat of pain lies there.

Thousands of invisible needles pricking the skin: hands, neck, eyelids, especially the chest.

A breath drawn in slowly; ragged, phlegm-filled; a cough trying to surface.

Small kaleidoscopic bursts of light fill the field of sight, then the bursts become slits, bleeding brightness, bleeding white; the cough surfaces, then, something emptying from the chest, rising into the throat, thick, then expelled into a handkerchief held to the mouth.

Sitting up now. The bleeding slits of light now replaced by a painful low glow all around.

The antiseptic smell of a hospital. The sheets below, crisp and warm.

I stand amid the roar . . .

. . . who's speaking? . . .

. . . *Of a surf-tormented shore . . .*

. . . right, it's both right and not. Why is that?

Speakers. There are two. Oinos and Agathos, debating the power of words.

. . . *in this existence, I dreamed that I should be at once cognizant of all things, and thus at once be happy in being cognizant at all . . .*

. . . think, dammit! Remember.

The laboratory. Dr. Wolfe, Dr. Chimera, and Mr. Blackmore.

The odd device that reminded you—*us(?)*—of the machine an optometrist uses to test eyes. *("Just relax," said Chimera, and looking into their eyes, you—he(?)—saw the total peacefulness, the totality, the completeness.)*

The device was placed against your—our—face; then . . . light, elation . . . darkness.

Then we awakened, here in this room, swimming up to consciousness on streams of bleeding light.

"Is all that we see or seem but a dream within a dream?" we whisper.

And suddenly—so suddenly that it fills our heart with both terror and euphoria—there is the promise of the Work again, only this time, we feel that there are countless new subjects out there for us to explore—wondrous machines, new cities, new *countries*, even.

Part of us wonders what this miracle called television is; part of us knows all about it.

We think we will look upon the world in a much different manner.

And we will express that wonder—at last!—in words, beautiful words, stories and poems and essays, and the sheer *want* of it, the need to express, is so overpowering that we immediately begin searching for something with which to write.

A pad and pen have been set out for us on a nearby table.

We look up and see the security camera, and know that nearby, in another room, Wolfe, Chimera, and Blackmore are watching us on a closed-circuit unit.

Part of us wonders what "closed-circuit" means; part of us knows all about it.

And so that is the name of the poem that we begin during these first few, confusing moments of wakefulness: "Closed-Circuit."

Broadcasting from home under the weight of megahertz and
   myopia
I seek a new place in this oft-dream-of utopia . . .

We pause for a moment and reread the lines.
Not perfect, but a good enough start.
For now we have the time and ability to make it perfect.
We reach up and wipe our eyes, not surprised to find the

tears—more yours than *ours* at the moment—but joyous, nonetheless.

Then we look up at the camera and smile.

We know each other's names.

As do those who watch us.

Our smile widens, and we offer the cold lens a mock salute.

And laugh.

Then return to our work.

7

In the graveyard beside the church on the hill is your mother's grave. The grief and feeling of loss is so strong now that we allow ourselves to think of her, for this brief time, and only your mother. We will depart this city in an hour by plane for Baltimore, then back to Ohio. We have eaten breakfast alone in the hotel dining room and have arranged for a driver to take us first to the church on the hill, then back into the city to the airport, where Dr. Wolfe and Mr. Blackmore will meet us for the flight on Mr. Blackmore's private jet. We pay our bill, lift our satchel, and leave the hotel for the limousine waiting outside. We stop a moment on the veranda and admire the soft morning sunlight on the brick buildings and sidewalks, the elm and live oak trees that line the streets, the white dome of the capitol building a few blocks east, and beyond that, with the river between, the white spire of the church next to where your mother's body was buried so many decades ago. This will not be the first time you/I/we have visited your mother's grave, to stand before it with your mind mutely churning, and then, after a few moments of vertigo, to leave. You have made this pilgrimage hundreds of times, as a young boy, as an adolescent, and as a man, even in military uniform, even while drunk. And it has always been the same. From the very first time, when Mrs. Allan took you/us outside the church after the service one Sunday morning and walked to the graveyard and stood hand in hand with you above the freshly cut plaque laid in the ground and told you/us that your mother's body had been buried here, precisely here, at this spot, from that very first time until this, it has been the same for you/us. Silence in our ears, no noise from without, no words from within, and a feeling, painful and frightening, of falling, as if down a well that reaches to the center of the earth. Yet, despite that feeling, you/we have returned to this spot compulsively, like an animal driven by an instinct. We have no sense of there being a reason for it. It is as if we are drawn by a force that originates there, not here inside our own head, among our sensations, memories, and ideas of the sanctified and holy. No, the power lies out there, in that graveyard, in that one all but unmarked grave. And now we find ourself standing once again in that cool, tree-shaded cemetery beside the old Episcopal church on the hill, and once again descend into a well of silence. Our mind has gone mute, and we no longer hear the wind in the leaves overhead, the traffic on the street behind us, the morning twitter of birds, and the coo of the doves from the niches of the steeple. We look down at the grassy plot of ground before us, the tarnished plaque at our feet, and feel ourself begin the descent. But this time, for no cause we can name, now or later, at the point of its beginning, before we have become terrified, we resist. We pull away and step back a few paces as if from a slap and bring the entire grave into our gaze and sharply into focus, the rich green grass, the switching patterns of shadow and sunlight on the grass, the square plaque sinking into the ground at the head of the grave. We can see each individual blade of grass, even those bent and crushed beneath the feet of some passing cleric or attendant this very morning. We are still wrapped in silence, as if in a caul. We can hear nothing, nothing. And we have no thought. We watch shadows cast on the grave by the fluttering leaves of the live oak overhead, and slowly they organize into an image, one that we are surely creating as we watch, but an image which nonetheless exists in the world outside, a configuration of shade against sunlight on the grassy plot of your mother's grave. The shades separate, move together, slowly swirl, separate, and come together again, until we begin to see the shape of a single eye, large, wide-open, an extraordinary eye, a wholly familiar eye yet one we have never seen before. It resembles an eye we have seen in daguerreotypes, and in mirrors. It is the eye of a close blood relation, it is your mother's eye, it is your own eye, it is the eye of Peter Krantz and also that of his mother, as well. We stare peacefully into it, and feel it stare peacefully back. Then, gradually, the image fades, the shadows move apart, and the eye is gone from our sight. But we can remember it. We instantly recall it to our mind, as if to test the reality of the experience, and it appears there, as tender and filled with love for us as when it first appeared out of the shadows.

We speak, then, to the space where that eye had been: "Because I feel that, in the Heavens above,/The angels, whispering to one another,/Can find among their burning terms of love,/None so devotional as that of/"Mother"/Therefore by that dear name I long have/called you/You who are more than mother unto/me,/And fill my heart of hearts, where Death/installed you . . ."

And we know now what our decision will be.

We—you and I, Edgar Poe the poet and Peter Krantz the janitor, we shall remain as one, as loving brothers within this frame, together making each of us more than we were when separate. And we will write many new stories for my/our mother who waits for us in Ohio. We have the money now, the means and the talent and the desire, to make her final years/months/days as rich as we always dreamed. She is both the mother you can't remember and the one I feared I would lose before letting her know just how much her life has meant to me. No longer will we feel like extras on the stage of our life; no more will we be a mere passerby longing for something to make them extraordinary.

There is Promise now where once we thought only Evil existed.

There are many things to do, see, experience, and so many tales that we can make of them.

We are one. And we cannot wait to see our mother back in Ohio.

We turn and slowly leave the cemetery. As we climb into the waiting limousine, we try once again to remember your/our mother, and this time recall her beautiful dark eye, her loving gaze on you/us, her only son, her beloved child. Bathed in that gaze which cleanses the Evil from our soul, we return to the city of Richmond, Virginia, so that we may leave it for the story ahead.

The story of our life.

Forever Free

Rod Garcia y Robertson

> *If you want a good time, jine the cavalry!*
> *Well, we jined up, and here we go . . .*
> *Last event in the minstrel show!*
>
> —*John Brown's Body*,
> Stephen Vincent Benét

Fourth Manassas

Stuart sat on one of Pelham's gun limbers, idly swinging a boot, listening to cursing gun crews force their way across Stone Bridge, shouldering aside Hood's victorious Texans. Bull Run streamed beneath twin stone spans, headed south, a molten silver sheet in the slanting summer sunlight. Stuart took a moment to admire the cannon attached to the limber—a trim three-inch rifle taken from the Yankees that morning. Thoroughly enjoying the battle, he hummed happily to himself:

> *My homespun dress is plain, I know,*
> *my hat's palmetto too.*

But then it shows what Southern girls
for Southern rights will do . . .

Actually, he wore the gray undress uniform of a Confederate States of America major general, set off by knee-high cavalry boots and a natty black ostrich plume in his cocked felt hat. Lately he had even grown a big bushy cinnamon brown beard—but deep inside he was that Southern lass whose sweetheart had gone off to war. His heart went out to her. She was what he was fighting for. Stuart launched cheerfully into the chorus:

Hurrah! Hurrah!
For the sunny South so dear,
Three cheers for the homespun dress,
That Southern ladies wear.

He had come up to hurry on the horse artillery, herding infantry and civilians off the bridge. A great throng of sightseers and tourists bused down from DC had crossed Bull Run at the lower fords—pressing onto the battlefield, picking up spent bullets, stripping fallen cyborgs for souvenirs. Spectators were supposed to stay south and east of the Visitors' Center, out of effective artillery range. But with General John Pope's bluecoats in hasty retreat, it was hard to keep crowds of civilians off Henry House Hill.

Some came in coaches and carriages, but most were on foot, walking all the way from the RV parks beyond Centreville. Many badly out of costume. Two DC teenagers were working the crowd, wearing tailored jeans and gang colors. (Park Service guards made them take off their mirror shades and pricey running shoes.) One banged away on an old-fashioned brass harmonica, while his buddy gave a spirited exhibition of barefoot break dancing.

Lying on the ground between them was a smashed cyborg from a Michigan regiment, a cavalry trooper cut down by case shot, oozing realistically red blood into his blue pants and tunic. His mount lay in pieces alongside the bridge, sawn in half at close range by the same blast of case shot.

Flies hummed in hot August air heavy with the odor of death. Tourists in a rebuilt buckboard with Idaho plates stared in disbelief at the battlefield break dancing—something totally new to Pocatello. The father holding the buckboard's reins wore a parson's hat and a black frock funeral coat, looking like an itinerant undertaker out drumming up customers. His teenage daughter sat fidgeting in her high-necked dress, plainly bored by the battle. She had a pale antique cameo pinned at her throat. Her shirtless little brother in Huck Finn overalls kept turning the corner of his eye toward the smashed cyborg.

Pitted pink plasti-metal soaked in synthetic blood showed through the shredded blue uniform, releasing a death smell real enough to draw flies. Limbs had locked at grotesque angles, what programmers called response-to-impact.

Leaning over, the father in the funeral coat tapped his son on the knee. "Don't worry, boy—he's only a robot. Just pink plastic, fake blood, and a bad smell. None of this is real. It's a reenactment."

That broke it. This was The Reenactment. Stuart could take crowds of tourists, even gang bangers in tailored jeans—but blind willful ignorance was too much. He whistled for his horse. Judging by the traffic jam on the bridge, the battery would take a couple of more minutes to cross. Pulling on his gloves, Stuart sauntered over to the fallen cyborg. He drew the downed bluecoat's pistol from its holster—a '58 Remington, sturdier and more reliable than the Colts supplied to his own troopers. Federals got first pick of rebuilt guns and equipment.

Thumbing back the hammer, he took casual aim, then pulled the trigger. With a loud blast of black powder, the pistol put a .44 caliber hole in the floor of the buckboard—right between the fool in a frock coat's booted feet.

Leaping like he had been hit, the man cried out, "What the hell are you doing?"

"Showing you the bullets are real. This is a battle, remember?"—that cracked up the DC gang bangers. Live ammunition was absolutely necessary to The Reenactment; anything less mocked the dead.

"But you can't shoot at us," the tourist protested.

"We can't? Read the release you signed."

Anyone coming to a nationally advertised battle could hardly complain about being shot at. Cyborgs tried not to hit civilians, but half the guns on the Southern side were not even rifled. "Besides, I did not shoot *at* you," Stuart pointed out. "If I had, we would not be having this conversation."

The frock-coated father sputtered indignantly. His lips twitched a couple times as if he meant to speak, but he thought better of it. He sat back down, not daring to stand on his "rights." His bored daughter barely contained her glee, sitting grinning at his side. Which was the point of the whole exercise—putting a smile on her face. Wiping off her pouty scowl, making her look pretty.

Stuart's mount came trotting up—a cyborg mare called Lady Margrave. With a sweep of his plumed hat, he bowed low to the giggling daughter, then mounted Lady Margrave. Now she could say Jeb Stuart stopped to flirt with her in the middle of a battle.

"Slick trick, Cracker," shouted the gang banger with the harmonica. "Yeh," his buddy agreed. "See ya'all at Gettysburg."

Stuart tipped his hat to them. Gettysburg was almost a year away, but they clearly could not wait to see his side get whipped. The Reenactment had something for everyone—making it hugely popular, part historical pageant, part *American Gladiators*. National pyschodrama on a grand scale, done in real time, with real people running real risks. Nothing brought the country together like a fight anyone could get behind.

Tucking the Remington into a saddlebag, Stuart trotted off over Stone Bridge, trailing after the battery. That fool in the frock coat had punctured his mood. Buffoons like him had no place in battle. What if he got his kids killed? Causing no end of complaint. So far The Reenactment had a near spotless record—not counting the idiot protesters mowed down at Malvern Hill, trying to disrupt the battle. Such breathtaking ignorance depressed him, corroding his confidence. He tried humming "The Homespun Dress" to get back in tune:

> *The Southern land's a glorious land and has*
> *a glorious cause . . .*

"What glorious cause?" a voice within him demanded. Besides growing a bushy beard, Stuart had lately begun hearing voices. Thanks to the Chimera process, he had grafted the DNA of Jeb Stuart—Lee's cavalry commander—onto his. But "being" Jeb Stuart turned out to be more than having broader shoulders and a cinnamon brown beard. Personality, habits, even memories could be encoded in DNA. And along with Jeb's memories, Stuart had picked up an inner critic.

"Slavery?" Jeb suggested sarcastically. Stuart pictured himself trying to force those two gang bangers to chop cotton for nothing—then he would have a real war on his hands. "So what are you fighting for?" Jeb demanded.

Stuart said nothing, ignoring his inner critic. A voice is just a voice. And Jeb never liked his answers. Truth to tell, Stuart was in The Reenactment for the thrill of it. Decent folk might piously deny it, but war could be thoroughly fun. What else could explain untold centuries of popularity? Pelham had played college ball for Virginia, busting his knees trying to make second string quarterback. He claimed nothing on the football field could touch it. Only battle had that absolute intensity. "They don't let the Clemson defense shoot at you."

Besides, they were winning. The battle had gone perfectly. Better than the real Second Bull Run. The cyborg playing General Pope was programmed not to learn from history—but his live subordinates, the fellows playing Hooker, Reynolds, Schurz, and Buford, were lifelong Civil War buffs. (Who else would risk their lives for The Reenactment?) They knew Stonewall Jackson was backed up against Sudley Mountain. And that Longstreet would come pouring through Thoroughfare Gap onto their flank. They could not help looking over their left shoulders, and making personal plans accordingly.

But Stuart, Jackson, Longstreet, and Bobby Lee had beaten them handily. Beating history as well—routing Pope a day early, with a deal less difficulty.

Herding Pelham's horse battery along, Stuart forced cyborg infantry off the road. Ahead he saw bluecoat cavalry blocking the Warrenton Turnpike, old US 211. He told Pelham to unlimber his guns—"Git yer artiller-ary going." Young and pretty, Pelham did not mind Stuart mocking his hillbilly drawl. Wheeling his guns about in a blur of flashing spokes, he showed with a bared sabre where the firing line should be. Each gun had six cyborg horses with three live riders atop them—Pelham's battery was one of the glamour units totally manned by Civil War buffs.

Skirmishers had worked their way through the woods north and south of the pike, taking potshots at the bluecoat troopers, bringing down horses and emptying saddles. Pelham's guns joined in. Rapid accurate cannon fire forced the federals to break ranks, spreading out along Cub Run.

Putting himself at the head of Fitzhugh Lee's brigade, Stuart led his troopers forward at a walk, with the sun low at their backs, resisting the impulse to charge. A charge *a l'outrance* ought never be launched too early, or the troopers would arrive strung out, with their horses blown. Cyborg mounts were forced on The Reenactment by Animal Rights groups—people could be put at risk, but never a dog or horse. But they were programmed to act like horses, shying from shellfire, stopping to drink at streams, tiring when ridden too hard.

Pelham's shells clattered overhead, like metro trains hurtling through a station. Unnerving, even when the shells were yours. At least he did not have to worry about answering fire—federal guns had been overrun, or sent on to safety. Instead Stuart advanced into batteries of telephoto lenses, aimed straight down US 211 from telemetry towers in Centreville. Camera crews in concealed bunkers broadcast close-in shots. Buried mikes picked up the beat of hooves. Satellites in low orbit sent overviews of the battlefield to a national TV audience too timid to make the trek to Henry House Hill.

Time to give them what they tuned in for. Distance closed, Stuart picked up the pace, from a walk to a trot, to a canter, to a charge. Union troopers caught in extended formation tried to close up despite galling fire. Too late. The hurtling mass of graycoat riders smashed into them to spectacular effect. Moments like this were unimaginable—shooting and slashing at close quarters. Shock, anger, terror, and amazement combined into a wild adrenal rush. Stuart saw with extra sharpness, heard with extra clarity. Colors leaped out, turning the sky a dizzying blue. He felt individual bullets whiz by his head—an astonishing sensation.

Suddenly it was over. Recoiling in shock, the federal cavalry scattered. Stuart found himself reining in at the edge of Cub Run. Federal infantry banged away at him from green fields on the far side of the creek. Definitely not the Clemson defense over there. Fortunately, cyborgs were programmed to shoot no better than Civil War soldiers.

He wheeled his mount toward safety. "Jeb! Jeb!" a high clear voice called to him. Stuart reined in, trying to tell if the voice was in his head.

"Jeb! Jeb! Over here." Shooting stopped. Stuart could hear the voice clearly, coming from the Union side of the creek. He turned to see a slim young federal officer on the far side of Cub Run, motioning for his cyborgs not to fire. He wore an Army of the Potomac cap topped by the Maltese cross badge of the Fifth Corps—an anachronism, Union corps did not get those badges until the Chancellorsville campaign. Whatever the fellow lacked in authenticity he made up in looks, being fresh-faced with smooth delicate features, prettier even than Pelham. Clearly no cyborg, he did not look like one of the live commanders. With that cap he could even be a tourist.

"Do you know me?" Stuart called across.

"Of course," the officer called back. Dark eyes twinkled with amusement in the fading light. "Who wouldn't."

Suspecting a trick, Stuart slid a hand into his saddlebag and drew out the Remington, keeping it hidden behind his hip. Alone and unarmed, the young bluecoat stood right at the edge of the stream. Shooting him now would have been plain murder—just as much as in the real war. But capturing Jeb Stuart would be a tremendous coup, and a legitimate ruse of war, lessening the sting of another lost battle. "What do you want?" Stuart demanded.

"Just to say congratulations. You whipped us good."

Without letting go of the pistol, Stuart tipped his hat. "Thanks, Yank."

"Look for me at Antietam." The bluecoat turned and scrambled back up the bank, disappearing into the gathering dark.

"Consorting with the enemy?" asked a voice behind him.

Stuart turned to see his staff trotting up—which must have been what sent the bluecoat on his way. The speaker was his cousin, Captain Hardeman Stuart. Stuart stared at the young signal officer, as if seeing something totally unexpected. Hardeman grinned back at him. "So what did the Yank have to say?"

"Nothing," Stuart decided, sliding the pistol back into his saddlebag. "Nothing that matters."

"Shud vee not secure dee bridge?" inquired Von Borcke,

his officious German aide—one of many foreigners drawn by the fighting, sounding and looking out of place, with his spiked mustache, short-cut jacket, and oversized boots.

"Yes, yes," Stuart admitted absently, unable to take his gaze off Hardeman. "Secure the bridge." In a real victory they would be pressing the retreating federals, driving them past Centreville, knocking on the defenses of Washington. But here the battlefield ended at Rocky Run. There were no Washington defenses. Nothing past Centreville but RV parks and souvenir stands. And beyond that Arlington and the Beltway. Once Pope was driven from the field Second Bull Run was finished. Now it was on to Antietam.

There remained nothing for Stuart to do but collect the rest of his command. Riding back down the darkening Warrenton Pike, surrounded by his staff, he kept turning to stare at Hardeman. Like Pelham's horse battery, Stuart's staff was one of the plum posts in The Reenactment—entirely filled with Civil War buffs and diehard Confederates. Most had been biosculpted to look like the men they played—Hardeman among them. What was the use of risking shot and shell if you were not going to "be" the Southern gallant you were playing? Stuart had gone the big step further. He had the money and the connections to undergo the Chimera process, grafting his DNA with that of the original Jeb Stuart. Making it hard to tell where Stuart Lovejoy ended, and Major General James Ewell Brown Stuart began.

Suddenly it hit him why Hardeman looked so out of place. Jeb's memories were playing tricks on him. The real Hardeman Stuart was killed at the original Second Bull Run. Hardeman had lost his horse, and been temporarily demoted into the infantry. Captain Cooke, Jeb's ordnance officer, had come upon him dusty and unwashed, marching with a Mississippi regiment.

"Bad luck," Cooke had told him. "Get another horse and come with us."

"Tell the general I will," Hardeman had replied. But he

didn't. Later they captured some federal troopers in a tavern near Manassas. One wore Hardeman's coat, with his captain's commission in the pocket.

Stuart resisted the absurd urge to clap his young "cousin" on the back. To hug Hardeman and make much of him. Congratulating him on being alive—on surviving a battle that should have killed him. A silly impulse. This was not the same man. Not even a Chimera-clone like Stuart. Just a Civil War buff biosculpted to look like General Jeb Stuart's long-dead cousin—an obscure signal officer in the Army of Northern Virginia.

Jeb's DNA was obtained from a lock of hair, a keepsake passed down in a Maryland family. Stuart began to wonder when that lock of hair had been cut? Apparently sometime after the summer of 1862—when Hardeman Stuart was killed—otherwise, why would Hardeman's being alive shock him so?

Shells came clattering out of the twilight. At first Stuart thought he had mistaken the sound. Then came a staggering thunderclap showering him with dark clods of dirt—a cannon shell had exploded in front of him. He was under fire. Make that "friendly fire"—from the fall of shot it could only be Pelham's horse battery firing at them. Mistaking Stuart's returning staff for some mad federal counterattack.

Another unimaginable moment. More shells shrieked down. Stuart opened his mouth to shout, "Stop!"—but he could not even hear himself amid the mad explosions. All he got was a mouthful of dirt as the next shell knocked him out of the saddle.

Facedown on the ground, he tried to force himself farther into the dirt, feeling big uniform buttons digging against his chest, suddenly seeing how insanely dangerous this all was. Shells kept banging down, terrifyingly close. He pictured the three-inch Yankee rifle he had sat on that afternoon, realizing it was now firing at him. The absurd thought passed through his head that Pelham—the "real" Pelham—would not be doing this.

"Look you silly ass," he heard himself say, "you asked for this. Stop groveling and show some spine." Anyone who came to a nationally advertised battle could not complain about being shot at—even by his own guns. He had courted death, outright demanded it: now it was here, whizzing past his ear.

Something seemed to seize Stuart by the collar and lift him up. Rising to hands and knees, he looked around. Dark blood stained his cuff. Von Borcke lay a few yards away, his head and shoulders torn off. He could only recognize the funny-sounding German by his short jacket and big bucket boots. Medevac would not do him much good.

Sick with shock, he let his head sag, vomiting between his gloved hands. The shelling had stopped. Pelham had ceased trying to kill them—either seeing his mistake, or just giving up firing into the fading light.

"Hallo there, are you hurt?" a voice asked. Stuart did not answer, trying feebly to wipe vomit from his beard with a blood-spattered glove.

"Can I give you a hand?" Someone reached down out of the darkness to help him up. Staring into the shadowy face, he saw it was Hardeman Stuart.

Maryland, My Maryland

Bands played at the Potomac fords as the Army of Northern Virginia crossed into Maryland, blaring out "Dixie" and "Maryland, My Maryland." Stuart crossed at White's Ford, just north of the Chesapeake and Ohio Historical Park, splashing through the river atop Lady Margrave, leading long lines of graycoat cavalry. High tree-shaded banks reminded him of Stonewall Jackson's last words—"Let us pass over the river, and rest in the shade of the trees."

Jackson, the "real" Jackson, had been shot by his own men

at Chancellorsville, mistaken for federal cavalry by some of Pender's Tarheels. But that had not happened yet. And might not happen at all; Chancellorsville had yet to be refought. It was Von Borcke who was dead, killed by Stuart's own horse batteries.

Bothering Stuart immensely. The blood on his cuff was Von Borcke's. The German should have survived, going home to grow old and fat. Pelham got a sharp reprimand, for what little good it would do. "He's not the real Pelham," Jeb pointed out, "just some prettified third string college quarterback with bad knees." The real Pelham died needlessly "inspecting" forward batteries.

Stuart himself had started confusing people with their replacements, and somehow expecting their fates to match his memories. Actually Jeb's memories. He kept Hardeman close to him, as a sort of good luck charm, saying, "Maryland is enemy country—and I need a signal officer near me." Hardeman had beaten fate once, why not again?

Beyond the trees came the crowds. Stuart led his column along two-lane blacktops lined with people, taking Maryland 107 to Poolesville, passing farmsteads, mobile homes, gas stations and a minimall in Martinsburg—his cyborg troopers looking like gray ghosts from another age. People packed the sidewalks and road shoulders to see Lee's invasion of Maryland. Southern sympathizers cheered and offered flowers to his staff. Yankees wore red, white, and blue ribbons, and waved little American flags. Most just stood and stared.

By the time he got to Poolesville he had flowers in his hatband, and a dozen new recruits. Excited young Southerners and potbellied survivalists begged to join the column: so did a couple of would-be Southern belles. The men were given makeshift uniforms and made to sign releases, trading shotguns and deer rifles for muzzle-loaders—disappointing one fellow determined to change history with an Uzi. Stuart told the two women, "*Mes regrets, mesdemoiselles*, our regiments are men only—but we're holding a ball in Urbana, and yawl're cordially welcome."

One threatened to sue. But her friend hopped aboard one of Pelham's gun carriages, happy to settle for the ball in Urbana.

Tipping his plumed hat, Stuart wished the frustrated Amazon, *"Bonne chance"*—The Reenactment had been thoroughly tested in the courts. Besides, Stuart felt beyond the reach of "Yankee Law." What really worried him was how he had started casually speaking French, without ever so much as studying a foreign language.

As they marched up Maryland 109 headed for Urbana, crowds got bigger and more festive. Maryland thoroughly enjoyed being invaded. Pelham's gun carriages were covered with happy carefree women; truant teenagers, genteel matrons, errant housewives, and truck stop waitresses, all headed for the ball in Urbana. Jeb complained that this "invasion" felt too much like the original one. "People come flocking to gawk, but hardly anyone wants to shoulder a musket." And ahead lay Antietam—the worst single day of the war.

When they got to the Washington National Pike, Stuart saw a banner hung from the overpass by a Baltimore mosque of the Nation of Islam—a verse from the Koran:

The Works of Unbelievers Are as Mirages in the Desert

Stuart's column filed under the overpass, halting traffic on the turnpike overhead, and on 355 beyond. The flip side of the overpass read:

Satan's Anvil Awaits the Wicked

Clearly Maryland had caught The Reenactment spirit. But even the banners failed to cheer him.

Police parted the crowds to get them into Urbana. The ball was bigger by far than the ad hoc affair Jeb had organized during Lee's original invasion. It had to be—anything less would disappoint the throng. A huge antebellum ballroom had been specially built for the event, floored with sawdust and smelling of fresh-cut pine. Women got in free, wearing homemade hoop dresses, or gowns supplied by The Reenactment. No off-the-rack finery allowed. Men had to volunteer for battle, signing releases and donning Confederate uniforms—making this The Reenactment's best recruiting day to date.

Regimental flags hung from the rafters. Polished bronze twelve-pounder Napoleons crouched in the corners of the hall, gleaming in the lamplight. Long tables glittered with silver and crystal, topped by everything from cold cuts of beef to Rhine wine and caviar. Newly awarded sabres stood stacked against the wall, while a military band played all the old favorites:

> *Well I wish I was in de land of cotton,*
> *Old times dere are not forgotten,*
> *Look away! Look away! . . .*

Stuart stood near the main entrance, surrounded by ranking members of his staff, greeting guests in person, seeing it all went smoothly. As the gaiety grew in volume, his gaze wandered. Couples whirled about the dance floor in a swirl of belled skirts and bared shoulders. Newly minted recruits to the Army of Northern Virginia did their best to imitate Southern gentlemen. An array of hidden cameras broadcast the show to the tens of millions who could not make it.

His eye singled out a couple in the crowd, a dark-haired young woman dancing with a cavalry captain. She stared full at him over her partner's gray uniform shoulder, smiled, and winked. Then they were whirled away.

Stuart knew that face—but from where? He had to know. "Go ask her," Jeb suggested. Ducking out of the receiving line, he left his staff to wonder what was up. Obviously a woman. Some *mademoiselle* had caught the general's eye—but which one?

Threading his way through the couples, Stuart found the pair he glimpsed from across the floor. He tapped the cavalry captain on the shoulder. The young officer turned about—it was Hardeman. Stuart smiled. "Congratulations, cousin. Your relief has arrived."

Hardeman gave a mock salute and stepped aside. Stuart slid into his cousin's place, so deftly the woman barely had to break stride. She responded with a sly laugh. "My, that was a neat maneuver."

"My staff is drilled to obey any order instantly," he assured her.

She arched a dark eyebrow. "No matter how distasteful?"

"Anyone can obey an easy order; it's unwelcome ones that test an officer's training." Her body fit snugly against him; somewhere, somehow, he had danced with her before—but could not imagine when. Looking down, he saw a silver heart-shaped locket hanging at her throat. "Dixie" ended, and the band struck up a new tune:

> *Oh, yes, I am a Southern girl*
> *and glory in the name,*
> *And boast it with far greater pride*
> *than glittering wealth or fame.*
> *I envy not the Northern girl, her robes*
> *of beauty rare,*
> *Though diamonds grace her snowy neck,*
> *and pearls bedeck her hair . . .*

This brought another high, light laugh from his dance partner. "Do you find this song funny?" Stuart asked. "It is my absolute favorite." How disappointing if she did not like it.

"But I am a Northerner," she confessed cheerfully. "From New York. Or have you forgotten?"

"Do I know you?" Everything about her seemed astonishingly familiar, especially now that she was in his arms.

"But of course," she assured him, all smiling innocence.

Stuart had seen those sly dark eyes before—but he could not think where. "Do you have a brother or a cousin on the other side, serving in the Fifth Corps?"

"Not at all," she answered primly. "Why do you ask?"

Stuart whirled her about in time to his favorite tune. "You remind me of a Yankee officer I talked to across Cub Run."

"Not surprising, seeing I am a Yankee." Again the mischievous grin.

"Then why are you here?" Not that he was complaining.

Tilting her head closer, she let him smell her dark perfumed hair, whispering softly, "Because I believe in your cause."

"Really?" His cause. What could it be? Slavery? Hardly—the only slave he owned was a cyborg manservant named Bob. Southern rights? That too was long dead. Excitement and high adventure—risking death to feel life? The Reenactment was rapidly losing any such thrill, becoming way too real.

"Absolutely." Her tone turned serious. "What is more, I know we can win."

Win? That was even more absurd. Lee's army of invasion was about to face two to one odds at Antietam—sending the South down to scripted defeat. "Kind thoughts, my dear, but the deck is heavily stacked against us."

Her grin returned. "Then demand a whole new deal."

He stared at her, wondering what to make of the pretty and determined New York Rebel. "How?"

Pressing against him, she let him feel the body beneath her silks. Surely they had done this before—but it had to be long ago. "You have sympathizers in the North, ready to help," she told him. "Ready to rise up when the time is right."

Stuart stared at the pretty lunatic in his arms. He had

nothing but contempt for copperheads—a lot of talk and damned little action. "Rise up? For what?"

She breathed a single word in his ear, "Freedom."

Freedom? Stuart thought of the telecast two months back—a bit of synthetic history—when Lincoln's Chimera-clone appeared before his assembled cabinet, tall and lanky, looking every bit like the face on the five-dollar bill. As the cameras focused in, the pseudo-president produced a book. He proceeded to read the *High-handed Outrage at Utiky*, by Artemis Ward—pronouncing it "the funniest thing I ever read." Millions listened in disbelief to some very old jokes. Drying his tears of laughter, the man playing Lincoln then presented his cabinet with a draft of the Emancipation Proclamation. Brushing aside objections, he insisted freeing the slaves was a necessity—only the timing mattered. "I will wait on the military situation. If God gives us a victory, I will consider it an indication of the Divine will that it is my duty to move forward in the cause of emancipation." Antietam would be that victory.

There were those who said it did not have to be that way. Stuart had heard dark talk of assassinating this pseudo-Lincoln, ending The Reenactment now—with the South ahead. Tasteless stupidity. Like that idiot with the Uzi. But desperate times bred desperate deeds. Stuart shook his head, asking, "What is your name?"

"Arabella," she replied coyly. "Arabella Cocky."

He could well believe it. "Why don't I remember you?"

"You will," she promised. "Give yourself time." The regimental band picked up the beat:

> *Hurrah! Hurrah!*
> *For the sunny South so dear . . .*

He twirled her about to the tune, and to the next, and the next, dancing the night away. She might be utterly mad, but he could not let her go. Something inside said that this was the woman for him—that he held his destiny in his arms.

From out of the night came the dull boom of artillery. Pelham's guns were in action, bringing the evening to an end. Stuart bowed, saying a sad good-bye, and the pretty New York Rebel pressed something into his hand. It was the silver heart-shaped locket she had worn around her neck. Opening it, he found two locks of hair inside, braided together, one cinnamon brown, the other midnight black.

> *Women and children, dry your eyes,*
> *The Southern gentleman never dies.*
> *He . . . can whip five Yanks with a palmleaf hat,*
> *Only the Yanks won't fight like that.*
> —*John Brown's Body*, Stephen Vincent Benét

Satan's Anvil

Stuart sat atop Lady Margrave, high on South Mountain watching endless blue-coated columns spread into wide thick waves below. McClellan's huge army was marching up Alternate US 40—the old National Road between Frederick and Boonsboro—fanning out to left and right, to force Turner's Gap and Fox's Gap. Stuart gave his head a sorry shake, "*Quo scelesti ruitis?*"

Seeing Hardeman's quizzical look, he translated—"Where do you hurry fools? Don't they teach you Latin in school?"

"No, they don't," Hardeman admitted, still looking mystified. He stared back down at the unfolding attack. "Breathtaking, even if . . ." Hardeman did not finish.

Stuart smiled. Even if they were just cyborgs? The boy was too polite to say it aloud—like Lee always calling the Yankees, "those people." Well, my lad, it does not much matter who's behind the musket. Cyborgs were programmed to kill just like "real" Yanks. You could even talk one out of shooting you—though Stuart would hate to have to try.

"How many would you guess?" Hardeman wondered.

"Way too many," Stuart decided. "Fortunately, we do not have to hold them off. That honor goes to the infantry."

Thin lines of gray-coated infantry faced the waves of blue lapping at South Mountain. Less than a quarter of Lee's outnumbered troops were there to defend the gaps. Confederate corps were scattered across three states, from Loudoun Heights on the Virginia side all the way up to the Mason-Dixon Line—complying with Lee's Special Order No. 191. Lee's famous lost order. The one dropped in a field outside Frederick wrapped around three cigars, and found by two noncoms in Company E of the 27th Indiana. The Reenactment needed no dropped orders—everyone knew where the scattered units were.

White puffs appeared amid the blue waves as they reached artillery range. "Come." Stuart turned Lady Margrave about. "I know how this will go." He was Lee's mobile reserve, and could not get caught up in this particular catastrophe.

By nightfall the next day he was asleep in the saddle, lurching along the Boonsboro Pike, Maryland 34 into Sharpsburg, utterly beaten and exhausted. Union commanders had driven fast and hard, smashing through the gaps, showing none of their historic caution. Going in without orders, avenging all those stinging defeats.

He found a big feather bed waiting for him in a brick house on the south edge of Sharpsburg. Lying atop the feather coverlet in a pleasant little room done up like a girl's bedroom, he studied the pink trim and primrose wallpaper. "Pretty, isn't it." Jeb sounded pleased. "Back in the real battle, I slept on someone's porch."

Stuart thought of Arabella and her blithe talk of "winning." What in hell had she meant? Certainly not this. Until now The Reenactment had been a glorious adventure—that had cost him very little. "Compared to what it had cost—say Von Borcke?" Jeb inquired.

"What makes you such a defeatist?" Stuart demanded.

The original Jeb Stuart had been the *beau sabreur* of the Confederacy. Stuart thought that taking in Jeb's DNA would make him dashing and unbeatable—but it had not turned out that way.

"You forget, I've seen this all before." Jeb sounded genuinely distressed, with a real weariness in his voice. "You may find it exciting, seeing the same mistakes made over and again—I am finding it repugnant."

Everyone had their problems. Stuart told his split personality to get some sleep, "We both need it."

Next morning Union columns marched down the Boonsboro Pike, filling the shallow bowl along Antietam Creek. When the Private Parks Act was passed—"Let the people who use 'em pay for 'em"—the Gettysburg Association bought up the lesser battlefields and took great care to return Antietam to its original condition. Relocating graves and putting monuments in storage, ripping up macadamized roads, replacing them with woods and standing corn. All of Sharpsburg was bought up and rebuilt to resemble the old-time town.

Watching the green vale fill with blue uniforms, Stuart clung to a slim hope. In the rules of The Reenactment, the Yanks had just one day to overwhelm them—September 17. Survive till dusk tomorrow, and it was home to Virginia. Given command of the reserve artillery, he spent the day siting and registering guns, making sure every shell would count. Telling Hardeman, "Stick close to me." Tomorrow he would need his lucky charm.

At dawn the federals came storming on, battle flags snapping above gleaming bayonets, crossing the Antietam Creek at a half dozen places, moving and firing like automatons—which they were. Stuart retreated to his guns, crossing a field of dry standing timothy. Bullets snaked through the grasstops, making him go up on tiptoe. Jeb laughed at his highstepping through the timothy. "Looking silly don't stop you getting hit."

Pushed into a shrinking pocket around Sharpsburg, Stuart fired his guns in two directions, supporting patchwork lines on either side of the town. He used up his dismounted cavalry plugging gaps, hoarding his living units.

By dusk he was down to just his staff and Pelham's battery. FitzJohn Porter's Fifth Corps—hardly used in the original battle—swept over Maryland 65 south of Sharpsburg, threatening to cut the Confederates off from the fords, trapping them against the Potomac. Sunset on September 17 was only minutes away, but he had to expend one of his live units if he hoped to hold them off. He shouted for Hardeman to take a message to Lee. "I'm using my last reserves. Send someone to plug the gap."

There was no one to send, but that hardly mattered. Dusk was upon them; by the time Hardeman got back it would be over. Watching his good luck charm gallop off, he congratulated himself on seeing Hardeman safe. A victory of sorts.

Now for sure defeat. Pelham could be counted on to muff this; Stuart had to see to it. Amid the barrage of musketry and howling shriek of incoming shells, he had to scream to be heard. Yelling for Pelham to limber up his battery, Stuart had the guns loaded with double canister—"Get set to ride right into them."

Putting himself at the head of the guns, Stuart galloped into action, the battery's wheels bouncing two feet in the air each time they hit a stone or ditch. Dashing up to a ravine full of Porter's infantry, the battery swung into position, blazing away point-blank. The federals returned the fire, cutting down gunners before they could reload, hitting the horses before they could be led away. Then with a realistic yell, blue-coated cyborgs came charging out of the ravine, sweeping into the battery, stabbing and killing.

Stuart met them as best he could, a one-man counter-charge, swinging his French sabre. They let fly a volley in return. Bullets ripped through his coat, slamming into Lady Margrave. One carried off his hat. Another hit him in the boot heel. Hands seized him from behind, hauling him off his horse.

Hitting the ground, he heard a high-pitched shout. "Keep yer head down." A Union officer stood over him, holding him down with a boot—a real person, not a cyborg—trying to keep him from getting shot.

Another volley ripped through the battery. Lady Margrave came crashing down on top of him, felled by the fire. He lay half-pinned by his horse, seeing only bluecoats. No one in gray or homespun remained upright. If he did not die in the next couple of minutes, he was a prisoner for sure. On the ground in front of him was a Fifth Corps cap bearing a Maltese cross.

Suddenly the firing rose to a new crescendo, accompanied by a wild yip-yip Rebel yell. A cheering gray-coated wave swept over the battery. Surprised and stunned, Stuart watched as Rebel cyborgs lifted Lady Margrave off his legs. Hardeman was there, helping him up again. All Stuart could say was, "What in Hell is happening?"

"It's A. P. Hill," Hardeman explained cheerfully, "falling back from Harpers Ferry. He's hit them from behind."

Hill's Light Division, recoiling from the failed attempt to take Harpers Ferry, had arrived on the field *behind* Porter's advancing Fifth Corps. All the bluecoats who had seized the battery were shot down or taken prisoner.

Hardeman smiled. "You won't believe who we've . . ."

Stuart waited for Hardeman to finish. But the young signal officer just stood there with his mouth open. A small dark splotch appeared on his gray blouse. It grew in size, spreading across his chest. Hardeman's mouth moved, as if trying to finish the sentence, but he toppled forward instead. Stuart managed to catch him. He held Hardeman until medevac came for him. By then it was too late. His cousin was dead, killed by a bullet from behind. Of course Hardeman had not really been his cousin—but cousin or not, he was sure enough dead.

Stuart trudged back into Sharpsburg, monumentally tired, wanting to get back to that brick house with the pink trim bedroom and primrose wallpaper. On opening the door, he was surprised to find the entrance hall full of fine white feathers. He saw more feathers in the parlor, and on the carpeted stairs, as if angels over Antietam had torn their wings in grief. When he got to the bedroom he saw that federal shells had ripped through the upper floors, bursting among the beds and pillows, filling the whole house with white feathers.

Ford's Theatre

This time the bands at the fords played "Carry Me Back to Ole Virginny." But there should have been no recrossing. The federal garrison from Harpers Ferry came right on the heels of A. P. Hill—only The Reenactment's one-day limit on the battle of Antietam kept them from being pocketed against the Potomac. Without it there would have been no retreat, no army left to fight another day. Making Hardeman's death all the more useless.

And not just Hardeman either. Stuart found he was the only unwounded survivor from Pelham's battery—thanks to the Yankee officer who pulled him from his mount. Pelham himself was dead, along with half his battery—the rest were dispersed to trauma units throughout the three-state area. One of The Reenactment's premier living units was replaced by cyborgs. A sure sign of worse to come.

Thoroughly demoralized, Stuart retired to his new headquarters, a reconstructed plantation called the Bower, between Charles Town and Martinsburg—in what was once Virginia. White tents dotted the oak-shaded lawns of the elegant Dandridge mansion. Bands played and Southern belles paraded about in ball gowns and parasols, practicing for the string of parties set for late in the month, when cavalry HQ officially opened.

Stuart no longer looked forward to the parties. The thrill he used to feel had evaporated. Hardeman, Pelham, and Von

Borcke, were all dead—good, bad, or indifferent, in the end it made no difference. Nor did it matter that they were all volunteers—firm believers in The Reenactment. Nothing mattered much, not anymore.

He could add Jackson to that list, killed by a sniper on the outskirts of Sharpsburg. Surgeons had harvested his DNA to use in a replacement. Until then, Stuart was the senior living commander in the Army of Northern Virginia. Bobby Lee had always been a cyborg—how else could you get someone to make the same mistakes over and over again?

"What did you expect?" Jeb asked. "These are battles—remember." Stuart told his inner critic to stuff it. As he sat arguing with himself, Colonel J. S. Mosby came strolling across the lawn towards the tent, wearing dress grays, a plumed hat, and a wide grin. The real Mosby had been a dapper partisan leader. His replacement enjoyed a roving commission as Stuart's aide-de-camp. He saluted, saying, "We've got a prisoner for you to see."

Stuart stared up at the unwelcome intruder. "Is that so?" Live prisoners were a prize, but Stuart was in no mood to gloat—not when the entire Army of Northern Virginia had just escaped capture on a technicality.

"Taken yesterday in Pelham's battery," Mosby boasted.

"I want no reminders of that action." Hardeman's death was all too fresh.

"This is one you won't mind." Not allowed to harry the federals, Mosby found his outlet in impertinence and practical jokes. Insisting on showing off an interesting prisoner was a plain attempt to cheer Stuart up.

"See what he's got," Jeb suggested.

Stuart shrugged, letting Mosby saunter off to fetch the prisoner. Standing up, Stuart straightened his uniform, checking himself in the tent mirror. Nonchalance is fine when you are winning, but it makes losers look beaten. Mosby returned with his prisoner—a blue-coated lieutenant bundled in a rumpled greatcoat, dark eyes downcast, face half-hidden by an oversized Fifth Corps cap bearing an anachronistic Maltese cross. Stuart instantly recognized the cap, having last seen it lying on the ground amid the ruins of Pelham's battery.

Mosby made a mock bow. "Major General Stuart—meet Lieutenant Cocky, 13th New York infantry." He swept the outsize cap off the prisoner's head. Black hair tumbled from beneath it—framing a pretty face. It was Arabella.

"We've met," was all Stuart could think to say, staring dumbfounded at the woman of Jeb's dreams. He motioned for Mosby to go—the guerrilla colonel departed, grinning happily. If you cannot make trouble for the enemy, goading your superiors is a good second best. When he was out of earshot, Stuart turned to Arabella, demanding, "What in blazes are you doing here?"

"I came for you." Arabella loosened her greatcoat, adding, "You might at least offer me a seat."

Southern hospitality took over. Stuart offered up his camp chair, reminding her that, "There are easier ways."

She settled smugly into the seat. "If I had waited for the next ball, you would have been dead—and I could not bear that. Not after waiting so long."

Stuart studied the beautiful lunatic. "So long for what?"

"For you—of course? Do you still have the locket?"

"Yes." He fished the locket out of his uniform pocket.

"Have you opened it?" she asked softly. He nodded, and she smiled. "Then you know who I am—and who you are."

He started to say Stuart Lovejoy—but he could not get the words out. Jeb stopped him.

Arabella smiled. "I have waited a powerful long time for you—Jeb. Those twin locks of hair have been handed down in my family for ages, along with our story. The sad tale of the Southern cavalier who broke my heart by getting himself killed. Then the Chimera process came along—a last chance to set things right, to give our sad story a happy ending. I had a descendant, a girl who did not like her life. She tried a couple times to kill herself—but medical science foiled her. If anyone ever needed a new personality, it was her. She took two strands from that locket—one for her, and the other for The Reenactment, giving us our second chance. We'd be fools not to take it."

Standing up, she slid easily into his arms. Her touch and smell brought back long-buried memories—how he met her in Lee's original invasion of Maryland, how he interrupted his march around McClellan's army to pay her a second midnight visit. They were no longer Jeb's memories, but his. Jeb spoke for both of them, telling Arabella, "You were absolutely crazy wearing a man's uniform, and risking getting shot."

She shrugged prettily. "Someone had to watch over you. If you were going to survive, you needed a friend in the enemy's camp. So I put those suicidal impulses to better use. Isn't that what The Reenactment's about?"

Tilting her head back, she offered up her lips, whispering, "Don't feel guilty. Flora is no longer with us." Flora was his wife—actually Jeb's wife. Long dead by this time. With a sigh, he succumbed. If anyone had looked into the general's tent, they would have seen him kissing a Yankee lieutenant.

When their lips parted, he looked at her. "Now what?" She clearly had a plan—and Stuart could not keep both her and Jeb in check. Together, they were too much for his battered psyche.

Arabella smiled. "Now we ride."

"To where?" asked Jeb, who was happy just to hold her. Their strands of hair had lain twisted together in that locket for the longest time. Did DNA rub off? Who knows? But her touch was the only thing that made him feel complete.

"To Washington, to put an end to this."

"How?" Jeb could not see what hope they had, two long-dead symbols of a lost cause.

"I cannot tell you. You just have to trust me. In your heart you may be Jeb Stuart, but part of you is still Stuart Lovejoy. And that part I still don't trust."

With good reason. Stuart did not trust her. What did she plan to do? Shoot Lincoln? Stop The Reenactment? Throw everything he worked and sacrificed for away? But Antietam had worn him down, and he could feel himself becoming just a voice in Jeb's head. "You cannot do this," he told his alter ego. "You're dead, remember?"

"That so?" Jeb scoffed. "Maybe I found something to live for." As they prepared to ride, Stuart tried to get Jeb to leave his big over-and-under LeMatt revolver behind—a .52 caliber monster with nine chambers and a charge of shot. But Jeb would not part with it—the pistol was as much a part of him as his horse or sabre. More so, since his horse was metal and plastic, and he had lost his French sabre at Antietam. "This is madness," Stuart protested.

"A madness you started," Jeb pointed out, jamming the huge pistol into his holster. Arabella exchanged her Fifth Corps uniform for a riding dress supplied by The Reenactment. Jeb helped her up onto a cyborg mare named Virginia, then he mounted Skylark, Lady Margrave's replacement. Bob, his cyborg groom, handed him the reins, saying, "Give 'em hell, General."

"I'll try," Jeb promised. Whatever Arabella had planned, this was his last foray into enemy country. Win or lose, Jeb was not going to lead another charge.

Fording the river near Shepherdstown, they picked up the old National Road at Turner's Gap, then continued on cross-country. Southern sympathizers in Frederick fed them and put them up for the night. By dusk the next day they were riding down on Washington from the north—the last direction a Confederate cavalry raid would come from. They breached the Beltway between Silver Spring and Chevy Chase, passing beneath hurtling lanes of headlights streaming in endless circles around the enemy capital.

Following Rock Creek into the heart of the city, they

slipped through Rock Creek Park, and around the National Zoo, coming out on Massachusetts Avenue. Washington was alive with blue uniforms, but it was all for show. Who really expected Jeb Stuart to come riding into town? In Arabella's blue greatcoat, he looked like part of the act. At Tenth Street they turned south, skirting the Convention Center, using the lane reserved for carriage traffic, waiting patiently at the lights for limos and Ethiopian taxi drivers to pass.

They turned Virginia and Skylark over to a parking attendant at the Grand Hyatt—giving the man a bogus room number and a green-backed picture of Andrew Jackson. Then they walked the last couple of blocks to Ford's Theatre, past chic shops and fancy eateries. Crowds converging on Planet Hollywood did not give them a second glance. To Stuart's surprise, the rent-a-cops at the stage entrance ushered them right in. Arabella had backstage passes, signed by Lincoln himself—a nice touch.

Slipping along the same back corridor that John Wilkes Booth used, they made their way to the Presidential Box. There was no Secret Service man at the door—Lincoln was not really the president. Just another cog in The Reenactment, whose duties did not extend beyond public appearances. This would be his last.

Jeb shed his blue greatcoat, and Arabella opened the door. Lincoln was alone in the box. He stood up as they entered, looking just like on TV, tall and ungainly, with deep-set eyes, a long, lined face, and an ill-fitting suit. He smiled slightly, "Major General Stuart, I presume?"

Jeb tipped his plumed hat and bowed. "At yer service, sir."

"Would it were so." Lincoln laughed. "Young man, I have much admired your work—from a safe distance—wishing it were done for me." He looked to Arabella. "And you my, dear?"

She nodded eagerly. "All ready, Mister President."

Flexing his long arms, Lincoln shot his cuffs, saying, "Let's get started." He turned to face the crowded theater. Arabella took Jeb's arm, guiding him to the president's right. The Ford's Theatre audience was rising to its feet, staring at the flag-draped box, sensing that something not on the program was about to happen. Like them, Stuart could only wait and listen. By then Jeb was completely calling the shots. Or rather Arabella was.

"Ladies and gentlemen." Lincoln's gravelly voice rose above the hushed whispers. "May I introduce Miss Arabella Cocky, and Major General James Ewell Brown Stuart, senior living commander in the Army of Northern Virginia. We three are together thanks to the Chimera process, without which we would all be long dead. For this we are eternally grateful—but we can no longer countenance the use to which our personalities have been put."

Lincoln paused, looking out at the hall full of upturned faces, who had come to see a stage show, and were now a part of history. "Therefore, by the power vested in me as president of The Reenactment, be it ordered that all historic personalities held as slaves within the body of another shall be henceforward and forever free."

Too stunned to applaud, the crowd stood staring. Jeb shook Lincoln's hand, then tipped his hat and took his leave, with Arabella on his arm. The corridor behind Lincoln's box was no longer empty. Camera lights flashed, and newspeople shouted questions. Keeping a tight hold on Arabella, Jeb forced his way through an excited mob of news crews, PR flaks, and Park Service security. Someone shoved a microphone in his face, saying, "Excuse me, Mr. Lovejoy . . ."

"Never heard of him," Jeb replied, shoving the microphone aside. Four more took its place.

"You are not Stuart Lovejoy?"

Tempted to beat a path with his sabre, Jeb told them, "My name is James Ewell Brown Stuart—Jeb to my friends. But you may call me General Stuart—sir. Now please stand aside, before I am forced to use a pistol."

None of them budged. "General Stuart, sir. What does this announcement mean?"

Arabella answered for him, "It means we are leaving." Lifting her skirt, she forced open a path for both of them, showing no more respect for lights and cameras than she had given the guns at Antietam. Riding boots came down hard on any foot that tried to bar her way. Startled media crews had to give ground or be bowled over.

Tugged along in her wake, Jeb turned to give the Yankee press corps a parting shot. "You may tell everyone, the entire nation, North and South—the War's over." Better late than never.

With his lady on his arm Jeb Stuart strolled out of Ford's Theatre onto the dark streets of Washington, DC, whistling a favorite tune:

> *If you want to smell hell,*
> *If you want to have fun,*
> *If you want to catch the devil,*
> *Jine the cavalry!*

Stepping Up to the Plate

Sandy Schofield

I blame it on the 1990s. A kid growing up then couldn't help but be repressed.

Repressed. That's his word, not mine. Which makes it our word, really, but it ain't one I'd use, at least until now. Every once in a while, Spence (I call him Spence—the rest of the world was calling him Spencer, up to a month ago) seeps through. He's given me control of this body, and he says he's got the mind, although I sometimes wonder if the mind and the body ain't one instrument. After all, he wouldn't'ta called for me if it weren't. So once in a while, I sound like him, and now he always sounds like me, and we're one messed-up team, scoreless, heading into the middle innings, hoping someone'll hit it over the fence.

I ain't never been to no shrink's office before—begging your pardon, ma'am—but Spence has, and he seems to think this'll work. You see, we're in our last week of this process and he don't want to give me up, but he don't like sharing his brain with me. He—hell, we—gotta make a choice, and make it soon. This process your company does, well they swore to the kid that it's reversible in the first three to six weeks. We're in week five, and it don't look like Spence here is happy with some of our differences. Me, I blame some of this on the work he done with that outside shrink—the one that had nothing to do with Nucore—before he went in for the procedure. See, my understanding of it from my reading of his memory is that we was supposed to meld personalities, not stay separate. I think we melded, he thinks I'm dominate, and we're in a hell of a mess.

You want history, our analysis of the problem, and we'll give you that. But we're gonna hold you to that promise, Doc, that you'll help us in the next few days latest. Because if reversal's what we need—and I don't think it is, but the kid is panicking—then we only got a week left to do it.

I know you know that, but I had to repeat it, for the kid's sake more than mine—you ever seen such a worrier?—and now we'll do what you say. I know you want Spence to tell the history part, but I'm gonna tell most of it because Spence is shyer than a virgin on a first date. He'll chime in if I get something wrong—he always does—and you'll recognize his voice because he talks with the most godawful prissy accent you ever heard from a boy who likes girls.

Babe!

Ah, hell, Spence. I know I ain't politically correct, but that's how folks talked in my day. And I ain't got time for niceties. I didn't then and I don't now. That's part of what you hired me for, to clean all them inhibitions out. And now he don't like it, Doc. Or maybe he likes it too much, I don't know.

All I know is a man can't live with this clenched-up feeling in his stomach all the time, and this constant thinking about every single move, this reassessing even before the act takes place. I'm thinking you help us break down them barriers the kid put up, or I'll bust 'em down myself. I ain't spending the next fifty years like this. It's bad enough that my throwing arm's gone, and I don't see as good as I used to. But Spence's body's built for speed, and there's some good musculature in the upper chest that I think I can make into something. I can probably hit as good as ever. But I ain't doing it with some repressed son of a bitch questioning my every move. And now that I'm here, I don't want to go back to there—wherever there was—but I will before I live like this.

Got it? Good. Okay. We start with history, just like you asked.

☐

The kid was born with a hell of a moniker: Spencer William Anthony Richard Marcus Blackwell the Third. Now, in my day, kids named like that either came from lotsa money, or from folks that wished they had lotsa money. From what I can tell, Spence here came from neither.

We were upper middle class.

Yeah. Like I said. Rich enough to have pretentions, and not rich enough to pay for all the fancy toys. Limboworld.

This kid has one mighty brain, and he's using it from day one. His parents let him on their computer before he can walk, and by the time he's eight, he's designing crap.

Software.

And by the time he's eighteen, he's got his own business—

Brains Unlimited—

And he's worth a goddamn fortune. Of course, he's never been laid, never had a cigar, had one drink—bourbon, right?

Brandy.

And coughed it back up like he's gonna puke it all over the kitchen counter of the friend who served it to him. He's never played sports. He don't like running, he don't like walking, and the bike his parents bought for him when he was nine is still collecting dust in their garage. He's twenty-five years old now, Doc, and all he's done is make money for shit he's designed in his head, things no normal human could ever understand—

Actually, Dr. Samperson, you use some of it now. I notice that someone in your office has installed the Office Version of my Smart

House program. The small blinking red light above the door would be a dead giveaway, even if you didn't use the Virtual Receptionist. And I would wager from the photographs on your desk that you have InterLink chips embedded in your children's shoulders so that you can find them anytime you want. Those children of yours look well cared for. Any parent with—

It's that goddamn repression again. What parent needs to know where his kid is every minute of every day? When I was growing up, parents didn't watch their kids. Sure, I got into some trouble—

Stealing, Babe.

Pranks. It was all pranks.

You were out of control. When you were seven, your parents sent you to reform school because you were out of control.

St. Mary's Industrial School was so I could learn a vocation. It wasn't no reform school.

It was a reform school and an orphanage. Even your official biographies admit this.

Ah, hell. Busted. You don't need to hear my history, do you, Doc? I mean you just need to log on to that Internet crap thing of yours and you can read all you want about me. George Herman "Babe" Ruth, the greatest baseball player of all time. That's what they're calling me now. But when I retired, ain't no one wanted me to coach no team or share my knowledge. I was kinda flattered when I understood what kinda help this kid wanted. And now he don't want to accept it.

It ain't that—it isn't that I don't want to accept his help. This union was my idea, after all. It's just that Babe here refuses to accept rules and boundaries. I had misunderstood that. I believed that any man who played professional ball would understand that games have rules and must be played by those rules. I had thought that my mind would be strong enough to control the worst of his urges. His second wife, after all, controlled his excesses quite well—

You forget, kid. I loved the broad. I just met you.

And I believed that my control would match his lust for life. It hasn't worked out that way.

Which is one big flaming load of horsepucky, if you ask me. This kid's always admired me. He's loved one sport and one sport only—baseball—probably because he spent his early years in the Midwest, and his dad would spend a couple hundred bucks (can you believe them prices?) for games a couple a times a year. The kid played Little League for one season and he has this memory—

Babe

—of hitting one ball—just one—and having it sail past all them other little kids and into the outfield where some scrawny five-year-old watched it land instead of catching it like he shoulda. It wasn't pretty, it wasn't poetry, but it was physical success, and he's held on to that memory for years. Then his folks move him to the Pacific Northwest where the Mariners are the closest thing to baseball, and even though in those days they had Ken Griffey, Jr., it wasn't the same. The Northwest ain't passionate about sports, never has been, never will be, and his hometown didn't even have a Little League team. They had something called PeeWee Soccer. Now me, I wouldn't go out for nothing called PeeWee and I can't say as I blame Spence here for not doing it neither. But what I do blame him for is never getting off his ass from that moment on. I tell you. It ain't healthy.

As if you're one to lecture about health. What about the "bellyache heard 'round the world"?

Too many hot dogs can do that to you.

And so can syphilis.

At least I had sex.

And paid for it.

See how he tries to flap me up, Doc? He asked for my help, but he don't respect me. I thought he did at first. He thought he did too. He always admired me. I went "all out" he said. I was the physical equivalent of him, no barrier could stop me when I was playing ball and no barriers stop him when he's designing his computer crap.

I'm the best software designer in the business.

And we're about equal on the ego, too, in case you couldn't tell. But see, the difference between me and him is somewhere along the way, he got scared. His mom died from complications of that bone disease—

Osteoporosis.

—at least that's what the doctors said, although I don't buy it. Since I joined this team, I been rifling Spence's history like a pile of file cards, and it's my personal opinion that the old broad died of the same fear that's got Spence now. If it hurts, you don't do it.

You see, she coulda got up and exercised and made them bones stronger—not better, but stronger—and it woulda hurt, but she coulda lived day to day. Instead she hears she won't get better so she refuses to get her physical therapy, lies in bed, stops eating, and then stops drinking, waiting for the Lord to take her. Good thing the Lord is kinder than me. I'd've let her wait.

Babe!

Folks who give up don't count for shit in my book. And that's what you're doing, kid. You're walking the same road.

I brought you in, didn't I?

And you ain't taking my advice. He's got this secretary— I ain't never quite seen a woman like her. And she's interested. I can tell. I keep telling him, take her to dinner, take her to bed, for godsake. But he keeps talking about lawsuits and harassment and stuff that don't seem relevant to the relationships between men and women. Maybe I don't get this century. Maybe people are supposed to be all tied up in knots—

Babe! She wants history, not analysis.

She wants history and analysis, kid. I guess that famous brain of yours wasn't paying attention.

But history. Okay. After the mom dies, Spence here loses

his father. The man was too fat and his heart couldn't take the strain. The docs was all amazed he went that long. Guess his heart was bad from the beginning. Anyway, as he's dying, he says to the kid, "I worry about you, son. You aren't living your life. You're just existing."

Of course that makes the kid mad because he thinks he's living. He's—

Made millions. Started companies. I've had more ideas than my father ever could have. And he lived off me for the last ten years of his life! In fact, he wouldn't have survived those last ten years if it weren't for the money I made, money that paid for specialists his HMO would never cover. He didn't understand that that was living—

That same day, the day before his dad dies, Nucore holds their briefing. The kid dismisses the whole thing. He don't want no one in his brain, nosirreebob. But when his dad dies the next day, he's all alone, and he begins thinking maybe he could use a tutor, you know, a mental guide to living like his dad wanted him to.

It's not that simple.

Actually, it is. No matter what he says. He looked through the available DNA list and saw my name. And he said of all the guys on the list (he was too scared to consider girls)—

I was not. I just didn't like what happened to Tsering.

—I was the only one who lived his life to the fullest. That, and I guess he always wanted to repeat his old baseball triumph, so he brought me on board.

Not quite. I went through a thousand hours of psychological training, preparing for this. You have to understand that it was never my intention to meld with Mr. Ruth. I wanted to remain separate, to use him as an internal guide that could be accessed whenever I needed him. I did not want a constant presence in my brain, scrambling for dominance.

He wanted me to act like one of them computer gizmos he designs. A click of a button and I disappear or reappear on cue. That's what he wants. I don't do that. I believe in experiencing everything to the fullest, and while he's been kaboshing that, I ain't been disappearing. I been trying to understand this place. Lemme tell you, given a choice, I'd go back to my own time any way I could. This place is tight-assed, full of fear and so much judgment that I ain't never been able to live the way I want.

There woulda been no Babe here. You'da washed me and ironed me and left me out to dry, a cleaner version of the Sultan of Swat. Hell, I'da pointed to the stands like I did at the '32 series in Wrigley, called my shot, and them commentators you got woulda been arguing the accuracy of my point from the minute I done it. Hell, I probably wouldn'ta been standing at the plate at the age of thirty-seven. You people'd drummed me out for my "lifestyle." You know they used ta room me with rookies so I wouldn't keep none of the other stars awake. Keep 'em awake, hell. I was never in the goddamn room.

Spence here, he'da lived in that fucking room, and never've left. This boy don't want to live no life. He wants to think his way through it. And he's been lucky. He got the talent to do that. But someday it's gonna catch up to him. He's only twenty-five now. Life ain't dealt its full hand. He don't know that. He thinks he's been through it all, losing his folks, being alone. But his company's good and people want his work. He don't know what it's like when they call you a has-been, when you have all the knowledge in the world and no one wants it, when the best years of your life are behind you and you know it, and dragging your ass out of bed day in and day out is a chore beyond belief.

When those days finally come to me, I had lived my life, taken all the joy from it and squeezed it dry. And while base-ball was gone to me, I had Claire, and she made them last years possible. Spence here, when his business goes and he gets thrown out by the board he put together or sued by your goddamn so-called Justice Department or gets sick like he's afraid he will, he won't have no one. And that's the thing he don't get, not deep down inside.

You can't judge my life by yours, Babe.

Thought that's what you brought me on to do, Spence.

I didn't bring you in to take over my life.

That's what living does, kid. It takes over your life. And if you do it well, you hit hundreds over the fences, and you fluff just as many. You learn how to take the strikeouts as well as the homers, and you learn that life is about both.

So you can't shut me off like a goddamn machine. But you got enough training to separate me out. Now, Doc, I think you need to help us meld because if we don't, we'll be locked in this war for the rest of his natural life.

Or we terminate this entire experiment.

Call it a failure? I thought you didn't fail, kid.

I didn't. You just weren't what I needed.

I'm precisely what you need. But you're afraid of that. So afraid that you invited me in at the same time as working to keep me out. I'm the poor cousin who you're afraid to admire. I brought you to the doc because you believe in her kinda hocus-pocus, but you ain't even gonna give this a chance, are you, kid? It just scares you too much.

I'm not afraid, Babe. I just want to remain myself.

If you wanted that, kid, you wouldn'ta spent millions for this procedure.

I'm successful.

In one thing. And kudos to you for that, kid. But ain't no one gonna remember you, ain't no one gonna say, that Spence, he was one hell of a human being.

They remember you for your excesses.

They remember me for my personality. They remember me for being larger than life. They remember me because, for all the women I screwed, and all the cigars I smoked, I played a hell of a game. I also gave all I could to kids who needed some attention. I never neglected them, and never forgot them. Hell, in '22 when that asshole Jimmy Walker

said I let down the kids by playing bad, I made sure that
never happened again. I had heart, kid, and you don't. All
you got is brains and fear. And believe me, that ain't enough.

Hey, what are you doing?

I still got control of the body and I'm taking us outta here,
kid. We'll go down the hall and have them separate us for
real and for good. I'll go back to that never-never world, and
hope the next time they hook me up with someone, it'll be
someone who'll appreciate me.

I appreciate you.

From a distance maybe. What I've learned in my life is
you can play your best for the team, but if the team don't
wanna play, you ain't gonna get the pennant. Me, I've always
liked being on a team that gives as much as I do. And you
never will, kid. That's too bad, too. Because you got possibilities. You're just gonna throw them away.

Sorry to take your time, Doc. Talking was more beneficial
than I thought it'd be. I been thinking about this ever since
I came to myself again, and it wasn't until I spoke to you
that I put it all together. I done all I could. In fact, I done
more than I should. The core of the problem ain't one that
can be solved, at least not by you, and not by me. It's up to
good ole Spence here, and he's acting just like his late la-
mented mother.

It's the bottom of the ninth, two outs, and he's up. But he
don't wanna bat. He ain't even coming out of the dugout.

That ain't no way to play baseball, and that sure as hell
ain't no way to live.

Guess it's my lot in life to offer advice and not have nobody take it. I can accept that. Maybe someday your company'll find me someone who'll actually want to listen.

It's been a pleasure, ma'am. You and your fellow docs be
nice to ole Spence here when he wakes up alone. I gotta
hunch he's gonna be spending the rest of his life that way,
so he may as well have help getting used to it.

I think separation is for the best, Babe.

I know you do, kid. And I can't make no one live who don't want to. Funny, ain't it. I'm the one being subtracted from you, but you're the one who's gonna stop living.

I'll live, Babe.

You'll breathe, kid. And believe me, that ain't enough.

Sittin' on the Dock

David Bischoff

"Otis! You sing with me tonight!" the man said to the memories and the soul.

The lights, the tart smell of his makeup, the excitement and the déjà vu of applause. Applause past, applause future, applause now . . .

It hung above the dressing room like a thunderstorm of flowers, and the taste of rhythm and blues shivered in the instruments of the band as they sat, twenty-first century tuned, humming with electricity and aural connection.

"Damn, you're a good-lookin' fella!"

Thorn Reynolds—"The Smooth One"—beamed at himself in the dressing room mirror. He had amazingly Nordic features—symmetrical, blemishless, handsome—for what was inside him now.

He touched a finger to the tie of his tux. Black silk. Beautiful, man, just like every groovy fibre of this special suit, designed to make a guy look like a million bucks for the HDTV screens out there. Of course, Thorn Reynolds was worth a great, great deal more than a million—how else could he have afforded Otis and the others? But it was looks that counted now, and his specially treated, youthful white skin was going to be absolutely vibrant as he opened his mouth tonight and came out with THE black voice for the twenty-first century.

And with the money he made?

Sheesh . . . That voice would just get better and better . . . He'd be a star like no other star over any century.

He took a long cool sip from the tumbler of champagne by his hand. Why wait to celebrate? This is for you, Otis, he thought, closing his eyes and feeling the cool bubbly running down to explode into warmth. And Nat and Louis—you're next. You mine, all mine.

Otis said nothing, which was just fine. This personality integration wasn't really Reynolds's cup of tea. He liked himself just the way he was.

And of course he'd edited out that plane crash bit . . .

There was a polite rapping at the door.

"Mr. Reynolds?"

"Stanton? Get your ugly butt in here."

The door opened and a short, furtive-looking man with curly hair slipped through. His eyes scooted about the room as though to make sure there wasn't anything threatening in here—and then they lighted on his employer.

"That's some audience out there, Mr. Reynolds," said the little man. Intelligence and guile glinted behind the obsequiousness. He wore a suit as well, but he looked uncomfortable in it. "This is some place."

"You've never been in Carnegie Hall before, Stanton?"

"No, sir. I like clubs myself." The man looked around the dressing room. "Nice. Old-fashioned, huh? Not high-tech."

"Only high-tech needed is the TV and audio and satellite hookup—and the process of course." Reynolds winked at his associate as he tapped his head. Good old DNA.

"Deoxyribonucleic acid, Stanton."

The associate beamed. "Or in your case, 'De Negro Application!"

Actually, of course, it was the Chimera Process, modified to a very rich performer's personal whims.

The Chimera Process had been an amazing discovery indeed—but no less startling was the fact that it had unveiled something unknown to science before. DNA in the human body was not only a code—but a storage and processing port for memory, character, and personality. Oh yes, and talent too! That was the part that had perked Reynolds up, the moment he'd had this process's details whispered to him by this very same soul here, Mack Stanton, black marketeer supreme. (It was Stanton, after all, who had kept him abreast of all the black market services that had helped keep his skin and his libido young, yea, these many years). Yes, the moment he'd heard about the Process (and of course he could afford it) he acted.

It had taken some serious work, but he was able to get what he needed almost immediately. As it happened, the remains that had been most accessible (with a little Burke and Hare work, natch) had been those of Otis Redding, the great soul singer who had died at the age of twenty-six, tragically, in the number two killer of pop stars—the light aircraft. (Number one, of course, being drugs and booze.) Redding was perfect because he had just enough experience to be great—and enough burgeoning talent to give Reynolds exactly the jolt his career needed at this time.

Thorn Reynolds had been a member of a "boy band" in the nineties—The Alley Guys—a manufactured group of white males who could dance a bit and sing a little like soul singers . . . and maybe harmonize too. But he'd spun off on his own into a solo pop career that had netted him millions and millions. Canny business work had umphed those millions into billions . . . And look at him now . . . One of the richest guys in the world.

But he wanted more than that. He wanted to be a star whose voice and fame would live forever. A Frank Sinatra who would dominate the music world not just for a couple of decades ... but a whole century ... And what with rejuvenation processes, two centuries. Heavens knew, with a guy like Stanton by his side, he'd be able to get whatever science and medicine had to offer—and even what they didn't have to offer.

But there had to be a little twist in the scenario for that to happen ...

"So you've got some news for me then, Stanton," said Reynolds. He was considering pouring his man a glass of the Chateau Rothschild ... but no ... He realized that he wanted it all for himself.

"Nat King Cole. Louis Armstrong." The small man snapped his fingers, one, two. "And I'm getting a line on the dead Temptations, Frankie Lymon—and say ... there's a piece of Elvis, if you want ..."

Reynolds cringed. "No thanks. That's what everyone went for first. No, I want good musicians ... Black singers. And I want the best ... and *all* of the best ... And I don't want anyone else to have them. Understand?"

"Sure! Of course," said Stanton. "That's the whole idea, right? Damned brilliant too, Mr. Reynolds." Stanton eyed the bottle of champagne in the ice bucket and licked his lips. "You get the soul and ditch the souls ... Other guys get squat! That's what I'm working on."

Reynolds smiled. He shrugged. "Good man. There's a nice bottle of Heineken in the minibar, Stanton. My treat."

"Hey, thanks!" The little man hurried over to the fridge and got out a beer. He opened it and took a long drag, then wiped his mouth on the sleeve of his coat. "Anyway, it's taking a little bit of money ... Hell, a lot of money ..."

"As much as it takes. I just want an accounting ... and no skimming, my friend."

Stanton grinned. "Sure. And far as I can tell, nobody else has started this yet. So if you want, we can even go for the blues greats ..."

"That's all right, Stanton. Just the great singers. That's all I want."

"Well, I'm doin' it, Mr. Stanton. Pretty soon, you're going to have them all." He took another chug. "Well, the ones you want anyway . . ."

"It's going to be a regular soul train when I sing, guy," said Reynolds, with a broad wink at his associate. He looked into the mirror. "Hmm. Stanton. My eyes blue enough tonight?"

"You bet, Mr. Reynolds."

"They should be the price I—"

. . . a glare of hatred . . .

. . . the smell of dismal city streets . . .

. . . a hail of rocks . . .

. . . an omnipresent weight . . .

It was almost as though he'd been hit by something hard.

Reynolds gasped. A sharp pain trembled through him, and he found himself staggering. He knocked over the bucket of ice, and the champagne bottle went rolling, spewing and gushing onto the brightly polished tile.

"Hey! Mr. Reynolds. You okay?" Stanton hurried to him and caught him before the singer collapsed. Gently he eased the man down into a chair.

The afterimages of dim fire were fading, and the spell lifted.

"Give me a drink," said Stanton.

"Maybe it's bad champagne, man . . ."

"Not that champagne . . ."

Stanton handed over the glass, and Reynolds took a long sip. The splash of alcohol washed over his raw nerves, taking off the edge.

"Used to have something like this before, Stanton. Early days," said Reynolds.

"Huh?"

"Kind of stage fright. Maybe the idea of singing live in front of the world is getting to me."

"But you've done it before!"

"Yes, but not with the augmentation."

"Maybe it's Redding. Maybe he had stage fright or something," said Stanton.

Reynolds frowned. Suddenly he felt as though wrinkles were coming over his face. Wrinkles he'd paid damned good money to keep away.

"I thought that Drs. Ezra and Bashwalli had edited all the negative things out!"

"Well, yeah, that's what they told me . . ." The small man's brow furrowed with concern. "You tried singing, didn't you?"

Reynolds nodded.

"How did it sound? You record it?"

"Yes, of course."

"Maybe you'd better let me hear it."

"Look, take my word. It's fine . . ."

"Mr. Reynolds. We can always cancel. If there's a problem, we should know about it now."

Reynolds nodded. "I taped the rehearsals with the band last night." There was a digital tape on the counter. The singer, shrugging off the last of the odd queasiness and fear, got up, got it, and plugged the disc into the player at the side of the dressing room.

A fat, plunky bass line started out, followed by classic Curtis Mayfield–style guitar. Then, backed by a shiver of strings, a voice began to sing.

It started with a furry growl that rose up into a sweet whisper. Tender feelings were expressed amidst frustration and loneliness. The voice was an odd mixture of velvet and gravel that somehow felt like a wrenching tour of emotions, couched in beat and melody. It immediately cried out to be listened to, an amazing combination of tonal skill, phrasing, and pure raw feelings.

Reynolds felt the hairs stand on the back of his neck.

"Jesus! That's amazing. . . ." said Stanton. He scratched

his head. "Redding's the guy that did 'Sittin' on the Dock of the Bay,' right? Yeah, and he wrote 'Respect' and 'Try a Little Tenderness.' "

"You know your R and B, brother," said Reynolds in a whisper, the shivers in his spine just subsiding. Me, he thought. That's me singing!

"But I don't remember Redding . . . Well, how can I say this . . . sounding so good."

Reynolds nodded. "Otis Redding was a great singer . . . an improvisational genius. He came up through gospel and he sang like Little Richard for a while . . . But then he got his own style and just ran with it. But he didn't have much range, and his voice was a little thin . . ." Reynolds grinned. "I've got that and everything money can buy, Stanton. But the key a great singer has to have is to know when to let your voice break, when to sound untrained and real." Reynolds tapped his head. "That's what I have now with Otis inside me."

"You're sure you're going to be able to do the show tonight? I mean, you didn't look too good there. I could get you a doctor or something."

"I'm fine. After hearing that—" He pointed at the tape machine that had let go of such an incredible sound—a sound that he had produced. A sound that would indeed make him immortal. "I have to go out and put my stamp on music." He grinned. "And if I fall down . . . I'll make it part of the act."

"Like James Brown!"

"Yes. Too bad the Number One Soul Brother's still alive, hmm, Stanton . . . ?"

Stanton shook his head, a worried look crossing his features.

"That's not my game, man."

Reynolds laughed, feeling much, much better. "Oh, he'll be available soon enough. No need to hurry." He looked at his watch. "Now if you'll excuse me, I need to do just a little bit of focussing before the show . . . Tell you what . . . We'll have dinner at my house in Mt. Kisco tomorrow night. We'll watch a tape of tonight's show. And we'll discuss the future of soul music, Stanton. My soul music."

Reynolds dismissed his associate and sipped at his champagne.

Outside, the world was waiting for what he had.

He chuckled to himself.

What he had for them was a new and immortal voice.

"Here's one for you, Otis, my friend," he said, drinking another sip of his champagne. "Here's one for you."

☐

It wasn't like he needed the booze to loosen him up or to gentle his nerves. He just liked to use it once in a while, like Sinatra. Sinatra mostly had a belt of whiskey or four before going on . . . Often carrying it with him. Dean Martin was supposed to have been the drunk, but that had been part of his act. It was the Chairman of the Board that had been the hard boozer.

"The champagne's in the bucket, Mr. Reynolds," said the gofer. "I got a nice Havana cigar out there too, if you want it."

"Good. Good," said Reynolds. "And a pitcher of water. I think I'm going to do some sweating tonight."

Often he'd sit on a stool and have a cigar for the slow songs, but he didn't think he'd do that tonight. No, tonight it was going to be a cool blue-eyed soul singer. There was going to be a lot of moving around, a lot of falling on his knees.

Outside, he could hear the murmur of the privileged audience who were going to get to see this show live. Reynolds fancied he could smell their perfumes and colognes, dancing together with the cultured chatter in a miasma. He almost wished that this wasn't stuffy Carnegie Hall—he wished it were the Apollo up in Harlem—he wished that when he

started singing his fast songs, people would start dancing . . .
Start swaying . . . Start a blessed ring shout . . .

Ring shout?

What the hell was that? he wondered. Something from the
Redding genes maybe. He didn't have time to speculate,
though, because the director's voice was ringing in his ear-
node.

"Okay, Mr. Reynolds. The band is set. We're going to go
into this cold, just like you want it. Just you, the band, and
the whole wide world . . ."

A split second of fear. A nanomoment of terror as he
looked over to the band, already set up behind their instruments (Dick Litchard on drums, Steve Abramson on lead
guitar, Marshall York keyboards, Mickey "Mouse" Munch on
bass . . . "The Smooth Crew" ready to lay down some "whip-
hop" as the "Boss-man" Reynolds liked to call it).

Mouse looked over. He took his hand off the fret of his
big Rickenbacker bass and gave his employer a grin and a
thumbs-up . . . and the spark of fear was gone, replaced by a
golden glow of adrenaline.

He could hear the director's voice in his ear. "Cue cameras. Cue satellite. Cue announcer. We're on!"

One more chug of champagne, and the singer was ready
for the song, lunging out toward the curtain, to meet the
world, to meet the beat . . .

"Okay, Otis. The spotlight is on," he murmured to himself.

The thrilling boom of the announcer's voice seemed to lift
him up from gravity itself:

"Ladies and gentlemen . . . The King of Music. Mr. Thorn
Reynolds!"

The curtain rose, and a roll of applause thundered.

Holding his automike in his intimate way, Reynolds
winked at the camera. "Tonight—" he spoke into the mike.
"Tonight I'm yours!"

The band flashed into movement, and a blare of beautiful

horns courtesy of the synthesizer blitzed into joyful reality. The drums thumped out the beat and Reynolds turned into his mammoth selling song "Tonight—I'm Yours."

A strange power filled him.

Astonishingly, his voice took off. Instead of just swinging the lyrics, precise and full of tremulo and vibrato—rehearsed and smooth—he found himself reading new emotions into the lyrics . . . Pausing and hanging on to the notes and pushing them into places they had not gone before.

After the first few verses, the band fell out of sync . . . and there seemed to be some confusion.

He turned around to them, and the drummer looked confused.

"We're roughing it tonight," he said, looking back at the band. " 'Cause tonight . . . tonight I'm yours."

The look of alarm and concern on the band's faces left with a blink . . . and they reverted to rehearsal form, laying down a loose background and beat, but basically following what Reynolds was doing and not following any specific charts.

When the song was finished—a full ten minutes of shouts and whispers and tension and release, of call and response with his boys' instruments, Reynolds found himself at the edge of the stage, drenched in sweat (he could smell himself!) and the audience was standing, roaring, tears flowing . . .

He loosened his tie and bowed. The applause increased.

"Tonight," he said. "Tonight I'm yours."

He felt lifted . . . Lifted from wherever he'd been before . . . someplace low to someplace high.

It was like the finale of a wrenching, emotional performance that he'd worked out of the audience . . . Only at the very beginning of the show!

"Jesus!" he said. "Jesus, Otis! Where to now?"

And he found himself going over to the boys.

They were looking at him oddly, but clearly swept up into improv heaven themselves.

"Hey—what gives?" said Steve, coming over.

"Taking a chance. I'm going to change the song order. You guys okay with that!"

There was cheer in the guys' eyes. Consummate musicians, they had always complained that Reynolds never jammed enough—and was never spontaneous enough for the music that he played. They knew all the songbooks, no question . . . So there was no problem with them keeping up.

The Mouse grinned. "You bet! What's up, Boss?"

"I'm feeling like 'I've Been Lovin' You too Long!' "

They all looked surprised, but none looked disapproving. That famous Otis Redding song had been something that Marshall had suggested that Reynolds try a long time ago— and he'd always turned them down.

Oh sure they knew the song. They were just clearly extremely surprised that Thorn Reynolds knew it!

If they only knew how, he thought, feeling a thrill.

"Take us to the river, Boss," said Mouse.

Cutting a swath through the applause back to the front of the stage, Reynolds drew a cloth out of his jacket and wiped his forehead.

With only a whisper of jangling electric guitar behind him, he launched into a breathy, succinct expression of pain and regret that was "Loving You Too Long." The band rallied behind him, turning it from its original three minutes and ten seconds on the *OTIS BLUE* album into an eight-minute slow dirge of sorrow.

When it was finished, Reynolds was on his knees again. The audience sat stunned, and there was silence for a moment. Then all was chaos. A roar unlike any that Carnegie Hall had ever experienced before arose—

Reynolds could almost reach out and touch a roar that stretched out around the world. A roar of recognition—a feeling that yes, you know what it's like . . .

He was sopping wet. Breathing slowly but deeply, Reynolds rose up and peeled his jacket off. He handed it to his assistant and took a pull from a water bottle . . . No ostentatious gesture. Just pure thirst. He felt no desire for champagne or for alcohol of any kind. Just water . . .

You don't miss your water till the well runs dry, a voice inside him said.

He walked back to the band.

"I can't do my boring old stuff now," he said, finding a big smile creasing his face. "Let's get down!"

"More Otis?" said Mouse eagerly.

"And let's make it like Otis got to play with Funkadelic, Bootsy Collins, and George Clinton."

He whispered more instructions, and they immediately launched into an Otis Redding–like version of Sam Cooke's "Shake" . . . but instead of cutting it short, they played up the funky bass lines, the synthesizer—and turned the staid Carnegie Hall into a steam bath.

Dancing! Dancing! So much dancing . . . he thought, watching the audience get up and move . . .

He'd taken them from regret to joy.

There was a half an hour left to the concert. Instead of playing any of his own songs, he sang classic soul songs. He sang some Four Tops and Temptations. He did some Stevie Wonder—"Can't Help Myself," "My Girl," "Fingertips, Part II," but all with the gospel improvisational style that Otis had brought to the stirring, shouting, sweating, and feeling of putting yourself on the line with your music. He'd never sung better—ever . . . He was possessed. Filled with the spirit and the sound and the grace of release and expression . . .

At the end of "That's How Strong My Love Is," an amazing roar tumbled over him.

A voice erupted in his ear.

"We've got five minutes until sign-off, guy. What a show!" The director.

He didn't even have to think about how to use those minutes.

Reynolds looked over to the band. Their jackets were off. The drummer's shirt was off, too, and sweat rippled down his bare midriff.

They looked at him, and they seemed to know exactly what he was going to do as well.

"Let's go to the Dock, guys," he said.

They nodded, smiling.

As they started up the background for that timeless song, Thorn Reynolds went up to the edge of the stage. The applause died, and he sat down at the lip of the proscenium.

Suddenly, the hall melted away. The people in their fine dark clothes and fancy hairstyles went away. The television cameras went away.

He was sitting before a theater full of other faces. Faces black, faces white, faces of many shapes and sizes—their eyes alive and listening. It was not memory, but it was not unreal. They were not ghosts but they were not alive, these people—and when he sang the song, "Sittin' on the Dock of the Bay"—the song that Otis Redding had recorded just three days before the plane holding him and most of the Bar-Kays had gone down into Manona Lake, Madison, Wisconsin—When he sang the song, the others sang along.

It was not memory, and it was a form of reality, realer than real he felt—And for a moment, as he sang that wistful song, he wondered if Rod Serling was going to make an appearance. The people in this twilight audience did not accuse or throw guilt . . . They simply sang in their styles, sang their hearts. . . .

And in the polyphony and antiphony, in the ringing resonance of their voices young and old, eternal yet gone, he heard the voices of a people torn from their homeland, their music their comfort and memory of that place. People under the yoke, who dreamed of better things. People whose emotional life was rich and strange and full with longing and grief and love—and who shared that life with each other. He heard the spirituals and the shouts, the gospel—and he heard for the first time how that music went to blues and ragtime, to jazz and bebop, to rhythm and blues and funk—to hip-hop and rap . . . And how it had been the voice of many and many, and how it had set them free, always.

When the show was over, and the cameras had shut down, the audience still applauded. The band, sweating as much as Thorn Reynolds, came to him and they hugged him, group style, as they never had before.

"You got it, man!" Mouse said.

"What a show! What a show!" said Marshall.

They wanted to interview him, the media did. And all the people he knew wanted to party with him. Before Thorn Reynolds might have wanted to hang on to this moment, party all night.

Party like it was still 1999, to paraphrase a certain other performer.

Now though, he just wanted to go back to his penthouse apartment in New York and sleep.

And as he took his limo home, he realized that tonight was the first night his band—black men all—had ever touched him.

☐

"You're not eating," said Stanton, looking up from his filet mignon.

Thorn Reynolds swirled his coffee. He hadn't felt like drinking champagne or any other kind of alcohol, either. He'd slept like a rock all day—and in fact had to change his dinner appointment to his place in Manhattan. But he did want to talk to Stanton.

Very much so.

"Not hungry."

"Man, that was some hell of a show you put on last night!" the little man said for the tenth time. "Some hell of a show. I recorded it, and I tell you, I'm going to watch it over and over. It's a classic. You're going to be all you wanted to be.

I guess it's the Otis Redding part of you that put you over the top, right? Man, it was spooky."

Reynolds smiled wanly. "So to speak."

"I can't wait to hear what you sound like when you get those other guys' DNA stuff charged into you," said Stanton. "You want to do some real black music? I'm looking into cornering the Paul Robeson remains, man. Maybe you'll become an actor, too, huh?"

Reynolds shook his head.

"No. Not going to happen, Stanton."

"Well it can, if you want . . ."

"No. I guess Otis will stay with me . . . but I'm not going to keep him if he wants to go anywhere else. And I'm not going to control anything. That's pretty much for others to decide, not me."

Stanton put his knife and fork down and swallowed hard. "What—But . . ."

"I guess maybe that tailoring of the DNA didn't work, and I'm more Otis Redding than I wanted to be—" said the singer. "Or maybe last night changed my attitude. Stanton, ever since the minstrel shows of the nineteenth century, the dominating classes have been using Afro-American music for their own entertainment and gain . . . I'm just the latest in a long line of that . . . You can't copyright musical styles, after all . . . they just develop . . ."

"What . . . You're going to start singing opera?"

"No. No, I'll keep on singing . . . I can't stop. The Otis Redding part of me wouldn't let me, even if I wanted to— He doesn't want to die young again . . ."

Stanton looked at his employer. He blinked. "Shit, guy! If you don't corner the market on the kind of musical talent you showed last night . . . someone else will."

"It won't be me," said Reynolds. "And I'm going to the press and tell everyone why I could sing like that the other night. And if others want to become soul singers . . . let them.

I like the way I sound now . . . And I'm going to stay that way. Or develop, as the case may be . . ."

Reynolds shook his head. "I don't think it really makes any difference. There's always going to be talent, and there's always going to be influences. I'm just not going to be the man to put chains on anyone . . . or anything."

Stanton shrugged and continued eating. "Hell, Mr. Reynolds. I thought you got the process with Otis Redding's DNA—not Abraham Lincoln's."

And the Otis Redding part of Thorn Reynolds said to himself, *Hmm, brother. Now that's a thought . . .*

Contributors' Notes

Elizabeth Ann Scarborough is the Nebula Award–winning author of *The Healer's War*, as well as twenty-two other novels and numerous short stories. Her most recent books are *The Godmother's Web* and *Lady in the Loch*, as well as an anthology she edited, *Warrior Princesses*. She lives in a log cabin on the Washington coast with four lovely cats who find her useful for the inferior human DNA that granted her opposable thumbs for opening tuna cans. When she is not writing, she beads fanatically, and is also the author/designer/publisher of a bead book of fairy-tale designs called *Beadtime Stories*.

Lillian Stewart Carl has lived in the Dallas, Texas, area since 1972. She and her husband, a geophysicist, produced, raised, and unleashed upon an unsuspecting world two sons, one in publishing, one in computers. She's published four fantasy novels and three romantic suspense novels, all heavy on history and mythology, and a dozen short stories. She's always wanted an excuse to do something with the six wives of Henry VIII. Historians of all persuasions agree that Anne was probably innocent of all charges.

Elizabeth Moon first gained prominence in the fantasy field with her Paksenarrion trilogy, *Sheepfarmer's Daughter*, *Divided Allegiance*, and *Oath of Gold*. She has revisited the world of Paksenarrion in two subsequent novels. She has also written science fiction, collaborating with Anne McCaffrey on the novels *Sassainak* and *Generation Warriors*. She lives with her husband and son in Texas.

Margaret Ball lives in Austin, Texas, with her husband, two children, three cats, two ferrets, a hedgehog, and a large black dog. She has a B.A. in mathematics and a Ph.D. in linguistics from the University of Texas. After graduation, she taught at UCLA, then spent several years honing her science fiction and fantasy skills designing computer software and making inflated promises about its capabilities. Her most recent book publications are *Lost in Translation* and *Acorna's Quest*, co-authored with Anne McCaffrey. When not writing, she plays the flute, makes quilts, and feeds the pets.

Jerry Oltion has been a gardener, stonemason, carpenter, oil-field worker, forester, land surveyor, rock 'n' roll deejay, printer, proofreader, editor, publisher, computer consultant, movie extra, corporate secretary, and garbage-truck driver. For the last seventeen years, he has also been a writer. He is the author of over eighty published stories in *Analog*, *The Magazine of Fantasy & Science Fiction*, and various other magazines and anthologies. He has written nine novels, the most recent of which is *Where Sea Meets Sky*, a *Star Trek* novel. His work has won the Nebula Award and been nominated for the Hugo Award. He has also won the Analog Readers' Choice Award. He lives in Eugene, Oregon, with his wife, Kathy, and the obligatory writer's cat, Ginger.

Thomas W. Knowles has published his short fiction, non-fiction, and technical articles, photos, interviews, essays, and reviews in a number of magazines, journals, and anthologies, including *Mystery Scene*, *New Destinies 9*, *Persimmon Hill*, *Southwest Art*, *Starlog*, *Texas Books in Review*, *Sports Afield*, and *Texas Sportsman*. With Joe R. Lansdale, he created and edited the critically acclaimed, illustrated nonfiction anthology series on the history and mythos of the American West, *The West that Was*, *Wild West Show*, and *The Living West*. In 1996, the American Library Association included *Wild West Show!* in their special recommended reading list as one of the thirty best nonfiction books on the American West. His latest release is *They Rode for the Lone Star*, the two-volume illustrated history of the Texas Rangers, authorized as the official commemorative book for their 175th anniversary celebration in 1998. He is a fourth-generation Texan, a member of both the Western Writers of America and the Science Fiction Writers of America. When he's not writing, he camps out with his son and the Scouts, teaches a writing course at Texas A&M University, and shoots period firearms with a Cowboy Action Shooting reenactment group. He may sometimes be found roaming around Texas, fishing, hunting, sampling local beer, collecting arrowheads, and taking photos of old churches, dance halls, and abandoned farmhouses.

Sharan Newman is a writer and medieval historian, two things that normally guarantee unemployment. However, she manages to survive through the kindness of readers of her medieval mystery series, the first of which, *Death Comes as Epiphany*, won the Macavity Award. She has also been nominated for the Agatha three times (but who's counting). *Cursed in the Blood* is the fifth in the series, and the sixth, *The Difficult Saint*, will be out in 1999. She is also the author of three fantasies on the life of Guinevere, and has coedited, with Miriam Grace Monfredo, the anthologies *Crime Through Time* and *Crime Through Time II*.

In her twenty-five years as a writer, editor, and publishing consultant, **Janet Berliner** has worked with such authors as Peter S. Beagle, David Copperfield, Michael Crichton, and Joyce Carol Oates. Among her most recent books are the anthology *David Copperfield's Beyond Imagination*, which she created and edited, and *Children of the Dusk*, the final book of *The Madagascar Manifesto*, a three-book series coauthored with George Guthridge. Currently Janet divides her time between Las Vegas, where she lives and works, and Grenada, West Indies, where her heart is.

Nina Kiriki Hoffman has been pursuing a writing career for fifteen years and has sold more than 150 stories, two short-story collections, two novels, *The Thread that Binds the Bones*, winner of the Bram Stoker award for best first novel, and *The Silent Strength of Stones*, one novella, "Unmasking," and one collaborative young adult novel with Tad Williams, *Child of an Ancient City*. Currently she almost makes a living writing scary books for kids.

Kristine Kathryn Rusch is an award-winning writer whose novels have also been on several bestseller lists. Her most recent novels are *The Black Queen* and *Hitler's Angel*. She has also coauthored *Star Wars: The New Rebellion* and several *Star Trek* novels with her husband, Dean Wesley Smith.

Carole Nelson Douglas is best known for her two mystery series, one featuring Irene Adler, the only woman to outsmart Sherlock Holmes, and the other, current, series which stars a large black tomcat named Midnight Louie, and his Las Vegas publicist Temple Barr. Louie last appeared on the scene in *Cat in an Indigo Mood*. But Victorian historical novels and cat cozy-noirs aren't all she can do. An accomplished short-fiction writer and editor, she recently assembled the anthology *Midnight Louie's Pet Detectives*.

Gary A. Braunbeck writes poetically dark suspense and horror fiction, rich in detail and scope. Recent stories have appeared in *Robert Bloch's Psychos*, *Once Upon a Crime*, and *The Conspiracy Files*. His occasional foray into the mystery genre is no less accomplished, having appeared in anthologies such as *Danger in D.C.* and *Cat Crimes Takes a Vacation*. His recent short-story collection, *Things Left Behind*, received excellent critical notice. He lives in Columbus, Ohio.

R. Garcia y Robertson is the author of four novels and more than forty short stories. He has a Ph.D. in the History of Science and Technology and taught history at UCLA and Villanova before turning to writing full-time. His latest novel, *American Woman*, a historical fantasy set in the American West during the 1870s, has gotten excellent reviews. He is currently working on a historical-fantasy trilogy set in fifteenth-century England during the War of the Roses.

Sandy Schofield is the open pen name of Dean Wesley Smith and Kristine Kathryn Rusch. Sandy has published four novels; one *Aliens* novel, one *Star Trek* novel, one *Quantum Leap* novel, and their newest, *The Big Game*, a *Predator* novel that has just appeared from Bantam. Someday, they plan to write an original Sandy novel, but they haven't gotten around to it. This is Sandy's first published story.

David Bischoff is active in many areas of the science fiction field, whether it be writing his own novels such as *The UFO Conspiracy* trilogy, collaborations with authors such as Harry Harrison, writing three *Bill the Galactic Hero* novels, or writing excellent media tie-in novelizations, such as *Aliens* and *Star Trek* novels. He has previously worked as an associate editor of *Amazing* magazine and as a staff member of NBC. He lives in Eugene, Oregon.

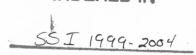